THEY STAY THE SAME

BY

TONI RICH

PUBLISH
AMERICA

PublishAmerica
Baltimore

First printing

ISBN: 1-59286-349-3
PUBLISHED BY PUBLISHAMERICA, LLLP
www.publishamerica.com
Baltimore

Printed in the United States of America

In memory of my parents,
Marie
and the *original* Tony Rich,
who gave me life and filled it with love.

Acknowledging my husband, Jack, who with his faith in me, love, patience and understanding resurrected my dead spirit.

Remembering the late Bette Hansberry and Bob Smith, Jr., two people who played an important role in my life.

Thanking Ken Basche, Ray Biondo, Steve Boder, Michael Kleine, Ph.D, Lil Male, Mary Kirka, Joe Rifice, Elizabeth Roncace, Pete Sallata and Susan Walker.

Circa 1928

"Stop, pig. Stop." The words were punctuated by the slobbering of the drunken Russian soldier issuing them.

Izzy Rosen, who was hearing impaired, didn't yield to the soldier's command. His son, Jake, grabbed his father's arm to alert him. They were on their way home from Friday night services.

Izzy and Jake turned toward the drunken soldier, who said, "Jew pig," as he spat in Izzy's face.

To further humiliate Izzy, the other military man opened his fly and urinated on him. This was only one of such humiliations Izzy had endured as a Jew. It was then that the senior Rosen decided to take his family and leave his beloved homeland and go to America.

Izzy Rosen and his family left their beloved land of Russia. He knew that Jake wouldn't have been able to have a peaceful Bar Mitzvah there.

Jake was approaching his thirteenth birthday and had dropped out of school when the family came to America. Compulsory education hadn't been a major priority of the lawmakers in that era. The Rosen family lived in the predominantly Jewish section of New York City, where Izzy's work as a tailor kept the family quite well until the depression. Upon coming to America, Izzy had sold all of his worldly possessions and invested it in the stock market. He lost everything. Izzy Rosen thought that he had uprooted his family for nothing and had failed them by making promises that he couldn't fulfill. Unable to pull himself out of despair, he took his own life, leaving a devastated family behind.

In 1931, Jake was chronologically 16, but a man of three years by Jewish doctrine. But by street doctrine, he was practically a senior citizen. He had become a bagman for the Jewish mob and was paid well for his efforts. The money, $25 weekly, was more than enough to sustain the family. His sister Sarah had married into the mob so she was the chief family benefactor.

Gertrude Rosen, the matriarch, fashioned clothes for society women but never recovered from the death of her husband. In 1932 she died. Jake always felt that she had willed herself to death.

7

Jake was overwhelmed with grief upon his mother's death but it gave him the impetus to follow her path in the rag trade. He had watched her cut fabric to gain the most yardage from a particular piece. He had watched her *stitch in the ditch.* He had also seen how she coordinated colors. Thus, he opened a fabric/design house called Russen, paying homage both to his beloved Russia and his surname.

It was through his newly formed business that he first met the love of his life, Becky. She worked in a department store that sold many Russen designs.

In 1934, at the age of 19, Jake married Becky at the very same Shul where he had been a Bar Mitzvah six years earlier.Jake and Becky became parents for the first time in 1935 when their eight-pound son Gary was born.

Al Mareno's family had migrated to America around the same time as Jake's. But their reason was to escape the Mafia. He grew up in a group of row homes consisting of ethnic purity.

Back then, people of similar backgrounds inhabited the same area. But it wasn't viewed as segregation. Each immigrant wanted to be surrounded by that which was familiar to him. The houses of worship built up around neighborhoods that they would service. Often people would speak in their native tongue, which was an embarrassment to the youth. They wanted to be Americanized.

Life expectancy was shorter then. The need for nursing homes was minimal. Families rallied around someone who was either ill or disabled so the infirm had home care.

In general, life was simpler. You worked hard, played hard, ate and slept.

Al, too, got into the rag business. He had been a school dropout. In those days, lack of finances and the need to subsist precluded the acquisition of an education.

Rita, who later became his wife, had a similar family history. She was an immigrant and likewise lived in the basically Italian neighborhood.

Al and Jake had an immediate camaraderie. It was because of their admiration and respect for each other that they became business partners.

To say the least, the friendship between the Marenos and the Rosens was extremely close. They were like a family unit.... Their different beliefs were intertwined like yarn in a well-knit sweater.

The kids spent countless hours together. The summer of 1945 was no different. As in past summers, Rita and Becky took their kids to the beach every day. This summer in particular, Becky was 6 months pregnant with her third child.

Tessa and Gary were playing in the water, as were Gary's brother Harry and Tessa's younger sister Treva. The two ten-year-olds were taunting their 8-year-old siblings. It was all in fun.

Tessa had a deep tan. Her brown hair was flecked with blond streaks. Her emerald green bathing was a vibrant setting for her potato brown skin and her hazel eyes. More often than not, her eyes and hair were identical in color. Treva was much fairer. Her normally blond hair was even blonder due to the ultraviolet rays to which it had been exposed.

Gary was a husky 10-year-old with dark brown hair and golden brown skin tone. Harry was the puny member of the Rosen family. His ribs were threatening to break through the skin of his all too thin body.

Becky and Rita were sitting at the shoreline, watching the four kids, who were now ducking each other and riding waves intermittently.

"Rita, it's a bit too soon to plan for Rosh Hashanah." Becky's pregnant belly illustrated the fact that she hadn't much longer to go before her newest family member made an appearance.

"But this is the very first time I'll be preparing it completely alone. I want it to be perfect. We don't know if you'll be in the hospital or not and my gang enjoys celebrating your holidays too."

"Well, if you're sure you want to do this it's okay by me," Becky said as she shifted her mountainous bulge, trying unsuccessfully to get comfortable

"Let's see. We'll have the usual stuff…. Chicken matzo ball soup, chopped chicken liver, and brisket of beef, kugel and veggies. Oh, I need your recipe for challah. I don't know if it will be as good as yours but I'll give it a try."

Once again, Becky shifted her weight as the beads of perspiration formed on her forehead. She added, "And honey cake is traditional as well as apples with honey for dipping."

"Neither will be a problem. Listen, I've about had it with the beach. Let's collect the kids and go home."

Becky, who had wanted to leave this uncomfortable outing, welcomed the suggestion. She began shaking out towels while Rita herded the kids out of the water.

"But we don't want to leave yet," they all whined. "It's almost August and you don't bring us down then."

Once again, Rita patiently explained that August was *polio* month and neither she nor Becky wanted to take a chance on the kids' health.

They begrudgingly left the water but rolled in the sand *accidentally* and had to go back into the ocean once again to get cleaned off.

Finally, the merriment of their day at the beach was over.

A few months passed. Little Jennifer Rosen was born. Rita was busy preparing the Holiday feast.

"What smells so good?" asked Al as he came home from work and brushed his lips against his wife's cheek

"Chicken soup. I hope it tastes as good as it smells." Rita said this as she mixed the matzo meal with the eggs and other ingredients for the balls.

The kitchen was a study of times long past. The table was covered with oilcloth. The sink was old but clean. The white stove was gas with four burners and an old oven, which did what it was supposed to do.

Tessa and Gary were in the family room playing ping-pong. They were going to help prepare tomorrow night's feast.

"Tessa, Gary, I'm ready for you to knead the dough for the Challah."

This was a task Rita gave to the kids for them to use up some pent-up energy.

They knew before coming into the kitchen that they had better surgically scrub their hands and nails.

"Okay, Mrs. Mareno. I'm ready." Gary playfully held up his hands as a scrubbed surgeon would.

Tessa, who followed closely on his heels, said, "Me too."

With that, they took turns punching down the dough while Rita was slicing onions for her chopped chicken liver. The livers were being sautéed in her cast iron frying pan, turning slowly from pink to the desired brown color. After chopping a hard boiled egg, Rita took the onion, cooked livers and some of the chicken fat in which she cooked the livers, mixed them with the egg, and then seasoned it to taste.

Gary said, "Mrs. Mareno, I think we've punched the dough enough. My mom always has it rise again."

"Yes. I know. Here, let's set it aside. Which one feels like beating the cake?"

"I do," they both said in unison.

This went on until they broke for dinner. The kids had lost interest. They didn't return to help.

Rita continued the preparations and everything was in readiness for the next night.

Al was seated at the head of the table with Becky to his right and Jake to his left. Rita sat at the opposite end with her mother, Rose, to her right. The kids sat on each side between the adults. Newborn Jennifer was in the portable crib in the den.

Jake blessed the Challah, broke it and passed it around. The meal was successful and the ecumenical mingling was fun for all.

How peaceful it was. The Catholic Marenos and the Jewish Rosens enjoyed another religious holiday together. They celebrated all of the Judeo/Christian holy days as a unit.

The holiday festivities continued into Thanksgiving. This time, Becky did the honors for the members of both households. This was the one holiday that fluctuated between the two houses. However, the religious observations took place at the home of the person whose religion was being observed.

As the years passed, there had been quite a transformation in the Mareno kitchen. The freestanding stove had been replaced by storage space where the oven once was. A stainless steel range top was above the storage area. Nearby was the double wall oven. The kitchen cabinets were oak with a pale green floor. A simulated wood table replaced the oilcloth-topped table. The walls were papered in beige and green. It denoted their upscale socioeconomic level.

Christmas of 1950 was special for Jennifer. She was delighted to help trim the tree. She loved it when Al played Santa for her. The other kids were really too old to believe in the jolly fat man but Jennifer squealed with delight when she saw him and got her presents directly from him.

How did things escalate so quickly? How did the peaceful coexistence become a nightmare? How could attitudes change so drastically? These were the questions soaring through Tessa's mind as she walked along the beach of Linfield … getting her facts together for the pending book.

Circa 1994

Bette Gilmar had heard her phone ringing throughout the day. She let the machine take her messages knowing that she would return them in due time. Her friends and associates knew that she had sequestered herself in her study while working on her novel, *They Stay the Same.* She had put much work into it with Tessa's complete cooperation.

As she sipped her wine and munched on her cheese and crackers, she realized that Tessa had glossed over some of the most poignant facets of her life. They were hurriedly explained and not embellished upon at all.

Bette felt that things that hurt the most were the things that most people wouldn't or couldn't conceptualize ... especially in a book. Most readers like to actually see things happen. If that were the case, the book would either be a quick read on the beach or possibly not be read at all. Bette had long ago decided to stick with Tessa's recounting rather than editorializing it. Tessa had to stamp her approval on each and every aspect of the book in which she was the chief source. She didn't want to antagonize Tessa in any way. Bette also realized that she herself was not a brand name but just a generic writer. She knew that she had nothing in her past to make her instantly famous. She had success in her own right. She was more than adequate as a wife, mother, friend as well as a nurse.

However, as she continued sipping her drink, she realized that she wasn't out to sell herself but was a conduit for a worthwhile story that bore telling. To see this type of prejudice under these circumstances was especially troubling. Her Italian grandparents had been victimized by prejudice when they landed at Ellis Island. Still later, her peers had problems with non-acceptance of their interreligious dating. Later, people had to deal with the stigma regarding crossing the color line. And then came the homophobes.

She finally turned off the ringer on her phone but could still hear the click of her answering machine as it picked up her messages. She continued to concentrate.

What had the effect of arousing Bette from her reflection was the incessant ringing of her doorbell accompanied by a machine gun-like knocking. She rushed to the door and saw Tessa through the peephole. She had no idea what to expect.

"Tessa," Bette said as she opened the door. "What's wrong?"

"Bette, we must stop the book. We can't continue."

"Wait a minute. Come in and sit down."

Bette took Tessa's coat and while motioning her to sit down, hung it up. Tessa lowered herself onto the lounge chair and sat back.

"Things have hit rock bottom. Althie dropped a bomb on Marc and Ali today. She's been married for a few months and she's six weeks pregnant."

"I should think that would make all of you happy. Just think, a great-grandchild."

"But you don't understand. She married Garrett."

"And?"

"Let's just suffice it to say that I do not want this story in print."

"But you already signed off on most of the work. You had approved of what we had done."

"Yes, but now I have second thoughts."

"Tessa, throughout these past several months I've admired your strength. You've always managed to keep your head and remain calm and cool where others may have resorted to hysteria. This is alien to you."

"Like I said, I don't want this to be published! This is done. Finished."

Bette could see that she was being dismissed so she got Tessa's coat. Tessa stood and started heading toward the door. She helped her into it and both women walked silently to the door. Tessa just left. She uttered nothing further.

Uncertain what to do, Bette decided to wait to see if she heard further from Tessa. When no other communication was forthcoming, she called her lawyer. After setting up an appointment for the following week, she began reading what she had completed thus far.

One

"Becky, listen to yourself. What's your problem? You're driving me meshuga!"

"It isn't just *my* problem. It's affecting all of us. Are you that dense?" Becky's face was as red as the ends of her dyed hair.

Jake zeroed in on the former. "That's for sure. Al and I are barely civil to each other. We speak only when spoken to. The whole environment has changed."

"Well, just imagine if they get married."

"Imagine what?"

"Damn you, Jacob. You really piss me off!"

Jake knew that she meant business. The only time she called him by his given name was when she was adamant about something.

"Tell me. Would it be so bad if they got married? I should think you above all people would approve. You and Rita are as close as sisters are. Gary and Tessa know each other better than a lot of people who are already married. The whole family has been involved in our lives for years."

"Friendship is one thing. I don't want to see a Christmas tree in my son's house. Nor do I want any snotty-nosed mackerel snappers under my roof. And I hate it when they speak Italian to Rose. Besides, religion is important to me."

"And who is it not important to? And what's the matter with them speaking Italian to Rita's mother? She has an easier time understanding that than she does English."

"But she should learn English. She's not in Italy anymore. Just what we need. A bunch of Wops talking Italian!"

"Listen to yourself. The Marenos happen to speak better English than either of us does. If Gary and Tessa do get married and have children, do you mean to say you won't love each and every one of them? Becky, don't do this. I know what prejudice is. I know what bitterness can do. I've seen more than enough in my life. Please don't draw a line here. Don't put a bridge between the two of us. Don't make me choose or take sides. We've always maintained a united front where the kids are concerned but this is a toughie.

15

I can't pretend something I don't feel."

"Jake, if you don't support me on this, I'll never forgive you."

Gary was walking past his parents' bedroom door after taking Tessa to the movies. As he walked past the closed door, he had heard the heated exchange.

At that point, the bathroom door slammed. He heard shower water running. That was his mother's way of both winning an argument and ending one. Speak loud and clear, then leave before a retort could be uttered.

He quietly walked down the hall to his room and got into bed. He put the radio on and listened to *Little Things Mean a Lot*. Sleep was elusive. He knew that Tessa had been going through the same thing at her house. They had discussed the situation often. However, he was ignorant of the fact that Tessa was *involved* in the discussion at the Mareno household. Neither one of them could fathom how their parents felt.

When Tessa got home, her father, mother and her grandmother, Rose, greeted her. Her grandmother stopped talking when Tessa came into the room.

"Hi Grandmom," said Tessa as she leaned over and kissed the older woman on the cheek.

"Hello child. Sit down. Your parents and I want to talk to you."

Tessa felt her stomach tighten. She knew what was coming. The fact that her grandmother was there meant there was something serious going on. She usually didn't come at night unless it was a special event.

Her father was the one who broke the stilted silence. He got right to the facts with no preamble. "Tessa, you know we like Gary a lot. But since he's Jewish, that places him out of reach for anything permanent. You're oceans apart with your religious beliefs. Now wait a minute; don't flash those eyes at your mother. Your mother, grandmother and I all agree on this." Even as he was saying this, Al had trouble believing his own words. But being a dutiful husband, he continued. "Do you have any idea at all about restrictions placed upon Jews? About any number of places that won't accommodate them? Do you know how many Anti-Semites there are in the world?"

"Three more than I thought," snapped Tessa.

"Don't get fresh. I don't think you have any idea at all what your relationship with Gary will entail."

Rita, who like Becky was the instigator behind this, could no longer stay silent. She had lived near a Jewish family when she was a little girl. She remembered all too well going to the Goldsmiths' house on Friday nights to light their stove. She remembered their darkened windows at Christmas when all the Italian families had lights glowing. She wondered if her daughter realized the significance of Judaism. They had only played at being Jewish during holidays.

"Listen to your father. You couldn't have a Christmas. You wouldn't dye Easter eggs. All of your basic traditions would be lost." Her mother looked at her imploringly.

"Figlia mia," Rose did prefer Italian to English. "I have loved you since I first saw you in the hospital." And while placing her hand dramatically to her chest, she said, "You are the flesh of my flesh. I want nothing but the best for you."

Tessa was about to say that Gary was the best when she remembered his admonishment. 'We can overcome these obstacles together. We know each other so well. We're used to the opposites in our religion. They're almost as much alike as they are different. Don't fight with them. We'll get through it together.'

Tessa waited before saying anything and then asked, "Is that all?"

And then the *plan* enfolded.

"Tessa," began Rose. "I want to go back to Naples this summer and as a graduation gift, I'd like to take you with me. We will leave a couple of days after graduation, June 17th, and come back in time for you to start college in September."

Tessa could feel the heat building up in her body. Tears were forming in her eyes. She willed them not to drop as she spoke. "What do you think I am? I'm not a chip on a Parcheesi Board waiting for someone else to roll the dice. I have my same job back this summer as a counselor at a girls' camp. But you already know that, don't you? I plan to have a good time with all of my friends before I go away.... Not just the Catholic ones."

"Tessa," pleaded her father. "Your grandmother really–"

"Don't tell me anything about real. The only real thing about this conversation is that it's happening. You're trying to rule me and hope that my feelings for Gary will magically disappear." Turning to her mother, she added, "I'm more surprised at you than I am with anyone. Mrs. Rosen and you have always been such good friends."

"Friendship is one thing. This situation is another. Why should it surprise you that I don't want my firstborn to have heartache if I can prevent it?"

"What heartache? Do you think a tree or dyed eggs are all there is to Gary and me?" Tessa wailed. She ran from the room with tears streaming down her face.

Up until recently, Tessa had enjoyed high school to the fullest. She was cheerleading captain in addition to being the secretary of the senior class. As long as she fit into her parents' mold with good grades, good friends and good behavior, everything was fine. However, graduation of the class of '53 was approaching rapidly and her parents were very vocal in expressing their dislike for the fact that she was spending too much time with Gary.

They had been raised together. That's why the reaction of both sets of parents was a complete shock to both of these young people. Gary wasn't faring any better at his home. These were the same people who shared each other's holidays.

Gary was an exemplary young person as well. He was not only captain of the football team but he was also senior class president. He was scheduled to enter college in the fall. Although his father would have liked him to join Al and him in business, Gary had shown no interest whatsoever in pursuing his father's means of support.

When she got to the sanctity of her room, she flung herself on her bed, crying into her pillow. The powder of the white bucks she was wearing puffed on the pink bedspread. Although she was usually neat, Tessa didn't care about the white coloring that was sullying her coverlet. They just didn't understand. They were too old to know what young love was all about. She and Gary wanted things to evolve naturally. She had wanted to go to college. Then, when she and Gary were in their last years of higher education, they would become engaged, getting married after they finished. She turned on her radio. Ironically the radio was playing *Little Things Mean a Lot*.

It was then that she heard a light rap at the door.

"Go away," whined Tessa. "I don't want to talk anymore."

"It's me," said Treva, her sixteen-year-old sister. "Let me in."

Tessa got up, opened the door and her petite blond sister came in.

"God, I couldn't help but overhear everything. Are you okay?"

"How can I be? I just don't understand this whole mess. They're so pigheaded!" said Tessa as she kicked off her white bucks and brushed the powdery white dust from her pink bedspread.

"What are you going to do?"

"I don't know. This is going to change a lot." Tessa was noncommittal.

"Such as?"

"Everything. I don't even know about college. Their reaction to Gary and me is so unexpected. They've never hinted at anything in the past."

"Well, listen. I'm bushed. I just got home. I danced my legs off at the 'Y' tonight. We'll talk in the morning."

"Okie dokie."

As Tessa locked her door, she looked down at her poodle skirt that she had gotten for Christmas. Somehow, the feeling of possessive pride disappeared in the throes of all else that had happened.

She got into bed after neatly pulling back her spread. She climbed into the safety of her private cocoon. She had a fitful night's sleep but came fully awake as the light of day was peeking through the bottom of her window shade. It was Saturday. She and Gary were going out in the Rosens' boat. His father had gotten a brand new one so he had given the other one to his sons. She knew she had to get up as she had promised to make them a picnic lunch. She finally roused herself enough to get out of bed. When she looked in the mirror, she saw her reddened swollen eyes. They bore no resemblance at all to her usual bright and shining ones. She walked to the bathroom.

Tessa knew that her dad had left early to go to the office. He always said that to be successful, a forty-hour workweek was not enough. Many were the nights he went to the office after dinner, checking the designs and fabric. Actually, she was glad there would be one less to bombard her this morning. Gary's dad would probably be at work too. They sometimes rotated their hours so the other could be free but with all that was going on, she had imagined that things weren't the same there either. She giggled to herself. Maybe the Rosens would send Gary to Russia this summer to visit relatives that were still there.

She bathed quickly, not luxuriating in the soothing tub as she usually did. She wanted to hurry and pack the lunch before rushing to the dock to meet Gary.

As she walked down the steps, she heard her grandmother's voice. Her mom and grandmother were talking about the vegetable garden that the Marenos always planted in their backyard.

"Hi," said Tessa as she went and kissed her grandmother on the cheek.

"Where are you off to so early?" asked Rose.

"I'm going boating. I want to pack lunch."

"Your mother has some boiled ham and Swiss cheese in the refrigerator. I'll get them out for you."

Tessa knew what would be coming but she smiled and said, "No thanks. I'll make peanut butter and jelly sandwiches. I think I'll pack some brownies too."

"But I bought the ham especially for you. I know how much you like it."

Tessa didn't take the bait but busied herself making sandwiches. She knew her mother was edging towards another confrontation.

"Did you hear what I said?"

At this, Tessa couldn't hold back any longer. "You know perfectly well that I'm going with Gary and he doesn't eat ham. Does that satisfy you now?"

"Oh, so you have to change what you eat now. All of a sudden what was

19

.

good enough before isn't anymore. What has your Yiddish boy done? Hypnotize you?"

"Please stop badgering me. I've never given you any trouble and I'm still not. You've created this whole problem. Now you're even brainwashing Daddy. How can he work side by side with Mr. Rosen? What does he do? Put everything in a Whitman Sampler box neatly labeled? Well, I won't pretend things are fine with all of you. I'm not a phony and until now, I never realized that you and Dad were."

The very Italian Rose spoke up. "Is that how you speak to your mother? Is that the way your bigmouth Jewish boy has taught you to honor thy father and mother?"

Tessa responded quite calmly, "I won't let you ruin this day. It's beautiful out. I'm just not going to let your pettiness spoil my day in the sun." That was all she said and since she wasn't arguing with them, they both maintained their silence.

She finished the sandwiches and went out the back door. She walked hurriedly to the dock. She was delighted to see that Gary was already aboard the boat. He looked so handsome with his light brown hair streaked with blond. When she got closer she saw the strained expression on his face, realizing that he must have had a similar encounter with his family. Becky as well as Rita was the instigator. Determined not to let anything spoil their day, she decided to put it out of her mind and not apprise Gary of the latest attack.

"Am I late? I thought I'd beat you here."

"No. I just wanted to make sure that the boat was clean. Harry took it out yesterday afternoon and he's a total slob. Hop in so we can get started."

They rode off. Their silence was only broken by the sound of the motor.

The couple cruised around for hours, pulled into their secret cubby and went ashore. They ate their lunch and nodded off, cozy in each other's arms. When they awakened it was 4:30. Gary was visibly shaken. He hadn't gone to Synagogue with the family that morning but had made a deal with his dad that he would be around for the Seder at the Synagogue Hall. Gary had been permitted to miss the morning services as long as he was back for that evening's celebration. That would have been enough of a time problem but the issue was compounded by the fact that it was Tessa's Holy Saturday and she was obligated to go to 6:30 Mass with her family. Still, if they hurried, they could make it. They cleaned up the remnants of their picnic and boarded the motorboat. Gary tried to start it but nothing happened. He tried again. Still nothing. Remembering that Harry had taken the boat the day before, he got a sinking feeling in the pit of his stomach. It was then that he checked the gas gauge.... Something he should have done before taking off. It was beyond empty. Just wait until he got his hands on his brother. He'd strangle him.

Finally, Tessa then let all of her pent-up emotion rise to the surface. She began to cry.

Gary consoled her. "Don't cry. The boat has oars. If we row together, we'll see other boaters who can probably spare some gas for us." In his heart he didn't believe this but he didn't want Tessa to be upset.

They began edging out of their cubby. After a half-hour, they were approaching an area where ordinarily someone may have seen them to offer help.

Suddenly, dark ominous-looking clouds rolled in. Not wanting to scare Tessa, he scanned her clothing looking for metal. She had no zipper on her shorts. Likewise, her sweater was void of lightning attractors. He checked her shoes and was relieved to see that her soles were rubber. As Tessa looked up into the threatening sky, the thunder and lightning combined for a colorful symphony. The cacophony was deafening. She let out a shriek as the rain came down with blinding fury. Quickly, Gary decided to get their life preservers. After helping Tessa put hers on, he put one on himself. The boat was taking in rainwater in addition to seawater. They clutched each other and began praying.

"Hail Mary full of grace," began Tessa

"Blessed God, on this first day of Passover."

"The Lord is with thee."

"Please protect us from the rages of the sea."

"Blessed art thou amongst women."

"Help us to survive the storm which we are now facing."

"And blessed is the fruit of thy womb, Jesus."

"Let one of your disciples lead us to safety."

"Holy Mary, Mother of God, pray for us sinners," continued Tessa.

"Thank you, Lord. And now I say...."

"Now and at the hour of our death...."

"Amen," they both said in unison.

With each clap of thunder and each flash of lightning a stronger bond was being formed between these two that nothing could dispel. They each knew that the God to whom each prayed would not abandon them.

21

Two

The storm lasted for what seemed like an eternity. The boat drifted aimlessly. Suddenly, there appeared to be a lapse in the storm. It was as if the sky decided that its wayward child had done enough harm and it was now time for penance.

By this time, it was approaching 7 o'clock and the tide was going into the shore. Luckily, in their wayward drifting, they had been slowly propelled toward their destination.

"Ahoy there," came from the coast guard vessel that seemed to appear out of nowhere.

"Ahoy," answered Gary and Tessa simultaneously. Their relief was evident. They hugged each other, silently thanking their own God.

"Is everyone aboard and accounted for?"

"Yes, it's just the two of us."

"Are either of you hurt or can you manage to grab a tow line?"

"Just throw it to us. We'll manage just fine."

Gary reached for the rope and pulled it into the boat. He tied it to the anchor while still grasping their safety tow. He held on to it as if their lives depended upon it even though the acute danger had passed. They were now relatively safe.

"What happened out there? Did your engine break down?"

"No. As stupid as it sounds, we just ran out of gas," Gary responded as he grabbed the blankets that the coast guard gave to them.

As Tessa looked at him, she felt all of the cold from the violent storm waters leave her body. In his eyes was the reflection of the same love and concern that she herself was experiencing. The two young people clutched each other's hands.

Neither had given any conscious thought to their parents or to their parents' reaction. Now the real world as well as all of its problems began flooding into their thoughts. The storm, which had threatened their physical well being, was nothing compared to the storm which would begin anew with their parents. Their drenched bodies were not the only reason they were shivering.

In the near distance, they saw the dock with a small group of people standing there. They were approaching it all too quickly.

Rita and Al were at one end with Treva and Rose. On the opposite end were Jake, Becky, Harry and little Jennifer. The physical division said more than any words could.

"Tessa, my God! We've been so worried," Rita called out.

Not to be outdone, Becky called out to Gary. "You're saturated. You'll catch pneumonia."

Gary and Tessa got off the boat, holding hands. They were torn between their love for each other and the compassion they felt for their parents.

Little Jennifer ran up to both of them. "Were you scared? Did the lightning hit the boat? Was it fun? Were you hungry? We all missed Seder."

"Yes, no, a little, no, I know." Gary responded to all of his inquisitive sister's questions.

Rita spoke to her daughter. "Come home now. You'll have some soup and hot chocolate. You can take a warm bath and get into some dry clothes."

"Al, I—"began Jake.

"No, Jake. Don't say a word."

"When will it be time to say something? My son almost drowns because Juliet wants to go boating." Becky said in a tone seeped with anger. It was an understatement to say she was agitated. Her flashing eyes and deep frown said even more than her words.

Turning toward his mother, Gary addressed her. "Mom, it was my idea to go out today. If Harry had left any gas in the boat, we would have been on our way before the storm hit."

Al spoke menacingly to Gary. "You mean that you stupidly endangered two lives because you were too careless to check the damn gas gauge before starting out?"

Jake ended his silence as he turned to Al. "Wait one minute. That's *my* son that you are berating. Becky and I are perfectly capable of reprimanding him. We haven't raised him to the age of 18 on a wing and a prayer. And I might add … a Jewish prayer."

"This has nothing to do with religion. Are you so blind to the severity of the situation that you resort to religious taunts? I never knew you to be so prejudiced. I—"

He never got to finish because Tessa screamed. "I'm so sick and tired of all of this bickering. How can you be so cruel? We could have drowned out there! We could have been struck by lightning! Don't you care? Dad, are you so worried that you didn't get to socialize after mass tonight? Do any of you do anything without thinking about public opinion? I hate all of this. I hate all of you!"

"Tessa," whimpered Jennifer. "I don't hate you. I love you."

Gary reached for his eight-year-old sister, drawing her close to him and whispered, "Tessa's just upset. You know how much she loves you."

At the same time, Al gathered his daughter in his arms. As she was uncontrollable and screaming, he had to carry her to the waiting station wagon.

Becky and Rita were still on the dock, apparently fighting to keep their anger in check.

Jake took Gary by the arm and said, "Come on, son, you have to get out of those wet clothes."

Gary shook himself loose, looked at his father and said angrily, "Dad. Let me alone. I want to apologize to the Marenos before they leave. I have to make them understand that I'd never hurt Tessa."

Gary jogged to the station wagon where Treva and Tessa were in the backseat. Although Treva was doing her best to calm her sister, Tessa was still screaming and sobbing.

"Tessa, please calm down," Treva was saying. "I hate to see you like this. Mom and Dad were petrified when Mr. Rosen called to see if Gary was at our house. They went to the dock and saw that the boat wasn't there."

"Can't you see?" wailed Tessa. "They're bigoted, hateful people! I'm almost sorry that I didn't drown out there. Nothing I do satisfies them anymore."

Gary got into the car and wrapped his arms around Tessa. "Shh. Shh. Everything will be all right. Together you and I will make it all right. They were just frantic with worry. Calm down please. The worst is over." But it wasn't.

"Ga ... ry, Ga ... ry. I don't know. I just don't know anymore. How can you be so sure? This whole day has been nothing but a nightmare," said Tessa between sobs. "If I have ever learned how not to behave, I've learned it well from our parents' example." Her breathing was still interspersed with sobs.

"I've never lied to you, have I?" Gary asked earnestly. "This isn't a fairy tale, but it *will* have a happy ending. I promise you that."

Tessa looked at him with overwhelming love. She kissed him on the cheek in between her lessening sobs.

Gary spoke to Treva. "Thanks for helping. I have to leave with my parents now."

"Don't thank me. She's my sister. She'll be okay. Don't worry about her."

Gary gave Tessa a quick kiss then got out of the car.

Rita and Al were approaching the station wagon as he was leaving it.

"Mr. Mareno, Mrs. Mareno. I'm truly sorry for all of this. I was careless, I know. I guess I had a lot on my mind. Please don't be angry with Tessa. She's really shook up."

"Gary," began Rita, who was never one to mince words even when the timing was inappropriate. "The two of you shouldn't have been allowed to continue dating. I blame myself more than anyone. You're too serious about each other. I don't want my daughter to have any heartache. I think that together the two of you will have nothing but that. You'll be torn between Passover and Easter; Hanukkah and Christmas; pizza and matzo; pizelles and bagels. There are too may differences, some much more serious than others. Your backgrounds are too different. You won't realize how many things are different until you have to make adjustments."

Gary didn't respond to her but extended his hand to Al and said, "Mr. Mareno, I'm truly sorry."

Al didn't extend his hand. Had he seen Gary's gesture?

Becky watched from the dock. She was livid about the entire incident. That anger was mild compared to the way she felt about the snub. She felt Al had deliberately delivered it. It was another slap in the face to Gary, whose face was already figuratively stinging.

Firmly Jake took his wife's arm as he was trying to steer her away from the scene.

"Did you see what he just did?'

"Come on, Becky. Let's go home. We have to get Gary warm and dry. Come now. Let's go."

"Who does that Wop think he is?" Becky ranted at full speed. "He can't shake my son's hand? The kid only wanted to make amends. Gary behaved more like an adult than anyone here today." When she saw Jake raise his eyebrows she acknowledged what he was thinking. "Yes, including me!"

They got into their car where Harry and Jennifer were already waiting. Gary came slowly to their car and got in quietly. The trip home was made in silence.

In both households, the parents tended to their cold, wet children.

Nothing could be improved by further discussion so after making sure that the boaters had something to eat and drink, both families did the same thing. They went to bed.

Three

Tessa rose the next morning and immediately remembered that it was Easter. The day that Jesus had arisen. She hoped that perhaps this would be a new beginning for her as well.

She got ready for Mass, wearing her new blue suit along with her new flowered hat. When she went downstairs to greet the family, she discovered that the entire house was empty. She saw a terse note that her mother had left for her.

> *Tessa.... Dad, Treva and I have gone to 8 o'clock mass and then to breakfast at the country club.... Mom*

Tessa was disappointed that she hadn't been awakened, as she always loved to go to the country club for Easter brunch. Her mouth would water for the Canadian bacon, French toast and creamed chipped beef. She could just imagine the taste of the fresh fruit with the sherbet on it. Gary's family didn't belong. Then it hit her, they weren't allowed to!

She put all of this out of her mind. She had to hustle to make the 9:30 mass.

She went to the refrigerator and as she got the carton of juice out, it fell to the floor. Having neither the time nor the inclination to clean it up, she left and began walking to church.

In the Rosen household, the scene was different. Becky had gotten up early as she and Jake had planned to go fishing. She wanted Gary, Harry and Jennifer to have a nice breakfast even though it would be Passover fare.

Becky was dipping the softened Matzo into the beaten egg. She already had the coffee brewing. The colored hard-boiled eggs were on the table. (She always felt the white shell was too plain and since she loved color, she diligently dyed eggs whenever she planned to serve them this way.) She got out the strawberry jam, tossed the salad and went to the refrigerator to get the whitefish salad out. Just as she was closing the refrigerator door, she heard the group coming down the stairs.

26

"Hi Mom," said Jennifer, bright and bouncy.

"My God, Becky. It's only 8:30, how long have you been up?" Jake asked as he gave her a good morning kiss.

"I don't know. Remember we all got to bed pretty early last night. There's only but so much sleep a person needs."

"Better tell that to Gary. He's still snoring," said Harry, who was waiting for the deserved reprimand he knew would be coming.

"It's just as well," sighed Becky. " I don't know what to say to him."

"Try not saying anything," suggested Jake, who knew he'd have to be Houdini to have that happen.

Becky busied herself squeezing orange juice from the oranges they'd brought back from Florida.

Jake went out and got the newspaper. Turning to the local news, he saw a small item....

The coast guard assisted rescuing a small craft from the sea last evening. Two young adults, Gary Rosen and Tessa Mareno, escaped harm from the electrical storm when they drifted toward the shore line after they had run out of gas.

Jake skillfully put that part of the news aside and just as skillfully placed the sales circular on top of it. Becky always went to sales and bought things that she just couldn't do without. Usually they were placed in the back of her closet or given to the Catholic Church for the poor families.

Since the fried Matzo was ready she began placing breakfast on the table. Then she said to Jake, "Let me see that. Oh, Flamingo is having a sale on cruise wear. We're going to the Caribbean in September, aren't we?"

"Probably," answered Jake. To him his voice didn't sound very convincing. With the latest development regarding the kids, he wasn't sure where his business interest would lie. Probably not with Al any longer.

Harry devoured his Matzo and whitefish salad in what appeared to be one swooping gulp.

Jen played with her fish but seemed to like the Matzo.

Becky and Jake had just picked at their meals. They were doing what they had always admonished their kids for doing.... Moving food to the perimeters of their plates to make it look as if they had really eaten more than they actually did.

Becky decided that it was time to have a private conversation with her older son.

After ascending the stairs she tapped at his door. She was only answered by Gary's loud snoring. After her second rap was met by continued silence, she opened the door and entered. One look at her son told her how sick he was. His forehead was stop sign red. When she touched his face she found he was burning with fever. She quickly got out the basin and alcohol that she had been taught to use for a fever. In a panic, she called down to Jake. He came up immediately.

"Gary's burning up. Put some ice in the icebag and bring it in here." To Gary, she said, "Honey, can you hear me?"

"Yes," he said faintly, pointing to his neck.

She took the ice pack from Jake and put it on Gary's head. She then began rubbing him down with alcohol.

"Jake, get me some aspirin and water. Please. And call Dr. Bosnac."

Before she gave him the aspirin, she gave Gary some water slowly. Once she saw that he could indeed swallow, she gave him two aspirin. She asked Jake to get her a pitcher of ice and water so she could get some fluids into Gary between alcohol rubs. After about a half-hour, she took his temperature.... 101^0. Managing to look into his throat, she saw pus on his reddened, swollen tonsils. She knew she should have listened more intently when he said his throat was sore. For Gary to admit that anything at all was wrong was an indication he was really sick. She thought about the past 48 hours, realizing that the stress hadn't done Gary any good. It probably worsened his condition.

She was sitting quietly in his room for what seemed like hours when she heard Jake open the front door for the doctor. She heard the pleasantries exchanged and was relieved to see Dr. Bosnac entering the room.

After listening, poking and questioning, he determined that Gary more than likely had a Strep throat. He gave him a shot of penicillin and one of Benadryl to keep his allergies in check. Before he left, he gave Becky instructions that were pretty consistent with what one did with a febrile child in the 50s. He also gave her a prescription for penicillin.

Becky accompanied the doctor downstairs, where Jake was patiently waiting.

"How is he?' His anxiety was evident in his voice.

"He has an ugly-looking throat but his chest is clear right now. Let me know if he doesn't seem to be improving."

Jake was glad to hear that his chest was okay because in the past, Gary had pneumonia a few times.

Becky was chastising herself aloud. "If only I had listened a few days ago when he said he felt sick. There is so much going on. We haven't been completely in tune with Gary these past few months."

Dr. Bosnac knew about the situation but said nothing to denote this. "I can't tell you how to feel or how to resolve differences but this constant haranguing isn't helping anyone. But right now, it's particularly detrimental to Gary."

Jake didn't utter a word. He knew a showdown was in the offing.

After they bid their good-byes, Becky spoke. "Jake, I hope that you don't blame me for all of this."

"Becky, I admit I don't want my son to be unhappy. I'll also admit that I don't think marrying outside of his religion would necessarily make him unhappy. It hasn't been easy on anyone. There is a schism between us and our son, not to mention the one between Al and me."

"Well, I don't know what you expect of me. I always thought Judaism was one of the most important things in your life. You know what slights we have endured because of our religion. Just look at the country club. Has Al ever proposed you for membership?"

There was no additional time to continue this conversation because Harry and Jennifer came into the room. They were anxious to hear about Gary.

Harry then braced himself for the inevitable.

"Harry, do you realize that your damned irresponsibility could have killed two people? This isn't as simple as not replacing toilet paper or toothpaste when you use the last bit of them. This was careless. It was a dangerous act, which could have had much worse consequences."

Harry just listened as his father reprimanded him. Although it was a short exchange, it was long by Jake's standards.. Becky usually did the disciplining.

While Gary was home ill, Tessa was returning from church. She felt sad but in a strange way, relieved. She was sure that the air would eventually be cleared for once and for all.

The door was opening as she was walking up the steps. She was glad to see it was Treva who greeted her.

"Hi. Are you okay? We loved breakfast. I'm sorry that you missed it."

"So am I. No one bothered to wake me up. What am I? An orphan? Why didn't anyone at least see if I wanted to go? You all know how much I love brunch at the country club."

"Mom thought it was better if you slept. And you know Dad. He rarely, if ever, bucks her."

"Well, no matter. I did a lot of reflecting in church as I sat all alone."

Treva looked questioningly at her sister but didn't ask what she had reflected or decided upon. She didn't have the time anyhow because the door opened and out came their parents.

"Girls, we are going to Grandmom Rose's house to pick her up for Easter dinner. We'll expect you both home by 5 o'clock.

Al fidgeted as Rita looked at Tessa when she said this.

Not in the mood to start WW III, Tessa just nodded while saying, "Okay. 5 o'clock."

As her parents sauntered to the car, Treva turned to Tessa and said, "Let's surprise Mom and start getting dinner ready."

"Okay. Let's start the gravy first. I think Mom has some canned tomatoes in the pantry. You get the garlic and onions. I'll get the sausage."

A half-hour later, the aroma of spaghetti gravy permeated the house. Tessa began setting the table while Treva tended the gravy and readied the ham for the oven. Tessa peeled the potatoes and together they made a salad. They made a cake in which they had put vegetable dye, turning it the desired shade of pink. They then iced it with pink and green icing. It didn't look half-bad.

When Al and Rita returned a while later, they were surprised to see what the girls had accomplished. Dinner was uneventful.

Four

A few days later, the charged atmosphere blew up. It happened in the offices of Russen. The worst part was the two men really respected and admired each other. But their wives weren't giving them any peace at home.

Al and Jake were sitting in the office to discuss ordering fabric. By the same token, they'd be assessing any damage that had been done to the business relationship. The furor over the kids had lots of fallout.

"No, Jake, I think we should definitely order fabric from a different supplier. Sew-Sew hasn't been that reliable lately. That's not doing our business any good."

"I know but I have Abe Weiss' personal pledge that they'll deliver on time."

"It's entirely too risky. I don't want to go through what we went through last order. I've spoken with Tony Bocca at Bocca Brothers. He's presented an excellent proposition."

"But I prefer Sew-Sew. They have a better quality."

"Not really. Have you seen some of their samples? They look vintage polyester."

"Let's cut the bullshit!" exclaimed Jake. "We're hop-scotching around the real issue. Our kids' situation has changed how we view things, namely each other's opinion when it comes to business decisions. Maybe we should put these discussions on hold. If this persists, I can't see any clear way to solve it. It looks as if our business relationship will soon be as dead as our personal one."

"I didn't realize that you had written our friendship off so quickly. Fine then. Let's make a clean sweep with no hard feelings. I'd like to dissolve the partnership."

"Are you that blind? Hard feelings is what started this whole thing."

"Maybe for you but not for me. I think it would just be better if we didn't have to be in close proximity any longer."

"I'm really pissed about the whole damn thing. Everything was good until this thing with the kids happened," Jake added.

"I never saw you go to the kids' defense. And if things were so great, how could all of this hatred and hard feelings have surfaced? I never knew you were so damn petty."

"And I never knew you were an anti-Semite."

As he uttered this last remark, Jake's face turned fire engine red. The veins in his neck were protruding. He reeled around and felt for his chair. He knew it was there but he couldn't see it in his blind rage.

Al went to his side. Jake pushed him away, shouting, "Stay away from me, you rotten bastard!"

Just then, Ida, the secretary, came bustling into the office with a glass of water along with one of the tranquilizers Becky had brought in for just such an episode. Jake's blood pressure rose periodically. But usually only under extreme duress. This certainly qualified high on the Richter scale for duress.

Realizing he had been responsible for this condition, Al was burdened with guilt. This wasn't something he had willed to happen. He never thought they'd have such a violent ending if an ending occurred at all. He quietly asked Ida, "Should I call for an ambulance? Should I call Becky?"

Ida held her hand up to have him stop talking.

In the meantime, Jake's eyes were closed. He was drooling. This must be the hypertensive crisis that he had been warned about.

Jake forced himself to relax. He thought about peaceful waters and the calm blue sky. Eventually he stopped gasping.

Al started to speak, but upon getting another silent signal from Ida, halted his words.

After an eternity, Jake turned to Ida and asked, "Can you drive me home now, please?"

Al and Ida's eyes met above the cause of their concern. Al mouthed that he would get Ida's car. He pointed to his keys to let her know that he'd get hers if she told him where they were. She nodded her head toward her pocketbook that was prominently placed on her desk.

He walked out of the office where he came face to face with a group of the concerned workers. Disregarding their questioning looks, he spoke. "Ida's driving Jake home now. He'll be fine. You should all go back to work. Jake wouldn't want to disrupt the day or your work. I'm getting Ida's car."

In the inner office Jake said to Ida, "Maybe I had better call Becky. I don't want her to overreact when she sees me coming home in the middle of a work day."

Ida dialed the phone and gave the receiver to Jake.

After two rings he heard, "Rosens, may I help you?"

"Mabel, this is Mr. Rosen. Is Mrs. Rosen around?"

"Just a minute." He heard her calling our, "Mrs. R? Mrs. R? Mr. R is on the phone."

Jake waited until he heard Becky's voice and began, "Beck-a-la, I'm coming home.... No, nothing's wrong. I'll tell you more when I get there."

"Well, how about it?" Ida said when he hung up. "Are you ready?"

"Yes," responded Jake. His color had lightened to a pale strawberry. His neck was no longer distended. His breathing and his demeanor were restored to normal. He picked up his briefcase and started out of the office. As he and Ida reached the door, Al opened it for them.

Al asked, "Do you need any help?"

Jake tersely replied, "No thanks."

Al asked, "Do you think you can manage him? I can get one of the guys to go with you."

Ida said, "I really think that would only aggravate him more. If I have any problem, I'll swing by his doctor's office or go to the hospital."

"Okay," Al answered. "I guess I can't do anything for him."

"I'll see you when I get back."

As Ida drove Jake home, the conversation was stilted.

"Jake, I make a left at the next light, don't I?"

"Right."

Ida turned left and Jake bellowed, "Ida, for God's sake. Why the hell don't you – or for that matter, anyone else – listen? I told you to go right."

"But Jake, I heard you say *right*."

"But I meant not a *left* but a right."

Ida said nothing further, made a U turn and then went straight, which would have been correct as well as right.

After about twenty minutes of silence, Jake said, "When we get to the house, there's no need for you to get out or anything. Becky probably thinks I'm half dead and if she sees you walking with me, she'll call Rabbi Goldberg to start my funeral arrangements."

Ida just nodded.

They pulled in front of the brick two-story house. Jake turned to Ida, saying, "Thanks." He got out of the car without waiting for Ida's perfunctory reply.

Jake walked up the pathway to his house and reached the door just as Becky was opening it.

"Jake, you look terrible. Come in. Lie down on the sofa. I'll get you something to drink." Shouting into the kitchen, she called out, "Mabel, Mr. Rosen's here. Please bring him a glass of orange juice and also the bottle of aspirin. Jake, how's your head? Take off your shoes. Loosen your tie. Take off your jacket."

Mabel came in with the juice and aspirin.

Becky said, "Mabel, will you please get a pillow?"

Jake was too exhausted from the morning to protest. He took the aspirin bottle from Mabel, opened it, and took out two. Then he reached for his juice.

After swallowing the aspirin, he dutifully loosened his tie, took off his jacket and shoes, then semi-collapsed on the sofa. He hadn't realized how tired he was until he was off his feet and safely ensconced in his womb-like afghan. Becky always teased him about his haven from the world. He asked her to pull the shades down, which she did before quietly leaving the room.

Meanwhile at Russen, it was approaching lunchtime. Al hadn't left his office all morning. The only conversation he had was with Ida. He had inquired about Jake but after hearing that Ida had gotten him home safely, continued doing his work.

His stomach was beginning to growl but he really didn't feel much like eating. He pushed himself away from his desk and reflected about the recent events. He knew that it was futile to try to make amends about the religious schism. No matter what else happened, the harsh words they had uttered couldn't be erased or forgotten. He wondered what would become of their business relationship. He knew that being partners in this hostile climate was out of the question. He was in a semi-alert state when the phone buzzed and Ida said that Rita was on the phone.

"Hello," said Al, knowing that she had an idea that something was amiss.

"Al, Mabel's sister is here cleaning and Mabel called saying that Jake came home from the office a few hours ago...."

"And?" interjected Al.

"I was wondering what was the matter. I hope you two aren't letting the business with the kids interfere with your business. After all, one thing doesn't have anything to do with the other."

"Rita, what planet are you living on? We all said a lot of things. Things that can't be taken back. Listen, I'm leaving early so I'll be home in about an hour. I really can't do anything here. I can't place any orders because I want to order from Bocca Brothers and Jake wants to give the business to Sew-Sew. Until we settle some issues, the business will be on hold."

Al bid Rita good-bye, knowing it was best not to prolong the conversation.

The work in the outer offices of Russen had come to a halt as lunchtime had arrived.

The piece workers, designers and the fitters all ate together. Russen had always been like one big, happy family rather than a faceless, nameless business.

Today, the hot topic for discussion was the argument they had been privy to. Jake and Al had been anything but discreet with their disagreement.

"Well, I heard the trouble began when Gary ran out of gas with the boat. I remember reading something in the paper about it."

"No, I don't think it started then. That was the proverbial straw."

"Both of our bosses are protective about their kids. Neither one likes the fact that Gary and Tessa are getting serious. They don't like the religious differences."

"That's stupid. They've practically been raised together. They went to school together and live near each other. They celebrate holidays together. What do you tell your kids? You can play together, go to school together, be friends, live in the same vicinity but turn off your hearts and get your brains in third gear so you don't fall in love?"

"Well, I'm sorry. I agree with Jake and Al. I think that Jews and Catholics shouldn't intermarry. No more than colored and whites."

"Why not? I don't see anything wrong with a religious difference. But I do believe that colored and whites shouldn't mix."

"I think it's none of our business."

"You are dead wrong. It certainly *is* our business because if it affects the partnership, it will impact on each of us."

"Well, as I see it, no one knows what religion you are but they can see the color of your skin. Religion's a private matter but color is right out there for everyone to see. Who cares if someone prays to Allah, Jesus or Moses? People do care about colored and whites though. I know that I wouldn't want any daughters of mine marrying a nig–"

"Don't say that word. Next, you'll be using wop, mick and other insulting nicknames. I used those two in particular because I'm half Italian and half Irish so I'm not offending anyone by using them."

"I think religion is very important. What religion will the kids follow if their mothers and fathers have two different beliefs?"

"That's up to them to decide when they're old enough."

"Oh, so you raise them as heathens until they're 7 or 8 then make them chose between their parents."

"Well, a mother gets stuck with taking them to church so she should have the kids raised in her religion."

"Why? How about if she doesn't go to religious services? Then who's *stuck?* And stuck with what?"

"It just goes back to what I always say; parents should stay out of their kids' lives. Before long, the kids are gone but hard feelings that develop among the adults last forever."

At that moment Al walked into the cafeteria with his briefcase in hand.

"Ida, I'm calling it a day. If anyone wants me, I'll be available tomorrow."

"Okay. Let me know if you won't be in, will you please?"

"I'll be here bright and early." And as he turned, he nodded at the employees who were just finishing up their lunches.

Five

Becky was aimlessly doing things to stay busy. She checked the closets for clothes to be cleaned and also began cleaning out her junk drawer in the bedroom. She saw a few photographs of Gary and Tessa playing alongside Harry and Treva. Becky reflected about the friendship she had enjoyed with Rita as well as with Al. It would be so easy if the kids were still young and in need of protection from the world. She was snapped out of her daydreaming by Mabel calling her.

"Mrs. R? Mrs. R? I've been looking all over for you. Mr. R. is awake. He asked me to come and get you."

She descended the stairs with a tight knot of dread in her heart.

"Jake, how are you feeling?"

"Much better physically but I'm emotionally whipped. I dread what's coming next. All of those years working side by side with Al are for naught. It appears as if the fallout is going to split us up."

"Maybe no. Business and pleasure were never supposed to mix."

"Are you equating this firestorm about Gary and Tessa with pleasure? It's been nothing but heartache. I never thought religion would be such a monumental issue with me. Or, for that matter, all of us. It appears as if *all* decisions, both personal and professional, are biased. For example, I want to continue our business dealings with Abe Weiss but Al is insistent about using Tony Bocca. We've always reserved the right to disagree but this has gotten way out of proportion. I just can't imagine what the future will hold."

Becky hesitated and then spoke. "What's next? Have you thought it through carefully?"

"I think the only rational thing to do is to call our lawyer and see what he can offer as a solution."

"Jake, I'll stand behind you whatever you decide. Maybe if we maintained a united front where the kids were concerned, we wouldn't be facing this now. Maybe we should have talked it over with Rita and Al. I kept begging you to pay attention but–"

"Becky, it's bad enough that I may be losing a business partner of many years. Let's not fix it so I'll lose another partner. Don't drive me away."

37

"But you must agree that I tried forever to tell you."

"How could I not agree with that?" Jake was getting agitated. "Can you leave me alone? I'm not made of iron. I have a breaking point too. Did you ever think if you hadn't always expressed a negative opinion about Gary and Tessa that it may not have been so appealing? Mrs. Perfect you are not!"

"Jake, I've *never* received support from you regarding the kids and their problems. Do you remember when Gary was in first grade and he didn't draw a picture when he was told? He was being defiant because he didn't like his teacher. You laughed and said he was just being a boy. How about when Harry–"

"What, did I miss something? Did you just declare World War III? This whole thing has gotten way out of proportion. I may have been the flour but you provided the yeast. Let's drop the whole thing. Let's just cool down for now."

"Good idea. Thing's will cool down. They'll cool down plenty. I'm going to get away from all of this. My sister has been asking me to come visit her in her new home. I'm going to Florida as soon as I can."

"Do what you want," retorted Jake. "Shall I have Bert draw up anything for us while he's at it?"

"Do whatever you want. At this point I couldn't care less. Put that piece of information in your fabric and sew it."

The kids came home from school and although they didn't hear any of this exchange, they knew something was up. For one thing, Jake was home early. The other thing was he was on the phone. Something he rarely did while at home. He said he spent enough time on the phone at work.

"Okay, Bert. Tomorrow at 9. Drop a dime to Al, please. If it isn't convenient, we'll schedule it later." As he hung up from his attorney, Bert Stein, Jake tried dialing another number that proceeded to be busy.

"Damn it to hell," he said. He stormed out of the living room, into the kitchen and poured himself more orange juice. He sat at the kitchen table and began pondering how in the hell things had gotten so very bad so very fast.

"Hi Dad," Jennifer said, bouncing into the room. "Where's Mom?"

Ah, Jake thought, the innocence of youth. The boys were discerning enough to know that something was awry and didn't stop in the kitchen but went right to their rooms. His little Jennifer was so happy that Jake was home she didn't even give it a second thought.

Jake said, "Mom's upstairs packing. She's going to see Aunt Reva's new home."

"But Daddy, the spring concert is next week. She always comes to hear the choir."

"I'll come, Jen. You can count on it."

Tears formed in Jennifer's eyes. As happy as she was that her dad was coming, her mom's planned absence overshadowed it. She walked out of the kitchen, up the stairs and knocked on her parents' bedroom door.

"Come in."

"Mom, Daddy says you're going to see Aunt Reva. Maybe you forgot but my choir is singing next week and you always come. Can't you go to see Aunt Reva's house later? Can't you go next week? Are you mad at me?"

"No, Jen. I can't go later. I have to go now." Rather than tell her the truth, she added, "Aunt Reva doesn't feel well and I'm going to help her for a while. Don't cry, Jen. It's important for me to be with her now."

Becky's heart was aching. She wasn't used to lying to anyone, let alone her baby. But she knew that if she didn't get away, she and Jake would do nothing but bicker and in the process say a lot of damaging things to each other. She felt that their marriage was facing severe turbulence now; not like the squalls they'd experienced in the past.

If absence didn't make the heart grow fonder, at least it would help Jake and her to evaluate the situation without constantly rehashing it. What had happened to their simple life? She was thinking all these thoughts as she hugged her crying daughter. Jen, who was eventually soothed, began helping her mother pack.

The Mareno household was quiet. The girls had after-school activities so when Al got home, he and Rita were alone. Mabel's sister Eunice had finished cleaning and had gone home.

Rita sat quietly on the sofa, glancing through the mail after she and her husband had exchanged greetings. The suspense was stifling and she was about to barrage Al with questions when the phone rang. Al answered it.

"Speaking. Yes, 9 a.m. Fine. I'll be there." As Al hung up the phone he said, "Son of a bitch!"

"Al, I've been more than patient. Please tell me. What's going on?"

"For your information, that was Bert Stein's secretary. My dear buddy Jake called him and set up an appointment for tomorrow at 9 a.m. I was *requested* to attend."

"My God! What's next? What brought that on?"

"You've got to be kidding. You couldn't be that oblivious to what's going on around all of us. Jake and I had a knock 'em sock 'em today. At one point I thought he was going to have a stroke. Ida had to drive him home."

In mentioning Ida, he remembered that he had promised to call her if he wasn't coming in. He dialed the phone and informed her of the fact.

Then he turned to Rita and said, "Rather than keeping the bickering going and harming the business, we'll probably have to have some kind of dissolution."

"What will happen? Who will operate Russen? If Jake does, what will you do?"

"Rita, I don't know the answers to any questions right now. Just have faith in me and trust me. It will all work out."

Rita remained quiet. Despite what Al said, she was worried about their future as well as Tessa and Gary's. If by some possibility they wound up together, where would both sets of parents fit in?

Tessa and Treva were walking home from school and talking about the upcoming senior prom. It was going to be held in two weeks. Tessa and Gary were slated to go together but she hadn't dared approach her parents for a dress.

"Why don't you just wear your blue dress from last year?"

"Tree," Tessa reverted to her sister's nickname, "I can't do that. This is my last big high school event. I'm just going to have to talk to Mom today."

The girls continued along just singing in harmony as they always did. Their house seemed to sneak up on them. They saw their dad's car in the driveway. That signaled a problem. They both went up the stairs and unlocked the door.

"Hi Dad. Hi Mom," chirped the girls, almost in unison.

After a mutual exchange, Tessa decided it was now or never. "Daddy, can I see if you have anything for me to wear to the prom at Russen's?"

"Sure. Rita, why not take Tessa there now? I think we have some things she'll like." He had an ulterior motive. Rita couldn't continue to question him about things he couldn't answer.

Rita felt as much like going for a dress as she felt like going to the dentist. Still, this was important to her daughter so she kissed Al and got her purse. With Tessa at her side she walked to the car.

"Mom, I certainly don't want a blue gown again even though I love the color. I'd like a pink strapless one. What do you think?"

"Tessa, let's just wait and see what's there. Don't get your mind set on one thing because then it will be hard to satisfy you."

They got into the car and began their trip.

"But if I don't have anything in mind, I'll never get something I like."

"Stop whining." Rita turned on the radio, effectively ending further discussion.

They came to Russen's Fashions, which was adjacent to the factory, parked the car and went into the building.

The guard at the door greeted Rita and ushered her into the evening gown section. Tessa was oohing and aahing over the gowns. She took six dresses into the dressing room to try on. Rita sat and was trying to look interested.

Tessa came out after each and every try on. Neither she nor Rita could agree on any of the choices. The manager said that she had two or three others, which were not completely finished, but she would let Tessa try them on.

When Tessa saw the pink-layered lace strapless gown with a crinoline slip attached, she flipped. It was just basted together and the zipper wasn't in but all agreed it was made for her.

"Gary will just love it," squealed Tessa.

Rita stiffened but ignored the remark. She asked when the dress would be ready. She also asked if they could get a swatch of the material so they could get Tessa's shoes dyed to match.

Mother and daughter left to go buy shoes. After accomplishing the purchase of both the shoes and the gown, they went home.

Tessa was bubbling over the dress. "Dad, it's great. I'm going to have Gary wear a pink tie with his tux. Tree, I just know you'll want to borrow it. We got shoes too. I'm going to wear the rhinestone necklace and earrings I wore last year."

Ordinarily Al would have been part of this exchange but today he just nodded. What a long way tomorrow at 9 was, he thought. But in some ways, not long enough.

Gary was doing his homework when his mother called him to the phone. He ran downstairs to pick up the extension. At the other end he heard Tessa's voice.

"Gary, I'm so excited. I got my dress for the prom today. It's pink and I'd love it if you wore a pink tie with your tux."

Gary was happy for Tessa. It seemed that the prom was the only bright spot they had to look forward to.

"Great. Listen, I'm studying for my chemistry test. If I get a chance, I'll call you later."

Gary was determined that nothing was going to ruin prom night. He kept calls to and from Tessa's house at a minimum so he wouldn't be on the receiving end of more lectures. It seemed strange but since the boating incident, he and Tessa had no longer been the focus of parental concern. They were in the eye of the storm. Something else must be occupying both sets of parents. But his thoughts were invaded when his mother called him

41

to dinner.

Gary took his seat next to Harry. Becky sat on one side of Jennifer and Jake sat on the other.

After saying the Motzi, Jake briefly addressed the business situation.

"Kids, tomorrow Mr. Mareno and I are meeting with our lawyer to see what we're going to do about the business. It seems that Russen may be divided but we're not sure. And if it is, we're not sure how. In the meantime, your mother thinks it's best if she has a rest from it so she's going to Florida."

"I thought you told me that Aunt Reva was sick." Jennifer stared at her mother.

Becky just glared at Jake over Jen's head, then turned to Jennifer, saying, "Aunt Reva had pneumonia last month and still feels rotten. She really needed me then but I couldn't get away. Now I can so I'm going to help her get caught up on her house cleaning as well as unpacking boxes."

Jake didn't feel that skirting the truth was the right thing to do but he didn't want to antagonize Becky further. Gary felt badly that he and Tessa were at the root of this but he couldn't help it. If things worked out the way they had been planning, their parents would just have to accept them as a couple.

The family continued eating while chatting about the weather and other non-volatile subjects. Jen asked her brothers if they would be able to come to her concert the following week. They both grimaced but each agreed to attend.

"Gary, bring Tessa too."

Uh, oh. Here we go, thought Gary. But to his surprise it went unchallenged. Gary didn't feel it required an answer so he began daydreaming again about the love of his life.

"Do you agree?" His dad had addressed him but Gary had no idea at all what the subject at hand was.

"What? Yes. I do. Oh, Dad. I'm sorry. I didn't hear what you said."

"I told Harry that he should take another year of Spanish so he'd have two years under his belt."

"Oh, yeah, that's right. Most colleges require two years of a language," said Gary. He was determined to pay stricter attention now to the dinner talk. However, as soon as the meal was over, he went back to study.

In the Mareno household Tessa could feel that something was happening. Strangely enough, no one was paying any attention to what they had perceived as a problem about Gary. It seemed as if they had a different conflict to deal with.

Before dinner, Rita had said to both girls, "Don't bother Dad tonight. He has a lot on his mind." But she offered nothing further in the way of an explanation.

At the dinner table, Rita tried to keep the conversation light but Al finally interjected that he had something to say. Tessa was completely focused on prom night in the hopes that everything would be resolved at that time. She was oblivious about what turn the conversation took.

"So we meet tomorrow," Al was saying as Tessa came back to the present. No one added anything to his last statement so the meal ended peacefully. Tessa had no idea what he said but thought if it was that important; she'd learn what it was.

After helping with the dishes, both girls went upstairs into Tessa's room.

Treva said, "I want to see your prom jewelry. Where is it?" She couldn't remember what it looked like.

"Right here." Tessa opened her jewel box to retrieve the rhinestone necklace and earrings. She had completely forgotten that her birth certificate was on top.

"What's that doing there?"

She lifted it out of the way but not before her younger and very observant sister saw it.

"Tessa, why is your birth certificate in your jewel box?"

"Because I'm such a jewel. Why else?" And without skipping a beat, Tessa added, "Actually, I'm going to Italy with Grandmom Rose and I have to apply for a passport."

The answer seemed to satisfy Treva and soon both girls began discussing jewelry.

Becky and Jake went to their bedroom early. They were both tired and didn't feel like pretending for the kids' sake that all was well.

While Becky showered, Jake looked at the three suitcases she had packed. Some short stay this was going to be! However, he chose not to explore the length of the visit when Becky emerged from the shower looking fresh and clean.

After so many years of marriage it had come to this.... An icy and yet, if possible, cordial silence. If they were passengers on a bus, they may have exchanged more words. It seemed their marriage was about to collapse and they were both powerless to do anything about it.

"What time are you leaving?" Jake broke the silence.

"I plan to take the early morning bus tomorrow. That'll get me to Florida the next day. Reva or Matt will meet me at the bus terminal."

"Do you need a ride to the terminal? I have the meeting at 9 but I can take you before I go."

"No, thank you. I'll just take a cab."

Becky got into bed, reached for her book and started reading.

Jake knew that he was dismissed so without further conversation, he went into the bathroom to take his shower.

When he came out, Becky's light was already out.

He was saddened to think of how they had always faced any problem together. But not this one. Should love beget hate? He thought that what people did under the guise of love could sometimes be intolerable. He got into bed and he, too, turned out his light. He just stared at the ceiling.

Becky felt tears well up in her eyes. She knew she hadn't given Jake the opportunity to bridge the gap that she had created.... Not only between Jake and her, but between Jake and Al as well. Life was so simple when the kids were still in their cribs. The most difficult part of being a parent was letting go. Perhaps she let go too soon. Maybe that was why this thing with Gary and Tessa had escalated so quickly. Heaven knows that the hostility surrounding them was blown way out of proportion.

Lying there in bed, she longed to twist her feet around Jake's. During cold weather or times of duress they always did this. It was comforting to know that the other was nearby. Lately, that harmony had been absent from their lives.

Jake was also restless throughout the night. He wasn't alone. Yet he'd never felt lonelier. Becky and he were both lying with their backs to each other. An invisible wall had been created and though neither of them had the desire to perpetuate it, neither tried to make it collapse. The silence filling the bedroom was so much louder than anything they could have said to each other. Daylight was a long way off so rather than toss and turn all night, Jake went downstairs and paced the living room.

Al went to bed before Rita. Although anger hadn't really been their undoing, a hopeless feeling engulfed both of them.

As he was lying in bed, he thought how poor they had once been. How they had used a bureau drawer for their newborn baby (Tessa). In some ways, affluence had brought on many of their problems. Life was much more basic when you had to worry about food and shelter rather than what color car to get or what style suit to buy. Rita and he had clung to each other emotionally then as well as physically. They'd been one surging force: almost as if apart they weren't whole. And now this. The morning would mark the end of an era: a partnership. More importantly, it would mark the end of a dear friendship. Without outside influences (God, he was thinking of Rita as an outsider), he and Jake may have kept on as they had all of these years. He asked himself when normalcy would ever return. Finally Al dozed off. He didn't hear Rita come in and she didn't try to arouse him from his slumber.

Six

The next morning Al and Jake pulled into the parking lot at the same time. Even in adversity they were in sync.

"Morning," Jake mumbled.

"Hello." Without saying anything more, they walked to Bert's office.

"Good morning, Al, Jake. Can I interest either of you in a cup of coffee?" Both nodded in assent. When this was out of the way, the meeting began.

"I understand that the two of you have reached an impasse with your business. Almost to the extent that you no longer want to be partners." He looked from one to the other. It was apparent this wasn't something they honestly wanted. They both just looked down at the floor, shrugging.

"I want you to understand that unless an agreement can be met easily, I can't represent either of you. This isn't just a matter of professional ethics. It goes further. I consider both of you friends. I'd like to continue those friendships."

Jake and Al exchanged glances. Each said it would be satisfactory.

"All right now. Let's begin. Is dissolution the only way out of this?"

"Yes," they said in unison.

"Okay. Do you want to cut everything right down the middle? That would mean one of you could buy the other out. Or do you want to divide all assets and have each of you start out on his own? How do you want to proceed? What do you have in mind?"

Jake was the first to speak. "Bert, we don't want to endure more hardship than necessary. Which do you feel would be less traumatic but by the same token, financially sound?"

"Perhaps selling the business outright and splitting the profits?" His voice went up in a questioning mode. "Then each of you could start over as a different enterprise."

"I don't know if that would be best or not." At this point, Al spoke up. "I like the location of the office and factory where they are now."

"And I'd like to maintain the name, Russen. It was my baby initially." Jake shot a quick look at Al and then continued. "Why don't I take the merchandise and name and let Al keep the location? We can make up

46

whatever difference there is between the worth of those two things."

"Al, is that okay with you? I'll draw up whatever you both feel would suit your interests. Personally, I prefer your selling the whole thing and splitting the profits. That way one can't harbor ill feelings if a new venture proves less than successful."

"Bert," Al said. "I honestly prefer Jake's idea. I'm willing to give up the name for the location. We can settle finances equitably."

Jake nodded as Bert added, "Are you two absolutely sure you want to do this? Is there any other way we can proceed?"

Al and Jake looked at each other. Despite the respect and devotion they felt for each other, beneath those feelings was a smoldering intolerance, which just wouldn't die.

They shook hands, patted each other on the back, wished each other well and instructed Bert to draw up the necessary papers.

As Al and Jake left the office, they spoke briefly.

"Good luck, Al. It's been a good ride."

"Good luck to you too."

With those few words, they got into their cars and drove off. They expressed no animosity nor did they express any respect for each other. It was over.

Jake drove to the dock and boarded his new boat. He planned to relax there while formulating plans for his future.

Al drove to his church, 'Our Lady of Hope,' where he lit a candle to the Blessed Mother. He prayed for her assistance with his professional life as well as dealing with whatever evolved between Gary and Tessa. There was something soothing in the walls of his church. He had solved many of his problems in front of Mary. Hopefully these would fall into that same category.

Meanwhile, Becky had boarded the bus for her escape to Florida. She felt like a traitor leaving Jake but she also felt let down by him, her beloved husband. Had he heeded her advice these past several months, he also would have seen that the kids were getting too serious about each other. As she listened to the rhythm of the tires she felt drowsy, but true to the past days, sleep was elusive. As she continued dwelling on the problem, her anger began to surface once again. It was all Jake's fault. You stayed within your own realm. Relationships out of that area should be discouraged. Some things just shouldn't be mixed on a permanent basis.... Catholics and Jews, oil and water, black and white. As her thoughts continued, the tires were now hypnotizing her.

At the beauty parlor, Rita was in deep thought as she got her hair cut. She couldn't pinpoint when the young people's situation had really come to her attention. All she wanted was happiness for both of her daughters and she wasn't completely sure that Gary could give Tessa that happiness. She and Al had certainly struggled but they were both from similar backgrounds with like expectations. They both were the products of Italian immigrants. Her feelings regarding her daughter and Gary had nothing to do with class distinction because if the truth were known, the Rosens were much more affluent than Al and she. With a name like Rosen, there would be no doubt to the religious leanings of the young couple. Could Tessa withstand the restrictions that society would put upon them? Right here in Linfield there were still country clubs where it was common knowledge that their policy was NJA (No Jews Allowed). Even their country club was restrictive. Tessa and Gary as a couple wouldn't be permitted membership in Linfield CC. But there *were* more important things than country club membership.

It was then that Rita came back to the conscious world, sighed and said, "Phoebe, where is your mind. I was telling you that I wanted my hair a bit longer than last time. You just kept cutting away."

"Oh, I'm sorry. It's longer than it was last time. Just let me even it off. I'm sure you'll be satisfied."

"Well, it's a good thing you came out of your trance. Where were you anyway?"

"I was just thinking about a conversation that Linda, John and I had." However, she didn't mention that Tessa's relationship with Gary had been the discussion. "Sorry. Look at yourself in the mirror. See. I told you it would be fine."

Rita nodded in assent, paid then left. As she drove by Our Lady of Hope, she saw Al's car. She pulled into the lot, parked her car, got out and went directly to the Blessed Mother. She lit a candle and knelt down beside her husband, who had tears running down his cheeks. She clasped his hand. They knelt, side by side, praying for peace of mind.

The calming effect was contagious. After a while, they stood up, squared their shoulders and left in silence.

Upon arriving at home, Al explained the result of the meeting to Rita. He would retain the building. Jake was getting the merchandise. He said the settlement would be fair. He had an idea to put in a raingear line in Russen. But now, he would do it as a single venture, independent of Jake as well as Russen. He planned to start small with women's apparel first. Then, later, he'd add a male line. He already had the name, 'Italian Mist'.

Rita listened attentively; realizing that starting a new venture would be somewhat difficult. Square one was never the easiest one to be at but together they'd prevail. She had complete faith in Al's judgment and his business acumen. Thus she knew he'd do well in anything he attempted. She also knew there were problems to be circumvented. She reassured Al that things would all work out and went into the kitchen to make him something to eat. Her mind was engaged in mental gymnastics. She was pondering over Gary and Altessa. She realized no one could drive two people in love apart. That didn't mean she was going to stop trying. She regretted the schism this was causing, not only between the business partners but on all of them as friends. The relationship between the two men was the most serious casualty.

"Rita, I've been talking to you but you were miles away."

"What? Oh. I'm sorry. What were you saying?"

"I was asking if you thought Tessa was going to Italy with your mother this summer."

"I don't think we should give her a choice."

"Are you talking about the same girl that I am? Tessa has a mind of her own in addition to opinions on everything. She may not always be right but she's always positive."

"Let's wait until after the prom. She's been under a lot of pressure. I'd really like her to be able to enjoy her last major high school event before graduation. We'll talk about it the Monday after the prom. How does that sound?"

They agreed to wait and sat quietly together, each lost in his own thoughts.

Gary and Tessa had just finished lunch and were going to class, excitedly discussing the prom, which was going to be a special night for them.

Gary assumed that Tessa knew about the pending partnership dissolution so he didn't feel the need to belabor that particular point. Besides, he didn't want to interject more negativism into their relationship. There was already enough peeking in at the perimeter.

They went their separate ways, planning to meet after school. Gary had to get home as soon as possible because his mother had left for Florida and Jennifer needed supervision.

As they parted, Gary thought how lucky they were to be temporarily out of the emotional storm. They were enjoying a respite from chaos.

Seven

Jake wasn't usually one to drink but he spent the afternoon on his boat, relaxing, nibbling on crackers and drinking wine. He single-handedly drank the better part of the bottle of Chablis which he found in the boat's refrigerator. He didn't feel the effects until he tried to get up. His feet were numb. He stumbled as he tried to stand. He tried to steady himself but slipped to the floor into oblivion. He remained that way for most of the afternoon, breathing erratically. He fell asleep.

As the sun's fury began to dwindle, Jake awoke to find he could not raise himself up. He knew he had to get home for the kids. He especially wanted the environment in the home to be as stable as possible for Jennifer. She was another victim in this affair. He, too, had been victimized. He knew Becky felt he'd added to the problem, thus inadvertently assisting the escalation. He also knew taking no action probably did more to fortify the kids' position than covert opposition.

He put all thoughts out of his head and began concentrating on the situation at hand. He had to get up. It was that simple. He grabbed on to the base of the table in the cabin and pulled himself slowly toward the seat. He finally managed to gain a sitting position. His legs were numb but the numbness wasn't as pronounced as it had been. And his breathing was better. What had he heard someplace? If the eyes don't weep, then the organs do. Well, it was something like that. He hadn't permitted himself remorse about the demise of the partnership. He imagined his blood pressure was taking a real beating because of everything going on. He knew the wine wasn't in his best interests but best interests be damned. He needed something to ease the pain of everything, including Becky leaving, however temporary.

He also knew he had to clear his head so he could plan his next course of action. He didn't feel he was capable of driving home. He didn't even attempt to rise nor did he try to make the journey to his car. He checked his watch. It was 4:30. The kids were probably all home by now. There didn't appear to be any activity on the dock so making noise or trying to go up to the boat dock wouldn't serve any purpose. He silently cursed his stupidity and weakness.

"Dad? Dad?"

Thank God, Jake thought.

"Dad?"

He heard footsteps and looked up to see Gary come into the cabin.

"My God, Dad, what's wrong?"

Though he tried, Jake found that he was unable to speak. He heard Gary cry out, "Sit tight, Dad." And since he was powerless to do anything else, watched as his son walked away.

It seemed like hours passed when Jake opened his eyes and heard Gary saying, "Dad, I called Dr. Gross. He's sending an ambulance to take you to Olive Tree Hospital."

Jake still felt powerless. The weakness had only temporarily subsided and even though he was vehemently opposed to hospitalization, he knew he had no choice. He really didn't want to subject his body to further harm. He was fearful his weakness would worsen. He was afraid he'd have a stroke.

His active mind was wandering. He was barely listening when Gary said he had called Becky's sister in Florida to let them know about Jake. Jake cooperated when the ambulance crew lifted him onto the stretcher. After steering him into the waiting vehicle, they took off for Olive Leaf Hospital.

In the meantime Gary phoned Tessa. "Mrs. Mareno, may I please speak with Tessa?"

When she picked up the phone, Tessa said in her cheery voice, "Hi Gary. What's up?" They had agreed to keep their calls at a minimum. She knew he had something important to say. She had ho idea it would be of such great magnitude.

"I need you to do me a favor. Can you go to my house and stay with Jennifer? Tell both Harry and her that my dad is being taken to Olive tree Hospital."

"My God. What happened?"

"He passed out on the boat today. Right now I'm so damn mad at my mother I could strangle her. She knew how upset he was about the business but she took off for the high ground. I called my aunt and told her to tell my mother to come home. I don't know if he's going to be okay." Gary added this last bit with a crack in his voice. This was out of character for him. He usually took everything in stride.

"Oh God, what's next?"

"Don't ask. Enough has happened to last all of us for a long time. I feel lousy about our part in this. I knew he was upset but I always thought of him as invincible. If anything is seriously wrong with him, I'll *never* forgive myself. But I honestly had no idea how opposed all of them would have been to us. They certainly concealed their feelings all of these years. What have we done?"

"Gary, we haven't done anything wrong. I'm sorry our parents have such strong feelings against us but we didn't do it to be obstinate or spiteful. Don't blame yourself."

As the siren of the ambulance sounded once again, Gary felt a tightening in his throat. He knew that if he continued the conversation, he would begin crying and not be able to stop. He just ended their dialogue, got into his father's car and followed closely behind the ambulance. All the time he was harboring guilt as well as his animosity toward his mother.

At the next bus stop, Becky decided to phone Reva.

"Reva, for God's sake," Becky said after listening to her sister's incoherent rambling. "What are you talking about?"

In mere seconds, Reva's husband Matt was on the line. "Becky, there's been a change of plans. Jake isn't well."

"Oh, my God."

"He's been taken to—"

"My God, what's wrong?"

"Becky, stay calm. As far as Gary knows, it's another episode of hypertensive crisis."

Becky dropped the phone. The bus driver, seeing her plight, came over, picked up the phone, identified himself and listened to what the voice at the other end was saying.

"Uh, huh. Right. Okay. I'll see what can be done. Sure. Olive Tree hospital in Linfield,"

Becky began to tremble. Then came the sobs. Soon she was crying uncontrollably.

The bus driver spoke to her loudly. When he got no reaction, he took a stern approach. When he got no reaction this time either, he grabbed her upper arms in his hands and gave her a shake. Then gently slapped her left cheek. This stunned her. The slap caused the desired effect.

She stopped sobbing, struggling to catch her breath. When he was sure that he had her full attention, the bus driver said, "Mrs. Rosen ... Becky. The other bus at this comfort stop is heading back north. I'm checking with the dispatcher to see if he can take you. I have to check with the driver first to see if there is enough room. Do you understand what I am saying?"

"Yes. Yes. Jake, Jake. How is Jake?"

"Conscious but in a serious enough condition to be taken to the hospital by ambulance," he said as he turned to one of the women passengers, asking her to look after Becky. He went to make the possible transfer.

The transfer couldn't be made on that bus but another was expected within the hour. The bus driver asked the manager of the comfort stop to look after Becky until bus # 371 of the Shore Line Bus Service Company came from the south to journey back north. This bus was going directly to Linfield, which was perfect. In her state, she'd probably have difficulty changing buses.

Becky was quiet and unemotional as her luggage was set down next to her. She was eating some chicken soup; not really tasting it.

Just as she was beginning to become agitated, the manager came over to tell her that bus # 371 had indeed arrived. He helped her up; then took charge of her suitcases. After he protectively escorted her to the bus, he turned over her baggage to the bus driver.

Becky went into the bus and dutifully sat down. She put her legs up on the vacant seat next to her, then turned her head so it was pressed upon the windowpane. She was willing the bus to go faster. Fatigue descended upon her but sleep was still elusive.

Eight

As the ambulance pulled up to the hospital, Jake's symptoms began to lessen. He was now able to respond verbally to questions. His eyes had lost their look of sheer terror.

The hospital attendant took over as soon as Jake was remanded to his care. Jake's blood pressure registered 192/110. His pulse was strong. His color was less red. Noting that Jake was hyperventilating, the attendant advised him not to put so much effort into his breathing. He told him to permit himself to relax. He told him not to worry … that they'd take good care of him.

Jake's mind was becoming alert. He'd slept off the effects of the wine. He was frightened. The doctor came into the treatment room and began taking his health history. The doctor's manner assisted in further relaxing Jake. The exam was thorough.

"Mr. Rosen, look straight ahead. I'm going to just shine this light into your eyes. That's fine. Now, I'll check your other eye. Continue looking straight ahead. Okay. Fine. I want to listen to your chest, so take a deep breath. That's fine. Now another. Okay. Let me listen to your back. Just do the same thing. Take deep breaths. Your lungs sound clear. Do you have any pain?"

"No."

"No headache? I can see that your artery in your temple area is pulsating strongly."

"I don't have a headache."

"Can you squeeze my hand?" asked the doctor as he took Jake's left hand in his. "Fine. Now let's do the same with your right."

With a little more effort, Jake accomplished this.

"Can you tell me exactly what happened?"

"I was on my boat drinking wine, which I don't ordinarily do. I woke up weak and couldn't maneuver."

"Did you hit your head or have a nosebleed?"

"Uh-uh."

"We're going to admit you to the hospital and–"

Jake became extremely agitated about this statement. "I can't go in the hospital. My children are depending on me."

"I understand from talking with your son your wife is coming home as we speak. Your health is my main concern You have slight weakness on your right side. Your blood pressure is elevated. We'll keep you on bedrest with sedation to help bring down your pressure. The nurse will be in with the sedation as soon as I go out to order it. And I'm going to speak with your son," said the doctor as he pointed toward the direction of the waiting room where a distraught Gary was waiting.

"How is he?" Gary couldn't hide the fear in his voice.

"He's calmer now. He's getting a sedative. The next 24 to 48 hours will be crucial. It seems as if this is a hypertensive crisis episode. If that's the case, he'll be here for a few days. After that he can go home with medication and modified activity. If he develops paralysis, we'll have to take it from there. It doesn't appear as if he's had a cerebral vascular accident, more commonly referred to as a stroke. Right now, we're treating this as a potential CVA."

"Does he know any of this?"

"He knows to a degree. At this juncture, it's pointless to add to his anxiety. He said he's been under great strain, both personal and professional. He didn't elaborate on it though. I told him that your mother was coming home so there was no need for him to worry about you kids."

Gary felt his jaw tighten at the mere mention of his mother. Up to this point he had kept his anger in tow, but the hostility came through as he answered. "I called my aunt. She's trying to reach her through the bus company's dispatch system. The earliest she can possibly be here will be sometime tomorrow morning." He held his arms at his sides as he spoke, clenching his fists while trying to control his surging anger.

"Why don't you go in briefly? You can tell him what you've told me. Don't stay too long. I'd like the sedative to take effect. Rest is the most important thing for him right now."

Gary went into his father's room. He was pleased to see that the agitation was disappearing.

"Hi Dad. I reached Aunt Reva. She said Mom should be back by morning. Harry and Jen are okay. I called them while the doctor was examining you. He told me not to stay too long because he wants you to rest as much as possible." Gary used tact. He didn't mention Tessa was at the house, helping with Jennifer. Some things are best left unsaid.

"Okay, son. Go on home. I'll see you tomorrow."

Gary went home, where his siblings and Tessa all were waiting.

"Gary, how's Daddy?" Jennifer cried. "Is he going to be okay? What happened?"

"He had a fainting spell at the boat. He's going to have to stay in the hospital for a few days."

"I want Mommy."

"She's coming home. She should be back before you go to school in the morning."

Tessa looked at Gary and said, "I told my mom about your dad and she was truly upset. She even suggested that Jennifer could go over there but due to everything else that's happened, I didn't think that was such a good idea. Your mom wouldn't like it."

"At this point I don't care what my mom wants or doesn't want. But since she'll be here in the morning, there's no point in moving Jen."

Tessa left and Gary was alone with his thoughts.

Becky was wakeful the entire night. When the bus finally pulled into the terminal, she relaxed. She felt as if she could sleep now. But it was out of the question. She wanted to see Jake. She *had* to see him.

At 6:30, Becky phoned her house. Gary answered.

"Gary, is he all right? Did you tell him that I was coming home? Can you come get me? Can I go to see him?" It seemed as if all of these questions were asked in one deep breath.

"Yes," Gary said tersely. "I'll be there as soon as I can."

When Gary got to the bus station, his fear for his father diminished when he caught sight of his mother. She looked ghastly. He knew her conscience bothered her and although he felt guilty for it, he was somewhat glad she was going through torment.

He kissed his mother perfunctorily. He then got her suitcases, putting them in the trunk of the car. They made the drive to the hospital in an uncomfortable silence.

Becky went over to the bed. She observed her sleeping husband. She pulled up a chair and sat vigil at his bedside. She loosely held his hand and occasionally wiped the sweat from his brow.

After a half-hour or so, Jake awakened. He blinked. Then blinked again. He rubbed his eyes as if he were erasing away a dream. Then he realized that yes, it was actually Becky and not a dream. She'd come home to him.

He broke into a smile while he extended his hands to her. She grasped them in hers and then moved closer to hug him gently. She kissed him.

She was crying softly as she spoke, "Jake. I'm so happy to see you. I've been so upset about you. It's my fault that you're in here. I should never have run away. If anything had happened to you, I'd never have forgiven myself. I should have known that running away wouldn't solve anything. I was acting selfishly. Can you forgive me?"

"Becky, I'm just glad you're here. The important thing is that we're together.... Together we can face anything. Let's not beat up on each other anymore."

With this, she began sobbing. "You're such a giving man. You give 100% of yourself all of the time. I withhold part of me. I was crazy with worry when I heard you were in the hospital."

"I'll be okay. Why don't you go home to the kids? I'm groggy. Besides, they'll be thrilled to see you. You must be whipped. You can come back later ... after you're rested."

Becky kissed him and bid him good-bye. Gary popped into the room to see his dad. They both left, allowing Jake to rest.

Rita watched as Tessa moped around the kitchen. She usually had a decent breakfast but this morning all she did was guzzle down a glass of orange juice and gulp down a piece of toast.

What turmoil! It was unbelievable. It was like a merry-go-round. However, there wasn't anything merry about it.

Rita heard Treva come down. She asked if she wanted to eat breakfast. Treva said she'd love French toast. Once again, Rita checked with Tessa, who still declined to eat anything.

"I can't even think about food. I just want to get to school, talk to Gary and see how his father's doing."

"You don't have to starve yourself in the meantime, do you?"

"You don't understand. The food just won't go down. I'll have lunch at school but right now I'm too jittery to eat."

Tessa went to school. She was disappointed to see that Gary wasn't there. She thought that he was probably beat because he had to pick his mother up this morning. Even though she knew the reason for his absence, waiting for news about his dad wasn't easy. She went through the day on automatic pilot. And it dragged.

At the hospital in the late afternoon, Becky was visiting with Jake. Gary had dropped her off. He was going to see Tessa. Although it had been his pattern in the past, he couldn't just drop in at the Marenos' house. He went to the nearest drugstore and used the pay phone.

"Hello," Tessa answered.

"Hi, it's me."

"Where are you? I've been so worried. How's your dad?"

"He's okay. I just dropped my mother off at the hospital to see him. He looks a lot better. His blood pressure is down a lot. I was wondering if you'd like to come with me while I pick out my tux?"

"Sure. Come pick me up."

Tessa was glad that Gary's father was doing well enough for him to be thinking about something as frivolous as the prom. She ran upstairs to get the swatch of the pink material she'd gotten when she bought the dress. She wanted it to be as close a match to his tie as it could be. Before long, they were on their way.

When Tessa walked down the stairs in her pink finery, both Al and Rita realized she was now a woman. She looked absolutely stunning in her gown. Both her parents were delighted that she'd have this fun-filled evening before going to Europe with Grandmom Rose. They hadn't pressed the issue but each hoped the summer away from Gary would help change Tessa's mind.

The doorbell rang. Gary was let in. Try as they may, Rita and Al couldn't view him as the *enemy.*

Rita said, "Gary, you look positively handsome."

When Gary saw Tessa, his face lit up. He whistled his approval.

"Tessa, let your father snap a picture of the two of you. Al, get a picture of Tessa opening her corsage."

Al said nothing but got the camera. He took a picture as Gary handed Tessa the wrist corsage. She opened the box and put the pink rose corsage on her left wrist. She then took out his carnation and pinned it to his lapel.

Al said, "Wait. Do that again. Let me get a picture of you pinning Gary's boutonniere on."

Then they left the Mareno household but didn't stop at Gary's. Gary said his father was resting and he didn't want to tire him. Even though Tessa saw through this flimsy excuse, she said nothing.

Upon arriving at the school, they went directly into the gym. The prom theme was 'Over the Rainbow' and the gym had been completely transformed. The decorating committee had done a fabulous job. There were clouds suspended from the ceiling of the gym with a huge rainbow covering the topside of one wall. The basketball nets were covered with gold filigree and there were fake coins pouring out from the sides. The gym floor was covered in green felt. A small fountain was in the center of the room and beaming spotlights of rainbow colors highlighted the water in the fountain. There were multicolored balloons wrapped around the poles in each area of the gym. The music stands of the bandstand were adorned with mini-rainbows. The entrance to the gym was colored with simulated yellow bricks.

Linda and Bette ran up to Tessa and said, "Tessa, your gown is really cool. And where did Gary get the tie? It's a perfect match."

"You both look great too. We got it at the place where he rented his tux."

With that Linda left to dance with her date, who had graduated the year before. He wasn't interested in making small talk with a bunch of kids.

Tessa turned to Bette and said, "Are you sure it's okay that I told my parents I'm staying at your house? I don't want to get you in trouble."

"Don't worry. My parents are away. My bossy brother won't be home 'til late. So he won't know a thing."

Gary came up at that point. "Bette, thanks for your help."

Bette didn't know what they were up to but figured it was pretty heavy. She knew Tessa would cover for her if it were necessary.

Gary went over to talk to his football teammates. They asked, "What are you doing later?"

He blushed and answered, "I'm not sure. Where are you guys going?"

"Linda is having an after midnight buffet at her house so we'll probably end up there."

"Okay. Maybe we'll see you guys there."

Lest he divulge his actual plans, Gary kept the conversation short and moseyed away from the group.

Toward midnight the voting took place for the prom king and queen.

It wasn't a surprise to anyone when the senior class advisor said, "This year's prom king and his queen are Gary Rosen and Tessa Mareno." Cheers from the crowd greeted this announcement.

After accepting their honor, Gary and Tessa danced alone on the dance floor to the tune of *Over the Rainbow*. When the music was over, they kissed each other on the cheek to the cheers of their classmates. So far their night had been beautiful and it had only just begun.

Nine

Tessa and Gary said their good-byes and told most that they would probably be at Linda's later. They got into Gary's car and drove to Elkton, Maryland. They had made preparations to marry. When the formalities were over, they went to a motel on the outskirts of Elkton … as husband and wife.

Despite what her non-virgin friends had told her to expect, her first time was beautiful.

Tessa went into the bathroom to put on her white peignoir. This was traditionally a shower gift from the bride's mother. It was also another tradition that it be worn on her wedding night. Naturally they had none of the traditional things.

As she entered the bedroom from the bathroom, Gary's eyes were brimming with tears. He told her how beautiful she was. Her peignoir was just transparent enough for him to see the outline of her small breasts, narrow waist and shapely legs.

Tessa slowly approached him, took his face between her hands, saying how much she loved him and how glad she was that they would always be together.

She could feel his bulge protruding from the front part of his pajamas. She met his kiss with tenderness.

As their arms went around each other, their kisses heightened. Their tongues began playing a sensual tag. She felt her knees go weak. He always did make her swoon but tonight she'd felt sensations she'd only fantasized about.

Still entwined, he guided her to the bed, removed her peignoir and assisted her into a prone position. She could feel her heart pounding. She was surprised that the sound of her beating heart didn't resound in the room. She watched as Gary took off his pajama top, and then lay down beside her.

She never realized how much his very presence unglued her. She experienced many different thrills as he caressed her body. He ran his hands all over her. She felt him start at her shoulders, go gently down her arms and by just using his fingertips, moved down the curvature of her body from under her arms alongside her breasts. She tingled as he moved his hands down her waist, down her hips. His caresses were sensual enough but he was kissing her too.

She responded by running her fingers ever so softly down his body, starting at his face, then his chest, across his nipples before reaching for his swollen appendage. She had never done anything like this before. She surprised herself at her brazen behavior. She heard him moan softly as she gently rubbed between his legs.

He then slipped the spaghetti straps of her nightgown off of her shoulders, lowering the bodice to her waist. He touched her high on the chest, slowly moving his hands down to her breasts. His touch was so minute that it felt as if a feather had moved across her breasts. She began to shiver. He used his index finger and thumb to teasingly stimulate her nipples. He lowered his hands to her hips and at the same time put his lips on her breasts, licking and nibbling on each intermittently. She began to purr like a kitten as he slowly moved his hands to the place that was her washcloth's domain. Her moisture made his finger journey easy.

He removed his hands from her groin area and helped her in taking off her nightgown. They just let it drop on the floor. Together they removed his pajama bottoms. The light in the room was just enough for her to see his pink, engorged penis. It fascinated her as she watched it grow bigger.

She was breathless when he trailed his tongue away from her mouth down to her breasts, to her belly. He tucked his tongue into her lint free navel, returning to her mint-flavored mouth.

Moaning with pleasure, she begged him to enter her and he did so with a possessive tenderness. The pain was excruciatingly beautiful. Each time he thrust within her, the pain was diminished while the pleasure escalated. They exploded in unison, spent and satisfied. They continued this throughout the night until they had to drive back from Elkton.

.

Ten

Several days later, Al met with Bert to set up his plans for 'Italian Mist'. There didn't appear to be any hitches with the settlement with Jake, though both families had to mortgage their homes to finance their single ventures.

When Al walked out of Bert's office into the waiting room, he saw both Becky and Jake sitting there. There was an icy stare on Becky's face but he couldn't discern what the expression on Jake's face denoted. What did the furrowed brow and pursed lips mean? Anger? Confusion? Or sorrow? He nodded to them, hoping that no one else in the room had noticed that he was snubbed. He hadn't dared speak to them because he was sure that they wouldn't acknowledge him.

Already feeling as if he'd lost a body part by splitting the business, Al felt even worse about the fond memories that were overshadowed in the wake of these new feelings. He hurried out of the office and went to his car.

Meanwhile Jake and Becky entered Bert's office.

"You're early today," Bert said. He wouldn't have scheduled the appointments that closely together if he had anticipated Al's running overtime and Jake catching the proverbial worm.

"Yes," Jake answered. "We had some shopping to do and since we finished sooner than anticipated, we thought maybe you could see us sooner."

"No problem," Bert said. "And by the way, my daughter told me that Gary was prom king. Congratulations."

"Thank you." Jake wanted no part of prom talk which would invariably include Tessa. "What exactly do we have to do today? Also, when I sign the final agreement, how soon do I have to pay the money to Al?"

"Have you applied for a mortgage yet? If so, we can do it within a week of the signing. If not, we'll have to give you a thirty-day grace period, which I'm sure Al will grant."

"We have applied for the mortgage but since I was in the hospital recently I have to get a statement from my doctor saying my health isn't endangered. He's on vacation until next week so it'll be at least 'til then before I can get my money."

"Okay. Read this over. I already showed it to A– The other party in this."

It was strange to hear Al being referred to as the other party rather than just plain Al. This maze of entanglement had drawn a lot of people into it. Most of them were innocent bystanders.

Jake listened as Bert began to explain the legal document. He only had a few questions to ask his attorney and was satisfied with the answers. Becky was more of a hard sell than Jake was. She asked endless questions. Bert was losing his patience. But perhaps the reason she was getting to him today was the fact he had been so uncomfortable about the two of them running into each other in the waiting room. Or maybe he was just saddened that two of his friends had chosen to end *their* friendship. It was like mourning a death. He knew that any social events would no longer be feasible with both couples in attendance. He also realized that as in divorce, many people would be forced to take sides or else alienate themselves from both couples. The latter alternative seemed to be the stronger possibility. That way both parties would be treated equally. People wouldn't have to make the choice of one over the other.

But on a personal note he wondered what he would do if his daughter chose to limit her affection to a Christian young man. He had always considered himself tolerant, but now, by being an observer in such a situation, he saw another aspect of his personality emerging. He hoped he wouldn't have to cross that bridge. The meeting ended and Bert continued with his busy day, no longer giving any thought to the rapid demise of an era. A tornado couldn't have come quicker nor could it have left more emotional destruction. How had this happened at all, let alone so very fast?

Graduation was slowly approaching but for Gary and Tessa, it couldn't come soon enough. Rose kept pressing the trip to Italy by dropping hints such as 'Oh, you'll meet my cousin soon'; or 'You'll see the pope.' Tessa sometimes thought she'd scream if Rose kept harping on Italy. She and Gary decided that to keep peace she would go with Rose. They knew that both families could use a cooling-off period.

Tessa went about getting her passport and mentally readied her wardrobe. She reflected on the cold reception she'd been getting on the phone from Becky. She also knew that Gray was subjected to similar treatment from Rita. She and Gary usually arranged their assignations while at school. Friday and Saturday were planned in detail after school on Fridays. Sundays were planned on Saturday. They were surprised at their free rein. They had some sadness about the old 'Russen' but were thankful for the focus being transferred from their relationship to something else.

Graduation was over; the partnership dissolved and it was now time to go to Italy.

The night before leaving, Tessa met Gary at Jake's boat. They planned what steps they would take to liberate themselves from their parents' grasp when she returned. They knew that the hurt would still be present no matter what approach they took. If necessary, Gary and Tessa would forego college. After all, neither Jake nor Al had a high school diploma let alone college. They had to make their own way together.

Although they were sad to be leaving each other, they thought their parents would see that they were adult in their behavior as well as cooperative *kids*. That night they clung to each other while tearfully saying good-bye.

Al, Rita and Treva went to the pier to bid Rose and Tessa Bon Voyage.

Tessa looked futilely for Gary. Although they agreed he wouldn't come to the dock, she had hoped he would've changed his mind. Apparently he hadn't.

The Trans-Atlantic journey was rough with both spending a fair share of time in their cabins. But soon enough they has crossed the Atlantic.

Upon arriving in Italy, they were greeted by Rose's sister Bella, who was fifteen years younger than Rose but looked like her clone.

They arrived at Bella's. There was a feast unlike any that Tessa had ever seen. There was an antipasto, Pasta Fagioli, spinach in garlic and oil, meatballs, pasta, parsley potatoes and steak, along with Italian bread. There was an Italian rum cake, cheesecake, spumoni, espresso and cappuccino.

It was a good thing they all spoke English. Even at that, Tessa didn't know how she was ever going to keep this enormous family straight.

Tessa enjoyed the feast and merriment. Before long they began doing the tarantella. She knew the basics but was given a quick tutorial. The festivities continued well into the evening. Tessa and Rose's circadian rhythms were off kilter so they went to bed while the party was still going strong.

Bella showed Tessa and Rose to their rooms after she realized they had enough of the dancing and music.

Tessa feel asleep as soon as she flopped on the bed. She woke up very early, feeling squeamish.

She lazed around for part of the morning and began feeling better. However, when she smelled the gravy cooking, she was overcome by waves of nausea. She had probably picked up a virus aboard ship. She went into the kitchen and had a cup of tea, waiting for her nausea to subside. She had always been resilient and in a matter of minutes she began feeling better. At the same time, Bella and Rose returned from visiting other relatives.

"Hi Tessa. You look better," said Rose. "Did you eat anything?"

"Well, I felt better but then the bug acted up. I got sick to my stomach again but I managed to eat something. I'm fine now. What're we going to do today?"

Bella said, "Some of my cousins invited us back for dinner tonight. We don't have to be there until 7 so we could visit the Catacombs first."

Tessa was thrilled. She was going to see a part of history that she'd studied about in school. She agreed. So the three of them went off to see the Catacombs.

Tessa loved it. She actually was glad that she had come to Italy even though she missed Gary terribly.

Eleven

As was his habit of late, Gary was daydreaming about Tessa. After taking a break he was walking back to work. He could practically walk the route with his eyes closed. *Seemingly* that's exactly what he'd done.

He stepped into the street, not observing any of the cars. He was certain that even if the right of way were not quite his, any car would surely yield for a pedestrian. What he hadn't anticipated was that the driver of a car might possibly be trying to stretch a light while it was still yellow. He looked up after hearing a loud horn blast in addition to the screeching of the tires upon the asphalt. Lucky for him it wasn't raining or else the car most assuredly would have skidded into him. The driver very aptly swerved and missed him by inches.

"Are you– Christ, Gary. It's you. Where the hell was your mind?" Al shouted.

Gary's face in no way registered the shock he got when he saw who was driving the car. His father-in-law had almost victimized him. He said to Al, "I'm sorry, Mr. Mareno. I was on my way back to Dad's. I guess I wasn't paying attention."

"That's for sure. You have a penchant for mobile problems, don't you? Both land and sea."

Gary let the remark slide. He didn't want to have a verbal confrontation with Tessa's father or rehash the boating incident. It was that very incident that had caused the domino effect.

"How's Tessa coming along?" asked Gary, heading for the high ground. But on second thought maybe it wasn't such safe territory.

"She's fine. They got there totally safe but neither she nor Rose fared too well on the ship going over. They were as sick as dogs. They've been doing a lot of sightseeing. The other day, they went to see the Catacombs. She said she'll probably gain weight while over there because every day they seem to have a feast."

Gary feigned ignorance to all of these facts.... No sense in antagonizing his father-in-law any further. "Well, I'll see you, Mr. Mareno." And he continued his trip back to his father's business.

Gary went about his duties, which were mostly arranging fabric on the shelves. The blues faded into light green, which became darker and then blossomed into red and so on. The prints were bold and beautiful and were all placed in groupings with flowers, stripes and like items placed together with the colors interspersed. The whole setup was quite appealing.

Jake brought Gary into the adjacent area, in which the cutting section was located.

"See, Gary. I have this area close to the fabrics and patterns so someone can either pick a pattern first and then get a suitable fabric or perhaps choose a snazzy fabric and search for a pattern."

"Oh, I see what you've done here. I know that when Tessa had her heart set on a color she would have to look all around until she found a pattern that she liked. This way it's a heck of a lot easier." Although Gary wasn't that interested in the business, he had to give his dad credit.

Jake was so proud of his new venture that he went on like he was doing a commercial. "We now have an additional feature here. We have designers who can draw up an outfit according to one of our customers' specifications. I know this will increase business once the word gets out."

What he didn't say was he knew Al wouldn't be in direct competition with him. Al was specializing in raingear only. He watched the progress of his former partner almost with a feeling of pride. After all, he had broken him in, hadn't he? He liked the name Al had picked for his new venture. He thought it was a clever marketing tool. He didn't wish his former associate/ friend any evil nor did he harbor any resentment toward him. Becky was another thing altogether. She spat venom whenever anyone mentioned the Marenos. The wound was too deep for her. Quite possibly it would never heal. He didn't have time for all that negative energy.

Gary was glad his father was excited about the new Russen. He didn't dare mention his close escape from an accident from a car driven by Al. He was nobody's fool!

Al was busy with his business. He was about ready to open. He had gone to Tony Bocca to purchase the repellant fabric, and then hired a skeleton crew to start the manufacturing of the rain attire. The letters in his logo were written in red and green like the Italian flag, ITALIAN MIST, and the background was white.

Rita had come in to help him set up. "Are you planning to arrange by sizes or color? That way you could intersperse the sizes throughout."

"I think by color. That way if I don' t have their size in a particular color, I can always get it made up. If we put the sizes together, people will be more hesitant to ask if we can get a different color in their size."

"Okay. I'll start with that." As interested as she was in Al's business, Rita couldn't get her mind off Tessa. Rose had written that Tessa was sick. Al needed her but she half wanted to go to Italy. She was sure there was something seriously wrong with her firstborn.

"Thanks. Honey, you look troubled. We're going to do just fine." He chose to pretend that he thought their finances were the reason she had that contemplative look on her face.

Getting back to business at hand, Al had chosen mostly neutral colors. Olive drab and gray were the predominant ones. He planned to add brighter hues after he got off the ground. He thought he'd later add matching hats and umbrellas but wanted to start off small. He could always increase his line once he got established.

Tessa was *still* not feeling well. Bella had taken her aside and asked her if she had anything she wanted to tell her. She assured her that it would be held in strictest confidence. Tessa thought somehow she'd found out about the secret marriage.

Then it hit her. Her aunt wasn't hinting about a wedding or anything of the sort. She was alluding to pregnancy. Tessa never even thought that was a possibility. Then came the dawn. This was the middle of July and her last period had been two week before the prom. If her calculations were correct, she was about two months pregnant. She was away from Gary and didn't want to share this news with anyone. She thought Bella would understand but she wanted Gary to know first. She thought about their wedding night. It was the most beautiful night of her life. She reflected upon that while trying to decide what to do.

Being practical, she came back to the real world and thought about her situation. She decided that she couldn't phone the news to Gary. Everyone would barrage him with questions about the call, putting him in an unfair position of fielding them alone. So she began composing a letter.

Dear Gary,
    Guess what? You are going to be a father.

No, she thought. That's too light and airy. This is something wonderfully beautiful. Therefore it deserves a proper introduction.

So she tried again.

My dear Gary,

Missing you has been horrible even though the trip has been wonderful. Aunt Bella is really cool. She and I have had lots of talks about you and our parents' reaction to us. It's too bad she doesn't live in America because she'd be a big help to us.

Gary, even though not being with you is painful, there's a part of you with me that's made everything easier. Something wonderful has happened. I just can't believe it. We've created a bond between us that will be a living testament to what we've shared. By now you probably know, we're going to have a baby, I wanted so very much to call you but then everyone would be standing around and you wouldn't have any privacy. By writing to you, I thought you could read this in your room and pretend that I'm there, in your arms, talking to you and giving you this wonderful news in person. I'm sending you a picture so you can see that I haven't gained any weight yet. At least not enough to show.

In a week or so, I'll tell Aunt Bella. She had hinted about this to me. She surmised I was pregnant before it dawned on me. I'm sure she'll tell Grandmom Rose, who I know will go completely into orbit. Watch how hot those phone lines will be from Italy to my house.

Let's wait to tell your parents together. Mine will probably know by then but the way things are, I don't think we have to worry about them communicating with each other.

I can't wait until we can be together. Nothing will ever part us again. We have so much to look forward to together.

All my love all my life,
Tessa

As Tessa was signing the letter, the tears fell. Happiness was intermingled with uncertainty. Overwhelmed she lay across the bed, crying herself to sleep.

Time was passing at a snail's pace for Gary. It seemed each day took a week.

One day in particular the sun streaming into his room awakened Gary. This was going to be a beautiful day. He knew today would bring news from Tessa with a probable date for her return. He worked diligently at his father's store and as usual went home for lunch. But the mailman was later than usual. So for the time being his hopes of hearing from Tessa were squelched.

After what seemed like an eternity, the end of the usual workday came. However, Jake had asked Gary to help him rearrange the bolts of fabric.

Naturally Gary couldn't say no, although he was dying to go home for his mail.

Gay agonized as the seconds, minutes and eventually hours passed. It didn't seem feasible all of this rearranging could take so long. Finally after a half-hour of this work, he spoke to his father.

"Dad, do you have any idea how much longer we're going to be? I'm famished."

"What? Oh, it's 6:30. I'll tell you what. Let's go home for dinner. We can come back after we eat."

Though he didn't feel like coming back, Gary said nothing. If the letter he'd been anticipating all day had come, he could read it and then willingly go back to Russen with his father.

Silently, they drove home. Each was enmeshed in his own thoughts.

When Gary and Jake both got home, they asked about the mail.

Becky said, "Jake, you got a few bills. Nothing much."

Gary waited impatiently for his mother to address him. When she offered nothing, he pressed the matter. "How about me?"

Offhandedly Becky answered, "Oh, yes. You got a few things. I left them in your room."

Gary took the stairs two at a time. Upon reaching his room, he saw the mail on his desk. There was a letter from College as well as one from the boy who was going to be his roommate. But most important of all, there was a letter he had been hoping for all day. It was from Tessa. He read the letter quickly at first. Then went back over it so he could savor every word. He was overwhelmed by Tessa's news. He didn't know if he was capable of keeping it a secret until she came home.

He came to grips with his emotions, realizing he could tell no one about this until they were together. Then they'd make both of their announcements together (the marriage and the pregnancy). He looked for a secret place to hide this special correspondence. Finally he decided to put it in his winter boots. No one would find it there either by accident or on purpose.

He went into the bathroom and washed up for dinner. When he went downstairs he tried to act as nonchalant as possible.

"Did you get anything in particular?" asked his mother.

Gary who had started eating said, "Uh-uh."

"Well, what did your roommate have to say?"

"I don't know. I didn't open it. I'll read it when I get back from work."

Becky was boiling. She knew he opened at least one letter. She didn't offer any further comment because her son and her husband were talking.

As Gary continued the conversation, he felt as if he would burst. He thought that his happiness must be evident. Somehow he managed to keep his cool.

The day that Tessa had mailed the letter she felt as if a burden had been lifted from her shoulders. Now she would be counting the days until she would be leaving for home.

When she returned from her errand, she was surprised to find Aunt Bella waiting for her.

"Aunt Bella, I thought you went with Grandmom Rose."

"No, Tessa. I had a headache and thought I'd stay home. That sister of mine has so much energy. If I'm not up to par, I could never keep up with her."

"I know what you mean. Even though she and I were seasick on the ship, she bounced around and didn't miss a thing."

"Speaking of being sick.... You're still sick at times, aren't you?"

Tessa realized it was futile to prolong the inevitable, so she decided to tell Bella what the older woman had already suspected.

"I think you know what I'm going to say," she began timidly. "I'm pregnant. My baby is due in February. After our parents put so many roadblocks in our way, Gary and I decided we wanted to be together forever, so we got married after our senior prom. Honestly, we didn't want to hurt or spite anyone. We just wanted to please ourselves. Our parents are upset because of our religious differences. We never thought of each other as different in any way. We were always friends. Then we fell in love. Our parents don't know we're married. You're the only one who knows. And other than the letter I sent to Gary, no one knows I'm carrying our first child. It's been so hard being away from him. He's decent, handsome and just perfect. Mom and Dad always liked him. Neither of us ever expected this." As Tessa was saying this, her tears spilled onto her cheeks.

When she finally did speak, Bella aid, "We're going to have to let Rose know. No. Wait until I finish. You have to get to a doctor. I'll make plans to come to America with the two of you. I'll say I can only go now because I have a wedding I must go to next month. Rose will believe this. At the last minute, I'll pretend to be sick so I won't be able to go. When you're at sea for a few days, you'll give your grandmother a letter from me. By that time she won't be able to wire the news because you'll already be on your way home. They can all be told in person."

Tessa was so relieved that she just put her arms around Bella and cried.

Twelve

Gary got through the days as a happy robot. He was surprisingly calm but since he was usually easy to get along with, his parents attributed his daydreaming to his getting ready for college. They also knew he was happy the summer was almost at an end and his Tessa would soon be home.

Shortly after the letter came about Tessa's pregnancy, he received another saying they would be home sooner than anticipated. This was due to the intervention of Aunt Bella.

As soon as he knew, Gary told Harry and Jennifer when Tessa would be home. Jake and Becky found out later.

Gary kept his secret from everyone. He had been tempted to tell his brother but was afraid that Harry wouldn't be able to keep something of this magnitude a secret. Not that he would do it deliberately but he might accidentally let it slip.

The time was fast approaching for Tessa's departure. Bella and Tessa had been very careful with the preparations. Bella had packed many clothes for herself even though it meant that she would probably have to iron them all by the time she got around to unpacking them. She was also helpful in concealing Tessa's morning sickness, which had an erratic schedule. It occurred at any time.

Finally, the day before they were to leave, Bella began feigning illness. She even went so far as to powder her face to make herself appear pale. The dark circles under her eyes were accentuated, making her look like a panda in reverse. Ironically, she did develop a fever, which added credence to her contrived story.

"Bella, you look like hell. What's the matter?"

"I really don't know. But I can't visit America just now. At this point, I don't feel well enough to face a long ocean voyage."

Rose offered to postpone the trip but Bella said she wouldn't hear of it. And besides, she did have a wedding in August.

"You and Tessa are packed and ready. I was young once so I know how eager Tessa must be to get home. Aren't you, Tessa?"

"I wish you could come with us. It's true that I'm looking forward to going home but I'm sad about leaving you behind. You've made our visit just great."

"Fine. Then it's settled. When I do come to America, you can both show me the sights."

All day long, Gary was jittery. Jake was constantly reprimanding him about his haphazard approach to his work. But Gary wouldn't let anything ruin the day. He corrected his errors and worked harder than before. He knew Tessa would be in around midnight. Treva had called to tell him that much. The entire family was driving to New York to pick up Rose and Tessa. Gary knew he wouldn't be welcome. He once may have been but.... He had to content himself with seeing Tessa the next day. Jake had given him the day off presumably to get ready for college. If Jake knew the true reason Gary wanted to be off, he didn't acknowledge it.

Al, Rita and Treva drove to New York in the early morning. They were going to eat lunch at Mama Leone's and Al was going to see his supplier. Bocca Brothers did service him locally but Al wanted a new and different rainwear color. He was visiting the mills to see what they had to offer.

Rita and Treva were going to shop for clothes at some of the wholesale houses to which Al still had access. Treva needed some new clothes for school. Rita just wanted a few things. Before long the day was ending. The ship would soon be docking. They were all excited as they awaited Tessa and Rose.

As they watched the ship come in to port, they were taken by the beauty of the scene. The Statue of Liberty welcomed all of the ships into the harbor. Al and Rita remembered how it had been for them.... Their first sighting of America. It seemed like a lifetime ago.

It took a long time but the ship was eventually docked. The gangplank was put in place and the passengers came down the ramp.

"There they are," shrieked Treva. "See. Over there."

Rita and Al saw them at the same time and just looked at each other. Tessa looked pale but radiant. Rose looked exhausted.

"Hi Mom. Hi Dad. Hi Treva. It's good to be home."

"Mom, are you okay?" the concern was evident in Rita's voice.

"Just a bit tired. It was quite a trip, especially the ride home. Just give me a day to relax. I'll fill you in on everything."

"As long as you're okay. Tessa, you look pale."

"I'm fine. Tree, I got you an Italian leather wallet. For you too, Mom.

Dad, I got you a leather belt. I'll give them all to you tomorrow when I unpack."

Tessa was relieved to see Rose had kept her word. She was going to let Tessa and Gary tell their own news. She was thinking about how upset Rose had been when she read the letter aboard ship.

Dear Rose,

Sit down. Calm yourself. Then read this.

This isn't an easy letter to write but I felt that I would rather you heard the news from me. There's no easy way to tell you, so I'll get right to the point. Tessa is pregnant.

I know you, your daughter and son-in-law don't approve of her relationship with Jake's son but he seems like an upstanding kid, notwithstanding the fact he's Jewish.

Sometimes things are made more appealing when they're forbidden.

This isn't meant to be a sermon but I'm asking you to help Tessa tell her parents. Or if not, help Gary and Tessa tell them. Maybe in some way, you can make it easier for the kids.

I really loved having you with me these past weeks. I do plan to come to America. However, I'd like to wait until after the baby is born. Perhaps for the christening, if that's okay with you.

Please don't be hard on Tessa. She's been through a lot this summer. I suspected she was pregnant so I confronted her.

Also, please don't be angry with the kids. They didn't have premarital sex. They got married the night of their senior prom. Their conviction to be together was stronger than any opposition.

The kids want to tell both sets of parents themselves so try to hold your tongue until they do. I know you will.

God bless you.

Love,

Bella

Tessa remembered Rose's face when she had come into the cabin and saw her grandmother holding Bella's letter.

She said to Rose, "Grandmom, you have no idea how happy I am that you finally know. I'm so relieved. Will you help me with Mom and Dad?"

"Tessa, why? You're just a baby ... just out of high school. What are you going to do with a baby?"

"Grandmom, I'm two years older than you were when my mother was born. I'm perfectly capable of having, loving and raising a baby."

"Do the Jews know yet?"

"That sounds hateful. Gary knows. That's all that matters."

"What do you expect me to say? Should I approve that you defied your parents?"

"Neither Gary nor I wanted to defy anyone. But no one bothered to listen to us. Nobody tried to understand. We love each other. I'm sorry you feel the way you do but I'm glad to be carrying our baby."

Rose started to soften her tone, "I'll give you until the day after we dock to tell your parents."

"Thanks. I can't ask for more than that. Honest to God, we'll be fine. Gary, the baby and I. We'll be just fine. You'll see. Thanks a lot." Tessa hugged her.

As the older woman returned the hug, she wished she could be as sure as her granddaughter was that their future would be rosy.

Thirteen

Though she was wide-awake at eight, Tessa didn't want to call the Rosen household. After breakfast of pancakes and sausage, which Rita made, she decided to go to the dock. If she knew Gary, he'd be there assuming she'd be there too.

She spotted him as she walked toward the dock. She ran into his open arms.

Gary hugged her tightly, then pulled back while saying, "Tessa, I'm sorry. I hope I didn't hurt the baby."

"Gary, don't worry. You won't be able to hurt our baby. You could never hurt anyone or anything. Anyway, I'm not made of glass," said Tessa, her eyes brimming with tears.

After they shared how much they had missed one another, they began discussing a more serious issue.

"Grandmom Rose knows about the baby. We have to tell my parents today or else she's going to do it. My father's not going to be working all day. How about your family? When should we tell them?"

"How about after the baby is born? Just kidding. My dad is only working a half-day today. He and my mom are going out of town later. Do you think we should be there when he comes home?"

"No matter how or when we do it, none of them are going to be happy."

"You're right. Let's go sit in the boat. We'll talk it over."

She took his extended hand. Together they walked onto Jake's boat and entered the cabin.

When they entered, they stood at arms' length, looking into each other's eyes. Finally, they walked toward each other and embraced. Their kiss began tenderly. Then Gary thrust his tongue into her mouth. The kiss rekindled all of the emotions, which had been first unleashed on their wedding night. They remembered the heat of that night all too well.

Gary carefully removed Tessa's blouse and bra, revealing her bigger, beautiful breasts. He touched them tentatively at first and then more vigorously.

"Oh, Gary. Oh, Gary. That feels so go-oo-od. I've missed you. I've missed your touching me."

She took off his shirt and rubbed her hands along his chest. She could feel his nipples harden as she crushed her breasts against his bare, sun-tanned chest.

He began licking her breasts, letting his tongue surround first one nipple, then the other.

They kissed again. Gary helped Tessa take off her Bermuda shorts. He looked at her belly as he observed the slight thickening. He admired his handiwork.

He ran his hands over her belly, then grabbed her buttocks. Although he was still fully clothed, he pressed her pelvis against his distended member. He took her hands, encouraging her to feel his maleness.

She unbuttoned his shorts, undid his zipper and in one swooping motion, removed his shorts along with his underwear.

They went to the bunk to lie down. He ran his hands all over her. His touch was both stimulating and sensual.

She took his penis in her hands, fondling it. He moaned. He massaged her pubic area before allowing his finger to enter her moist, hot cavity. After he removed his finger, he put it into his mouth, tasting her juices.

"I need to feel you inside me *now.*"

He teased her some more by running his tongue over her body while exploring her inside with his fingers. She cried in delight and she reached for him. She grabbed his penis and impaled herself with it.

They were in such a fevered pitch that within seconds they reached mutual satisfaction. They just lay there staring at each other.

Within minutes, he was ready again. This time they made love slowly and deliberately.

Then they both fell asleep. Upon awakening, they decided it was time to talk to their parents.

They got into their car and drove to Gary's house. Jake pulled in right behind them.

"Hi Dad."

"Hi, Mr. R."

"Oh hello, Tessa. I forgot you were coming back today."

They all walked into the house, where Becky was siting in the kitchen having some soup.

"Hello Tessa," said Becky flatly. "Would you like to join us for lunch?"

"No thank you, Mrs. Rosen," said Tessa as she took Gary's hand.

"Mom, Dad, Tessa and I are in love and wearegoingtohaveababy." This was said so fast that the Rosens didn't quite get it.

"What? What? Did I hear what I think I heard?" Becky was the first to react. "Do the Marenos know yet?"

"No, my parents don't know yet," said Tessa.

Jake just walked out of the room.

Becky raised her right hand and took a menacing step toward Tessa. Gary stepped in her way and forcibly, yet gently, held her hand before it could find its mark. She glared at both of them, said nothing, and then followed Jake out of the room.

Gary and Tessa stood for a moment longer and then they just walked out of the house.

"I told you she'd get her hooks into him one way or another. I told you she'd make sure he wouldn't forget her. I told you to stop this before Gary got roped in. I told you–"

"Becky. I don't know whom you're talking about. I don't know any Gary. My son Gary is dead."

He took out his tallith, his yarmulke and his prayer book and said a prayer for his dead son.

Becky sat in the living room crying.

Tessa and Gary were both shaken by the Rosens' reaction. They expected it to be bad but ... if this was a preview of coming attractions, they were almost tempted to let Rose do the dirty work. Uncertain of what to do next, they went back to Jake's boat and went to sleep. Sleep was always a form of escape for Tessa. She definitely needed her emotions brought down to get ready for the next would-be unpleasant encounter.

As the day passed they both became more anxious. Finally, unable to stall any longer, they set out for the Marenos.

When they got there, Rose and Rita were sitting in the kitchen having a cup of tea. The cups were nearly full so Tessa realized that they had just sat down. Grandmom Rose had kept her promise and had given the young people a chance to break the news themselves.

"Hi Mom. Hi Grandmom. Where's Dad?"

"Hello," said Rita. "He's upstairs changing his clothes. He has some things to do around the house."

"Hello children," said Grandmom Rose. "Sit down. Would you like something?"

"No thank you," said Gary.

As Tessa shook her head no, Al came into the kitchen in his jeans.

He nodded at his daughter and Gary then questioned his wife. "Rita, have you seen my pliers? I thought they were in my workshop but when I looked, they weren't there."

"As a matter of fact, they're here on the counter." She got up, grabbed the tool and handed it to Al.

Tessa reclaimed her voice and spoke up. "Dad, can you stay a minute or so longer?"

"Sure." Gary walked closer to Tessa, reached for her hand, looking at her as she spoke.

"Mom, Dad and yes, you, too, Grandmom. It's no secret that Gary and I are in love. We have been for some time now. But there's something you don't know.... We're going to have a baby."

"Oh, dear God," said Rita. "I thought I had instilled better morals than that in you. Tell me, Gary, why'd you take advantage of her? Wouldn't any Jewish girls put out for you?"

"Mom, your words are cruel and unfair. What do you think there is between us? Just sex? Did you think I ignored your sermons on virginity? We happened to have gotten married prom night. Not that you deserve any explanation."

"And you expect that to make everything all right?"

"Rita," Al interrupted. "That's enough." Turning to his son-in-law, he asked, "What kind of planning have you done to insure my daughter's happiness as well as that of the child she is carrying? You have to stop going through life with a *damn the torpedo* attitude. Isn't there anything worth waiting for? Did you think this was going to miraculously change the way your parents, Mrs. Mareno and I feel? Do you think any of us will change our feelings by this announcement? I think you'd better leave now."

"No. If Gary goes, so do I."

"Tessa, there's your suitcase." Al pointed to one of the bags that had been emptied but not yet put away. "Take what you can now. We'll see that the rest gets delivered."

Tessa's eyes filled with tears. After eighteen years of doing all her parents had wanted her to, this *evil* deed negated everything.

Rose broke the silence. "Al, Rita, I must tell you. I found out about this on the ship coming home. My sister Bella guessed Tessa's condition. She was responsible for our early return. She wrote me a letter, which I read on the journey home. I, too, am disappointed. But she's my granddaughter and I love her. Tessa, to ease things for everyone, why don't you and Gary come to live with me? I'm sure that your parents and Gary's would want you safe."

"You can do whatever you want," said Al. "I wash my hands of the whole thing." He picked up his pliers and stormed out of the room.

Rita's eyes as well as Tessa's were filled with tears. She couldn't think of anything to say to ease their pain nor for that matter did she want to. She had half hoped that Italy would create a miracle. But deep down in her heart she knew that Tessa felt about Gary the same way she felt about Al. Damn it all! Her thoughts began to spin wildly. She realized she would have a Jewish grandchild. All she could think of was how Al had played Santa Claus for both their daughters and the Rosen children. She came out of her reflection as she heard Gary speaking to her.

"Mrs. Mareno, please try to understand. We didn't do this *to* you or to my mom and dad. We weren't being spiteful. We just did what was right for us."

"Gary, I can't talk about this now. I'm going to church to light a candle and pray I'll be able to come to peace with this whole thing." She turned to Rose. "Mom, do what you want. I'm not willing or ready to cope with this problem. You've had more time to come to grips with it. Perhaps, one day, Al and I can." Turning toward Gary she asked, "Do your parents know yet?"

Without belaboring the scene they had gone through earlier, Gary said, "Yes, they know." Suddenly he remembered he hadn't told his parents they were married. Wistfully he thought perhaps it would make a difference.

Rita left without uttering another word.

Rose put her arms around the young couple. For the first time since she'd gotten the news, she cried … for the end of a childhood, for the division of the families and for the trials and tribulations her firstborn grandchild would have to face as an interreligious couple.

When they got Tessa's belongings together, the three of them went to Rose's house. Rose and Tessa began to make things ready while Gary went back to his house to get his things.

The house was unusually quiet. When he went into the den, his mother was siting there quietly in a chair. She didn't acknowledge his presence, ignoring him as he greeted her.

Jake was nowhere to be found but he saw Harry and Jennifer upstairs.

Harry asked his brother, "Well, what have you done now? What's going on?"

Jennifer asked where Tessa was.

It was easier to answer Jennifer's query so he tackled that one first. "Tessa is at her grandmother's house. Tessa and I got married prom night. We're going to have a baby."

"Goody!" shrieked Jen.

"Holy shit! No wonder the seniors are acting so weird. Dad was saying the Mourners' Kaddish. I asked them both who died. Neither of them answered."

"That explains why Mom just ignored me. I'm dead but just too dumb to lie down. Well, let me get my clothes packed and get out of here. The Marenos aren't overjoyed either. Tessa and I are going to live with her grandmother until we get things sorted out. I'd better hurry. Since I'm dead, he may think he's seeing a ghost." Gary's quip was by no means indicative of the heartache he felt. However, it was better than crying.

The days passed slowly. Tessa finally got to an obstetrician. Neither she nor Gary had any contact with their parents. Harry and Jennifer had stopped by Grandmom Rose's house. Likewise, Treva had come by. The young people called periodically to see how the newlyweds were doing.

Gary hit the pavements looking for work. He got a job at the gas station down the street from Rose's. He also got a paper route in the morning. On weekends he was bussing tables at a local restaurant.

Rose didn't charge them room or board so he was at least able to save some money that would help defray some of the medical expenses.

Tessa got baby-sitting jobs, which would help finances slightly. She felt at least she was contributing something.

Rose pampered them both. She got to know Gary well. Each day she saw how tenderly he treated Tessa. She was pleased to see firsthand how respectful he was to both Tessa and her. She often wished her daughter and son-in-law could witness this relationship.

Before long, Christmas came. Gary enjoyed helping Rose and Tessa trim the tree. He went Christmas shopping with both of them, happily carrying all of their packages. Tessa's pregnancy made her even more beautiful than ever. Gary thought she glowed brighter than the lights on the Christmas tree.

Christmas Eve, Rose always had the family over for the traditional fish dinner. She made the call to Rita, inviting her, Al and Treva.

"No, Mom. Al and I won't be there, but Treva can come."

Rose just sighed and said good-bye.

Treva came with presents for Rose, Gary, Tessa and her niece or nephew. Al and Rita sent nothing. Tessa had knitted a scarf for her father and had baked cookies for the family. She had bought her mother a pair of gloves in the new blue color which would complement the blue that Al had started using in some of his rainwear.

After dinner, the four of them went for a ride to see the Christmas lights. They had planned to go to midnight mass together and were filling in the time until it was time to go.

They arrived at church at 11:15 so they would be able to get a seat. Gary

81

dropped them off and went to park the car. As he was walking back from the parking lot, he saw Al pulling into the lot. Gary couldn't tell if Al saw him but he hastened his pace rather than let his father-in-law catch up with him.

Upon arriving back at the church, Gary spotted Tessa standing alone. He soon found out why. Treva and Rose were talking with Rita. Tessa had been snubbed. He felt his anger rising.

Taking Tessa's arm, he walked her slowly down the aisle. "Where does your family usually sit?" He then turned left into the usual Mareno pew, leaving enough room for Rose, Treva and also, if they were so inclined, Al and Rita. Gary hoped if they were going to bury the hatchet it wouldn't be planted in his back.

Treva came down the aisle followed by Rose. They sat down next to the young couple.

Al preceded Rita down the aisle and surprisingly turned left into the same pew, and sat next to Rose.

Abruptly Gary leaned over the three ladies siting next to him and extended his hand to Al. "Merry Christmas."

Al expressed his thanks. He gave Tessa a kiss on the cheek. Truly a Kodak moment!

Rita leaned over and kissed Tessa on the cheek, wishing her a Merry Christmas. Since eyes were definitely on them, Rita extended her hand to Gary, saying nothing. The choir began singing. There was no further interaction.

After midnight mass was over, the parishioners always went into the auditorium/gym and had hot chocolate and cookies. The Marenos never missed this festivity. Rose and Treva were going. Rose said, "Tessa and Gary, you're coming for cocoa, aren't you?" Without giving them a chance to answer, she took Gary's arm and ushered him into the auditorium.

Rita and Al were already there when the other four came in. Although he realized that Tessa's family believed strongly in appearances, Gary was somewhat apprehensive.

Rita called out. "Why don't you come and join us?"

Rose guided Gary first. She let Tessa and Treva follow them to the table.

"Hello," Gary almost whispered.

Rita and Al both responded.

Treva tried to bridge the gap. "Mom, you should see how pretty the baby's room is beginning to look. Gary painted the walls sunshine yellow. Grandmom Rose bought yellow carpeting for it. Tessa made the cutest yellow café curtains for the windows. The crib's in, too."

When no one said anything, Treva continued, "You'll have to come see it, unless you'd rather wait until the baby's here."

Although this wasn't actually directed to him, Al responded, "We'll see."

Tessa felt her throat tighten. Ever since she was a little girl, she equated 'we'll see' with no. It was a stalling tactic her mother had used, hopeful that the desire for something would pass.

Rita looked at Tessa, studying her long and hard before she spoke, "I hope you feel as good as you look. Do you?"

"I feel great. The doctor is pleased with my weight and my whole condition. I'm a little tired of maternity clothes though. February is just around the corner. Thank God. Do you think you can come to visit your grandchild when either he or she is born?"

Rita just ignored the question, although she did pat Tessa's hand reassuringly. It was still a deep hurt to both Al and her. Perhaps the next couple of months would help in mending the tattered relationship.

Tessa was trying to make Gary feel more comfortable. Although her efforts weren't a complete failure, they fell short of the mark.

When the end of the social came, Treva went to Gary's car to retrieve the gifts Tessa had gotten for all of them. She then went to join her mother and father.

That night Tessa and Gary felt perhaps the wall was being broken down … bit by bit. Even Rose felt the evening ended on a positive note.

The rest of the holiday season passed virtually uneventfully. Gary and Tessa went to dinner on New Year's Eve and spent midnight sound asleep like old married people.

"What the hell is he trying to pull?" screamed Jake to Becky when she mentioned Gary was seen at midnight mass with the Marenos. "We don't hear from him on any of *our* holidays. This is way out of line."

"But Jake, we both made it clear to him that we didn't want anything further to do with him."

"That doesn't mean he has to rub our noses in it, does it?".

"I don't think he's doing it to us as much as he's doing it *for* his wife." At this point Becky didn't mention she had heard Gary was seen waiting in the long lines to have packages wrapped. When he had them done, they were in Christmas wrapping. She also neglected to tell him she had heard Gary had gone to mass a few other times before Christmas. Becky didn't actively seek news about her son but longed to hear any tidbit at all that was passed along to her.

Jake knew his wife missed their son. So did he. He never told her he had seen Gary on the street but rather than meet him face to face, he crossed to the other side. So what was Gary supposed to do?

The days passed quickly and the month of February had arrived.

* * *

Bette took a respite from her reading and was reliving the conversation she had had with Tessa while they strolled along the Jersey coast on that brisk October morning prior to beginning their book.

"But I'm not sure if writing this book is going to be the right thing. Maybe we can do some good with it for others to learn by our mistakes. I just don't know. It may be so emotionally exhausting I'm afraid I'll have an exacerbation of my Chronic Fatigue Syndrome."

"Sometimes it's more exhausting to keep things impacted within your brain rather than talking them out. I'll let you dictate. You can sign off on the pages you feel are okay. You can likewise withhold your signature on any that don't have a right feel to you."

"Do you think it's saleable? I'd have to devote a lot of time to something with an unknown result."

"If you wanted a sure thing, you wouldn't have opposed society and married Gary. And in case you hadn't noticed, prejudice is alive, well and flourishing even now."

"Okay, let's go for it. I might have trouble getting my thoughts in chronological order but I'll muddle through it as best I can. You already know much of it. After all, you covered for us on prom night." Tessa felt as if she owed Bette something.

* * *

Fourteen

Gary was working long hours. If he wasn't delivering papers, he was pumping gas, if he wasn't pumping gas, he was bussing tables. The tips in the restaurant were pretty good. Gary was training to be a waiter. He was proud of this, as it was more or less a promotion. It was a far cry from the future he'd planned. But he willingly sacrificed that to be with Tessa. He did have some bad days though.

"I'm a little scared about supporting a wife and baby. I know if I wait tables full time, I'll have some money. Maybe I'll keep my gas station job for days off at the restaurant. I won't have much time for Tessa and our baby though."

"I'll help take care of your baby and do what I can with money. Maybe Tessa will want to go to work."

"Geez, that would be super. I don't imagine we'll hear anything at all from our parents, let alone get any kind of help from them."

"Not to worry. I'll lend you money if you have trouble with the hospital. Just stay healthy." Rose was always there whenever he was down.

Tessa was getting anxious about labor and delivery. She knew this was something she was going to have to do for as well as by herself. She could no longer tie her shoes and she was extremely awkward with steps. She held tightly on to the railings and sidestepped the stairs so her belly wouldn't propel her downward. She followed her doctor's orders explicitly. She and Gary skirted many issues facing them, not the least of which was the baby's religion. She wanted to feel him out this one day so she engaged him in a conversation

"Gary, do you think that Aunt Bella will come over for the baby's christening?"

"I don't even know if there'll be a christening. We never discussed that."

"Oh," responded Tessa. She thought she wouldn't dare broach the subject of allowing a boy to wear her christening dress. No point starting that particular discussion until they knew what the baby's sex was. She held her tongue … so as not to open up a potential wound.

The morning of February seventh, Tessa awakened to a damp bed. Frightened at first, she realized that this was the beginning of the baby's journey into the world. By this time, Gary had finished his paper delivery and was busily pumping gas at the service station. Tessa decided that Grandmom Rose could take her to the hospital if necessary. However, when she went downstairs, she discovered a note from Rose saying she had gone shopping and would be back around noon. Tessa began feeling a cramp-like sensation, which escalated into a firm contraction. It nearly took her breath away, partially because she was frightened and alone but also because she didn't know what the next several hours of labor would be like. There was a good ten-minute time lapse between this one and the one preceding it. At this rate, she thought she'd be in labor forever. Frightened and uncertain what to do, she called her mother.

"Hello."

"Hi. Are you busy?"

Rita didn't' recognize the voice at first but the panic in it registered all too well. "Who is this?"

"Me. Tessa."

"What's wrong? Is it my mother?" Rita exclaimed with alarm. Tessa hadn't called since the day she moved out.

"No, Mom. She's fine. It's me. My labor's started. And I'm home alone." Tessa was whining.

"Where's my mother? Where's Gary?"

"Grandmom went shopping. She won't be back until later. And Gary's working."

Rita didn't offer anything either in the way of advice or help. She felt that any suggestions should come from her daughter.

"Do you think you could come over and keep me company?"

"Have you called the doctor yet for instructions?"

"No, should I?"

"Is your bag packed yet?"

"No, I thought that I had a couple of more weeks to wait."

Rita sighed audibly at the other end of the phone, upset that her daughter hadn't readied herself for the actual birth of the baby. "Listen to me. I'll come over now. Don't try to do anything except time your contractions. Oh, yes and for God's sake, call your doctor to alert him. See what he has to say."

Rita decided against calling Al. She'd deal with him later. Her daughter needed her now. She reflected upon all that had happened over the past several months but put all thoughts aside. Right now, she had a more pressing situation to deal with.

Upon reaching the house, Rita let herself in and called upstairs to Tessa, "I'm here. I'm coming up."

Tessa acknowledged Rita's presence but was busy timing another contraction. This one lasted longer than the previous one but was still a good ten minutes after the one before. She had gotten her robe, slippers and nightgown ready. She was getting her toiletries together.

Rita entered the bedroom and asked Tessa where the suitcase was. She then got it off the closet shelf and started putting Tessa's things into it. "Did you reach Dr. Martin yet?"

"Yes. He said I probably have a way to go. He told me to wait until my pains are steady at three to five minutes apart. He said a first baby almost always take longer. Does it always hurt so much?" Tessa was back in her whining mode.

"Tessa, you have no idea at all what to expect. You're just a baby yourself."

"Please. No lectures. I called you because Grandmom Rose is shopping and Gary's working. I tried calling the gas station but I think they take the phone off the hook when both of the mechanics as well as the gas pumpers are tied up. I should have asked you to stop there to tell Gary that our baby has started making its way into the world."

"Tessa," Rita continued, ignoring the bit about a lecture, "perhaps we can get him, or at least let him know when we're on our way to the hospital. Do you know when grandmom will be home?"

"She said around noon but I don't know what time it is. I'm using this old watch for my contractions but I didn't bother setting the time. I just wound it."

Rita just rolled her eyes. "While you were winding it, wouldn't it have been just as easy to set the proper time? How much more effort would that have taken?" Rita was not saying what she wanted to. She was thinking that if Tessa was acting so put upon by just setting a watch, what would she do when she had someone dependent upon her 24/7?

However, biting her tongue, she suggested, "Let's go downstairs. I think that maybe you should have something light to eat. It will be a long time before you have anything else."

"Don't I have to be fasting?" Rita didn't answer so Tessa followed her mother down the stairs like a dutiful little girl instead of a woman about to give birth.

After making some toast and pouring orange juice, Rita sat down next to Tessa. She encouraged her to eat the light snack.

Tessa ate a bit ... just enough to satiate her appetite. She got up to put the dishes in the dishwasher but got another pain. She said nothing but stopped midway until the pain subsided and then continued cleaning up.

Once that table was cleared, Rita and Tessa sat in the living room, just looking at each other as well as the wall clock. It was slightly after noon when they heard Rose's key in the lock.

"Tessa, are you okay? I saw your moth– Oh Hello, Rita. What's going on? Is it the baby?"

"Yes, Grandmom. I called Mom because you weren't home and I couldn't reach Gary."

"How far apart are your pains?"

"They are still irregular," Rita answered. "Coming at seven to ten-minute intervals. Why don't you go tell Gary while I stay with Tessa?"

"Fine." Rose grabbed her purse and keys then scurried out of the door.

Gary was pumping gas. There were three cars waiting in line. Rose decided the best thing to do would be to get in line and get gas. She could tell Gary while not taking him away from his duties.

When her turn finally came, Gary said, "Hi, GM. How much do you need?"

"Actually I don't need any. I came to see if you could get off. Tessa's in labor."

"Oh. Oh. Oh, my God. Is she okay? Is she in the hospital? I'll check with my boss," said Gary, who didn't wait for an answer to either question.

Gary was back in minutes. "I have to wait until they can get the relief guy to come in. I'll be home as soon as I can. Don't look for me before an hour and a half though."

"Don't worry. She's still got a way to go. Her mother is with her."

Gary hurriedly said, "Good-bye." His mind was in turmoil. They hadn't even decided on a name yet. The list was still as long as an encyclopedia. He went back to his duties, mindlessly performing them.

As Rose was driving home, she saw Becky leaving Russen. She resisted the temptation to tell her the news. She didn't want to be viewed as an interfering old lady.

Meanwhile, back at home, Rita was encouraging Tessa to walk around, hopefully to enhance her progress. As well as pass the time. She had gone to see the baby's room. She had found it to be as adorable as Treva had said.

When Rose arrived she imparted the news. "Gary was busy at the station. He has to wait for his relief. He said not to expect him before two hours." She lengthened the time in case there was a holdup and he couldn't make the suggested time frame.

"I hope you told him to go to the hospital, didn't you?"

"No. You'll probably still be here with your irregular contractions."

"I hope not." Tessa was beginning to grate on her mother's nerves.

Rita didn't know whether to call Al, so she did nothing.

Rose got Rita aside and told her about running into Becky. Rita concurred with Rose's decision about not telling her. If Gary wanted to he'd call his mother himself ... either now or after the baby was born. They were discussing this very thing as Gary walked into the house. He said a quick hello then sat down bedside Tessa.

"Well, how's it going? Any time soon?"

"It's too soon right now. That much I know. It really does hurt though. I hope I can get through this. I wasn't ready for it to hurt so much."

"You'll be okay. Try to relax as much as possible between contractions. You'll have more energy later and the delivery will be easier." Gary remembered what he had read in the doctor's office when he'd accompanied Tessa to her appointments.

Tessa tried not to show how annoyed she was at Gary. Relax.... It was easy for him to say. He wasn't the one who had to propel this baby into the world. She tried to think of pleasant things but couldn't right now. Her mind began wandering through the years.

It seemed as if it was just yesterday that her mom and dad got angry with her for going to see *Forever Amber*. It was on the Catholic church's banned list. To her and Treva, that was a sure way to boost sales. She thought it was silly her parents got so angry. She thought her punishment for this and many other infractions had been unjust. She tried to focus on anything but labor.

Then a doozy came. When it passed, she remembered how she was never allowed to go to sleepovers especially if the girl's parents were going to be out and wouldn't be home until late. And also she was remembering how she would always get scolded for something that Treva had done. She was admonished, 'She's only a baby.' Well, she was hopeful that when she and Gary were raising this baby she'd never offer that explanation for bad behavior. She was going to be a good mother. Well, not that her own mother wasn't a good one.... She lost track of time but was jolted by another contraction.

"Gary, I think we should go to the hospital now. This one came about 5 minutes after the last one."

Deep in his own thoughts, Gary didn't hear her.

"Gary, Gary," Rita said. "Tessa's talking to you. She's' ready to go to the hospital."

"Okay, I'm ready. Let me get your suitcase. Come on, Tessa. Let's go."

89

"Can we come?" asked Rose.

Tessa looked at Gary, then at her mother and grandmother. She was about to answer in the affirmative but Gary beat her to it. "Sure."

Shortly after, the three of them were ensconced in the waiting room in the maternity ward. Tessa was in the labor room.

Rose was looking at a magazine but wasn't really absorbing anything. She was remembering when Rita was born as well. Likewise, she remembered the joy surrounding Tessa's birth. It was too bad there was so much controversy about this baby. She tried to put herself in her daughter's place as well as Becky's but couldn't fathom turning her back on a child of hers. Was Rita cold-hearted? Or had Al forbidden her to interact with Gary and Tessa? She always felt that the woman in the house set the tone so she had to place some of the blame on her daughter's shoulders. She wished Al and Rita could've witnessed the mushrooming love between the two kids. Even though they were young and innocent, they had learned to accept their orphan-like state.

Rose looked up to see her daughter staring out the window with her hands clasped in her lap. She noticed the guilt-ridden expression on Rita's face.

Rita saw Rose watching her. She knew her mother, although usually nonjudgmental, was silently chastising her for the schism in the relationship with the kids. What her mother didn't know was Al had given her a free rein with the kids. He told her to handle it any way she wanted but not to expect anything from him. Al had been deeply hurt by the lack of interaction both personal and professional with Jake. His business was doing well but Gary and Tessa were a constant reminder of what once had been.

Rita felt, in good conscience, she couldn't turn her back on her husband. She kept hoping he'd come around. She saw the ice melting at Christmas but nothing else had transpired these past 6 weeks. Rita thirsted for news about Tessa and was glad that both Rose and Gary were unavailable when Tessa went into labor. She knew that Rose would've told her of the birth. But she felt by being here, she undid some of the absence from her daughter's life.

She glanced at the clock. It was 4:30. She knew Al usually wrapped up work around that time. He would go back to the office in the evening if it proved necessary. He usually worked weekends too. In the past, he and Jake had rotated weekends. She was putting off the inevitable but knew she had to call Al to let him know where she was. He always knew where she was if he should get home before she finished her day of activities.

"Do you want some soda or juice?" asked Gary. "My mouth is dry."

"Oh, yes. Get me a coke please," said Rita as she handed him a dollar bill.

Rose said, "Me too, please."

"Use my money. Is it enough for all of us? Here," she said as she handed him a couple of more dollars. "Get some crackers too."

"No thanks, Mrs. Mareno. I have enough." Gary was too proud to take a handout from anyone, let alone someone whose favor he was courting.

After he left, Rita confided in her mother. "I have to call Al but I'm not looking forward to it."

"A baby's birth should be a happy time. Instead this one is clouded by turmoil. The kids have been treated like lepers or criminals."

"I really don't need a lecture now."

"Well, maybe I should have spoken up sooner. I raised you to behave better than this. The kids have behaved better than the adults."

"Please. I have enough to contend with. Just drop it. I dread making the call."

"Do you want me to do it for you?"

"No thanks. I'll do it," Rita said this as she walked to the pay phone.

"Hello," said Al, a little breathless at the other end.

"Al, it's me. Listen. Tessa called today because she went into labor with no one home. I went to Mom's house and stayed until Mom got there. I waited with both of them until Gary got home from work. I'm at the hospital awaiting the news."

"Okay. Is that all?"

"For now, yes."

"Okay. I'll take Treva to Luigi's for dinner. See you later."

"Al, wait," Rita added, but she was talking to a dial tone. Al's tone wasn't nasty but he was curt. Rita sensed the interest underlying his feigned indifference.

Forlornly she went back to where Rose was sitting. Gary arrived with the snacks and sodas for them.

The wait was horrible. They skimmed through magazines aimlessly. At one point, Rita's was upside down. Although this didn't go unnoticed, neither of the other two mentioned it.

Light-years later, Dr. Martin came into the waiting room, looked at Gary and said, "Congratulations. You have a seven-pound six-ounce baby girl." He shook Gary's hand.

Rose and Rita hugged each other. Then Rose embraced Gary and kissed him.

Timidly, Rita went to Gary, took both of his hands in hers and spoke, "Gary, I'm so happy."

Gary spontaneously gave her a hug and said, "Thanks, Mrs. Mareno. I know Tessa's glad that you were a part of this. She's really missed her family these past several months."

"Maybe we can rectify that." Rita went once again to the public phone, eager to reach Al. She deposited her money, dialed her number and heard Treva's voice.

"Hi Aunt Treva. It's Mom. Where's Dad? Tessa had the baby." Rita wanted the pleasure of telling Al he had a granddaughter. Knowing how crazy he was about his daughters, she figured he wouldn't be able to contain his joy.

"Dad went back to work. What did she have? How much did it weigh? What's its name?" All of Treva's words ran together.

"She had a little girl. Seven pounds six ounces. I don't know what her name is yet. I'm going to call Dad at work. I'll talk to you later."

As she dialed, Rita hoped that Al wouldn't dampen her spirits.

"Italian Mist," said Al.

"Hi, it's me. I'm so excited. Tessa had her baby. A little girl! She weighs seven pounds six ounces." When no response came Rita questioned, "Did you hear me?"

Choking back tears, Al said, "Yes, have you seen her yet?"

"Not yet. We're going to in a little while. I'll see you later tonight."

A short time later, Gary, Rita and Rose went to the nursery to see the baby. Her face was still puffy. She had peach fuzz hair, which appeared to be a light reddish brown. She was crying.... The only one in the whole nursery who appeared to be doing so.

All of them were overjoyed at seeing this special newborn. Rose and Rita got ready to leave to let the new parents have their first encounter in private. Gary went down the hall into Tessa's room.

"Tessa, did you see her? She's a beauty. Thank you. Thank you."

"No, I haven't seen her yet. I'm exhausted. Where are Mom and Grandmom?"

"They left so we could visit. We have to get busy on names."

"Actually I came up with one. How about Jakali? It's a contraction of our dads' names. We could call her Ali for short."

"That's cool. Anything in the middle?"

"I'd like to give her my Aunt Bella's name in the middle. What do you think?"

"Too many l's. Jakali Bella. Nope. No good. How about Beta? Our moms' names will get into the act that way."

"I like that idea. Okay. It's settled then, right?"

"Right. I'm going to go home and let you rest. I love you, Altessa."

"Oh Gary, I love you too ... so very much." They kissed and he left.

Gary went home, where Rose was boiling eggs to make a quick egg salad for dinner.

Gary begged off, still too excited to eat. He went to the phone to call his parents but not before he told Rose the baby's name. She offered no comment as he was already dialing the phone.

The phone was picked up immediately.

"Hello," Harry answered.

"Hi Uncle Harry."

"Gary, no shit? The baby was born. Was it a boy or a girl?"

"A little girl. Do you think that Mom or Dad would come to the phone to talk to me?"

"They're not here. Just Jen and me. Shall I tell them or do you want to call back?"

"Let's play it by ear. See how it goes when they come home. Call me and let me know."

A few hours later, Harry called to say he'd delivered the message to almost deaf ears. However, he and Jennifer would like to see both Tessa and their niece.

Gary shrugged off this latest snub. Before he got off the phone, he told Harry they'd be more than welcome.

The day finally came for Tessa and Ali to leave the hospital.

Gary and Rose went to pick them up. Tessa was dressing Ali as they arrived. The three of them finished the task and they all went home.

To their surprise, there was an arrangement of flowers from Al and Rita. No acknowledgment had come from Gary's parents. However, this surprised no one.

Fifteen

After deliberating, Gary and Tessa decided to have Ali christened in the Catholic Church. Other than Gary, there were no involved Jewish relatives. If anything happened to both parents, the extended Catholic family would take over the religious upbringing.

Rita and Al were invited to the christening. Ali wore the same christening dress her mother had worn nineteen years earlier. Treva was Ali's godmother. She doted incessantly on the baby. The christening went without incident. Although the relationship was strained, both Al and Rita attended. Jennifer and Harry did not. Although they'd seen the baby more than once, they felt by attending a religious ceremony they'd be betraying their parents.

In early September 1954, when Ali was almost seven months old, Bella came to visit. Gary and Tessa met the ship while Rita took care of Ali.

"There she is. There she is," screeched Tessa.

Gary had never met Bella but knew immediately who she was. "My God, she looks like Rose's twin sister."

"I've been telling you that. Aunt Bella. Aunt Bella! Over here."

"Tessa, it's so good to see you." She turned to Gary and said, "It's great to meet you at last. I've heard so much about you, I feel like we're old friends." She hugged them both.

"Tessa told me how super you were to her while she was in Italy. I can't thank you enough."

"I'm just happy that things are working out for the three of you."

"We have so much to do here today. Gary, get Aunt Bella's luggage." As he went to do this, Tessa continued, "We have to go to the Empire State Building. Do you want to go inside the Statue of Liberty?"

"No. Why don't I do that when I come back to get the ship to go home? I'm anxious to see the Empire State Building. Is it as tall as they say?"

"Just wait," Tessa answered her.

After seeing the Empire State and other sights, they left New York and drove back to Linfield. Rita, Al and Rose were going to take over the sightseeing.

"We have reservations near Plymouth Rock. Even though none of *our* ancestors came over early, it's still impressive." The newly appointed tour guide, Rita, said this.

"I'm in your hands. Take me there and any place else you think I should see."

The next day, they went to Washington, D.C.

While at the Lincoln Memorial, Bella said, "This president of yours was a good man. People shouldn't be deprived of their dignity and sold like cattle. It's too bad they had to fight a war to accomplish it."

Al was impressed at how knowledgeable she was. "Where did you learn about American history?"

"You people aren't the only ones who learn about foreign countries. Where else but in school? Do you mind if I suggest a place I'd like to see?"

"Shoot." Al was willing to take her anyplace.

"Philadelphia."

Early in the morning they went to see the Liberty Bell and the Franklin Institute. Bella was quite impressed with some of America's history, even though the US was just a baby compared to Italy.

The visit lasted for three months. She arrived home before Christmas.

Shortly after Bella left, Rose received a Trans-Atlantic phone call.

"Rose, this is Vito."

As soon as she heard her brother's voice, she knew something was wrong. "What happened?"

"It's Bella. She died last night. We don't expect you to come to the funeral but thought you'd want to know just the same."

Rose started crying softly as she asked, "How did it happen?"

"A heart attack."

When Rose hung up, she called Tessa first, then her daughter.

"I have some bad news," she said when Tessa answered the phone. "Aunt Bella died last night."

Tessa was hit hard by this news. If not for Aunt Bella, she would have been apart from Gary for a much longer period. She felt as if she'd lost a grandmother. Gary, likewise, was saddened by Bella's death. They were glad that they'd had the visit with her.

The days, weeks and months went by with still no word from the Rosens. Ali's first birthday was approaching. Tessa decided that enough was enough. She dressed Ali warmly, took out the carriage and walked to the senior Rosens' house.

Timidly she knocked at the door.

"Just a minute," she heard Becky call through the door.

The door opened and even before Becky could react, Tessa said, "Mrs. Rosen, I'd like you to meet your granddaughter."

Becky couldn't believe her eyes. "Come in out of the cold."

Tessa maneuvered the coach away from the door. She lifted her baby, then entered the house.

"Is Mr. Rosen home?" Tessa was timid.

It was lunchtime. Tessa remembered when Al and Jake were partners, they'd often go home for their noon meal. As a matter of fact they would rotate going to each other's houses.

"No, but I do expect him soon. May I hold her?" Becky couldn't wait to get her hands on her granddaughter.

"Certainly. She's an extension of you. I'd never deny you that pleasure."

Becky took the baby in her arms while asking, "What's her name?"

"Jakali Beta Rosen."

The symbolic contraction didn't go unnoticed by Becky, who added, "That's clever. What do you call her?"

"Ali."

They both heard Jake's key in the door.

"Jake, is that you? Come in the kitchen." Becky had been preparing lunch when Tessa had knocked at the door. She had ushered both Tessa and the baby back there so she could continue her task.

"Becky, did I see a coach outside? Are you baby-sitting for those kids down the street again?"

"No, Jake. Something better."

As he entered the kitchen, his mouth dropped open. He feasted his hungry eyes on the baby. Becky was still holding her. He was taken completely aback.

Not sure he could contain his emotions, he finally grunted, "What's for lunch?"

"Here," said Becky. "Hold Ali while I finish slicing the tomatoes." Giving him no chance to protest, she thrust the baby into his arms.

Jake couldn't resist cooing at this pink-faced, brown-eyed brunette who had inherited the best features of both of her parents.

Becky's eyes started to tear. It was as if the tomatoes had onion properties. She silently prayed that the eighteen-month exile of her oldest child was coming to an end.

Jake inquired about the baby's full name. Although he didn't acknowledge it, he was glad he and his former friend were united in something once again.

Tessa spoke up. "Mr. Rosen, Mrs. Rosen, we're having a birthday party for Ali's first birthday next week. We'd like the both of you as well as Harry and Jennifer to come."

Becky looked from Jake to Ali to Tessa. Her pleading eyes returned once again to Jake.

"Well, Beck-a-la, what do you think?"

It was that simple. Becky knew the healing process would now begin. Tessa had extended an olive branch to them. They'd be fools not to grab it.

That night Tessa recounted the story to Gary.

"That took a lot of courage.... Just picking up and going to my parents' house. You didn't know if they'd even let you in the door."

"It's not as if I was alone. If nothing else, they had to be curious about their only grandchild."

"You're amazing. Not only about this but the way you handle everything, especially Ali. I was actually afraid of her at first. I thought she was like my mother's porcelain dishes and would chip if I wasn't extra careful."

"She's the same as we are.... Just more dependent, more needy, smaller and unable to communicate her needs."

"Oh sure. *Just* like us. Why don't you write a manual, *How to Discern Your Baby's Need*? It would be a best seller."

"Don't tempt me. I just might."

After the first birthday party, at which the Hatfields and the McCoys called a truce, it became easier for the families and former friends/business partners to interact.

Gary and Tessa opened a bakery, which they called 'Baking and Crust'. The similarity to banking was denoted in the name. After all, they both worked with dough. Neither of them had any business experience so this venture didn't last too long. Jake had offered Gary a position with Russen. He and Tessa chose to be more independent. Rose came up with a great idea.

"Why not open a submarine sandwich shop? Both of your fathers could help you set it up. I'll co-sign a loan for you."

They consented to this. Thus 'Down Under' was initiated.

Since they had already baked bread, they decided that they could save money by baking their own for the subs. They started out small. They rented a place on the dock, figuring that they would get business from boaters who were going fishing but didn't want to take time to prepare food. The first summer, it rained all the time. But even at that, the business held its own. They decided to expand their basic submarine sandwich (provolone cheese, prosciutto, salami, lettuce, tomato, onions and hot peppers) to include a steak or cheese steak sub with fried peppers and onions.

And before long, it became a main attraction of the waterfront.

Their lives were kept busy. The business took a temporary backseat to the fact that Tessa and Gary were expecting their second child in June. They were hoping for a boy this time and began getting the room ready in their new apartment. They had chosen one halfway between their parents. This seemed to be convenient as well as non-controversial. Even though the families were mending their fences, there was no point in antagonizing either side. They were careful how they divided their time as well as Ali's between them.

In March of '56, Tessa was rushed to the hospital, bleeding uncontrollably. The placenta had pulled away from the uterine wall and she lost the baby, which was the boy they had hoped for. She continued bleeding, so Dr. Martin had no choice but to perform a hysterectomy. She also had to receive a few units of blood. Thankfully she pulled through and was discharged from the hospital.

Although Ali was happy to see her mother, she had oodles of questions. Not the least of which was, "Mommy, how did you lose my brother? You always make me hold your hand."

Gary answered the question. "He's an angel now. He was too small to live here on earth so God took him up to heaven."

Ali didn't completely understand this but she said nothing else.

When Tessa got home from the hospital, Gary had a surprise for her. He had bought the dream house they had looked at and fallen in love with. It had a huge kitchen, three bedrooms, two baths and a nice yard in which Ali could play. But even this couldn't cheer Tessa up. She was so despondent that those who loved her feared she might do something to herself.

One day when she heard Gary on the phone speaking to Rita, it hit her why everyone was hovering around her. She lit into Gary when he got off the phone.

"What do you think I am? Some kind of nut? Don't you know how much I love you and Ali? Do you actually believe I'd do something so stupid as to cause irreversible harm to myself? Can't I be upset about my little boy? Can't I be upset that I can never have another baby?" She gave vent to the tears she hadn't permitted herself to shed.

Gary just held her, saying, "Tessa, don't you think it has been hard for me, too? My heart hurts like the devil. I wanted that little boy as much as you did. You're not the only one who's been affected by this. Even Ali asked when her mommy was going to be playing with her again. Our parents are upset too. If you remember, this was going to be their turn to help with a newborn grandchild. They didn't get to do this with Ali. No one wanted you to lose our baby. No one wanted you not to be able to have another. I've never seen you like this before. I can't take the sadness in your eyes anymore. You're such a wonderful mother and it pains me that you won't have the opportunity to be one to more children. I feel lousy enough without your sadness. I'm the one who talked you into this pregnancy. I should have waited until you could have taken it easier. I know that sometimes these things happen no matter what, but oh God...." Gary began to cry.

Tessa looked at him for a long time and finally retorted. "Gary, I know that it wasn't anyone's fault. Don't dare blame yourself. If I hadn't been wallowing in self-pity, I'd have seen the pain I was putting all of you through. Let's get on with our lives and be thankful for our precious Ali."

Tessa got up the next morning. For the first time in a while, she applied makeup. Now she cared about the image that she was projecting to the world. She wasn't quite ready to go into work but instead concentrated on getting their house ready.

She went to see her father-in-law at Russen so he could help her gain access to fabric distributors. She was flowing like a faucet with her decorating ideas. Ali's room was going to be pink, Gary's and her room was to be blue, the guestroom was going to be black and white. She referred to that one as her integrated room. Jake was so happy to see her like this that he hurriedly made arrangements for her to get to the wholesalers.

99

Sixteen

As the months went by, Tessa was once again back to doing all the things she'd done prior to losing her son and having a hysterectomy

She and Gary were planning a housewarming. She fussed over the menu. They decided they'd start with an antipasto. Pasta would be next, along with chicken Parmesan, meatballs, roast beef, baked potatoes, asparagus, Italian bread and lots of different pastries for dessert. The staff at the sub shop were being paid to serve this feast.

The guest list was a mini version of their class in high school. Linda and her husband were invited. Linda's mother was still working in the beauty parlor. She was still doing Rita's and Becky's hair, so she, too, was included. Both sets of parents were going to be there as well as Gary's brother and sister. Treva and Rose were other family members included in the guest list. There were few single friends because many of their classmates had gone away to college. Everyone there knew everyone else.

The party was in full swing. The only thing that wasn't quite kosher was that Linda was coming on to Gary. At first Tessa thought she was imagining it but when she saw Tom (Linda's husband) practically drag her home, she knew that her perception had been correct. She wondered if subconsciously Gary was viewing her differently because she couldn't bear him more children. But then she thought she really couldn't blame *him* if someone was making a play. It was how she handled the situation that would make the difference. She decided to pretend ignorance. Even the next day, when Rita mentioned it to her, she only said that Gary, Linda and she had been friends for a long time and Linda had too much wine. However, she did take Rita up on her offer to take Ali overnight.

That night when Gary came home, Tessa was wearing her sexiest nightgown.

Gary came into the house, exhausted. Business was good in the sub shop so he had hired a few more sets of hands. He knew what Tessa was doing. Although she hadn't alluded to the Linda episode, she'd have to have been stupid not to have picked up on it.

He asked Tessa to open a bottle of wine. He would shower then join her in the bedroom. He said he'd already eaten but she still cut up some cheese. She wanted to satisfy all his appetites.

When he went upstairs to take a shower, he saw there were candles lit all around the bedroom. He laughed to himself. He hoped their fire insurance was paid up.

Upon stepping out of the shower, he saw that Tessa had put out a large towel for him and had removed his pajamas from the bathroom. He grabbed the towel and went into the bedroom. There was Tessa in a very sexy black nightgown that left nothing much to the imagination. During the past two years, they had been so busy with business their lovemaking had become mechanical. He could see tonight wouldn't be a rushed encounter. The wine carafe was by the bed on the night table with two glasses.

"Gary, I've missed our lovemaking. It used to be so good. I don't mean to imply anything other than we haven't allowed ourselves enough time. Everything is centered on the business and Ali. We've almost lost ourselves in the shuffle of everyday living. Mom took Ali tonight to give us a break. And much as I love our daughter, let's not forget that if it weren't for what we shared, she wouldn't be here."

"Tessa honey, I'm sorry things have progressed to this point. But we've gotten through a lot more than this. I know we'll see our way back to our marriage ... together."

Tessa poured Gary a glass of wine and offered him a slice of cheese. They sat on the bed and chatted about insignificant things. He put his glass down and began caressing her face. He looked into her eyes and saw her love. He hoped she saw love emanating from his.

He put his arms around her and kissed her with passion. Although it wasn't new to them, it had been dormant for quite a while. She responded to his kiss as he ran his hand gently down her body. He began at her shoulders, softly over her breasts and back up again. She felt a fire ignite between her thighs. He then let his arms trail lazily down her again, touching her waist, hips, thighs and legs without stopping between her legs. He slowly lifted her nightgown over her head and helped her lie down. Loosening his towel, he encompassed her in it. He heard her moan as she felt his total commitment rising to meet her.

Tessa reached into the drawer of the nightstand. She seized a piece of marabou she had been using for some project with Ali. She ran the marabou down his neck, over his chest, onto his abdomen, down his legs, tantalizing him further by skipping his engorged penis. Then, ever so slowly, she ran the fabric up and down his manhood while she continued to kiss him. It was then his turn to moan.

Gary grasped the marabou from her and ran it all over *her* body. She didn't know which spot was more stimulated. He ran the cloth between her legs. He was nibbling her breasts. She was frantic. She wanted him to enter her but didn't want him to stop what he was doing.

She was in such a pitch as she screeched, "It's time. Now!"

He thrust himself inside her. They satiated their passionate lust simultaneously. They continued pleasuring each other throughout the night.

The next morning, Gary awoke to an empty bed. He looked up and saw Tessa walking through the bedroom door with a tray containing his breakfast as well as the morning paper. She looked so luscious to him that it wasn't long before they resumed their nighttime fun. But then the real world descended. He had to get ready for work.

Before long, Tessa and Gary had opened another 'Down Under' in the same building which had housed the restaurant Gary had worked in during Tessa's pregnancy. Since the other sub shop was so successful, they decided to keep the same theme. They perpetuated the red, green and white color scheme. They called it "Down Under II.'

Ali had an insatiable curiosity about everything. She was forever asking questions about everything.... Especially injustices.

Ali had made friends with Mabel's granddaughter. For Vera's fourth birthday, Ali and her parents went to Mabel's house for a small party to celebrate the occasion.

The rented house was clean despite the fact that the linoleum was worn down to bare wood. The adjacent houses were dirty. Mabel's windows sparkled. The clothes on her line were white unlike the surrounding tattle tale gray on those of her neighbors.

Vera showed Ali the double bed she shared with her grandmother. Although there was another bedroom, there was no furniture in it. In their shared bedroom, they used painted cardboard boxes for storage. These were arranged sideways, having a similar effect as a dresser.

When they left, Ali hit them with a deluge of questions. "Why do they use those boxes for their clothes? Why doesn't Vera use that other room? Why are those houses so dirty? And...?"

Gary looked to Tessa for help.

Neither of them could offer an adequate explanation.

Another time they were passing dilapidated houses.

"Who lives there?" And as she said this, Ali wrinkled her nose.

"Colored people."

102

"You mean like Mabel?" Ali had been exposed to colored people ever since she was born.

"Yes. Well, maybe not exactly like her."

"But look at that trash? Doesn't anybody get rid of it?"

"Probably not as often as they should." They didn't know what else to say. They had accepted the fact that this was how the coloreds lived.

Another time, they went to the movies as a family unit. She noticed that the men with the slicked-back processed hair sat on the sides. There were no colored people in the center.

"Why don't they sit where we sit? Don't they like the center?"

Once again, Gary and Tessa were stuck for an answer. What could they say? They just shrugged.

She asked why they were called colored. She opened her parents' eyes to many of the inequities she saw in the environment of those people as opposed to her own. Tessa and Gary always accepted segregation in their city as a part of life. Not Ali. In her innocence, she viewed it as unjust. They were amazed at her grasp of the conditions, which in the 50s were prevalent regarding colored men and women.

She had adopted Mabel's granddaughter Vera as her *bestest* friend. Ali was colorblind. Vera was present at the Rosen household for all festivities. They were inseparable.

There was one area where they weren't together. That was school. Vera went to a colored school while Ali attended the all-white school. Vera probably had a superior IQ to Ali's but her formal education was not even close to what the kids in the white school got. Gary and Tessa asked Mabel if they could obtain guardianship for Vera. That way she could go to the other school … the white one. Of course, Mabel consented.

Thus, Gary and Tessa went to the school board president, Floyd White, who was a borderline Ku Klux Klansman.

"Mr. White, you don't know Vera Green but she's a good friend of our daughter. We are obtaining guardianship from her grandmother. We'd like to enroll her in first grade here next year."

"Where does she go to school now?"

"Dover Road Elementary."

Mr. White sputtered, "Well, uh, well what are you telling me? Is she a nig– I mean is she colored?"

"Yes, does that matter?"

"Only to most people on the board including me."

"That's too bad because our lawyer has assured us that the legal work will be completed by the close of this workday."

Mr. White almost had apoplexy. "Then you're not asking me, you're telling me."

"I guess that you could put it that way."

The board president knew he could possibly forestall the plan, perhaps even squelch it entirely. However, since the Marenos and Rosens were an integral part of Linfield's *Who's Who,* he acquiesced. Needless to say he wasn't the least bit happy.

Upon entering school, Vera was frightened. The kids in the school were accepting. After all, she was a novelty. However, the parents of these kids were up in arms. They didn't want this little *nigger* attending school with their precious white lilies. Surprisingly enough, the major supporter of Vera was Joanne White, the daughter of the school board president. It was because of his daughter's attachment to Vera that he informed Gary and Tessa that their business was going to be picketed in protest of Vera's school attendance.

He called Gary at the sub shop.

"Down Under."

"May I speak with Gary Rosen please?"

"Speaking."

"Don't say I didn't try to dissuade you from getting involved in this colored/white issue."

"Who is this?"

"Floyd White from the local school board."

"And…."

"And I thought I'd give you a heads up that 'Down Under' is going to be picketed around lunchtime."

"Why? Certainly not because a little girl is being given a better education!"

"You left out one major word…. Colored. Don't say I didn't try to tell you."

After Gary hung up, he actually felt sick to his stomach thinking about people such as the ilk of the picketers.

Gary and Tessa went to work together, earlier than usual because they knew that it would be difficult getting past the picket line later in the day. About 11 a.m. they looked out of the door of 'Down Under' and saw a large group lining up outside. Most of them were carrying signs that were typical of bigots. The junior Rosens were surprised to see some of their friends among these hate mongers, not the least of whom was Linda.

Since they were apprehensive, they called the police so they'd be ready in case violence ensued. They also wanted to be sure their customers, who were brave enough to face the crowd, weren't harmed.

As the lunch hour approached, they were heartened to see Rita, Al, Becky and Jake appear in the sub shop to help. Gary had let his help go home so they wouldn't have any problems.

The lunch business suffered. Otherwise the noon hour was uneventful. At about 1:30, Tessa came to life and remembered Ali's class was coming to the dock on a field trip. It was now too late to notify the school of what was happening outside their sub shop. Tessa went outside and saw the bus had already dropped the children off. Her heart thumped wildly when the teacher led the kids toward the dock area.

Smiling at the pseudo parade, Ali and Vera were leading the group, which was walking double file, holding hands. Tessa ran over to where the children had started their journey but had gotten there too late to turn the group of children back. Vera and Ali were still in the lead.

The jeering started up again. The mob, almost ready to disperse, saw the group coming, with Vera in the forefront. The kids thought it was fun. To them, it really was like a parade. Up until now, the mob had been fairly peaceful. But now, a bottle was thrown from the crowd. It landed inches away from Ali and Vera. Furious, Tessa sought the person responsible. The mob, which was becoming more agitated, closed ranks around Tessa, jeering and insulting her.

"What does this do for you?" yelled Tessa. "Does it make you feel important? Are you proud of the example you're setting for your children? Take a good look at the object of your venom. She's a *little girl.* And she has as much right to the same advantages that you and I have. You should all be ashamed of yourselves."

"Wait a minute, Mrs. High and Mighty," someone said. "You're the nigger lover, not us. You're the one responsible for her being in the same school as our kids. You're nothing but a troublemaker who should have minded her own business."

Tessa looked to where the voice was originating. She realized the person wasn't even a localite.

"You don't even live here so how could you begin to know the facts? What I'm telling you is you're the one who should be minding your own damn business. Are you getting paid to heckle and jeer? Go back to where you came from and take your hatred and despicable tactics with you. There's no room for you here."

By this time, Vera's grandmother, who had been working at the junior Rosens' house, had arrived at the dock. She forced her way through the mob and threw her arms around Tessa, shielding her from thrown debris.

"Don't bother with the likes of them," she said. "Let's just make sure the little ones are okay."

"Oh lookee who's here. I declare it's Aunt Jemima. Lordy, who's coming next? Uncle Tom? Or did you all leave him at the cabin?"

Tessa was about to lunge for the man who spoke these words but Gary came and grabbed her. Mabel was standing, just watching the scene when Vera came up to her.

"Don't pay him no mind, Grandma. He's just stooooopid!"

The man lunged toward Vera.

"Come on over here, little nigger girl and I'll show you which one of us is stupid."

As Vera took her grandmother by the hand, the man threw another bottle, which landed squarely between Vera's eyes. The crowd had stopped its jeering and looked at the scene in total disbelief. Some of the women in the group began crying. The thump of Vera's head on the curb was deafening.

The whole idea of the day hadn't centered on violence. These so-called concerned citizens just wanted to prove a point. They didn't want any niggers in their school.

Vera fell back. Her head hit the curb. Her yellow hair ribbons were streaked with blood. Her eyes fluttered and she looked at Mabel and said, "I love you, Grandma." She appeared to be still breathing but not for long. The trauma was too extensive. Her brain had filled with blood. The subsequent pressure caused a cessation of breathing. She took a deep breath and died in Mabel's arms. Her young life was over within seconds.

Tessa was inconsolable, feeling that the whole thing had been her fault. She had never confronted an angry mob before, nor had she ever witnessed anything so ugly.

Gary made sure the other children, especially Ali, didn't get too close to the scene. He had the bus pick up the kids across the way from where they had been dropped off. Al, Rita, Becky and Jake just stood, watching in total disbelief. Mabel was still praying over Vera when the ambulance came.

"No, don't you touch my baby. She don't like to be with strangers. She's okay with me. Take your hands off her. She'll be scared. Let me carry her to the ambulance. Here, I'll sit next to her. I'll hold her hand while we ride to the hospital."

Gary supervised the children and saw them safely onto the bus. When they asked where Vera was and why the ambulance was there, he told them Vera had fallen and hit her head. Ali began to cry and the others joined in. The teachers were overtly upset but did their best to camouflage their feelings so as not to further alarm their charges.

Tessa was watching Mabel accompany her granddaughter to the hospital. The police had the drunken man under control, cuffed him and put him in the patrol car. The mob just stood, quietly talking amongst themselves. An angry mob truly has no conscience.

Gary approached the remaining group of protesters and spoke. "In case there should be any doubt whatsoever in your minds, the *nigger,* as you described her, is dead. Not that you care. In your eyes, it's just one less of them. I'm appalled at the way you acted toward a defenseless little girl. I'm ashamed to say that I called some of you friend." As Gary spoke, he saw Linda and her crowd had gone. He wondered if they'd been around for the literal kill. He noticed that most of his other friends had also gone. He hoped they weren't a factor in Vera's death. In his mind, they were all accessories.

Members of the group remaining tried to speak with him but he turned his back on them, saying, "Leave well enough alone. I've nothing further to say except I hope to see all of you in court. I hope you all get tried as accessories to murder."

Tessa was still in shock. Gary decided she had to get home and be put to bed. He'd have Rita or Becky take her home, then phone their doctor. He wanted to get her on an even keel before Ali came home from school. The men went to the hospital to be with Mabel. Rita and Becky went to wait at the house for Ali to come home.

When the men got to the hospital, they were chagrined to see that Mabel was not allowed to go into the treatment room. This was allegedly because she was so upset. This probably would have been handled differently if she were white.

"Look at that." Gary was the first one to speak. "Even under conditions like these, there's a color barrier."

They were concerned for Mabel. They still weren't sure if she knew that Vera was dead. When she saw them, she swooned and fell to her knees. She knew all right.

"Mr. R., my baby's dead! The good Lord needed another angel so He just up and took her from me. What am I going to tell her mamma? Why did this happen?"

None of them could give an explanation because they, too, found the day's happenings unbelievable.

Al and Gary went to the emergency desk to see about getting the body released. While they were inquiring about a time frame, Jake asked if Mabel could view her granddaughter before leaving. This was granted.

"Vera, honey. I love you. God will watch over you now." She kissed the cold little face and tearfully left the hospital with the Rosen and Mareno men.

Seventeen

Back home, Tessa was lying in bed waiting for the doctor. She was staring blankly at the walls of the blue bedroom.... A room which she had loved dearly until today. She dreaded facing Ali, as she knew this would be her first encounter with death. Although she knew this wouldn't be her last, she hated the fact that it had to be this one little girl ... especially under these circumstances. They had thought the best thing would be to be as truthful and succinct as possible. At least this much.... Someone had thrown the bottle and it hit Vera. She fell and hit her head. That's all they were planing to say. They felt there was one consolation.... Vera probably didn't feel any pain. If that could be called a consolation.

The doorbell rang. It was Tessa's doctor. He also doubled as a family friend. Since the story had been on the local news, he knew what had transpired at the dock. In as much as he agreed with the junior Rosens that Vera deserved a chance, he wouldn't have been the one to orchestrate it. He never would have had the courage that both Tessa and Gary had exhibited ... to obtain guardianship as well as admission to the school.

He was ushered into the bedroom by Rita while Becky stayed downstairs to make some tea for her daughter-in-law.

Dr. Martin commiserated with Tessa as he administered the sedative.

"Bob, what have we done? I'm devastated!"

"Tessa, you didn't do anything except give a little colored girl a chance to better herself."

"What are we ever going to tell Ali? They were inseparable."

"Maybe you had best leave the telling up to Gary. What are all of the other children going to be told?"

"An abbreviated version of the truth. At least that's what I hope."

Rita chimed in, "I'll call the school principal and make sure the story is simplistically unified." With that she walked out of the room to accomplish this.

After Rita left, Tessa, who was blaming herself, cried to Bob Martin. "I feel so empty. It's almost as if I did the orchestration. If only I hadn't approached that horrible man, little Vera would still be here with us. If only

108

I had remembered that the class was coming to the dock on a field trip. If only—"

"Tessa, you can't blame yourself for all the evils in the universe. Those people must look to themselves, not just the bottle thrower, but the entire group. On the news, they said he doesn't even live here in town. I'd like to know who enticed him to join their cause. Maybe I'm crazy but I feel sorry for the others in the group who can't think for themselves. You've always had spunk. You've always stood up for what you believed in. I'd take you on my team any day. Don't ever be afraid to stand up for what you believe in."

He looked at her and realized that between the emotional exhaustion and the sedative, she was falling asleep.

Gary and Al went into the waiting room to get Jake and Mabel. They didn't want to discuss the plans that they'd been formulating to get Vera's body nor the thoughts that they had for the funeral.

Mabel's eyes were glazed over. She was practically non-seeing. The three men managed to help her into the car and took her to the senior Rosens' household. It didn't seem to be a good idea to take her to Tessa's house.... It would have been entirely too painful for her to see Ali.

Jake told Mabel he would call her daughter in South Carolina but Mabel said it was her place to do it. She first called her daughter's minister to go to the house. When he arrived there, it would be time enough to break the news.

Jake got on the phone with the minister and made preparations for Mabel's daughter, Vickie (Vera's mother), to come to New Jersey for the funeral. He and Al would foot this bill for her trip as well as the funeral. However, funeral arrangements couldn't be finalized until Vickie and Mabel gave their seal of approval.

Ali came home from school. "I have a note from Mrs. Richards. Shall I give it to Mommy? Where is she anyway?"

Becky looked to Rita, who spoke softly to her granddaughter. "Mommy has a bad headache and is lying down."

And then came the expected deluge of questions. "How is Vera? Is her head okay? Is she okay? Everybody was so scared because someone said a mean man threw a bottle right in her face and cut her eyes to pieces. Is she home from the hospital yet? Is her eye okay? Can I please see her?"

Rita and Becky looked at each other. Then after taking a deep breath, Rita said gently. "Ali, do you remember how we always talk about angels? Well, it seemed that God needed another little one so He took Vera to heaven with Him."

"But He can't do that. She's my *bestest* friend and I want her here with me. That's not fair! Was it because I didn't share my new doll with her? I'll share it with her all the time now. Can I go to church and tell God to give her back?" And then the tears flowed.

It was Becky's turn to console her precious granddaughter. She had remained silent when Rita was talking about angels. She didn't want to interfere in the religious beliefs they were instilling in this adorable child. She knew she had no right to meddle in her granddaughter's religion. After all, a miniature form of what had happened today had taken place when Gary and Tessa had broken the news of their marriage to their parents. Becky got the chills when she thought of the day's events. She was ashamed of her own intolerance a few years back. She decided the best thing to do was hold Ali and let her cry it out, knowing that the worst was yet to come.

When Gary and Al came into the house, Ali ran into her father's arms.

"Daddy, Daddy, Vera's an angel. God took her from me. What am I going to do without her? Can't you fix it, Daddy? Remember how you fixed my dollhouse? You can fix anything, can't you?"

"Honey, if I could fix it, I would. God has already taken her to heaven and I'm sure she's looking down on you wishing you weren't so sad. Come and sit on my lap. I know how terrible you feel. We all feel awful. I'm so sorry I can't make this right for you. I wish I could."

"But Daddy, it's so mean of God. If He wanted to take Vera for an angel, why couldn't He have taken me, too? Then she and I could still be *bestest* friends."

Gary looked to Al, Rita and his mother for support. The very thought that perhaps Ali could have been injured or maybe even killed today in the incident was then too much for him to handle. *He* began to cry.

Ali said, "Daddy, don't cry. It's okay. Vera always loved you. I know she wouldn't want you to be sad; she's looking down on you, too, smiling through her missing teeth. Please, don't' cry."

The next day, Vera's picture was on the front page of the newspaper. Ali asked Gary to help her cut it out so she could put it on the bulletin board at school.

Before Ali left for school, the police sergeant called and asked the Rosens to come by with her to give an official statement.

Gary and Tessa picked Mabel up. She had spent the night at the senior Rosens' house. They had closed the sub shop, at least until after the funeral and perhaps longer. They went to the police station, where they were put through the necessary questioning. It was deemed unnecessary to question all of the children but since Ali had a bird's eye view, they wanted to bring her in. Although the police had gotten some information from the mob and the instigators, they still didn't know who had enticed the bigmouthed murderer to join the *parade* ... a name that the kids had all given it.

The police interviewed Ali in the presence of her parents.

"She was my *bestest* friend in the whole wide world. I didn't know that kids ever, ever died. I thought God coated us with something so we wouldn't.

"Vera and I were first in line going to the dock. And we were the first to see the parade. Vera said, 'I hope the band doesn't play very loud. I hate loud music, don't you, Ali?' Vera's grandmother came up to us. Then people were calling Vera a nasty name ... one we don't use in our house."

"What was the word?"

Ali looked to her parents. "Is it okay to say it?" when she received their non-verbal assent, she whispered, "Nigger."

"Do you remember what happened next?"

"Somebody threw a bottle and Vera fell down. She made such a loud thump I thought she was going to be upset that the drum was so loud."

"And then?"

"Her clothes turned orange when she started to bleed. At first, I thought it was cherry soda. Then the car with all of the Christmas lights came and took her to heaven."

Gary and Tessa looked at the officer and protectively embraced their daughter as if to say enough is enough.

Tessa was the one within the family unit to rally first. She was the cohesive force that held the group together. At first, she blamed herself unmercifully. She finally came to realize that in the long run, if they hadn't taken Vera in, she would have been shortchanged.

"Who knows what her life would have been like if we hadn't interceded?"

"But she has no life now. Doesn't that make us wrong?" asked Gary.

"For what? Caring for her? Loving her? Believe me, her life was way too short but what there was, was good. Could you have stood by and watched her be stymied?"

Gary had to concede that Tessa's rationale was much more logical than his emotional reaction.

The day of the funeral was a chilly one. It had been decided that it was going to be held on a Saturday to make it easier for the school staff and students. The Baptist church was within walking distance of both the school and the colored cemetery. Rather than have a caravan of cars, the consensus was that the adults would walk behind the casket, which was followed immediately by the family. The children in Vera's class wanted to go also. With much deliberation, the decision was reached that they would make the journey on their tricycles.

The entire community was aware of the events that had occurred in the normally quiet town. The news media had seen to that. Mabel even received a letter from the White House. It read:

Dear Mrs. Green,

Mrs. Eisenhower and I were horrified at what happened to your granddaughter. We want you to know that we join the rest of the nation in sending our condolences.

Please be advised that your government has begun a full investigation into this untimely and baseless death of your granddaughter, Vera Louise Bell.

There are really no words that can erase the suffering you and you entire family are enduring.

With heartfelt sympathy,
Dwight David Eisenhower

Initially, Gary and Tessa had second thoughts about Ali going to the funeral. They came to the conclusion that the only way she would accept the death of her friend was to see her put to rest.

They got Ali's tricycle out of the shed and also the one they had given Vera for her birthday in July. They had planned to drive to church. After the service, the group would go past the school and then to the cemetery.

Ali insisted they let Vera wear the same yellow outfit she'd worn on the day she'd been killed. She was afraid God wouldn't recognize her in different clothing. She gave her own yellow ribbons to be used in Vera's hair since hers had been ruined by blood.

It was now time for the procession ... on foot for the adults ... tricycles for the kids. The class consisted of twenty children and they were going to ride two abreast. This gave enough room for one parent to be on each side of their child. Ali led the procession flanked by Mabel, Vickie and Vickie's older son, Marc. Gary and Tessa were towing Vera's tricycle by two yellow ribbons.... One tied to each handlebar.

Ali kept looking at the empty tricycle and expected to see Vera with her toothless grin riding it. She just knew her friend was okay and Ali'd wake up and Vera would be there.

In memory of Vera, whose favorite color was yellow, all the children had on a yellow blouse, shirt or sweater. They each wore yellow socks. Their tricycles were adorned with yellow streamers. For them, it was like a parade.... It was filled with some fun.

Death not being a stranger to them, the adults' reaction was an entirely dissimilar one. They were overwhelmed with grief when they saw the riderless tricycle. Those who had taken part in the picketing felt profound guilt. Those who were silent throughout the tug of war over Vera's placement in the school felt deep regret. Those who supported her being in the school were blaming themselves for not affording her better protection. The tears were flowing freely. It was a day that would be imprinted forever on those little people who were in attendance as well as the adults who accompanied them.

After the minister spoke a few words at the grave, he asked if anyone would like to say something. Ali indicated that she would.

Before she spoke, Ali studied the teeny box that Vera was in. She was upset there were no holes in it so Vera could breathe. She remembered how they would play in the back of this very cemetery. They'd collect fireflies, put them in a jar with holes poked in the top and then use the jar as a flashlight. They would frolic gleefully, not giving thought to the fact that there were dead people a short distance from where they were playing.

"Vera, I'm sorry that God needed another angel but I know you'll make sure that everyone in heaven will help you get it ready for us. I'll take care of your grandmother and mother ... so don't worry. You can just take care of God."

By now, almost everyone was sobbing. As the mourners filed by the not yet lowered casket, each of them left a yellow rose and quietly walked to the exit of the cemetery where they prepared to go to 'Down Under' for lunch ... courtesy of Gary.

The town was not quick to recover. Some members of the mob were prosecuted, but the only one who got a substantial sentence was the bottle thrower. Since he was inebriated, he was charged with involuntary manslaughter. He received a sentence of twenty years while the Green and Bell families received a life sentence without Vera. Since Vickie was discovered to be a drug user, Marc came to live with his grandmother.

In August, before the start of the next school year, the Linfield Board of Education held a regular meeting.

"Is there any new business?"

Gary took the podium. "We have a few new families living in the apartments over 'Down Under' and they have children. There are three of school age who will be ready to start kindergarten next month."

"But families enter all the time. What's so unusual about that?"

"Nothing really except to bigots. The families are colored. The students entering are colored."

President White had to pound his gavel as shouts of *nigger lover*, *not again* and *over my dead body* resounded loud and clear.

"Order. Order. Please. Order. We'll have no further outbursts. Each person will be given three minutes to present his argument for or against Mr. Rosen's proposal."

"The chair recognizes Linda Eckers."

"Mr. President, members of the school board and friends. God never meant for people who are different from us to live among us, let alone go to school with our children. We saw what a public outcry there was last year when just one colored was allowed entrance into one of our schools. Do we want our children to see more violence? Do we want another life lost? Do we want to call more unfavorable attention to our community? I say, vote this proposal down now and squelch it once and for all. This is unnecessary and unwarranted. I move we decline their admission to our all-white school."

The cheers were resounding. If there had been a seismograph available, the uproar surely would have registered a 10.

Once again, Floyd White admonished the crowd. He was heartened to see that someone had alerted the police. There were a few uniformed officers present.

Gary went to his mother and father, briefly spoke with them and after receiving thumbs up, requested to speak next.

"I'm not a stranger to prejudice. It has been with me for my entire life. Many of you know how hard it was for Tessa, as a Catholic, and me, as a Jew. We surmounted untold difficulties.

"The most surprising and unexpected opposition came from both sets of our parents. How our fathers could work side by side and our mothers socialize together and then abandon us when we chose to spend our lives together as man and wife was a bitter pill to swallow.

"Was her Catholic background going to contaminate or defame Judaism? Hardly. Would either of us turn our backs on traditions that we were born into? Probably not.

"Evidently, I failed as a son. My father said the prayer for the dead for me when Tessa and I married. However, at eighteen, if I had married anyone else other than Tessa, I know I would have been a divorce statistic.

"There was one shining light of hope in our relationship. That was my wife's grandmother, who showed us what true acceptance is. Who knows what would have happened to us if she hadn't given us shelter, love and, most important of all … that very acceptance?

"Why not let Linfield be the light to show the way for other communities? True, all men are created equal only in the eyes of God, however, aren't we all God's messengers? That's also true.

"This may call attention to our community but I, for one, feel this attention would be positive."

Gary sat down amidst silence. He had never publicly discussed his private conflict before. In the front row, Becky and Jake along with Rita and Al Mareno stood and applauded their son(-in-law). The rest of the audience, save the Linda contingency, did likewise. The board voted against Linda's motion 7-0.

Gary and Tessa left the meeting with their parents, went to the apartments over 'Down Under' and assured the colored parents that their most precious possessions would be afforded the opportunity such as the constitution assured them.… Life, liberty and the pursuit of happiness.

The day after Labor Day, Mabel went to the school with the Rosens and the Marenos.

The local police were present at the white school since it was the first day of school for these kids. They had a look of expectation on their faces. Their eyes were shining. They all sported broad grins. The adults were the only ones experiencing trepidation.

There were ropes on each side of the pathway leading to the school. They proved not to be necessary. The gathering crowd recited the Pledge of Allegiance together.

Gary carried a small American flag and along with the parents of the three new children escorted them into the building. Mabel, in tears, held her head high with renewed hope in her heart.

Vera's death had not been in vain.

Eighteen

Tessa came to the conclusion that she wanted to do more with her life than just help Gary at the sub shops, which were both doing a booming business. After much deliberation, she decided to go to the local hospital and take up nursing. Gary had hired additional help so her presence at their business wasn't as critical as it had been.

When Tessa was just beginning to get her experience in the local hospital, her Grandmother Rose was admitted to the floor on which Tessa was working. It was a difficult ordeal for Tessa because she was taking care of Rose when she took her last breath. Rose had high blood pressure for years and was resistant to taking her medication. She had suffered a severe stroke.

Hence the family had another death to face. Even though they were heartbroken, somehow this was less difficult for them to abide. It was in keeping with the laws of nature. The older should depart from the earth before the children.

Tessa was heartbroken over the death of her grandmother. The two had been very close. The family pulled together and got through this. Once again, they busied themselves with the task of everyday living.

Tessa was doing exceptionally well in the nursing program. She was astute. Not only did she capably measure a patient's vital signs, she was quick to assess when an imaginary panic button had to be pressed. She was excellent in her classroom block of time and was able to put what she learned into practice.

Finally graduation came. The whole family attended. It was a beautiful ceremony. Al and Rita were especially proud of Tessa. She had certainly accomplished a lot since the day she and Gary had imparted the news of their marriage. They realized now how much they had overreacted to the announcement. Thank God that Rose was tolerant as well as loving enough to help the kids.

Since Tessa was number one in her class, she was class speaker.

"...and so I would like everyone to partake in a moment of silence for those who couldn't be here today ... two of whom I'd like to publicly acknowledge, little Vera Bell and my grandmother, Rose Donado."

After the silence, Tessa continued, "Hopefully there will be considerable improvement in health care. And those less fortunate than we will be able to receive that which we take for granted. I'd like to take time to thank my husband Gary, who has encouraged me throughout my studies and without whom my life would have been altogether different. I would also like to thank my mother and father for their patience throughout the years. And finally, I want to tell my daughter, Ali, how very proud I am of her and how much I love her."

Gary had been daydreaming when he heard his name. He was thinking of everything they had gone through and in such a short time. What a long way they had all come. Now his parents even came to Christmas dinner at his house. Although Ali was being raised in the Catholic faith, she was also part of her father's Judaism and even went to Synagogue on different occasions. Gary thought of Grandmom Rose and fondly remembered how she brazenly included him in the first Christmas Eve festivities.

Becky was deep in her own thoughts. She, too, was proud of her son and daughter-in-law. They'd shown such determination despite all the obstacles which were put in their path. She knew it was right to raise Ali in the Catholic faith although she would never admit it to Jake. It had always been her belief a child should adopt the mother's religion. She didn't object to the Christian aura around her son's house. With pride, she witnessed the tolerance this young couple displayed to everyone.

Ali was proud of her mother. When the cloud went behind the sun and out again, she just knew that Vera was peeking at the graduation.

Jake looked at Becky and thought, I bet she's thinking of what the past several years have brought about. How foolish it now seems that we were such hypocrites. We've covered a lot of ground making up for the past but I don't think we can ever really make true amends. I hope we'll all think a long time before we ever pass judgment on anyone else again.

Life was peaceful. Ali was an excellent student. In first grade she read on a fourth-grade level. And now that she was in fourth grade, her excellence persisted. Gary was doing well at his business. Tessa had begun working at Linfield General. She was a great nurse. She had taken her state board exams in July and was awaiting notification. Beginning in August, Tessa rushed to the mailbox looking to see if her results came in yet.

One day she screamed up to Gary, "Gary. I passed."

"So what's new? You didn't actually expect to fail, did you?" He came down the stairs and hugged his elated wife.

After passing her nursing exam, she was in line to be assistant head nurse of the medical floor in the new wing, which was opening in January. She was doing quite well. The doctors valued her clinical opinion regarding their patients. Some of the older nurses were dissatisfied with what they felt was a slight to them. Thus, they began a gossiping campaign to discredit Tessa. They linked her with various deeds, which weren't in keeping with her marital status. According to the grapevine she was seeing one of the doctors on staff. He was also married.

Tessa was aware of the gossip but refused to be drawn into trying to disprove it. How can you prove a negative unless it's a math problem? She kept her silence. More than once she had apprised Gary of the situation.

Because of her innate ability, she was on demand to assist doctors when they did treatments on their patients. Not only did she have excellent rapport with the patients; the families were also her fans. She was willing to work on whatever ward she was needed. Thus, she became the floating nurse, filling in as needed. When she was busy, the doctors were understanding and tried to ease her caseload by doing things for themselves. The hospital worked like a well-coached team.

A rumor was planted that drugs were missing whenever and wherever she worked. She knew she hadn't done anything illegal but started to pay more attention to what transpired when she was on duty.

It seems Dr. Jasper, who coincidentally was the doctor that Tessa was having the alleged affair with, would assist the nurses dispensing pain medication to his patients. He offered when, apparently, they were busy. She remembered one situation in particular. It occurred when the place was a madhouse. Tessa didn't have much help that day.

"Tessa," went the comment, "Mr. Brooks wants something for pain."

The patient in question had just come back from surgery. Dr. Jasper was his internist.

He continued, "If you get the Demerol ready, I'll give it to him."

Tessa, who welcomed the extra pair of hands, got the prescribed dosage and gave it to Dr. Jasper to administer. You can imagine her surprise when she went in to Mr. Brooks and saw him writhing in pain.

"Mrs. Rosen, when can I have something for pain?"

"But Dr. Jasper just gave you something."

"No. He said he was going to have you give me something."

Tessa was befuddled. She thought perhaps the man was confused due to the narcotic that he had received. She didn't know what to do. She couldn't pretend that she gave medication to someone else to see that Mr. Brooks got what he needed.

She lucked out, however, when she noticed the Demerol bottle had more remaining than it was supposed to have. Evidently someone had carelessly signed out a dose and failed to give it. She then gave Mr. Brooks his shot.

She picked her brain to recall other similar incidents. The previous scenario had occurred more often than not. She knew Dr. Jasper was having marital problems. However, she was the one with whom he was having the said affair. She knew *that* wasn't true.

However, the complaints similar to Mr. Brooks' were a frequent occurrence. The problems were falling on Tessa's shoulders because they seemed to occur on her watch. It was easy to pinpoint when and where this occurred. She became chief suspect because the shortage was in tune with her floating status.

Her jealous counterparts were having a field day with this abuse. Tessa didn't want to discredit anyone else's reputation so she was reticent to say anything about Dr. Jasper. She thought she'd set a trap for him rather than go to the Directress of Nurses. However, the opportunity never came.

Upon reporting to work, Tessa was surprised that Mrs. Brown, the D.O.N., wanted to see her after her tour of duty. She went through the day happily anticipating what she thought would be notification of her planned promotion. The meeting opened.

"Sit down, please." was the ominous greeting from her supervisor.

Tessa didn't need a second invitation to sit because her knees were so shaky she thought she'd fall flat on her face if she didn't do it right away.

Carol Brown continued, "It distresses me to have to say this. It seems as if there's been a problem for the past several months. A good number of patients have claimed they have asked you for sedation but even though you signed the substance out in the narcotics register, the patients claimed to have never received the medication. Your record has been exemplary so far ... so much so that your name was submitted for a promotion when the new wing opens."

"But I've never even take an aspirin from the med room."

"To continue, I've no other recourse but to suspend you pending a thorough investigation." Her tone was icy.

"But I've never even thought about doing anything like that. You've known me since I was a teenager doing volunteer work here. I'd never do anything to cast any shame on my family."

"I really must admit I'm surprised, but nonetheless, drug abuse, as you know, is intolerable. Especially one involving medical personnel. I must do this. I promise I'll reinstate you when and if the finger is pointed in another direction."

"But I could lose my license. I'll never be free from suspicion if that happens." Tessa's hazel eyes flashed angrily but she held her tongue in deference to the position of authority. She didn't want to defame Dr. Jasper. She wasn't thinking clearly. Her palms were sweaty. She was so overcome with emotion she became dizzy. Nausea engulfed her. She knew the sweat on her brow plus her general demeanor gave credence to the suspicion of drug abuse. When she regained a trifle bit of her composure, she was ready to speak.

However, Carol Brown interjected, "Your license will only be suspended if you're found guilty of tampering with the narcotics book and taking these drugs illegally." With that the D.O.N. stood.

Knowing the meeting was over; Tessa kept her chin high as she left the office, her eyes brimming with tears.

Tessa was more than aware of the enemies she had at Linfield General but never thought they would resort to something like this. The other rumors didn't interfere with the performance of her duties so the administration, if they even knew about them, remained silent.

That night, after Ali was in bed, she asked Gary to pour them each a glass of wine, as she wanted to discuss an issue with him. Gary obliged. Together they sat down in the kitchen. Tessa began to cry.

"Gary, you know how much I've always wanted to be a nurse. You also know that I was called in today for what we thought would be notification of my promotion. Well, that wasn't the case at all. It seems they think I may be illicitly taking drugs from the medication cabinet. I have an idea who's doing it but I can't prove it. Can we call Tom Lange and see what I can do? I want to prove my innocence. And by the way, if you need any help in the sub shops, I'm available. It seems I am now on a vacation of sorts."

"Tessa, if you know who's doing it, why in God's name didn't you tell Mrs. Brown? Why should you take the fall for one of the other nurses?"

"Because I know how it feels to be accused of something you're not guilty of."

She went on to explain how Dr. Jasper was always volunteering to give his patients their sedation. She told him it was possible it was the doctor's problem. She also told him how people said she and the doctor were having an affair.

Gary put his arm around his distressed wife. "I was and still am very proud of you. You're a helluva nurse. Most hospitals would love to have you. It's inconceivable this one chose to suspend you!" He was livid to think she had been censured for the actions of someone else. "We'll fight this together. Don't lose sight of that fact. We'll weather this storm and come out on top. Don't lose sight of that fact," he repeated.

"What should I do? How can we fight this?" asked Tessa as her fraught nerves raised her voice an octave. The tears flooded from her eyes.

"Don't give up. Please don't cry. I'll call Tom Lange tomorrow. We'll go see him together to get his legal advice."

Two days after, Gary and Tessa were sitting in Tom's office to discuss what measures could be taken to vindicate Tessa and get her job back.

Tessa did have friends on the nursing staff, one of whom was Bette Gilmar. She was also a R.N. She and Tessa had been friends for many years. With her help, Tom laid out a plan to set a trap for Dr. Jasper.

"...so anyhow," said Tessa as she spoke with Bette and some of her other nursing contemporaries who were willing to help. "The blame has been put on my shoulders."

"That's ridiculous. For God's sake! What can I do for you? I know you're no junkie!" said an irate Bette.

"Well, I hate to say this but I think Dr. Jasper's the one stealing the Demerol. So the next time he offers to give his patient Demerol, let's give him a placebo."

"But what will that prove?"

"He'll have to go to another floor to get the real stuff," someone else chimed in.

"Yes, but if I don't sign it out and give it to him, I'm not going to be a suspect."

"But the next nurse who unwittingly gives it to him will be unless someone intercedes. Can't you see? The whole nursing staff's in jeopardy."

"Yes, but when patients complain to the med nurse, she'll have to report it to her supervisor."

"But that's not enough to prove he's the guilty one."

"My lawyer is going to get his investigator insinuated into the hospital as a member of the cleaning staff. They are faceless to a lot of people who work there, so Dr. Jasper won't pay any attention to a person buffing the floors."

"Oh, I get it, when he doesn't go to the patient's room, it'll show he's lying about taking care of the patient's pain."

"Gad, it's like an Alfred Hitchcock movie."

"Except this is real and there's no Cary Grant. In addition to that my nursing license is riding on it."

They kept documentation daily for a month prior to Tessa's hearing. They covered every floor on which Dr. Jasper had a patient. It gradually became clear he didn't go back to the various patients' rooms with the sedation. Instead he went into the doctor's lounge. The times and dates were well documented. A pattern of his errant behavior was established.

Before Tessa's hearing date, Tom Lange submitted documentation to the drug enforcement bureau as to what was happening. At that time the local police department took over the sting operation. Arrangements were made for an undercover cop to follow Dr. Jasper into the lounge after he was seen getting the injection from the floor nurse.

Dr. Jasper went to the fourth annex, where his patient, Sam Gross, was housed. Mr. Gross had a kidney stone and was in a lot of pain. Dr. Jasper asked the nurse to give him a syringe with the 75 mg. of Demerol which had been ordered. He, in turn, would administer it. The nurse was in on the sting operation, so after she prepared the syringe, she called the extension where the undercover cop was awaiting notification. He was advised that Dr. Jasper had the syringe allegedly to give to Mr. Gross.

However, Dr. Jasper walked into the lounge where he amicably greeted everyone. By this time, he had begun to perspire and was feeling nauseated. One of his associates began talking with him about a patient. Then, suddenly changing the subject, he said. "John, you look ghastly. Can I get you anything?"

"What? Oh, no thank you. I have a bit of a gastrointestinal upset. If you'll excuse me, I have to use the lavatory."

Dr. Jasper went into the stall and pulled the syringe from his coat pocket. He was getting ready to inject himself when the police officer broke into the stall, saying, "Dr. Jasper, you are under arrest for violation of the narcotics act."

Dr. Jasper dropped the syringe on the floor and fell down, sobbing. "Please help me. I think I am dying. Please, give that back to me." He was pleading with the police officer, who had at this point gotten the syringe.

The lounge was in an uproar. Some of the doctors quietly left, but some of them stayed to watch sadly as one of their own was taken away in handcuffs.

Tessa couldn't help but be angry with Dr. Jasper. She blamed him for her suspension. He had caused many sleepless nights for Gary and her. He was the cause of the whispers she had to endure when she came back to work following her reinstatement. If this was how loyalty was rewarded, she wasn't sure she wanted to continue being a nurse. However, she didn't have much time to ponder this as her mother had called and said Al was seriously ill. He had been treated for a gastric ulcer, which was not responding to treatment. Surgery was indicated. Rita asked if Tessa could take care of him while he was in the hospital. She quickly agreed. Thus momentarily all thoughts of a career change took a backseat.

Tessa went in to Mrs. Brown requesting time off to care for Al. Since she didn't have enough vacation time accumulated, she asked for a leave without pay. She didn't want to abandon her father but felt that working her shift plus staying with her father would have been physically and emotionally draining. She had been on an emotional roller coaster for quite a while now. It seemed that when one problem was solved, another reared its ugly head.

Nineteen

Al's surgery, a gastrectomy, was scheduled for the following week. Tessa had an uncomfortable feeling about Al. She had noticed his weight loss but attributed it to his work as well as his concern about her suspension. As she looked at him closely, she noticed that he was jaundiced.... Something that she hadn't seen before. Rita was unusually silent about her concern. That frightened Tessa even more. When her mother was most alarmed, she was apprehensive about putting it into words.

The night before surgery, Tessa said to Gary, "I don't have a good feeling about this. My mom's awfully quiet about Dad. And I know Dad just updated his will. Treva came in from Michigan. It just doesn't feel right."

"Don't look for trouble. Let's just wait. We'll see what happens after the surgery. Then we'll know more. I hate to see you get so worked up. Besides, there's nothing more you can do. Try not to be negative. Above all, don't let either of your parents know how upset you are. What has Treva said about all of this?"

"Not that much, but I know she's worried too."

To make matters worse, it rained the day of surgery, which contributed to Tessa's despondency. The day was eerily dark and depressing. Rita was keeping her silence. The surgery was scheduled for 8 o'clock and Tessa, Rita and Treva got to the hospital at 7 for a short visit with Al. Then they went into the visitor's lounge to wait.

After a few hours, Dr. Dean came into the lounge.

"Hello Mrs. Mareno. Hello Tessa."

"Doctor, how's my dad?"

"Not well, I'm afraid. His condition is a lot worse than we had anticipated. We found a malignancy in his stomach with metastasis to his liver and pancreas. I'm afraid there isn't anything we can do except keep him as comfortable as possible."

Rita appeared as if she were going to faint. Tessa gently helped her mother to a chair.

"Can you give us any idea as to a possible time frame?" asked Tessa, surprised at her own calm. Gary had often told her she was great in a crisis,

124

only allowing herself to fall apart when those around her were okay. She hoped this would prove to be the case now.

"At the outside, a few months."

"Should we tell him of his illness?"

"No, definitely not," cried Rita. "He shouldn't have to bear this burden. His will is in order. Even if it wasn't, who cares? I don't want him to know!"

"But Mom, that isn't right!"

Treva, who had remained silent, spoke up, "What exactly isn't right?"

"That Mom doesn't want Dr. Dean to let Dad know how sick he really is. I don't think that's fair."

"Well, what do you think is *fair?* Do you think it's fair that Daddy's sick? Do you think it will give him any peace to know he's dying?"

"I only know that if I were the one who had limited time, I'd want to know. And I think that Daddy would too."

"Who died and left you boss?" Treva cried out. She was unaware of her poor choice of words and continued, "Just because you're–"

"Girls, girls, don't bicker. We have enough to worry about without the two of you going at each other."

"I've never lied to Daddy before and I don't plan to start now!" Tessa looked pleadingly at the doctor. She wanted him to intercede.

Dr. Dean's face turned crimson. He was embarrassed to be in the midst of this family encounter. "Uh, well, I kind of feel the patient should know."

"But why's that necessary? Shouldn't their feelings count? Shouldn't their feelings be protected?"

"The only thing wrong with that is, uh, it's hard for the family to hide the truth from a loved one. I know that, uh, your intentions would be to protect him, but, uh, sometimes the patient just knows by body language; by sadness in eyes; by whispers when the family thinks he's asleep; that he's a lot sicker than, uh, he's been told. It might be good if, uh, he could talk about, uh, his impending death with someone close to him. However, I'll do whatever all of you decide. I won't speak with Al candidly unless that's what you want." Dr. Dean was always more articulate than he now appeared but he didn't usually find himself in the middle of a family fracas.

"Thank you." Rita continued, "We can't expect more than that."

Al's condition plummeted in the recovery room. His bleeding time was lengthened due to the liver involvement. As the bleeding continued, his blood pressure was dropping. He, himself, realized that the end was near. He looked at Tessa as she sat by his side in her white uniform, looking so professional. He was very proud of her. He looked at his beloved wife and mouthed the words, "I love you" to her. His gaze then went to his fair-haired Treva. She looked so sad he thought he'd cry. He didn't fight the sedation. He just allowed his body to float as if on a cloud. He thought of his parents and Rita's parents. He even thought of Vera, realizing that he would be joining all of them soon. Rita and Treva left the nurse to take care of her most precious patient.

The act of dying didn't take Al long. He was pain free. Tessa saw to that. He felt as if he were in a dream state. She was holding his hand when the end finally did come at 5 in the morning.

She quietly walked out to the nurses' station and said, "Mr. Mareno apparently CTB'd. Can you call the resident to pronounce him?"

The nurse on the floor knew that it was her father. They complied with her request. After Tessa called the undertaker, the nurse told her to go home. They would ready him for the funeral director.

In her trance, Tessa remembered a poem that one of her classmates in nursing had penned. Through her tear-filled eyes, she wrote it down, wanting to be sure that she could remember the whole thing before the stress of the next few days set in. She wanted it to be read at her father's funeral.

The nurse went in to aid the sick man.
He recognized her and clutched her hand.
The look on his face was not denying,
His illness was fatal, he was dying.
The tears were evident in her eyes so true.
What could she possibly say or do?
He slumped over, apparently dead.
She looked at him and bowed her head.
The scene was heartbreaking and very sad
For the elderly man was the nurse's dad.

Tessa left the hospital and went to her parents' house to break the horrible news to Rita and Treva. They sat together for a while. Then Tessa went home to tell Ali and Gary.

"Grandpop died today, honey."

Ali began to wail. "Mommy, I knew it as soon as I saw you. Your eyes are all swollen and puffy. Like they get when you cry."

Tessa couldn't believe her daughter was behaving in such an adult manner. She listened as the pseudo adult continued, "I'm really sorry about Grandpop Al. But now Vera will have someone there who she knows. Just think, Mommy, we have another angel to pray to." With that, Ali cried and cried, thus acting how Tessa had imagined she would. Ali had been close to Al.

By this time Gary was at work so Tessa went to 'Down Under' to deliver the news to him.

"Honey, what's wrong? I thought you were going to do private duty for your fath– Oh, my God. Don't tell me."

"He died. Just like that." Tessa snapped her fingers as she said this. "I can't believe it. My father, always so robust ... dead!"

What surprised Tessa was how hard Gary took the news. He was stunned by the news. He sat in a vacant booth, put his arms on the table, lowered his head to his arms and sobbed silently. It was actually the movement of his racked body that let Tessa know he was crying.

When composed enough to speak, he said, "Ya know, even after all that's happened between your father and me, I always admired him. Generally he was a straight shooter. We'd gotten so close after Ali was born. These past several years have just about erased any hard feelings I'd harbored toward him. I see how much I want to protect Ali, so it made me see our marriage through his eyes." The tears were still streaming down Gary's face. He told his manager the reason he was leaving. He went with Tessa.

The funeral was a huge one. Ali asked Tessa if she could recite the poem. Everyone agreed to let her read it (Actually she had memorized it). She made all of them proud of her ... especially when she controlled her tears until they went to the cemetery.

Rita surprised everyone by her demeanor, but she'd never been a believer in any public displays of emotion. It wasn't until she got back home that she allowed herself to fall apart.

Later in the week, Bert Stein contacted Rita. They arranged a time for the reading of the will. It was no surprise that Al had left everything to Rita, including the business. After much discussion, Rita, Treva and Tessa agreed to let the sisters run the business.

Tessa decided she would continue nursing after all. A schedule was arranged to accommodate all parties. Jake offered to help in any way.

'Italian Mist' had done well over the years. The colors and style of the rainwear were superior to any other company's. The family took great pride in this business which Al had started. It had evolved into a large, successful business. Somehow, as long as 'Italian Mist' was around, Al would be too.

Twenty

Rita was taking Gary, Tessa and Ali to Florida for the Christmas school break. They had reservations at the Miraflor in Miami. When it came time for them to start the long train ride, Rita was sick and couldn't go. So the three Rosens left for their vacation in the sun.

Upon arriving at the reservation desk at the Miraflor, Gary was met with veiled resistance.

"We have no reservations for Rosen."

"No. They are in the name of Mareno."

"Oh."

"Mrs. Mareno couldn't come with us as she was sick."

"Well, that presents a problem. We have reservations for Mareno for four people. Now you tell me there are only three and the name is *Rosen*." The disdain in his voice was evident.

Gary, who was used to this, understood immediately. No Jews allowed!

Tessa didn't or else wouldn't get the picture. "Well, now you'll have another room to sell."

"It's not quite like that. Um, we only honor the reservations the way they are made. I am sorry but since that isn't the case, we'll not be able to honor your reservations."

"What do you mean you can't honor our reservations?" Tessa yelled. "We've traveled over 1000 miles on a train and now you tell us you're putting us out on the street. I've never heard of anything so ridiculous. My daughter is exhausted. For that matter, so are we. Let me see the manager at once."

Gary had been trying to signal Tessa what the real problem was but she wouldn't give up. "This is one welcome we'll never forget. My mother always stays here. I repeat, call the manager." She was livid.

"The house phone is there, ma'am. Right against the far wall." And he went on to service other guests.

"Now I know how Mary and Joseph felt when they were told there was no room at the inn."

"Well, perhaps you can find a stable also." The clerk was anything but cordial at this point.

Gary grabbed Tessa by the arm and edged her away from the desk. "Come on. We'll find another place."

"But we already have a place."

"For God's sake, are you that dumb? It's restricted."

Tessa caught on and followed Gary out of the lobby amidst comments like 'bigmouthed Jews.' So much for aplomb.

They drove to a roadside motel called Flordette. Gary had cash so he registered them under the name of Rosa. Then they called Rita.

"Hi. Mom, if you try to reach us we aren't at the Miraflor. We are staying at a place called Flordette but when you call here, ask for Rosa, okay?"

Rita didn't completely understand. She knew they weren't elaborating because Ali was right there. She'd probably seen as well as heard enough already.

The rest of the vacation went without incident but the event they had faced on their first day was forever imbedded in their minds; and more was to come.

Ali was being tantalized at school. There wasn't a high Jewish population in Linfield. In fact, there was only one Synagogue as opposed to several Catholic churches, as well as various Protestant ones. So most kids hadn't any idea about the Jewish faith.

One Monday in school, a classmate of hers said, "I saw you coming out of the building with the funny star on Saturday."

Ali innocently answered, "Oh, the Synagogue."

"What's a Sin 'o' God?" another kid asked.

Rather than correct this mistaken pronunciation, Ali said, "It's my father's church."

"I know what it is," said a savvy other.

The first one asked, "Well, what is it?"

"It's for the Jews. You know. They're the ones who killed Jesus."

"You know. In the catechism, it says that Christ was crucified. That's why we have Easter. That's when He moved the rock from His grave. I'm glad He did because I love my Easter candy."

Ali didn't know if she should say anything so she kept quiet.

"What were you doing there?" asked another as she wrinkled her nose

"I went with my dad." Less is best.

"Yuk." And that appeared to be the end of it.

However, the kids continued to tantalize her. They said she probably didn't even have a Christmas tree. Although they had been at her house numerous times, the visits never coincided with Christmas. It got to the point where Ali dreaded going to school.

She now had frequent stomachaches. She often wanted to stay home from school. When she noticed this increasing reticence to go to school in the mornings, Tessa investigated. It was through a friend of Gary's that she learned what was happening.

That night, she and Gary had a discussion about this latest problem.

"This is something I would never have dreamed of."

"But you had to know that it was a possibility. I've lived with prejudice all of my life so nothing surprises me anymore."

"But these are just kids."

"Tessa, where do you think they learn this behavior? Yes, hatred and prejudice is definitely a learned behavior."

"Well, Easter is coming up. Why don't we have an Easter Egg hunt at home? We'll have Easter baskets for the kids coming to the hunt."

"Okay. You set it up. Invite all of the kids in her class. That way no one will have anything further to use against her."

And yet another problem was solved.

Ali was growing into a beautiful young woman. She was fast approaching her thirteenth birthday. She continued to do well in school. She had numerous friends. She continued taking piano lessons and performed at several recitals. Her mother and she clashed on occasion but probably no more than any other mother and daughter.

Tessa appreciated her own mother more and more when she went through confrontations with Ali. She thought if the pre-teen years had been a bit rocky, what would the actual teen times be like? She was soon to find out.

The years after Vera died were hard for Ali. She had felt responsible for her friend's death. She thought if she hadn't kept bragging about how smart Vera was and how she wished Vera went to her school, Vera may still be alive.

Ali was colorblind in picking her friends. This was an attitude that her parents also adopted. She hung around the black kids as often as she did the white ones. One of her best friends was Vera's brother, Marc. He had been living with his grandmother, Mabel, shortly after Vera's death. One reason was his mother had gone back to her drug-enhanced street life. Thus Mabel was his legal guardian.

Ali was doing well in eighth grade and was scheduled for the enriched classes in the local high school.

She had developed a crush on a ne'er do well…. Barry Brown. Tessa was not the least bit happy about this.

"Where are you going?"

"To the movies."

"With who?"

"Barry and some of the gang."

"Do you know that he's been in reform school?"

"That was a long time ago. He's okay now."

It was with great trepidation that Tessa watched her only child go off to God knows what.

"Hi," said Ali as she saw Barry.

"Hi. It doesn't look as if the rest of the kids are coming."

So they went into the movie theater together.

Ali hoped against hope Barry would kiss her in the movies but he didn't. It was as if she had a 'no trespassing' sign on her forehead. But she thought maybe he didn't try because he was too macho to face rejection. But would she have rejected him? She pondered how she would handle any sexual advances, as harmless as they may have been. She wouldn't have wanted to hurt anyone's feelings. But she was ambivalent about being touched … other than casually.

Looking back on this brief interlude, she realized he was toying with her. He was making himself look good by hanging out with a better crowd. He went back to his old gang, thus leaving a heartbroken Ali behind.

She wrote a poem about their brief encounter, making this entire episode of her life more than it was.

It's hard to forget a love that's true. …
Not to recall fond memories of you.
Harder still to look in open space. …
And not be greeted by your smiling face.
I'll never forget the fun we've had. …
I'll recall the times, good before bad.
I said it wouldn't end, they said yes.
I should have known that they knew best.
Our love is a story, old and new. …
From Adam, Eve, and Juliet too.
It's cruel to say that it has ended. …
After two lips have fondly blended.
Words can't express my feelings toward you,
Or how I feel now, brokenhearted and blue.

Maybe someday I will again do. ...
All of the things I had once done with you.
My love for you I'll never forget,
But losing you, I'll always regret.

And with one broken heart behind her, Ali entered high school. When she entered the tenth grade, she was the leader of modified rebellion. She had always questioned why this and why that. Her parents had encouraged her to be assertive but she was in overdrive.

The relationship between Marc and her was growing. They were inseparable. Although Gary and Tessa had misgivings, they kept their opinions to themselves. They knew all too well how the tentacles of prejudice impede things. *They* had been victimized and *they* were the *same* color.

"I can't believe that our daughter's apparently ready to take on the world."

"Why? In the 50s, we swam against the tide. If you'll recall, no one was overjoyed about us getting together. Now the color thing is the big issue. The adage, 'the more things change, the more they remain the same' is certainly true."

Actually Gary and Tessa were glad to see Ali connecting with someone because she had misgivings about establishing strong ties with anyone. It was as if anyone she befriended would meet a fate similar to Vera's.

There was a party at one of Marc's classmates' house. She had permission to go. She had no way of knowing that the crowd was going to be a mixture. She didn't know there would be an older group there. At any rate, there were no chaperones present. This was Ali's first encounter with such an event.

The music was loud, the food plentiful and the liquid refreshments were more than Coca-Cola. Ali saw that everyone was drinking the fruit punch so she joined in. When the first sip passed her lips, she knew the taste was different. Ali was now having second thoughts. She knew she shouldn't have come to the party because there appeared to be things going on which she didn't want any part of. But she was just a kid. And she wanted to be like any other kid. So she sought Marc out.

"The punch tastes funny."

"For God's sake, Ali. Don't be so stupid! There's booze in it."

"I am *not* stupid. I resent you saying that."

"Well, why did you come to the party if you wanted to be goody two shoes?"

"I'm not goody two shoes. I just don't think I need to drink liquor to have a good time. I want to go home."

"If you want to be a drag, they won't invite you again."

"I'll stay if you hang out with me."

"I didn't come to baby-sit you," said Marc as he walked into the other room.

Ali felt deserted but decided to stay to prove to Marc she wasn't a baby. She also knew her parents would play a game of twenty questions if she came in before 11 ... her curfew time. As the night went on, the group got less lucid. Soon, she and Marc were just about the only sober ones there. The party had wound down.

Marc went to get the car while Ali waited inside the house. As she waited, she was approached from behind. Before she could turn to face the guys who were talking, one of them grabbed her from behind while another covered her eyes. She never saw who was talking to her.

"Hey, baby, how about if you and us get it on?"

She froze, thinking she should have gone home earlier. She thought she recognized one of their voices but she still hadn't seen their faces.

Trying to remain calm, she said, "I'm waiting for someone to pick me up."

"Who? Nigger boy?"

"How can you talk about Marc like that?"

"Why not? He's nothing to us. We just like the white meat he always manages to bring to all of the parties."

Ali tried to pull away but the boys grabbed her tighter. She heard a click. Apparently one had gone to lock the door while another managed to blindfold her with some kind of cloth. They dragged her into an adjacent bedroom and flung her onto the bed. They turned the music up louder and louder so if she chose to scream, it couldn't be heard. Terrified, she did just that. It did prove to be futile.

Ali tried to disassociate herself from what was happening. She felt one of them run his rough hands across her back as he unhooked her bra. Another one ripped her pants off.

The next sensation was an olfactory one. She was aware of the strong smell of alcohol which had permeated the room.

She tried to remember what she had been told about violence. She thought if she shouted and begged them to stop, it would be a turn-on for her assailants. She gritted her teeth just as they were beginning their fun.

Ali knew it was futile to talk to them so she just braced herself for what was the inevitable.

"Do you have the soda bottle ready?" she heard one of them say. "Make sure you shake it up good. I want that nigger juice washed out before I put my cock in her."

"I have my thumb over the neck of the bottle so it doesn't splash until it hits the right spot."

Sick laughter abounded throughout the room. Ali tried to completely detach herself from the ugly situation. She met with only a minimal amount of success.

Suddenly she felt a cold, hard penetration in her vagina. When she thought she could no longer endure the pain, she felt a gush of fluid splatter into the vagina. It burned her for a bit. Then the beasts removed the bottle from her, laughing all of the time.

"My, my. It's a cherry soda! Who would have thought the nigger's whore would be a virgin. Let's go. This isn't as much fun as I thought it was gonna be."

Ali couldn't believe it. They were actually leaving. She had never experienced anything so vile before. She was quaking with fear. She was relieved her virginal state had spoiled their pleasure.

As she heard the door close, she took the blindfold from her face and began to sob. She had no idea how much time passed before she heard Marc's voice as if from a great distance.

"Ali, what happened? God, you're bleeding. Ali, do you hear me? Ali, listen to me. It's me, Marc. Ali. Look at me!"

Ali was flailing her arms, crying, unable to speak. She couldn't form a coherent thought, let alone a sentence.

"Shh, shh," Marc whispered. "I don't know what happened here but I'm taking you to the nearest hospital."

"Noooo. I can't go there. Please don't take me there. I just want to go home. Daddy will take care of this. Please, Marc. *Please!* Take me to my daddy."

Marc couldn't believe what he was hearing. His self-assured, independent Ali was crying for daddy. Not knowing what else to do, Marc did as she asked.

"Ali, wait, I'll get a blanket from the car."

"No! Don't leave me alone."

"Okay, come on." Marc put his arm protectively around Ali and ushered her into his car. He got her safely into the front seat. Then he went to his trunk to retrieve the blanket. Even though it wasn't cold, Ali was shivering and her teeth were chattering.

The ride home was horrible. Marc silently blamed himself for leaving Ali alone with those pigs.

Ali was reliving the night, realizing that she should have gone home as soon as she became aware of the spiked punch. She didn't know how she could have possibly gotten herself into that situation.

As they were getting closer to her home, they saw a police car stopped beyond the curve in the road. Marc debated whether to stop and try to get help for Ali. He decided it would just be better to get her home so he continued driving.

When they pulled up to the Rosens' household, Marc hurried to the door and rang the bell. He looked up to see the light go on in Ali's parents' bedroom. They were at the door in seconds, bombarding him with questions.

"Marc, what are you doing ringing the bell at this hour? Where's Ali? She has a key. Has something happened to her? Marc, you look like hell. What's happened?" Gary and Tessa were taking turns with questions.

Gary looked to Marc's car and saw Ali. Relief flooded through him and he walked over to the car. The relief quickly turned to fear then anger when he saw his little girl, disheveled, with tears streaming down her face.

"Ali, Ali, baby. What happened? Did you have an accident? Ali, honey, answer me! What happened?"

"Oh, Daddy," began Ali but all she could do was wail.

Gary was really shook up when he saw his distraught Ali. After he saw Ali's tattered clothing, he called back to Tessa, who was standing at the doorway. "Get an afghan and bring it here to me."

Tessa came out to the car with the afghan and gasped when she saw the condition of her baby. She quickly and efficiently helped wrap Ali in the warmth of the blanket. Despite this, the intensity of Ali's shivering increased.

As Marc was walking to the car, Gary said, "I can't handle her alone. You're going to have to help me carry her. She's too rambunctious." Ali began flailing her arms again, as if to ward off more insults to her body.

"Get away from me. Get away!" Ali was in a frenzy.

Marc went to Gary's aide ... not a minute too soon. Ali's knees were like jelly and her tremors made it futile for her to even try to walk by herself.

Noticing the blood trickling down his daughter's legs, Gary whispered to Tessa, "Call Dr. Martin."

With Marc's help, Gary maneuvered Ali to the sofa, which he had covered with another afghan. Tessa hurried to the phone.

"Hello, Bob. Forgive me for calling you so late but I think Ali's been raped." As she said the words, Tessa began to cry. She still couldn't believe it. In between sobs, she tried to tell Dr. Martin what she thought had happened.

135

"Tessa, calm down. I can't make hide nor hair of what you're saying," Dr. Martin said. "Where's Ali now?"

"She's here at home. Marc brought her. She has blood running down her legs. She seems to be in shock. She hasn't spoken a word since she came home. She just stares blankly into space. And she can't stop shivering."

"Tessa, take her to Linfield General. I'll see you there."

"I don't want everyone staring at her and talking about her."

"We have to have her examined properly as soon as possible. It's for her own well-being as well as to substantiate any case we may have. I know it's hard but you've got to listen to me. Take Ali to the emergency room. I'll meet you there."

"I don't know if Gary will go along with that."

"You have no choice. Nor do I, for that matter. The law is explicit in this type of case. If there are subsequent charges to be filed, we've got to follow proper procedures."

Hanging up the phone, Tessa regained control of herself. After all the years in nursing, she was able to handle almost any emergency … even those close to home.

She motioned to Gary that she wanted to talk to him.

"Bob wants us to take her to the hospital. He'll meet us there."

"That's unthinkable. I won't subject Ali to all of that public humiliation!"

"Calm down. We have to do what's right. We can't sweep this under the rug. I didn't want to go at first, but after I talked with Bob, I realized we really have no choice. I don't know exactly what happened tonight, but I'm certain our baby has been victimized. I, for one, don't plan to stand by and let this happen to anyone else's baby."

Marc was sitting on the floor in front of the sofa, holding Ali's hand. He left Ali and joined them. He filled them in as best as he could. He'd only surmised what had happened. "When I went outside, some of the bums attacked her." This was the succinct explanation which Marc gave. "She wasn't making any sense. She just kept saying she wanted her daddy. You can see her clothes are torn away plus she's been bleeding." He went back to Ali. He resumed holding her hand.

Tessa flashed her eyes at her husband, who then said, "It's not that I don't want to get to the bottom of this. But I can't see how it will do any good to relive what she's gone through tonight." Gary explained his reticence.

"She's going to have to relive this subconsciously for the rest of her life. We have to do what's best in the long run and not think about ourselves or what people may think."

"Do you think that's what's stopping me? I'll admit I don't especially want people to know this probably hasn't been her first sexual encounter. I don't especially like the fact I'll hear people say a nigger originally deflowered her. That's how I'm sure it will be told and retold. And it will get juicier and juicier each and every time."

By this time, Tessa could no longer hide her annoyance with her husband. "Well. I'm taking her to the hospital with or without you. Maybe the nigger will drive us there. It's your call. Which do you think will raise fewer eyebrows? You or Marc taking us?"

"You make me sound like a bigot. I only used the word because I know what the town will say about our little girl. I'm just not ready to have her reputation sullied because of this." Gary went to the closet and got lightweight jackets for Tessa and him.

Tessa went back to where Ali was lying. Marc was still sitting on the floor, holding her hand. He had the same helpless expression on his face.

"We're taking Ali to the hospital. There's no point in your coming with us but I'm sure that the police will want to ask you what happened at *that* party."

"I honestly don't know what happened. When I went to get my car, I helped some of the other kids too. Then when I came back, Ali wasn't able to tell me."

"Do you have any idea who did this?"

"Not yet. But you can be sure I'll find out." Marc was clenching his fists as he said this. "I saw a car tear ass away…. Excuse me…. Drive away. I got the license number."

"That's a good place to start. Why don't you go to the police station and report exactly what you do know?"

Gary appeared in the room and wrapped his arms protectively around Ali. He told her they were going to the hospital. In childlike obedience, Ali moved to an upright position and was going to attempt to walk. Gary and Marc gently lifted her and carried her outside, putting her into the front seat of the car. Tessa scurried into the back and they were on their way to Linfield General.

After watching them pull away, Marc drove to the Linfield police station.

When Tessa went to give the facts at the emergency desk, she was glad to see one of her friends was the intake clerk. The woman knew Ali was coming in. Dr. Martin had called to alert them.

As Tessa was walking away from the admitting desk, she saw Bob Martin coming into emergency room. Relieved, she said, "Thank you so much for coming. We're still in the dark about what happened."

"Was anyone with her when it happened? Perhaps someone else could give us the details."

"No. Marc was at the party with her but he was outside at the time."

"All right. We'll see her first and then deal with finding out what happened. Is Gary here?"

"Yes. He's in with Ali."

As soon as Bob walked into Ali's room, she began to speak.

"Oh, I'm so glad to see you. Please, can you help stop the soreness?"

Bob didn't say anything but asked, "Do you want your mother to stay while I examine you?"

"Maybe that's not such a good idea. Mom, can you and Daddy go to the waiting room?"

Tessa yielded to Ali's request. She and Gary walked out, hand in hand, giving Ali a quick kiss before they left the examining room.

"Okay, little lady, how about if you tell me exactly what happened tonight. At least the part that has you here, bleeding and sore."

Ali filled the doctor in on the gory details. He just nodded sympathetically, encouraging her to continue talking.

"I didn't do anything to warrant this." Ali defended her position needlessly. "My skirt wasn't short. Nor did I have on tight pants or a low cut blouse. They said, when they used the bottle that they wanted to wash all of the *nigger* juice out of me. But Marc and I have never even had sex. We're good friends. When they found that out, they stopped and left."

After Ali told him the major portion of what had happened, the nurse came in to assist with the exam. Dr. Martin was glad Ali kept talking because it was would be easier for him to do the examination if she wasn't paying full attention to him or the nurse.

They both eased her into the stirrups. He examined her as gently as he could.

When Dr. Martin was finished, he spoke, "I would like to bring your parents in now. We have to let them know what's going on and what happens next."

"Okay."

When Gary and Tessa entered the room, Ali began crying again.

"I'm sorry you had to go through this, too. But honest to God, it wasn't my fault. It wasn't Marc's either. But I think I know who a couple of the guys were."

"Tessa, we have to call the police."

"Do you want to do it, Gary, or do you want me to?" asked Dr. Martin.

"I'll do it, Bob," said Gary. "I just wanted to make sure that my little girl was okay first."

138

"Well, as far as I can determine, she has multiple vaginal abrasions but no apparent tears. She has told me what happened and, well … it's not very pretty. They used a soda bottle."

Gary and Tessa looked shocked and disgusted. But before they could speak, the doctor continued, "But at least there's no need to worry about a pregnancy or a sexually transmitted disease. Thank God for that, at least. It could have been much worse. But apparently when they discovered that Ali was a virgin, they lost interest."

Gary felt both relieved and guilty. How could he ever forgive himself for suspecting the worst of his daughter? The tears were welling in his eyes as he hurried to call the police.

Tessa went to Ali and cradled her in her arms while Ali cried silently.

"Shh, shh. It's all right. Everything will be okay. We'll let the police handle the incident. I can't tell you how sorry I am that this is how you lost your virginity. But the important thing is you're okay. I wish this whole thing hadn't happened but since it has, we'll get you through it together … all of us … Daddy, Marc, you and I."

"I hope Daddy doesn't blame Marc. And I hope he's not disappointed in me. There wasn't any way either of us could have known that this would happen. They thought that Marc and I were having sex. They lost interest when they found out I was still a virgin. I can't tell you how glad I am they stopped before one of them put his dirty thing in me." Ali sounded rational but her eyes were wild. Her face had big red blotches all over it.

Although Gary was gone but a short time, it seemed like an eternity before he returned.

"The police already knew about the situation because Marc had gotten there and had already reported it. But it seems they have an accident on the Curly Drive section of town. Evidently kids were driving too fast and they failed to initiate the curve in the road."

"Where's Marc? Is he still at the police station?"

"Yes."

"I hope they don't blame him for any of this. He doesn't even know what happened. He was outside."

"They did at first. When I called, I set them straight. I told them that he was as much a victim as you were." Turning to Tessa, he said, "I'm going to the police station to check on Marc. Can you and Ali manage?"

"Sure. But I have to make sure it's okay for her to go." She looked at Dr. Martin.

"There's no reason why Ali can't go home now. I've given her a bit of a sedative so she'll get some rest. I want her to have a sitz bath three times a day, though. Also, I'll give you a prescription for an analgesic ointment to ease the soreness. If she has any severe pain or runs a fever, don't hesitate to call me … either at home or through the office. Are *you* okay? I know how hard this has been for you."

"I'm fine. I'm just so glad.… Well, that things didn't get further out of hand. Thanks for everything."

They said their good-byes. Tessa went to get the car while the aide put Ali in a wheelchair, which was standard hospital procedure.

On the way home, they passed Curly Drive and saw a group of police cars as well as two ambulances. The scene didn't look too promising for the occupants but neither Tessa nor Ali commented on the situation.

Twenty-one

As Gary got out of the cab and began to enter the police station, he saw that Marc was in handcuffs. He was dumbstruck. He had been assured that Marc was not a suspect.

When Gary approached the officer who had Marc in custody, he said, "I hope you haven't violated any of his rights because I was assured they believed him and realized he was only giving them the facts as he knew them"

"Mr. Rosen, am I glad to see you!" Marc said. "They believed me at first but the with the change of shifts, the atmosphere changed. I don't know what they expect me to say any different than I did before. I only know what I know. I can't give them any gory details. I don't know what to do."

"It's okay. Ali's okay too. Her mother's taking her home now." Turning to the policeman, he said, "I demand his release. He's done nothing wrong."

"Hold on a minute, Bud, he *swung* at me. He's cuffed because of that…. Not for the fairy tale that he tried to snow the other guys with."

Looking at Marc, Gary knew it was true. He had indeed swung at the officer. He could only imagine what had provoked it. After all, hadn't he, himself, thought the worst of these two kids? Wouldn't a stranger be inclined to believe the same?

"Officer, could you possibly uncuff him? I'll vouch for his behavior. You'll have no further problem with him."

The policeman looked from Gary to Marc, shrugged his shoulders and said, "What the hell. He's your problem now."

Gary nodded, laid his hand on the back of Marc's neck and ushered him into a side room.

"What's the matter with you? Have you lost your mind? Why would you even try to use force on a cop? Were you going to erase everything that happened tonight by punching someone's lights out?"

"He was saying some terrible things about Ali and me … doing things together. I couldn't listen to him anymore. You wouldn't have wanted me to sit back and listen to him either."

Gary couldn't look Marc squarely in the eye. He felt a gnawing in the pit of his stomach. How could he absolve himself of having the same thoughts that the officer had confronted Marc with? He finally regained control of his emotions and his thoughts. He found his voice again.

"Marc, I don't think you're aware of how serious your actions were. You tried to strike an officer of the law who was performing his duty. It doesn't matter how antagonistic he was. You're still in the wrong. Now we have to go to the next step, which is to get you out of here and finding out the least amount of damage we can expect from what you did. Let me see if I can post bail for you or if you can be released into my custody. In the meantime, sit tight. Don't stir up any more problems. For now, you needn't answer any further questions."

Gary went to see the officer of the day, which turned out to be an acquaintance of his. He wasn't surprised when he was told the *boy* was going to have to post bail or spend the night in a holding cell.

"Let's get something straight right now." Gary began. "If it was any other kid in that room, you'd release him to a responsible adult. Your decision couldn't have anything to do with the fact that Marc is black, could it? I'm telling you right up front that I'll bring charges of racial discrimination, even if I have to go all the way to the Supreme Court. As petty as you may think this is, it's a violation of his constitutional rights. I, for one, will not stand by while this happens without doing all in my power to correct it."

The officer said, "Calm down, Gary. The fact that Marc is black has nothing to do with anything. He tried to assault an officer who was performing his duty. You can go to Kingdom Come with all of your allegations but the fact remains constant. The boy barely missed hitting an officer. How would most Americans, both black and white, feel about that?"

"I'm not disputing that fact. But I can just imagine the incidents that led up to it. What I'm objecting to is the manner in which this first offense is being handled. For God's sake! Are you that much of a racist?"

"My actions are none of your business. But look.... There's a bail bondsman in the other room, arranging bail for another nig– Negro. Why don't you wait with the kid and I'll send him in to you when he's finished."

Gary knew there was no reasoning with him further so he left and went to rejoin Marc.

Finally, when bail had been arranged, Gary and Marc left the police station together.

Marc was overwhelmed with gratitude toward Gary. He realized both he and Tessa were live and let live people. They didn't demand allegiance to their thoughts or actions. They just want to be treated with respect. And respect is exactly what he had for both of them.

That night, he learned how truly good the Rosens were. At first, as a southern boy, he had viewed them as damn Yankees. He considered them polite to as well as superficially solicitous of blacks. He realized they didn't have an agenda ... nor did they want pats on the back for the goods they did.

It was because of how supportive Gary had been in the police station that Marc began viewing him as an adjunct parent.... Like the father that he never really knew. His own father was grazing in who knows what greener pastures.

Marc still hadn't contacted his grandmother, so Gary accompanied Marc home and stayed while Marc explained to Mabel what had happened. Although Mabel was upset about Marc and his trouble, her compassion was all for Ali and Tessa.

"How is Miss Tessa holding up? How's my poor Ali? It's a frightful thing what those pigs did to her! Do the police know yet who they are?"

"Ali thinks she knows two of their names. I imagine they'll gladly give up the other names when they realize unless they do, they're going to take the entire blame themselves."

Since there was nothing left to say, Marc drove Gary home in silence.

As Gary crawled into bed, Tessa reached for him. Not wanting to rehash the night's events or hear, 'I told you so,' Gary said, "I honestly thought Ali and Marc had been having sex. Isn't it a sin her first sexual experience was such a violent one?"

They lay entwined for a long time, crying together.

The next morning, as Marc read the paper, he saw the destroyed car, which he had seen, belonged to Dick Johnson. Two people had been killed as a result of the accident but their names weren't being released until the next of kin had been notified. Marc couldn't feel any pity for the accident victims, because he was sure they had been the same bunch that inflicted both pain and humiliation on Ali.

Likewise, at the Rosen household, Gary read the news in the paper. He surmised these were the culprits who had hurt his daughter. His only regret was the *entire* group wouldn't be brought to justice.

Ali slept well into the morning. When she awakened, she took her bath. She had her breakfast. Then she learned about the accident. It was Tessa who broke the news to her.

Ali looked at her mother in disbelief and asked, "Mom, do they know yet who was killed in the accident? How many guys were in the car?"

Tessa said, "They haven't released the names of any of the people in the car, either the living or the dead, until they let the families know. The paper did say that there were six people in the car."

"What happens now, Mom?"

"That depends on a lot of things. If Dick Johnson and Paul Peterson are the boys who are dead, it looks like you won't have to worry about a day in court because you really can't positively identify the others who were involved. If they're alive, then we have to decide what to do next. For now, the most important thing is how are you today? Marc called any number of times already. He and your father are at the lawyer's office now, trying to see what the next step is to be."

"But, Mom, you said we won't know anything until we know who's dead and who's alive."

"I know but Marc got into some trouble at the police station last night. He was overwrought and…. Well, he did something he shouldn't have."

"Why is it I seem to cause nothing but trouble for his whole family?" Ali wailed. "First Vera, now Marc! He's one of the kindest, most gentle people I know. Whenever he's around me, I cause him nothing but trouble."

"That's not true. Why don't you go and lie down for a while? We'll talk more about this later."

Ali agreed reluctantly. Tessa was weary. She was glad to see there'd been no mention of Ali's rape in the newspaper even though her name would have been redacted. At least one thing had gone right.

In the lawyer's office, Bert began, "You're off base about this. I may agree with you that they baited and badgered him because he's black but his conduct was still inexcusable."

Marc was sitting in Bert's office, with his elbows on his knees, resting his forehead in his hands. To say he was dejected was an understatement.

"That's stupid rhetoric. You know how they treat minorities in our Linfield police station. I'm surprised no one has complained officially."

"Tell me. How would that play out? Most things are just innuendo. Marc, did they issue any racial slurs at you? Did they utter the word *nigger*? Just exactly what did they do that provoked you into such a fever pitch?"

At this point, Marc was having a hard time separating fact from fiction. He knew his objective judgment was impaired during the interrogation because of his concern for Ali.

"Well, no. Not nigger but they kept calling me *boy*."

"How old are you?"

"Almost 18."

"So you're 17, isn't that right?"

Marc just nodded in agreement.

"Technically you're still a boy." Bert held up his hand to prevent Gary from interrupting this exchange.

"But they spat it out."

"Intonation with one word is difficult to turn into a hate tactic."

Marc's lips began to quiver as he recalled the emotional horror of seeing Ali reduced to an incoherent, defenseless blob. He always referred to her as a bitchy spitfire. He couldn't fathom what rape was like but figured it had to be horrific.

"But you should have seen her," Marc was defending his actions. "It's something I'll never forget. Even if I had a lobotomy, it would still be imbedded in my brain."

"That's not the issue. Actually your feelings really shouldn't come into play during the interrogation. How does it matter that you're upset about the rape of your girlfriend when all they wanted were the facts?"

Marc hesitated, looked at Gary, began to speak, but decided against it.

"Would you feel better if I left?" asked Gary.

"Yes," answered Marc, quickly, obviously relieved.

After Gary left, Bert said, "Okay shoot."

"Uh, I don't know where to begin," said a distinctly embarrassed Marc.

"Believe me, anything you say is probably no worse than what I've heard before. Just begin and let the words flow."

Bert and Marc got into the actual interrogation full speed ahead.

"Well, they kept saying things about Ali being.... You know, like she and I would do unnatural things. They asked if she took it up the ass. They wondered if that was why the boys *allegedly* broke her cherry. They constantly said *alleged* this and *alleged* that. I know they were trying to rile me up. They said we'd gone too far this time and maybe we had second thoughts. Mr. Stein, Ali was raped with a *soda bottle*! How can they think I'd do something like that? If I'd been anyone else, they would have treated me different. My grandmother always says since I'm black, I have to be more careful than white boys at school are. I always have been. But I'll never get over this. And I don't think Ali will either." With that, Marc put his head in his hands and started crying. "When I think of it, I get sick to my stomach." And he ran into the adjacent bathroom retching.

When he came back into the office, Bert went to the outer office and said to Gary, "You can come in now. The kid's really shook up."

Gary went over and put his hand reassuringly on Marc's shoulder.

"Calm down, son. It'll turn out all right."

The word son wasn't lost on Marc. He looked at Gary with such admiration. Even Bert sensed the depth of Marc's feelings toward Gary.

145

"Okay, here's what we have. In all likelihood, Marc will probably be placed on probation, since I'm sure the hierarchy of the police department doesn't want a probe into their practices.

"In regard to the actual rape itself, didn't you tell me the boys were involved in an auto accident and some were killed?"

Gary nodded in assent.

"Well, let's find out who the victims were."

"In other words," interjected Gary, "if the only ones Ali could identify were killed, there'd be no court action."

"Yes. And as much as I like to see vicious acts punished, in the long run, it'll be better for Marc."

"I'll check to see who the victims were. Then I'll work on a possible defense for Marc."

Marc and Gary left Bert's office and went to see how Ali was doing.

Ali was sleeping when they got there. Tessa was busy doing things around the house and hadn't heard recent news. It was through the twelve o'clock news that they learned who the victims and survivors were.

When Gary heard that Dick Johnson and Paul Peterson were the dead boys, he was ambivalent. He knew that Ali wouldn't have to go to court, nor would Marc have to repudiate the testimony of the white boys. He regretted that the other boys would not be punished for the horrible treatment of his daughter. He didn't know how Tessa would feel, but he was certain that Ali would feel the same as he.

Until now, Marc had kept his emotions pretty much under control since last night's difficulty. But now that he was free of the burden of telling his story to bigots, he began to shake and some more tears fell. He told Gary he didn't want to have to repeat all of those things that had transpired with the police during the interrogation. He hadn't even scratched the surface with Bert Stein. He was too embarrassed to do so even after Gary had left the room. Bert sensed this and didn't push the issue. He was all too familiar with overzealous interrogation tactics.

True to her Italian heritage, Tessa suggested they have lunch first and then go tell Ali what had happened while she was napping. When Tessa was upset or nervous, she had to keep busy doing things. This morning, she had made potato salad, cole slaw, a cake and cookies. She had bought corned beef at the grocery store the day before so it was sure to be deliciously fresh.

Neither Marc nor Gary realized how hungry they were. Eating was not high on their to-do list. All of the legal activities had kept them busy for the past several hours.

"Gary, has Marc told Mabel yet about what's happened?" Tessa asked when Marc went to wash his hands.

"Do you know, I forgot about that. She doesn't know about the death of the boys, or should I say animals? After we talk to Ali, I'll go with Marc to see her. I think she's off today."

"Boy! That corned beef sure looks good. I'm famished now."

All conversation was at a standstill while they ate.

"Mom, who's downstairs with you? Did I hear Dad and Marc? And what's for lunch? I'm starving."

"Ali, honey," Gary said, "Marc and I are finishing lunch. We'll bring something up to you in a minute."

"Thanks, Dad."

Upon reaching Ali's bedroom, Marc got cold feet. He didn't know how he could face her. He'd let her down. He didn't know if she could or would forgive him. Gary practically pushed him into the room.

"Hi, Marc. Are you okay?"

He couldn't believe his ears. After what had happened to her, she was asking how *he* was doing. If she didn't blame him, perhaps eventually he'd be able to forgive himself.

"My God, that looks so good. I'd like something to drink. Water or something but no soda."

Marc and Gary froze. Finally Gary said, "Fine, honey. Whatever you want."

Though Ali was usually talkative, today she was more quiet than usual.

After she had finished eating, Gary said, "Ali, as you know there was an accident last night after the party. Two of the boys were killed. They were Dick Johnson and Paul Peterson."

"Now they won't have to pay for what they did. Their secret died with them!"

Tessa, who had heard the commotion downstairs, ran up into Ali's room.

"Gary, Marc, Ali, for God's sake, what's going on?" Tessa asked as she put her arms around Ali, trying to soothe her.

"We just told her that Dick and Paul were the victims of the car accident," Gary said. "I thought she'd be relieved."

"Gary, why don't you and Marc go downstairs? I'll stay with her for a while."

Marc and Gary went quietly down and back into the kitchen.

"Mr. R., I don't think Ali's with it today. If she were, she'd realize that no punishment is worse than death."

"She went through hell last night and nothing short of hell would be good

147

enough for them in her eyes. We just have to be patient with her. This isn't just going to disappear because they won't have to be confronted by the truth. In a way, it may have been better for her if she had her day in court. But she doesn't realize in the long run, this is much better for you both. You saw firsthand how they could make a victim look like a perpetrator. Your word would have been negligible in a white man's court with a white jury, white judge, white lawyers as well as white spectators. I can't apologize for the world but I do hope that someday it will be different."

"But Mr. R., don't you think that anyone would believe me? I've never been in any kind of trouble. A lot of people in the community know me well. Do you really think they'd turn their backs on me and stand up for those animals?"

As much as he hated saying it, Gary countered with, "You're leaving out one very important fact. They are white animals. Look, I'm not trying to be cruel but facts are facts. I don't see any point in pulling any punches."

It hurt Gary to see the pain in Marc's eyes, but he knew Marc had to face reality. Gary, himself, had faced numerous acts of prejudice during the years, not the least of which emanated from his own parents.

Upstairs, Tessa was saying to Ali, "Honey, you've been deeply hurt. I can't undo that. Nor can Daddy. The abrasions will heal soon enough but the emotional scars will heal only if you let them. Let's talk about this whole thing. If Marc was the only witness, think about how they would have torn his testimony to shreds! He had a problem at the police station last night because they kept implying perhaps it was he who *raped* you and he was using others as scapegoats for his actions. Ali, who do you honestly think the jury would believe? You're old enough now to face the facts. Daddy and I have permitted you free rein with your friends. We believe we've raised you well enough for you to make many decisions on your own. Perhaps that was too much responsibility for you.

"But we've nurtured your friendship with Marc because he's a fine young man. People, in general, don't view that friendship the same way. But I'm not ready to let other people dictate who my friends should be any more than I want them to influence your friendships. When we do things which people don't understand, we subject ourselves to grief. Hopefully, that grief will be shortlived and infrequent. I, for one, am glad that we don't have to subject either you or Marc to public scrutiny. I'm not playing ostrich, but I don't believe in going out on a limb while someone is at the other end sawing it off. As you get older, you'll realize what I'm saying is true. Sad, but true."

Ali wiped a tear from her eye and said, "Mom, I don't know what I'd do if I didn't have Daddy and you for parents. You always help me no matter what the trouble is. I'd like to see Marc alone now if that's okay with you."

When Marc walked into the room, he saw that Ali, who was usually vibrant and effervescent, looked a little smaller and paler. When she saw him, she gave him a weak smile, which he returned in kind.

"Hi, Marc. Mom told me everything. She tried to make me see it was for the best, but I still don't think it's fair. I know they wouldn't have gotten the death penalty, but this way, everyone will mourn them as some tragic heroes in a paperback book. But I know what kind of animals they really are."

"I know, but it's probably better neither of us have to testify and relive that horror. At first, I was disappointed, too, but when your parents explained how the situation would be viewed, I was relieved."

"Marc, do any of the kids at school know about this?"

"I don't see how anyone could. And now, no one has to ever know. The two of us were the only ones left at the party and the hospital certainly won't go public with it. And since no charges will be filed, it'll probably remain a secret."

"All of you make it sound so simple. But none of you had to go through what I did. None of you understand anything!"

"Just a minute! How can you say we don't understand? Did you see your father last night? Did you see your mother? Do I always have circles like this under my eyes? Just because we don't scream and carry on doesn't mean we don't understand. I know you're in pain, but so are the rest of us. I'm sorry for what happened.... We all are. But you're not the only one affected. Where do I fit into the picture? For that matter, where do your parents fit in? I'm leaving. If you want to talk to me or see me, you know how to reach me."

"Marc, Marc, wait!"

But Marc had already gone down the steps, taking them two at a time.

"What happened? Why is Ali calling you? Have you upset her? Haven't you put her through enough?" Tessa screeched.

"Not you too, Mrs. Rosen! I thought you knew I'd have given anything to have been hurt instead of Ali. If she wants to see me, she can call. I was victimized, too. I'm sorry if that's not what all of you want to hear, but that's just the way it is." He stormed out of the house, slamming the door behind him.

149

Twenty-two

Tessa was stunned into silence. None of Ali's friend had ever challenged her or Gary before ... especially not Marc. He had always known his place. As Tessa reflected she wondered about the implications of her thoughts. Was his place one of respect, or had she subconsciously relegated him to a position of a second-class citizen because of his color? Looking at herself now, she wasn't completely happy with what she was seeing. Was she a hypocrite? Or was that too harsh a word? Did she feel superior to Marc? Could that be why she'd encouraged the friendship? She could almost feel the rejection which Marc must be feeling. Years ago, she and Gary had endured a similar situation at the hands of their parents.

That Marc was born black and they were white was simply the way things were. No one could perceive a situation unless they were in that exact one. How many times had she said, "If I were you, I'd...." It was easy to solve another's problems. Not only were you detached from them but also you wouldn't have to live with the consequences of the solution. Was she one of those perfect do-gooders who had the answer to everyone's problems, even if the answer was unsolicited? These thoughts and more were converging upon her all at once. When she heard Ali crying upstairs, she was relieved to have a respite from her reflection. She went into the kitchen and made some hot chocolate. There was nothing more soothing to Tessa when she was a little girl than hot chocolate ... especially on a cold day. The warmth of the chocolate always reassured her that all was right with the world.

After preparing the drink, she pushed back her hair, squared her shoulders and went up the stairs. She and Ali needed to talk.

When Ali saw her, she said, "Mom, Marc said some pretty rotten things to me. I always thought he was my friend. Now, I'm not so sure."

"Ali, a friend isn't a rubber stamp for all of your thoughts and wishes. A friend sometimes says things you may not like. That doesn't make those things wrong. A friend is someone who knows your faults and likes you anyway, who stands by you when times are tough. A friend isn't a blind mute either. He or she can see and hear exactly what you do but perhaps see things from a different perspective. If their view doesn't coincide with yours, they

150

still have a right to express it. Wouldn't it be dull if everyone always agreed with you?

"Maybe your dad and I have given you a slanted view of the world. We never meant to infer that you're the ultimate in decision making. We gave you free rein but always reserved the right to overrule you if necessary. Now is one of those times.

"You didn't see Marc last night the way we did. You don't know what he was put through. Naturally you were concentrating on what was done to you. What happened to you was terrible, awful, and far worse than I can ever imagine. But that doesn't take away from the fact that Marc was injured too. Do you have scars from this? Yes. Are they permanent? I hope not.

"And what about Marc? Will his wounds heal? Will you be there to help him through his heartache? None of us in White America can possibly comprehend what the one *mere* fact of color does to a life. When my ancestors came into this country, they also were the victims of prejudice. However, they lost some of their accent and were Americanized. People can't tell just by looking if one is of Italian descent. But this isn't so for the blacks. In the summer, white America runs to the shore to darken its skin. Why is it the same look of darkness is associated with laziness as well as shiftlessness in those in whom the color is permanent?

"Maybe Marc will never set foot in this house again. Maybe you and he will grow apart. You have more control over how this incident affects your long-term relationship with Marc. You have a lot of sorting out to do. I have faith in your judgment. Daddy and I will support you in whichever way you go with this. Don't let the brutal, vicious acts of others bring you to end something which has been so good and meaningful to you."

As Ali felt the warm, soothing taste of the chocolate in her mouth, she knew that all would once again be right with her world. She realized that much of what her mother said was true and in fact, was something she'd already told herself. How could she let anyone know that she had felt so betrayed by all of them that she was irrational with her judgment? Although the hot chocolate was a welcome solace, this was not something as simple as a skinned knee. This was an occurrence that could alter her whole life.

She was half-awake and half-asleep when she said, "Mom, with the help of all of you, even Marc, I'm sure I'll be okay. Right now I just want to sleep. When I wake up, maybe I'll find this was just a nightmare. I'll call down to you when I wake up, okay?"

Before Tessa could answer, Ali had already fallen asleep. Tessa took the cup from her daughter's hand and quietly walked out of the room, knowing that the first battle of the war had been fought and won. Exactly how may more battles would be necessary was beyond her control. She only hoped that with God's help, Ali would resume her life and enjoy it as she had before the entire episode.

Ali slept so soundly when Gary came into her room to see if she wanted anything for dinner, she was momentarily startled. She'd been dreaming of Vera. She identified even more than ever with her deceased friend. Vera had also been a victim of circumstances beyond her control. Ali thought at least her own life had been spared. She owed the fact that she had gotten home safely to Vera's brother. Just as no one had blamed the Rosens for Vera's death, she couldn't and shouldn't blame Marc for what happened to her. She'd call him in a few days, when she was better and was up for a conversation.

"So anyhow, princess, what would you like for dinner? Mom says she'll make you anything you want."

"I think I'd like eggs and toast. I've been in bed all day so I feel like having something *breakfasty*. Bacon, too. Okay?"

"Sure." Gary decided not to discuss the taboo subject, figuring time would be a great healer.

His avoidance of the predicament did not go unnoticed by his astute daughter. She knew her father and mother would give her what they had often referred to as breathing room. If she needed air, they would give it to her. However, if she needed verbal reflection, they would be her sounding board.

Later that night, Tessa came into the room and spoke with her daughter. "How are you feeling? Is your bottom very sore? Have you made any peace within yourself?" Tessa was distressed about how wane and fragile her daughter looked.

"I'm a little sore but it's not as bad as it was. Do I have to go back to see Dr. Martin?"

"He said if you felt okay and don't run a fever or have excessive soreness, there's no need to schedule a regular appointment. Though, when you feel better he wants you to come by on your own. He wants to examine you and discuss the incident. I'll take you but I won't be there for the conversation. I'm still too angry. It's best you talk with someone who's more objective than I."

"Mom, Marc made me see how very selfish I was being. I didn't like the way he did it though, but he was right after all. I'm going to call him in a couple of days. Deep down I know he wasn't to blame in any way. I still feel pretty rotten about everything. I'm sure he and I can work this out." Ali paused thoughtfully for a moment, then added, "I dreamt about Vera and she asked me not to desert her brother. She said he was only trying to be helpful. She likened it to how we tried to be helpful when she came to my school with the rest of the white kids and me. You know none of her family ever pointed a finger at any of us. It's funny how sometimes dreams seem to make things all right again. I think I'll call Marc and let him know I still care about him. I don't want him thinking that we all hate him now."

"Honey, I'm sure Marc realizes that we're just upset about this whole thing. His grandmother will help him put things into perspective. She has such strong faith in God that she entrusted her future and that of her family to Him. Even Vera's death and her daughter's drug problem didn't shake her faith. Tomorrow I'll call her to let her know our feelings and respect for Marc are still intact."

"It'd make it easier for me to call Marc if she intervened. You know, I'd like to come downstairs tomorrow. Is that okay?"

"Sure. Let's see how you feel in the morning." Tessa put out Ali's light and went into a waiting Gary.

"I feel like I've spent 24 years in 24 hours! I just want us to get on with our lives. I think Ali's made of strong stuff and that's what's coming to the surface."

"You're right, but now, I need us to take a break from being a mother and a father and once again just be two married lovers."

He reached for his wife and she responded eagerly.

Twenty-three

Although Ali did call Marc, they didn't resume their past friendship. She still had to come to grips with the rape and the part that he did or did not play in it … even though deep down she knew it actually wasn't any fault of his. They grew apart. Ali began rebelling against anything authoritarian.

She began spending time with Barry again.

"Ali, my uncle lent me his car. Would you like to take a ride with some of the gang?"

And so they were riding along when a police car's strobe lights flashed behind them. Some of the kids in the car were smoking pot.

"License and registration please."

"Just a minute. It's right here." Barry fumbled for the imaginary registration.

The car had been reported stolen, which was the reason they were stopped.

They were taken to the police station.

Hence the phone rang in Gary and Tessa's bedroom.

"Mr. or Mrs. Rosen, please."

"This is Mr. Rosen."

"This is Officer Staley at the Linfield police station."

"Has there been an accident?"

"No, sir, but there's a problem. Since your daughter's a juvenile, we need you to come down to the police station as soon as possible."

"Right away." Gary said, but he thought, as long as she's not hurt.

Gary and Tessa quickly got ready and went to the police station.

"Where is she?" asked a breathless Tessa, after she and Gary introduced themselves.

"In the interrogation room."

"What happened?" asked Gary.

"It seems that she and a few friends went for a joy ride in a stolen car."

"No, there must be a mistake," interrupted Tessa. Gary put his arm around her shoulder and whispered to her to listen.

"It seems she and the group also had marijuana in their possession."

"Oh, no," bemoaned Tessa, who couldn't believe her baby was into illicit drugs.

Gary asked, "What's the procedure?"

"We can remand her to your custody but she'll have to appear in court to face the allegations."

"Can we please see her now?"

"Follow me."

Ali was near tears in the interrogation room but when she saw her parents, she put on a brave front.

"Mommy, it was so stupid. I thought Barry had borrowed the car from his uncle but he didn't. He stole it from a mall. When I asked him later, he said since he planned to return it, he really was just *borrowing* it. When I asked him about his uncle, he said his uncle had a car just like it so it was like he got it from him." Talk about a convoluted explanation!

Gary couldn't believe what he was hearing and tried to remain calm while he said, "Fine. And how exactly do you explain the marijuana? Were you doing research for science?" He spat these words out, which was a departure from his usual demeanor.

"Barry? Barry, who? Barry Brown?" screeched an out of control Tessa. "I thought you were going somewhere with Marc."

"Marc's boring. Barry's lots of fun."

Tessa restrained herself, not offering anything else. She was in total disbelief.

"Let's go home now," said Gary, as he dragged his daughter by her elbow through the station house to their car. The ride home was made in deafening silence.

In the morning, Gary called Bert. He thought at this rate, so soon after the rape incident, he'd be better off putting Bert on retainer.

The court date came quickly.

"How do you plead to marijuana possession?"

Bert, who was standing next to Ali, said, "Guilty, your honor."

There had been an agreement that she wouldn't be charged with stealing the car because the other kids gave the same story that the car belonged to Barry's uncle. Barry was the antithesis of Ali and the other kids involved. None of them had ever been in trouble with the law before.

The judge decried, "I adjudicate you a juvenile delinquent and suspend sentencing at this time."

Ali got placed on probation, which was okay with her.

A few months later, Ali and her new gang went to the local department store to try on clothes. When she saw something she liked, she left it on under her own clothes and walked out of the store.

Thus Gary and Tessa received another phone call from the police department.

"Mr. or Mrs. Rosen, please. This is Officer Staley calling."

Gary's heart rate increased as he answered, "Yes, Officer, this is Mr. Rosen. What can I do for you?"

"You had better come down to the police station. There's been a problem with your daughter."

Dreading what they would learn when they got there, Tessa and Gary, as dutiful parents, went to headquarters.

"What seems to be the problem?"

"Ali and some of her friends went on a shopping spree. However, they didn't have any money but that didn't deter them. They put the store clothes on under their own and walked out."

"So she's being charged with possession of stolen goods." Gary's jargon was sounding legalistic due to his encounters with the law: compliments of Ali.

"That in addition to marijuana possession."

"Can we see her now?"

"Yes. I'll get the paperwork up to snuff so she can go home with you."

"Hold off on that please."

Astonished, Tessa looked at her husband. "What do you mean.... Hold off on that?"

"What don't you understand?"

"Well, we're going to take her home, aren't we?"

"I'm not sold on that. Sometimes you have to be cruel to be kind. I don't plan to, nor do I suppose that you plan to keep coming back here."

"How do you propose to accomplish that feat?"

"Watch me," Gary said as he led her into a waiting Ali.

"Daddy." Ali began crying.

After saying to Tessa, "Give our daughter a tissue please," he turned to Ali and said, "Is there anything you'd like to try to snow us with?"

"I planned to pay for them tomorrow. I was going to ask you for the money."

"That's not good enough. I think it'd be a good idea if you cooled your heels tonight in a detention center."

"You won't do that to me. Mommy, don't let him desert me!"

When Tessa said nothing even though her heart was breaking, Ali whined, "You can't do this to me. I promise I won't do anything like this anymore. Mom, you've *got* to make him listen."

156

Tessa, who knew she was about to cry, turned her back on her daughter for the first time ever, both literally and figuratively. She stoically walked out of the room, got outside of hearing range then began to cry. She was completely astounded by Gary's actions but not as shocked as she was by her daughter's behavior.

"There's no refrigerator here. No TV. What am I supposed to do? I'll be locked up like a common criminal. The room is so small; it's a cubbyhole. I want my own bedroom. I want my creature comforts. I want to be able to talk on the phone. I want—"

"Enough. This isn't about what *you* want anymore. It's about what your mother and I *don't* want. We don't want to get another call from the police citing your undesirable behavior. We don't want you to associate with the likes of Barry Brown. Even though he's in jail, you follow his friends as blindly as you followed him. When you're ready to abide by home rules and regulations, to say nothing of society's, you'll be welcome back into our lives again. Tonight, without all of your creature comforts, you'll have ample time to reflect on your behavior. But remember, we love you and we'll be happy to welcome you with open arms when you return to the girl we have known and loved these past seventeen years."

Although the Rosens and Marenos were distressed about Gary's decision, they knew that Ali was on a collision course. Marc couldn't believe what Ali's parents had done to her when he found out about it. What he didn't realize was that they did it *for* her.

For a good portion of the night, Ali was hopping mad about being abandoned. But when her parents came for her, she was happy to be allowed back into her familiar way of life. Ali was herself once again. The cohesiveness of the family unit was once again restored.

Twenty-four

With her incarceration behind her, Marc and she began spending more time together. She called him and asked if he'd go for a walk with her on the docks. He agreed to go.

She brought up the rape, "So you see, I never really blamed you deep down. I'd never been a victim before. I didn't know what to do."

"Ali, I'm sorry about what I said to you. I've been the victim so many times, I guess I was upset that when you were put in that position I should have been able to stop it."

"What happened wasn't your fault in any way. I think I knew that even then. It's just I had to have someone to blame and you were the closest one. Can we go on the way we were?"

"We can never go back to the way we were. This thing has made our bond stronger. I've always liked you but now, I feel more protective of you. I want to make sure that nothing like this ever happens to you again."

"What do you plan to do? Put me on a leash and have me heel all the time?"Ali giggled.

"Stop teasing and be serious for a change. It's good to have you and your devilment back again, but I need to get my point across to you."

"I was just teasing. I've never seen you this intense before."

"Maybe it's because I took our friendship for granted. I know now things can't always run smoothly. I guess I always knew that, but somehow, I thought you'd be insulated from the world's ugliness. Ali, I–"

Just then a big clash of thunder roared and the sky opened up with a punishing rainfall. Ali and Marc ran the two blocks to 'Down Under.'

"Hi, you two." Gary was happy to see them together. "What would you like to eat?"

"Hi Dad, I'd like a steak sub. How about you, Marc?"

Marc was chagrined he didn't have the time to tell Ali what was really on his mind. Now it seemed as if the moment was lost.

"I'll have the same," Marc said.

"Has Mom been by yet? I know she and Aunt Treva were working this morning on some new rainwear. They're really going crazy with colors. I can hear grandpop Al now…. 'But Tessa, rainwear is supposed to look more drab than that. You aren't supposed to make people glad it's raining.' And Mom would say, 'But Dad, why go around glum and morbid? The weather is enough of a downer, why should they look like the world is coming to an end just because the grass is getting watered?' Isn't that the way the conversation went?"

"I didn't think you'd remember all that chatter. I used to stay out of it. I'm not one for getting in the middle of two hotheaded Italians."

"Who are two hotheaded Italians?" quipped Tessa as she and Treva strolled into the sub shop.

"Oops, Ali, now look what you've gone and done."

They had a good laugh, something they hadn't done in a long while. It seemed that things were getting back to normal. Finally!

Twenty-five

Marc and Ali were spending more and more time together. They, like her parents before them, were doing the unthinkable. They had crossed an invisible line. For all intents and purposes, they had fallen in love. They had spoken of marriage but knew that the timing wasn't right. No definitive plans had been made since Marc was in his senior year of college, and Ali was in her first year of nursing.

Although Gary and Tessa didn't positively know this, they sensed Ali and Marc's future would be spent together.

Tessa was so busy between the hospital and 'Mist' that she had virtually no time at all for Gary. He was feeling truly neglected.

"You never seem to have time for us to do fun things together," pouted Gary.

"But I'm wearing so many hats that it's getting harder and harder to juggle my time."

"Just once, I'd like you to do something spontaneous, like call out of 'Mist' and the hospital and say to me, 'let's go away to a romantic hideaway.'"

"I can't even think of romance let alone a getaway. I'm barely able to do all I'm expected to do. I can't do anything as frivolous as take time off right now."

The neglect proved to be a catalyst for problems in their marriage. It was time for their twentieth class reunion and Tessa couldn't make the committee meetings with any regularity. However, she urged Gary to attend them. Whenever Linda was stuck for a ride she encouraged him to pick her up. She almost orchestrated what came next.

One night, when the meeting had been at Gary and Tessa's house, Linda came with a friend who was a classmate. The girl got a phone call and due to an emergency, she had to go home. Tessa volunteered Gary to take Linda home.

As he pulled up in front of Linda's house, she turned, fluttered her eyelashes and said, "Gary, since I took you out on a chilly night, why not come in and have something hot to drink? Or maybe some scotch would warm you up."

"Okay, Linda. Sounds good. Tessa was tired and she was going right to bed."

"Hmm, that doesn't sound like a bad idea."

Linda got her keys as they approached the front door. Gary was glad he had a full-length coat on because she had aroused him with her innuendo. He hadn't felt this nervous since his first time with Tessa. No, he wouldn't … couldn't think of her now. She had set her priorities straight. In her eyes, he was three or four. Well, maybe one time wouldn't hurt.…

"Gary, why don't you make us a drink while I get out of this dress. It's a little tight, as much as I hate to admit it. Can you get the zipper for me? Thanks. I'll get something more comfortable on."

Gary immediately went over to the bar with his coat still on. It was good camouflage.

The reason for this wasn't lost on Linda who said, "You can hang your coat in the closet or put it over a chair if you'd rather."

He knew she was aware of his predicament. He realized she was silently delighting in it.

His coat was draped over the chair in the den, across from the bar, when Linda reappeared in the room.

She had on a black peignoir set. It left nothing to the imagination. He feasted on her. She was in super condition. Her five-foot-four frame was lean.… Just a luscious body. Her face was another story. She had a ski jump nose and a huge overbite. But in a strange way, the buck teeth were sexy.

Linda came up behind him as he was readying their drinks. "Do you have a hankie? I think I have something in my eye." As she spoke, she reached into both pockets of his pants.

He could hardly contain himself. He thought for one awful second he'd ejaculate on the spot. He tried to ignore the sensual feeling of her breasts boring into this back: tried to ignore the gentle but insistent pressure of her hands on his penis as she was still searching for that hankie. Just as he thought he would explode, she removed her hands, claiming to have found the handkerchief.

Thanking him for the drink, she motioned for him to sit down on the sofa next to her. She leaned over, just enough for the pink of her nipple to peek out from under her nightgown. She knew exactly the effect that she was having on him. He was making inane conversation. She was staring at his bulge while licking her lips.

She said, "Gary, don't be uncomfortable. I don't bite." She giggled as she added, "Well, not hard, anyway."

She put her glass down. Seductively, she walked to a painting, which she had done several years before.

"Gary, have you seen this?" She ran her hand suggestively up her breast and let it rest on the hanging beach scene.

"Come and look at it. I won first prize for it. You can consider this your private showing."

In a semi-hypnotic state, he walked over to the painting, thus lessening the distance between them.

"Do you like what you see?" she asked huskily.

"Oh, yeah." His voice was deep and throaty as he looked from the painting to her nipples. They were so inviting.

"I thought you would."

She bent down and unzipped his pants. "Does that feel better?" she asked. She eased his erect member out; gently touched the tip of it.

"My, that could be considered a lethal weapon. Are you ticklish there?"

With her fingertips she slowly encircled the head of his penis. When he moaned, she did it faster and harder.

He didn't know whether to fling her down and thrust himself into her; push her face into his waiting prick or lift up her gown and taste the sweetness between her legs. He didn't have too long to ponder. Linda got to her knees and took him into her mouth. She was licking him tenderly with her tongue while letting her buckteeth graze over the rest of his shaft. He had never felt this before. At first she was gentle with her tongue and teeth. Intermittently she would bear her teeth down hard. He thought she'd emasculate him right then and there. She continued to bite him and at the same time she put her hands on his buttocks and pushed him further into her mouth. Right before he spilled over like an erupting volcano, she stopped, pulled him to the floor and urged his head toward her private parts.

"No, not there. Do it here," she cried hoarsely as she put her hands where she wanted his tongue to be.

She took his pants and shorts off, and then helped him take off her peignoir and nightgown. She slid her arms around his neck, encouraging him to carry her into the bedroom. When they were on the satin-sheeted bed, he looked down at her. He couldn't believe the flame she had lit in him. One he never knew existed.

They kissed but he wanted to taste her sweetness again and have her taste him. He and Tessa had never done this. Nor had he stayed erect for so long. When he was younger, he and Tessa had climaxed quickly. Now that they were older, sex had become perfunctory. No, he must stop thinking of Tessa.

This encounter was something completely separate from their relationship.

They brought each other to climax by oral stimulation. Then they looked at each other and kissed; both of them keeping their eyes open. Gary laughed to himself as he thought that her eyes weren't the only things that Linda had opened to him. Wow. Her lust was insatiable. He found his was too. As he was thrusting within her, he lost himself completely. There was no Tessa, no Ali, and no business. There was just Linda and this pure, animalistic sex. When they both were fulfilled at the exact moment, Gary knew this wasn't going to be just a one-night stand. And it wasn't. It lasted throughout the months of the preparation for the reunion.

Tessa went about doing all of the things that made a house a home and a business successful. She didn't even notice Gary's reticence to make love. Nor did she pay any heed as to how late he was coming home from committee meetings.

Twenty-six

An electrical charge was in the air as it came time for the June class reunion. It was to be held in a local Linfield hotel. The committee had decided they would follow the theme of the senior prom and call it 'Over the Rainbow.' The decorations were a bit more sophisticated this time as there was no ugly gym to hide nor any basketball nets and backboards to camouflage. The committee had mini rainbows at each table and the bandstand was decorated in gold filigree and rainbows. The hotel was an elegant one so it didn't need too much to add to the festive atmosphere of the night.

Gary and some of the committee members were going to take part in a verbal skit of nostalgia; entitled 'Do You Remember When?' He and the other guys wore their letter sweaters with Levi's, penny loafers and Wig Wam socks. Linda, who wasn't a cheerleader, borrowed Tessa's sweater. Gary had volunteered it with Tessa's full approval.

The moment she saw Gary and Linda together she knew. They were having an affair. She sat like a robot throughout the entire skit. The cleverness of the presentation was lost on her. Gary and Linda jitterbugged to the tune of *Shh Boom*, which was popular when they were kids. It was then that the group started their quips.

Do You Remember When…?

A cop out was an outdoor policeman?

People danced in each other's arms?

The difference between the sexes was enjoyed and not MS-directed?

High heels and purses were just for women?

When lack of support meant money and not bras?

How about when batting was more than just a skill on a baseball diamond?

How about when people got married and then had a baby?

How about when people got married?

Divorce was scarce?

The air was clean and sex was dirty?

Sex was not for the single girl?

Being gay was being happy?

A butch was a haircut?
'Streaking' was something done to your hair?
We thought that paint was the only thing that streaked?
'X' was an algebraic term and not a movie rating?
Abortions were illegal?
Uppers were false teeth?
Speed was a traffic violation?
Horse was a four-legged animal?
Grass was a lawn?
A nickel bag was candy?
You had to pack to go on a trip?
A pot party was a progressive dinner?
Mainlining was living in suburban Philadelphia?
Getting stoned was having rocks thrown at you?
Smoking before the Surgeon General said it was hazardous to your health?
There was dancing in the gym instead of havoc in the halls?
Kids actually went to proms?
Teachers were respected?
Police authority meant something?
A pig was a four-legged animal?
Fuzz was something on a peach?
Crabs were something you ate?
Coffee was only a nickel?
Trolleys ran on Atlantic Avenue?
The mile stretch was Ventnor's answer to the Indianapolis Five Hundred?
Trains ran to Atlantic City?
Rolling chairs on the boardwalk were humanized and not motorized?
Linfield had an ice hockey team?
Joni James performed here?
We got carded at Weekes'?
The Four Aces weren't just a poker hand?
Jesus, before He was a Super Star?
Wheel of Fortune was a song by Kay Starr?
The moon was thought to be made of cheese?
The generation gap just meant being old-fashioned?
Being ripped off was having torn clothing?
Things were cool and neat instead of fly and fox?
Four-letter words were nice, good, okay and for those who couldn't spell
… groovy?

Mother was one word and not part of one?
Parents told kids what to do?
A punk was a weed in your yard, now he's a kid in a classroom?
A hang-up was something you did with a phone?
A pick was used to chop ice?
Only sailors wore bells?
Clothes had to be ironed?
Dishes had to be washed by hand? (Linda held up her hands and said, "Mine still are!")
The yeast in bread soared, not the price?
Life was a magazine and not a hassle?
A wet dream was not a hole in your waterbed?
Being possessed was going steady?
Marlon Brando's character rode motorcycles?
Desire was a streetcar?
Tea for Two was an innocuous song?
Happiness was a thing called Joe?
Denim was farm wear?
A platform was a political view and not an elevated shoe?
Watergate was just a canal?
Wigwams were something you wore with your saddle shoes and not found at Wounded Knee?
Kids went to school in daylight?
Gas was more than a rumble in your stomach?
A subpoena had to be answered?
Being bugged was just being annoyed?
In the fifties, a demonstrator was a Fuller Brush man?
A freeze was an Italian water ice?
But the most important thing to remember is:
We're not getting older, we're getting better!

The members of the class chuckled aloud often as they, too, remembered these and other things prominent in the 50s way of life.

Tessa didn't realize the huge part she had played in setting this heartache up for herself. She was always happiest doing for other people, but would never have guessed her kindness to Linda would result in the affair. Little did she suspect when she was throwing Gary and Linda together this would be the end result. She only half heard Gary speaking to her.

"Tessa, did you like the skit? We put a lot of work into it. Sometimes,

Linda and I even met by ourselves to make sure we could cover a lot of the changes from 1953 until now without dragging it out too long."

"Yes, I'm sure you both put a lot of everything into it."

"Tessa, we had a part for you," Linda said, "but Gary felt that you were too busy and too stilted to come out with the one-liners."

Afraid of what might come out of her mouth if she opened it, Tessa stared icily at Linda while remaining silent.

When it was time to say goodnight, Tessa didn't know how she was going to play it. Should she prey on Gary's sense of decency? No. Evidently he no longer had decency. What should she do? She didn't know if she could remain married to someone who took his vows so lightly. In the past, she'd known about men who had strayed. She often wondered how their wives could ever forgive them, let alone take them back.

She decided that she would do nothing tonight. She was upset with herself because she had thrown them together. Part of her was smarting because if it was obvious to her, how many other people had picked up on the affair tonight? And how many had known about it since its inception?

The ride home was silent. Tessa, who usually ran headlong into a situation, decided to wait before doing anything. She had many years invested in Gary. She wasn't ready to throw it away by being tempestuous. She realized that she'd been somewhat remiss in being a wife to him. She was a daughter, sister, businesswoman, mother and a friend. She had allowed her relationship with Gary to lapse into obscurity.... Their paths seldom crossed anymore ... let alone their libidos. She knew that if it weren't Linda, someone else would have been there, teasing and cajoling Gary into a sexual encounter. She tried to decide what bothered her more; the affair or that others might already know about it.

Finally, they arrived home. Gary busied himself with getting the souvenirs from the backseat while Tessa got out of the car. She let herself into the house. She wasted no time going upstairs and into their bedroom. She hastily undressed, got into bed, turned her back to Gary's side of the bed and closed her eyes. The night had been such a roller coaster ride she fell asleep almost immediately. She didn't even hear Gary when he finally came into the room.

The next day, Tessa woke up early; dressed and went to 'Mist' even though she wasn't expected this Saturday morning.

Tessa didn't want to share Gary's indiscretion with anyone but knew she needed a sounding board, some advice. She made an appointment with the priest for later in the day.

The priest, while not condoning Gary's actions, helped Tessa work out an approach to the problem. She was to bring Gary in and the three of them were to sit down and thrash things out.

However, the formulated plan never came to fruition. When Tessa returned to 'Mist' there was a message from Dr. Martin, who had called at Ali's request. He had visited Ali at home. Frightened, Tessa went directly home. She entered the house, breathless and harried to see that Marc was also there.

"Sit down, Tessa," instructed Gary. "This will make you get a little weak in the knees."

"Mom, Dad already knows what I want to tell you. I had suspected something was wrong so I went to Dr. Martin earlier this week. I saw him in the hospital when I had my obstetrics rotation after my classroom block. He offered to see me then and there. He confirmed what I thought. I'm pregnant. You know Marc and I planned to get engaged soon but wanted to wait to get married until after my nursing education. This just speeds things up."

"Ali, with your training, you certainly know about as well as have access to birth control. Whatever was on your mind that you didn't use something?"

"Mom, this one night I was upset about something. Marc began consoling me and one thing led to another. Bingo, it happened."

"Ali, what could have possibly upset you so much that you parked your brain outside of your body?"

Tessa then saw the look passing between Gary and Ali. Ali knew, she thought. She knew about Gary and Linda. That's what had her so very upset.

"You pig!" Tessa yelled. "Because you couldn't keep your fly zippered, our daughter had to suffer."

"Mom, please. Don't fight with Daddy now. He's really sorry about all of it and I–"

"Oh, so I'm just supposed to forgive him, right? Wonderful! Now we all play 'Let's Pretend', eat our Cream of Wheat and wait for the baby. This is a trashy beginning for a little baby."

"Tessa, watch it, that's our future grandchild that you are equating with trash."

"You should know all about trash. It's been keeping you comfortable for a long time now."

"Tessa, now is not the time to discuss that situ–"

"Will there ever be a right time to discuss it? Is there anything you can say that can change the facts? You cheated on me! How can there ever be a satisfactory explanation for that? Tell me, if you can. I can't imagine even *you* can be that glib. How many people have been walking on eggshells around me so as not to tip me off? How many other lies have you told me? How many people did Linda tell about your affair? Does it make you feel

168

more of a man because you had a little piece on the side?" By now, Tessa was screaming. Her face was red. Her neck veins were bulging. Everyone in the room was silent as she resumed her tirade.

"Have you been that unhappy all these years? That you had to resort to thinking below your belt? Has our life been so terribly dull, so without pleasure that you had to seek fulfillment outside? Don't you care about anything other than your own selfish needs? How dare you disgrace me in this way! And how dare you carry on with poor, pitiful Linda. Tell me, Gary, just how pitiful is she? All men seem to come to her defense. How many other visits to how many other whores have you made throughout these years? Who has consoled you and comforted you all of these years? *ME!*"

She stormed out of the door, started her car and drove away.

Ali was absolutely stunned. Never in her 19 years had her mother spoken to her this way. She looked from Marc to her father and began crying.

Gary was the first one to regain his composure. "Okay, kids, the ball's in your court. Tell me what I can do to make things easier for you."

"Daddy, abortion is definitely not an option." Ali took Marc's hand in hers. "We've never ever approved of it. It's completely out of the question. We can wait to get married until after the baby is born or we can get married now. Do you think Mom has washed her hands of us?"

"That remains to be seen. However, you and Marc must face this together. It's not like anyone forced you to have unprotected sex. Now, let's see. Where are we? Square one. You both want to get to square two, but how?"

"Mr. R., I think we should get married right away. Ali is only one month pregnant and although we didn't plan to do it now, why not? You and Mrs. R. have always made me feel welcome and I'm sorry if this has lessened your opinion of me. I hope I can rectify that by being kind to Ali, our first baby and any others we might have."

"Marc, I'm not asking you to don sack cloth and ashes. I just want you and Ali to accept full responsibility for what you've created together."

"Dad, do you think that Mom will come to the ceremony?"

"I have no way of predicting that but since you are one of the most important people in the world to her, I'd be stunned if she missed it."

"We should go to city hall, now, and apply for our license."

"Marc, it's Saturday. You'll have to wait until Monday. Ali, do you think you can get your blood tests today? Also, would you like me to call an official to marry you? We have to set this up as soon as possible."

"That'd be perfect. How about Judge Stein?"

"Sure. Shall we set it up for Thursday? As long as you can hurry and get your blood tests there shouldn't be any problem." He looked to Ali as he said this last bit.

"I'll go and call."

"Mr. R., I haven't told my grandmother yet. As soon as Ali comes back, we'll go to tell her."

"Okay, Marc."

Ali came back into the room, saying, "It's okay. We got a green light for our blood tests today. Sue Downs is working. She said she'd be happy to draw our blood."

"Ali, let's swing by my grandmother's and tell her before we go to the hospital."

After the young people left, Gary had a feeling of déjà vu. Although he and Tessa prided themselves on being open-minded, they still believed in love, marriage, and then children. He was glad he could give the kids emotional support. He was almost sure Tessa would eventually come around. They had to make their plans quickly. He thought Ali's bomb of the 70s was not that far removed from his and Tessa's bomb of the 50s. Once again the past was rearing its head. The major difference was how the parents of this young couple reacted. He was determined not to be rigid. Although Ali and Marc were of different races, he always felt they would share their lives together. The only factor which was completely unexpected was Ali's pregnancy.

But for now, he couldn't permit himself the luxury of reflection. It was time for action. He went to the phone and called Bert Stein, who agreed to perform the ceremony. That done, he phoned a catering service .He arranged to meet with them on Monday morning. He thought twice about calling Rita, Treva and his parents. They, of course, had to be told. He ordinarily would either leave these things to Tessa or else they'd do them together. He couldn't exercise that option until he found out if Tessa was planning any involvement

Since there was nothing further to be done, he decided to go and check his sub shops. His managers, as usual, had probably kept things running smoothly but he wanted to make an appearance. Just as he was about to leave home and start for the shop closest to him, the phone rang. He hadn't heard Tessa's car drive up nor did he hear the door open. Unbeknownst to him, Tessa and he answered the phone simultaneously.

"Hello," said Gary.

"Gary, I'm so glad that *she* didn't answer the phone. How are you? Can you slip away?"

"You have a helluva nerve calling here, especially after last night. Of course you must realize Tessa knows about our screwing around."

"Wait a second, Gary. You make it sound dirty."

"Well, what do you call it? Back street? And what makes you think it wasn't dirty? You fulfilled a void in my life these past several months, but I want to make amends with Tessa. My future is and always has been with her. I don't want to see you ever again."

"Fine. Is that all it was? I thought it was pretty sensational. If you were being truthful you'd admit that to me as well as yourself."

"You can delude yourself into believing whatever you want. What it boils down to is that it was just sex with no thoughts above my waist or above your neck. It's *over*. I'm sorry if I hurt you. However, I'm devastated I hurt Tessa and Ali. Please Linda, don't call me again. I won't lose everything that's nurtured me for the past 20 years for a roll in the hay."

"You lousy son of a bitch. If that wife of yours is so great, why the hell did your cock rise like a charmed snake whenever we were together? You know, Gary, out of all the men I've had, you were the weakest lover; the one without endurance … the one who needed prodding … the one who took all of my energy to bring to fulfillment."

"Then you'll have more time for others."

Rather than continue this inane conversation, Gary hung up the phone. In a matter of seconds, it rang again.

"Hello," answered Gary.

"You lousy son of a bi–"

Gary hung up the phone immediately. He listened for a dial tone, then took the phone off the hook.

Tessa picked that minute to walk in on him. She felt somewhat sorry for Gary but still couldn't erase the scene from last night.

Before she spoke, Gary said, "I called Bert Stein. He's going to marry the kids on Thursday. I'm meeting with a catering service Monday morning. Will you come? Ali and Marc went first to tell Mabel and then to Linfield General for their blood tests. I didn't call your mother or sister because I didn't know how you wanted to handle it. I was planning to go to my mom and dad's now. If you'd like, we can go together and then to see your mom and Treva."

"Gary, I'm emotionally overloaded. Give me a few minutes to take a shower, get my bearings and then I'll go with you. Does this predicament remind you of anything?"

"God, yes. The main difference is we're going to be supportive of our kids. They'll have enough obstacles to overcome. I'm sure our parents will rally behind them too."

"We all learn by our mistakes, Gary. You're probably aware of that now

171

more than ever."

Without waiting for a reply, Tessa went up to take a shower.

The scene at Gary's parents' was subdued. They were concerned about Ali finishing nursing and Marc finishing college. Gary and Tessa assured the Rosens they'd help the young couple as much as possible.... Arrange for babysitting; allow the newly formed family to live with them, etc. Becky and Jake listened attentively.... History was being repeated.

From there, they went directly to Rita's. Although she didn't say anything, her furrowed brows showed her true feelings. She agreed to be at the wedding on Thursday, as had the Rosens. Treva, who had been apprised of the situation near the end of the day, was also planning to come.

The next few days went without incident. On Thursday morning, the sun was shining brightly. Tessa had been up since dawn in anticipation of the wedding. She had shopped for a dress a few days earlier. She'd settled on a peach silk suit with an ivory shell.

Gary was going to wear an ivory suit with a peach shirt and ivory tie.

Ali had gotten an ivory dress with a three-quarter length sleeved jacket. She bought ivory shoes and purse. She was going to wear the diamond stud earrings which her parents had given her when she graduated from high school. She also planned to wear the diamond pendant, which became hers when her great-grandmother Rose died.

The family agreed to keep the guest list down. A few of Marc and Ali's friends were on the list, some of Gary and Tessa's friends and business associates, and a few friends of the senior Rosens and Rita. Despite that, there were going to be 100 people coming to the Rosen household. A tent had been rented to extend guest mobility. A violinist would provide the music. Marc had asked Gary to be his best man. Even though he was the father of the bride, this wouldn't be a conflict of duties. Ali had asked her Aunt Treva to be her maid of honor.

The Rosen lawn and yard looked beautiful. Everything was decorated in peach and white with balloons of that color being placed in and around the tent. The tables had the same color scheme. And to think it had only been planned in just a few days.

At six o'clock, the guests began arriving. Gary, Tessa, Mabel, Rita, Becky and Jake greeted all of them and showed them to the tented area where the ceremony was to be held. At six thirty, the violinist began to play the wedding march. Mabel entered with Marc, then came Treva, Gary entered with Ali; Rita, Becky and Jake had already been seated down front.

Ali's and Marc's eyes were brimming with tears. At the end of the ceremony, the judge introduced Mr. and Mrs. Marc Green to their families and friends.

During the ceremony, the members of the immediate families were in tears. Some in reminiscence of another wedding twenty years earlier which no one had attended; some in sadness for those not present; some regarding insecurity of the integrated couple's future. Some were shed in disappointment that the pregnancy had overshadowed the commitment of these two young people. And some were just shed in pure happiness for the newlyweds.

Throughout the evening, the various servers brought around hors d'oeuvres of sesame chicken, miniature quiches, stuffed mushrooms, meatballs, miniature onion rings, spinach balls as well as many other tasty pick up foods.

There were a few serving tables set up.... One with pasta dishes, one with bagels, lox and whitefish salad, and one with fried chicken and collard greens. There was also a cheese, cracker, fruit, vegetable and dip table. The wedding cake was iced in both chocolate and vanilla. The reception was simplistically elegant.

Before long, Ali went up to change into her going-away outfit.

.

Twenty-seven

Now was the time for Gary and Tessa to discuss their differences, mainly the Linda ordeal.

"I know I screwed up big time with my thing with Linda. Honestly, it was just sex … nothing else. I had no thoughts above my waist. You and I had gotten so blasé about our sex life. It was like, *Okay, we're supposed to do this. Let's get it over with and do something important.*"

"But you're the most important thing in my life!"

Between the longing in Tessa's voice and remembering the sensual pitch with Linda and him Gary felt himself becoming aroused. He timidly put his hand under Tessa's chin, saying, "I've never loved anyone else. You are and always have been my whole life." He kissed her tenderly at first. Before long, their kisses heightened into a burning passion which had been dormant for years.

Gary possessively ran his hands along the curves of her body. He could see that the years had not put much weight on her. What was there proved to be just as enticing as her 18-year-old body.

Tessa gently ran her hands over his chest, stimulating his nipples. She then ran her tongue over them amidst his groans of pleasure.

He longed to nibble on her breasts, so, once she took a break, he turned to her. She began massaging his lower abdomen and while fingering her moist cavity, he kissed her breasts.

She remembered all of the sensations they shared in the past. She was experiencing them now, not only languishing in memory. She was responding to the here and now of his touch. She hadn't allowed herself the freedom from responsibility for so long that this unbridled passion made her feel like a novice.

Gary looked into her eyes, which were open and filled with tears, saying, "Are you as ready as I am?"

"Yes, yes, *yes.* Please!" urged Tessa.

He plunged deep within her. They were both completely satiated within minutes. They embraced tightly; taking a brief respite from what they knew would be their very special night to savor.

They both knew they had survived the Linda ordeal and had come out a stronger couple because of it. Their commitment to each other was renewed.

Twenty-eight

Meanwhile, Ali and Marc had driven to Niagara Falls. Ever since Ali had been a little girl, she anticipated going there for her honeymoon.

When Marc and Ali arrived at their room, Ali went to the bathroom to get ready for their first married encounter. Tessa had bought Ali an ivory peignoir trimmed with the same peach color that had marked their special day.

Ali had let her hair down before emerging from the bathroom. Marc caught his breath as he saw her with the moonlight shining in her hair. He, in turn, went into the bathroom. When he came out, Ali was sleeping soundly in bed. Marc tried to do the same. This was not the way either of them planned to spend their wedding night, but they both knew well that things don't go always as planned.

Sleep was elusive to Marc. As he lay looking at the ceiling, he remembered their first night of sexual bliss.

They had gone to a local restaurant and Ali had looked at him and said, "Look, there's my dad. Over there … with *Linda.*"

Marc feigned indifference, "Oh, I guess they're working on their class reunion." What he didn't say was he was suspicious that Gary was having an affair with Linda. He had occasionally seen his car parked at Linda's. Of course, he could always use the excuse he was delivering something from his shop. In a way he was definitely delivering.

True as the song that Eydie Gorme sings, Ali saw two people at the bar who were so much in love that she could see it from across the room. Ali headed blindly for the door, tears spilling over. *She* wasn't the wife as the song goes, but nonetheless, she was an injured party.

Marc followed her to the car. He drove to a quiet area where he parked the car.

Ali was in tears. Marc just held her, comforting her as best he could. They began petting and before long, Ali reached for his erection. She had never done anything like that before. He thought his penis' blood supply would be terminated due to the tightness of his jeans. He knew that Ali surprised even herself. She looked at him and said, "I'm acting like a hussy; just like Linda."

"No way, Ali. I've always wanted you to do that."

Marc recalled how rapidly things began progressing. Even though he hadn't a condom, they consummated their relationship right then and there in the car. He was stupid not to have protection with him but they had never even come close to having sex before so who figured?

He decided he had better allay those thoughts because his new bride was sleeping and he was just taunting himself. He hadn't been a virgin, but other than the soda bottle incident, Ali was.

As he reflected in the quiet of his marital chamber, he knew although they had jumped the gun on starting a family, they just hastened the inevitable by getting married sooner than originally planned.

He remembered when he found out she was pregnant.

"I'm late."

"No, I was early."

"I'm late."

"Pay attention. I was early."

"No. *You* pay attention. I'm *late.*"

"Oh my God! You mean like in period late?"

"You're right on target."

"Has this ever happened before?"

"Maybe once or twice. But it never mattered before because those times I couldn't have been pregnant."

He also relived the day they told Gary and Tessa. Ali's father was more understanding than Tessa was. He remembered her as being a real bitch. He and Ali discussed it later.

"My dad was a sweetheart about it, wasn't he?"

"It's a good thing because your mother was anything but."

"I can almost understand. She had displaced anger. Instead of directing it to my wandering daddy, she took it out on us." She had just completed her psychology block of education.

"Next you'll be telling me that sex is external for a male.... That since a penis is outside the body, he can disassociate himself from what it is doing. So he can do the horizontal rumba with an easier conscience than a woman can."

"Maybe. But don't you get any ideas. I know there's no brain beneath the waist, but if you whore around, you'll have nothing beneath the waist to disassociate yourself from after I get through with you."

After dinner, they drove to another out-of-the-way spot. Since she was already pregnant, they had another sexual encounter.

Twenty-nine

Tessa had been experiencing extreme fatigue after the wedding. With work and other stresses, she thought she just needed some additional rest.

However since her symptoms persisted, she went to her doctor.

"I'm so exhausted all of the time. My muscles ache so badly that I can't even lie in bed at night. I sit in a chair and hope I'll eventually fall asleep. My insomnia is a real problem. This isn't like me. And to tell the truth, it has me scared."

"I'd like to do an Epstein Barr Titer on you. You may have Chronic Fatigue Syndrome."

The titer confirmed her doctor's diagnosis. "Tessa, you should delegate some of your responsibilities to other people. Also, you must try to eat properly and get some exercise."

"Exercise! You've got to be kidding," Tessa laughed at this. "It takes all my energy just to take a shower. I shower, go back and lie down until I can muster enough energy to wash my hair."

In a few months, Tessa was beginning to feel more human. She learned to pace herself and not to be dragged down by stress. She also allowed herself to rest whenever she got tired. It had become commonplace for her to turn off the phone and take a 30-40-minute nap in the afternoon. Not only did this recharge her battery physically, but it gave her the impetus to achieve her mental pursuits as well.

One of the underlying factors behind Tessa's stress was a topic which she didn't discuss with anyone. She barely even admitted it to herself. Linda was pregnant. Tessa had a deep suspicion the baby was Gary's. Little did she know this was factual.

Gary tried to keep his pending parenthood a secret, but by the same token wanted to assume his financial responsibility. He talked it over with Marc.

"I need your advice with a legal problem."

Marc, who was going to be a lawyer, was flattered that Gary would consult him. He was expecting the forthcoming announcement. He said nothing and waited for Gary to continue.

"I'd like to set up a small trust fund for Linda's baby."

Marc offered no response.

"Aren't you curious?"

"I feel you'll tell me what you want me to know."

"Is this confidential?"

"Certainly."

"Well, the baby is mine. Linda's husband thinks it's his. Linda always used a diaphragm but this one night.... Well, we hadn't planned on even meeting, let alone do anything. I'd like to put $15,000 in stocks ... making it a one-time pay-off."

Marc knew how difficult this was for Gary.... To have a child and not acknowledge it. He and Tessa had always wanted more children but....

"Linda is going to tell her husband an aunt passed away. Before she died, this imaginary aunt wanted to do something for the new baby. The aunt wanted to leave it some money. She supposedly said people often forget a caboose. This baby certainly falls into that category!"

"Okay. Let's talk to Tom Lange. I'm sure he'll draw it up."

"Thanks a lot. I don't think Tessa ever needs to know. I've put her through enough but the thought that someone else is carrying a child of mine that she couldn't...." Gary rubbed his forehead, "...might send her over the edge."

And that was that.

Thirty

The next months went by quickly and before long, Chad Zachary Rosen Green (who would be known as Czar) made his appearance on February seventh.... 20 years to the day that his mother had entered the world. He was the light of Ali's life. He was very special to her, not only because he was truly a love child, but also because he was the first of what she hoped would be many.

Marc called Mabel to tell her of the birth of her great-grandchild.

"That's wonderful, honey. But you sound so sad."

"I was just thinking about what people are saying. If they're counting, since he wasn't a preemie, they're probably saying, 'Well, what do you expect from a nigger and a nigger lover.'"

The conversation over, Ali walked up behind Marc and asked, "Is that what's troubling you?"

"For me, not really. I'm so used to the word nigger it doesn't bother me anymore. When you hear a word so much, you become inured to it. Not to go off on another tangent, but it's like the word *fuck*. After a while, because it's used so much, you don't even realize it's been said. It has lost its shock value. I just don't like you or our son being tainted by ugly words."

Since Ali couldn't feel what he did, she put her arms around him, showing total acceptance. There were no words she could offer. She just kissed him.

Gary and Tessa were ecstatic about the birth of their first grandchild. Gary bought him miniature golf clubs...Tessa knitted incessantly for him. To them, he was like a replacement for the boy they had lost. Of course they had a lot more time to devote to their grandson, as well as a lot more money. Besides, they could pick and choose the times they spent with him, returning him to his own crib in his own home after devoting as many hours as they wanted to him.

They showered him with gifts all of the time. So much so it was making Marc uncomfortable. He told Ali that there was more to being a grandparent than buying material things all of the time.

Ali confronted Tessa about this. "Mom, can you and Dad lighten up a bit with all of these gifts? Marc and I don't want Czar to associate your arrival with gifts. Before long, he'll be speaking and he'll look directly to your hands and ask 'what did you bring me?' Neither of us wants that. Special occasions are different."

"My goodness, Ali. You're overacting. He's just a baby. He's too young to know what's going on."

"But Mom," Ali continued talking as she looked at Czar, who was sitting on the floor playing with a ball, "he won't always be too young. By that time, it may be a habit you'll find hard to break."

"Okay, but you're going to have to tell your father yourself."

Later that day, when Gary came by, Ali relayed Marc's and her feelings about constant gifts. Gary, who was generous to a fault, couldn't see what was wrong with a few gifts. However, since Czar was the second generation of his group of Rosens, he acquiesced to his daughter and son-in-law's wishes.

He didn't like a lot of what his daughter's life was about. He didn't like the fact they were living in a basically black development. But if he were being totally honest with himself, he wouldn't like it if she were living in an all-white development with people of a similarly low socioeconomic level. He tried to come to grips with the fact that the man sets the socioeconomic standard for the family. This was currently all Marc could afford.

When he went home, he spoke to Tessa about his uneasiness.

"Tessa, there's something amiss in that house. It's intangible. I can't quite put my finger on it. They're living in substandard housing. But that's not it. Since Marc won't accept any help, I thought buying Czar things would take some of the pressure off. However, I agreed not to bring any more gifts."

"I feel uncomfortable whenever I visit there. Marc seems preoccupied most of the time. Ali just isn't used to living like that. I assume that a black/white union doesn't have much choice when it comes to public housing. All we can do is be patient and offer help when they need it … and will accept it. But that Czar…. Isn't he adorable with his curly blond hair and green eyes? You'd never know he was black!"

"What he looks like doesn't matter to me but it will probably make his life a little easier."

"Gary, it really does make a difference, doesn't it? I've been deluding myself into believing this was going to be a lot easier than it has been so far. I've seen strangers stare a lot at Marc, Ali and Czar. Although at a glance, Marc doesn't appear black, it's evident he is. However, Czar doesn't bear the badge of blackness. Hopefully, he'll be able to make his way in *White* America."

181

"Did you ever imagine we'd be talking like two bigots?"

"We're not actually. We've just taken off our rose-colored glasses since we've gotten a glimpse of the real world."

Ali and Marc were having a discussion also.

"Marc, I told mom and dad about showering Czar with gifts. I agree with you on that. What I don't agree with is the way we're living. I feel as if we're in exile. The neighbors don't talk to me. I know they speak to you because I heard them say you're a *brother*. If I'm your wife, shouldn't that make me a sister? And people say white people are prejudiced!"

"Ali, you can't possibly comprehend what it's like to be black. All these years, you've naïvely believed that the only difference was in appearance. Well, that's just not true. The white man has betrayed blacks. We're accepted in limited situations under limited conditions. Think about it. Your mom and dad pride themselves on their liberal views, but how many black people do they intermingle with? I'm not talking about the hired help, because that's a different relationship altogether. It's still like the pre-civil war days. I still have to appeal to the plantation owner with no hopes, at this time, of owning my own plantation...."

"You sound like a militant, ignorant, white hating nig–"

"Go ahead. Finish it. You're thinking it. That's as bad as saying it. Your thoughts are put into actions in a covert way. Deception isn't something you do well."

"Why are you allowing a simple discussion about housing develop into a dissertation of 'Blacks in White America?' I'm not going to allow one conversation or our arguments to turn into a sociology lecture. You people are more clannish than we. You're more apt to shut out non-blacks than we are to shut out non-whites. I'm not naïve enough to think love conquers all, but I do know hate destroys all. Can't you at least concede I'm not accepted here? Can't you swallow your pride and let my parents help us upgrade our lifestyle?"

"You just don't get it, do you? The man dictates the socioeconomic level for his family. Right now, this is all that I can afford."

"Are you saying you have a closed mind to financial help? Czar deserves better."

"Ali, so do I. Can't you see that? So do *I*!"

Marc stormed out of the apartment.

Ali began crying ... not from anger, but from frustration. She loved Marc so desperately and until now, she'd put on a blinder to his militant side. She'd believed that she could change him; mold him into her image of what a husband, black or white, should be.

The phone startled her. She ran to get it before it woke up Czar.

"Hello," said Ali.

No response. Just breathing.

"Hello. Who's there?" asked a now frightened Ali.

Still no response.

"Please, this has been going on for too long now. Answer *me*. You've called every night for the past month. Are you sick or what?"

She heard laughter on the other end.

"I guess it's or what," said a deep male voice. He was still laughing as he hung up the phone.

Frightened, Ali decided she'd call the phone company the next day and have them intercede. She had written down the dates, times and messages of the calls. There seemed to be a correlation. Whenever Marc was out of the house, the calls came. Did that mean there was someone lurking outside her door? Someone in her neighborhood? Someone stalking her? She double-locked the door. And since her emotions were more intense than usual, she grabbed a knife before proceeding upstairs to Czar's room. Sitting in the rocking chair, she was on guard duty.

Marc was at another of his meetings. This one was later than usual. He didn't get home until one a.m. He was surprised to view the scene in his son's room. He gently and quietly tapped Ali on the shoulder. She woke up startled. She began brandishing her knife at him. He did his best to restrain her, but the knife tore into her flesh, near her shoulder.

It was upon feeling the pain that Ali completely woke up. She saw the would-be intruder was Marc. She fainted.

Marc applied pressure to her wound and when Ali was again conscious and alert, he guided her into their bedroom, where he called Gary and Tessa. He gave a hurried explanation of why he called, saying he was taking Ali to Linfield General and asked if they could come over to stay with Czar.

Gary and Tessa didn't ask any questions but rushed right over to Ali's and Marc's.

"What the hell!" said Gary when he saw Ali and her blood-soaked shoulder.

"Daddy, calm down. It was all my fault."

Tessa said calmly, "Gary, go in and make sure that Czar is all right. Ali, I'll drive you to the hospital."

"No, Mrs. R. That's my responsibility," Marc said.

"It seems you're responsible for a lot." She checked herself and said,

"Okay. You two go. I'll stay here with Gary and Czar."

Marc carefully helped Ali down the steps and out to the car.

Upon reaching the hospital, Marc dropped Ali off when an attendant came with a wheelchair. After parking the car, he went to the ER.

"I'm Marc Green. My wife is here."

"No, sir. I don't believe that she is."

"I know that she is. I dropped her off myself. She has a lacerated shoulder."

"But she's wh– Oh, oh. Okay. She's back in cubicle two but no one is–"

Marc didn't wait for the standard 'No one is allowed to go into the treatment area.' He rushed to where Ali was.

When he got there, he saw the doctor had already begun to inject the wound with novocaine.

"Marc, wait outside," Ali said. "You know how you hate the sight of blood."

"Ali, maybe I can help," said Marc as he grabbed her right hand.

"This is a pretty nasty cut. How did it happen?"

"I was cutting vegetables for soup. I didn't see my son's ball on the floor and I tripped over it. When I fell, the knife went directly into my shoulder."

"You were cutting vegetables in the middle of the night?"

"Doctor, I have a six-month-old baby, so I don't always get the chance to do things at a reasonable hour."

"Anytime there's a knife wound, gunshot wound or anything else out of the ordinary, it must be reported to the police. It's not a matter of distrust, it's the law. I have no choice in this."

Ali looked at Marc above the doctor's head. Even if she had known the doctor, he would have still been required to report it. Ali realized she'd have to divulge the fact of her phone calls now. Perhaps she should have already done so.

Marc said, "Okay. Do what you must. I want to make a phone call. I'll be back in no time. You're almost finished anyway."

"Tell them I'm okay," said Ali, assuming Marc was calling her parents.

Within minutes, Marc was back … just in time to be questioned by the police.

"Yes, Officer," answered Ali. "It was definitely an accident."

Surprisingly, the policeman looked at Marc and said, "We'll need a statement from you, too."

"Certainly. But I'm sure Ali explained what happened."

"Yeah, and I'm the King of England. Now, you tell me, what actually did happen?"

"Are you doubting my veracity?"

"Excuse me," interrupted the nurse as she entered the cubicle. "Are you Officer Harley?"

"Yes, I am."

"You have a phone call at the desk."

"Continue, Bob," said Officer Harley to his partner, as he left to take his call. "I'll just be a minute."

"Come on now. Let's hear what really happened. Did you always have a bad temper? Do you always beat up on women? Come on, boy, answer me!"

"Listen, you tin pan alley cop," Marc hissed. "I don't have to stand here and take your bullshit. If I were a honky, you'd treat me differently. You arrogant–"

"Officer, like it or not, that's what happened." At this point, Ali interceded. "All the badgering in the world won't change that. Why don't you go out and solve a murder or something instead of harassing two law-abiding citizens."

Rick Harley reentered the cubicle.

"Okay, Bob. Let's go. We've just about wrapped this up. They evidently won't change their story." And turning to Marc, he menacingly said, "Let me give you both a word of advice. The next time you accidentally get cut in the middle of the night, go to another hospital. If you ever come back here again, under circumstances like these, we won't be as lenient."

"But I'm not finished," said his partner.

"Yes, we both are," said Officer Harley.

Without further comment, they left.

"I wonder why they left so suddenly," quizzed Ali.

"Who knows?" Marc said though he did. "Are you finished here?"

"Yeah. What did Mom and Dad say?"

"Actually, I couldn't get near the phone. It looks as if everyone in Linfield needed the ER tonight."

"Well then, let's just go home. I'll tell them all about it when we get there."

They got into the car and Ali said, "Marc, I've been getting phone calls whenever you're not around at night."

"What kind of calls?"

"Well, at first, they seemed to be tantalizing, harassing. Now, they're more threatening."

"What do they say? Man or woman? Black or white?"

"Sometimes nothing. Man. Black, I think," answered Ali.

"Is there any special time? Is there any special pattern?"

"I did write down the times and messages, if there were any."

"What are the messages?"

"Well, mostly like, 'Hi baby, lonely?' and something like 'Do you want to get it on?'"

"Ali, why haven't you told me about this before?"

"You've been under so much stress with school and work, I didn't want to burden you further."

"Ali, honey, I don't think of you as a burden. No more than I think of Czar as one. I'm afraid I haven't been completely in tune with you. Listen, you're not going to be able to lift Czar for a week or more, so why don't you stay at your parents' house? In the meantime, I'll have the calls checked. That is if they still come when you're out of the house."

"Marc, please. I don't want to feel as if I'm deserting you. I don't have to go to my parents' house."

"Let me be the judge of that," said Marc, turning off the car in front of their complex.

Ali felt so guilty because she was actually relieved to have a reprieve from squalor.

Tessa had been impatiently waiting for them.

"Ali, are you all right? How many stitches did you get? The baby's an angel. He's still sleeping soundly. Did they have to call the police?"

"Yes. Twenty. Good. Yes." Ali answered, not wanting to expound on anything.

"Mrs. R.," Marc said, "Can Ali and Czar stay with you for a while? She won't be able to lift Czar at least until her stitches come out."

"Of course, Marc. You, too," Tessa offered, but at that point she couldn't have cared less if he took her up on the invitation or not.

"Actually, I'm better off here. Summer school is almost over. I have a project I have to finish."

"Okay. I'll go and pack up the baby," said Tessa, greatly relieved that Marc wasn't coming. She didn't know all of the facts. But this incident on top of Gary's and her uneasy feelings didn't endear her son-in-law to her.

"I'll go with Ali and see what she wants to bring." Marc went up to help his wife.

After packing enough clothes for months for Czar and almost as many for Ali, Marc bid his wife good-bye and carried his sleeping son to the car. He couldn't figure out if Czar was in exile or if he was.

After a few days, Ali had bounced back. Tessa was once again reminded of the resilience of youth. Marc came by often, sometimes for lunch or dinner, sometimes just to say goodnight to his wife and son.

Marc had deep circles under his eyes. Ali was aware something was going on but wasn't sure what it was. Marc assured her everything was fine, also adding that no more calls had come to their home.

Marc skipped contact for two days in a row. He hadn't called or come to the house. Ali got no answer when she phoned him. She was frantic.

It was in a TV news bulletin on the third day that Ali was appalled when she saw Marc with a group of unsavory-looking characters surrounded by some members of the Linfield police department.

Ali hurriedly turned off the set, mindful of Tessa in the adjacent room.

"Ali, what was that I just heard? Something about terrorists being caught here?"

"I wasn't paying attention. It'll be on the six o'clock news, I'm sure."

"It looks like no one is safe anymore."

"Uh, huh," said Ali, who was finding it extremely difficult to remain calm. The phone rang.

"Hello. Oh, hi Gary. No, I didn't see the news. Okay, honey. I'll see you soon."

"That's odd," remarked Tessa.

Ali remained silent; afraid she would scream or burst into tears. She was thinking, Marc, why did you have to screw up? We could have been a happy family despite our divergent races. Why did you have to join a subversive unit? She went upstairs on the pretext of having to get something, hoping to be composed enough when her dad came home.

She heard the front door open and Gary calling. "Tessa. Tessa. Where are you?"

The frantic tone of his voice jolted Tessa and she knew she was going to hear something she wouldn't like.

"Gary, what happened?"

"It's Marc. I saw him on TV with a group of black troublemakers. The police were surrounding them."

"What's it about?"

"I'm not sure, but from the bits and pieces I got it seems to indicate that this group was about to bomb city hall!"

"But I don't understand. Why would Marc tie in with them? He's never been militant."

"We've both noticed a change in Marc these past few months. Apparently, someone or something got to him. Tessa, there's no way I can condone his part in this no matter what he claims to be his reason. I'm afraid that he's gone over the edge. Right now, I'm more concerned with Ali and

187

Czar. What will happen to them if he goes to jail?"

"They'll stay here with us, of course."

"I know *that*. But what about long-term action? Ali should get a divorce.... Start a new life."

"Gary, it seems drastic to suggest that right now. Let's see what this is all about. Let's help her through this for now. One step at a time."

They stopped talking as Ali entered the room.

"Mom, Dad," said Ali. "I saw Marc on TV earlier. I know that's what you were talking about. At first, I couldn't believe it was him. But of course it was. I can't believe he would have any part in subversion. He always says change is better accomplished by evolution not revolution. There must be something else.... Something we're missing."

"Wait a minute, Ali." Gary snapped his fingers as he remembered. "You're right. I don't know why I didn't see it clearly before. Marc wasn't wearing handcuffs. The others all were but not Marc."

"That's right, Daddy. Oh, God. What time is it? Almost six, isn't it? Let's put on the TV."

With trepidation Ali turned on the TV.

"Next on the six o'clock news, more about the overthrow of the B.A.D. group.... Blacks Against Dictatorship."

After endless commercials, the news came on at last.

"Good evening, fellow citizens," began the mayor of Linfield. "I'm addressing you personally so I can give you as clear a picture as possible of the facts as we know them to be at this time. For several months, we have closely monitored the BAD group. For those of you not aware, this group, Blacks Against Dictatorship, have been vocalizing their displeasure about four of their members being held in the Linfield jail awaiting trial for a crime they claim they did not commit. We will not discuss this crime here and at this time, as I do not want to do anything to jeopardize this case. Today, several arrests were made. Many explosives were found, which were allegedly to be used to bomb city hall as well as to assassinate Police Chief Jenkins and myself. Several large trucks were also confiscated, which were allegedly going to be used to limit access to and from the city limits.

"We were able to circumvent all of their aggressive actions due to the efforts of many, but mostly due to the effort of one Marc Green, who for the past few months has been working on behalf of the police department. He managed to infiltrate the group. He gained their confidence. For the past few days, no one had heard from him. We all feared the worst. His contact had no knowledge of his whereabouts or what he was doing.

"At six o'clock this morning, he *accidentally* inflicted a knife wound to his own abdomen, knowing he'd need medical attention. It's through his quick thinking he was able to let us know what was happening. He knew the hospital would have to report the incident to the police. While the police were on their way, Marc was also able to get a message through the nurse to his contact that an additional message would be coming. This nurse knew Marc so she had no qualms about doing this. She alerted the contact to expect further information from the police, who were investigating the knife wound. Because of this, we were able to gear up for our raid. Without divulging evidence, furthermore without endangering other lives needlessly, let me just say that Linfield is a safer place tonight because of Mr. Green."

Ali thought Marc had become radical. He had always reminded her of her father until these past few months. He was as honest and trustworthy as Gary was … save the Linda thing. She loved both of these adult males, almost worshipping both of them. Ali was now crying audibly…. The result of both relief and pride.

Tessa and Gary once again had pangs of guilt for doubting their son-in-law.

The news continued and a reporter was interviewing Marc.

"Was the subterfuge worth it, Mr. Green?" the reporter asked.

Marc thought for a moment. "As hard as it was to have my wife and in-laws think ill of me, I'd have to say yes. Anything that would make our city safer for my wife, son and the rest of my family and friends, would certainly be more than worth it."

"What gave you the idea to cut yourself?"

"A few weeks ago, my wife got cut accidentally and the police were called in. I knew they'd have to be called to investigate. Luckily I was able to get the nurse to alert my contact to expect further news. The rest you know. Now, if you'll excuse me, there's a certain baby boy and his mother I have to see. Honey, I'm on my way home."

The phone rang incessantly. It began the minute that the newscast was over. Tessa had toyed with the idea to take the phone off the hook but decided against it. After all, why not hear the accolades for Marc? She and Gary had to defend him for the past several months. People would comment on seeing him about town with undesirables.

Ali went upstairs and got Czar dressed, then she called down to Tessa to come and carry him downstairs. She was pleasantly surprised when Marc came into the room, having been escorted home by the police.

"Hi, honey. I'm so glad it's over. Forgive me for all of these months. I know I've put you through hell. I couldn't let you know. It wasn't that I didn't trust you. I just couldn't compromise my cover. The last few days were horrible.... I've never been so scared in my life. For a while there, I wasn't sure if they had found me out. Then I realized they just wanted to keep all of us intact until the time was right. How are you? How's your shoulder? How's our big boy?"

"Let me catch my breath." Ali laughed. "I'm the one who should be asking forgiveness. I doubted you. I'm really sorry for that. I didn't understand what had come over you. I couldn't imagine why the sudden change, why you seemed to have become so militant. *Now* I understand! That night at the hospital, you went to call someone, who called off the police, didn't you? I couldn't understand why all of a sudden they just stopped the questioning and let us go. For a while, I thought you were going to assault one of the cops. I was suspicious though when you said you couldn't get to the phone, because the ER wasn't busy that night. Answer me something though. Was it one of the BAD gang who was making those calls to me?"

"I think so. The gang knew you had gone to your mother's but they thought you'd left me. I didn't let them know anything about the knife incident. I figured if they thought you actually did leave me, it would make things look more realistic. Ali, I still believe I should be the sole provider for you and Czar but if your mom and dad want to *lend* us money until I can provide for you in the way I would like, I'll accept … with a written agreement of terms. I don't want to feel like a charity case. I didn't like the way you and Czar were living. So have your dad get the papers drawn up."

"It won't be for that much longer. As long as I know you're the same guy I married, I won't mind where we live. It's just with the conditions, phone calls and your emotional distance, I couldn't cope. Who cares if the neighbors speak to me or not? If you'd rather stay there, I can put up with anything."

"Let's not talk about this now. I just want to enjoy you and Czar. There were times when I thought I'd have to give up the undercover work because I couldn't bear the look in your eyes. For that matter, I couldn't stand your parents' disrespect. You know they've always been such an important part of my life and I wouldn't want to disappoint them any more than I'd want to disappoint you."

The three of them went downstairs where Gary and Tessa had chilled champagne.

When it was popped and poured, Gary proclaimed a toast."To our hero, our son-in-law. We are now and always have been proud of you. There were times during these past several months we doubted you but that's a thing of the past. Please accept our congratulations as well as our gratitude for caring about the welfare of our daughter, grandson and the rest of us in Linfield."

"Thank you, Mr. R.," said a blushing Marc.

Tessa opened the door for less formality. "Marc, why don't you call us something other than Mr. R. or Mrs. R.? Make it whatever you feel comfortable with.... Mom, Dad, Gary Tessa, whatever. Mr. and Mrs. sounds so formal. I admit I, too, had definite doubts about your behavior these past months but I would have felt the same way if the change had come over Ali."

"Well, Mom, I guess you're stuck with me now. It looks as if I am going to be around for quite a while. I'd like to propose a toast. To the closest I've ever been to having a mother and a father.... To my mom and dad. Thanks for your trust, and most important of all, thank you for your daughter."

Thirty-one

Czar grew overnight. Marc was doing well in school and Ali was near the top of her nursing class. They opted to stay in the subsidized housing. Since the BAD group was jailed, the neighbors now were cordial to Ali.

Eventually, Ali graduated from nursing. She began working at Linfield General. Marc had graduated from College early. He was attending law school. All was going along smoothly. Marc and Ali purchased a house near Gary and Tessa. Gary had loaned them the money. The loan was done properly.... Notarized, interest, and all of what Marc wanted to be included.

Ali was looking at furniture for the house and was finding it thrilling picking out colors as well as styles. Marc had no real interest in decorating so she had a free hand.

Their bedroom was going to be done in various shades of blue. Ali wanted to buy a white carpet for their bedroom but decided if she wanted to wear shoes in her bedroom, she didn't want the carpet to have to suffer. Czar's room was going to be furnished in pine furniture. He still was in a crib, but Ali bought bunk beds and was going to store them in the attic until he was ready to be put in a bed, probably soon. That room was going to be in blues and greens. The other bedrooms were done in shades of beige, browns and oranges. Ali felt if they had more children, they could always adapt the room to suit. The master bath had the same wallpaper as the master bedroom. Since Ali loved vibrant colors, one wall of her living room was painted orange with the other three papered in a white and orange print. The dining room was somewhat formal with a crystal chandelier, large oval oak table, side bar and china closet. Orange and white were prevalent in this room. Ali always felt so very alive with bright colors. She didn't want anyone else decorating her home so she opted not to hire a decorator. If a visitor in the house thought something was an eyesore, she wanted it to be something she both liked and had picked herself.

A few more years went by. Marc had finished law school. He was currently working in the District Attorney's Office. He was so good at his job there was talk that he'd replace the present DA upon his retirement. Ali was an

192

O.R. nurse. She liked it because she basically had her weekends free; save one per month when she was on call.

Czar had celebrated his fourth birthday and according to Tessa was greatly advanced for his age. All was going along smoothly until one day.

Czar came home from nursery school with some poignant questions.

The one that hit Ali was, "Mommy, what does *b-l-a-c-k* spell?"

"Black, Czar, like the darkest color in your crayon set."

"But Mommy, how come I heard one of the mothers say that's what I was? My skin is light like yours. And Daddy's, too."

Ali didn't know what to answer. She was just formulating a reply when the phone rang. Literally saved by the bell.

It was Treva, asking Ali if she knew where Tessa was. It was time to look for the summer line of rainwear. Ali remembered that her mother had a doctor's appointment and told Treva approximately when she could be reached at home.

By the time she had gotten off the phone, Czar's interests were elsewhere. But Ali knew since this subject had come up, it would appear later. However, she didn't expect it to be so soon.

"Daddy," Czar began. "Today I heard some lady saying to the others that I was *b-l-a-c-k*. I asked Mommy what it spells and she said it spells black. I'm not like the crayon. What does it mean?"

"Czar, God made people in different colors. My mother was black and my father was white. That still makes me black. Since I'm black, even though your mother is white, that makes you black, too. The darker color dominates."

"I don't understand. My skin is the same as Mommy's."

Marc looked to his wife for help.

"Czar, it's hard for most people to understand. I'm sure when your little brother or sister comes, he or she will be as light as you are."

Marc's ears picked up. "Are you saying what I think you are saying? Is another baby on the way?"

"Yes. I've suspected but you know how irregular I've become. I found out today when I went to Bob Martin."

Czar was so happy about hearing the news that his attention was temporarily diverted from the touchy subject.

That night, after Czar had gone to bed, Ali and Marc talked about Czar's dilemma.

"Ali, I'm at a loss for words. How can I explain it to a four-year-old?"

"We knew this would eventually become an issue, but my God ... so soon!"

"This is all new to you. I've lived with it for years now. There's no way we can insulate him. The best thing to do would be to act nonchalant and give him all the emotional support we can."

Ali knew by Marc's tone that the subject was closed for now.

The next day, she and Tessa were meeting after work to go shopping. Tessa, always in tune with her daughter's feelings, knew something was troubling her.

"Aunt Treva liked the silk look rainwear. I agreed. So we ordered it."

"Great, Mom."

"Your father was arrested for rape this morning and I'm being sued for embezzlement."

"Well, Mom, those things happ– What?"

"Ali, what's wrong, honey? You're so preoccupied."

"Oh, mom, I'm so upset. Yesterday when Czar came home he asked what *b-l-a-c-k* spelled. Someone at school said that's what he is. And if that wasn't bad enough, last night at dinner, he asked Marc about it."

"My God, what did Marc say?"

"He told him that since Marc's mother was black and even though his father was white, Marc is still considered black. And even though I'm white, the fact that Marc's black makes Czar black also. Marc told him that the darker color dominates."

"Well, that was succinct enough. How did Czar respond?"

"He said he didn't understand. Marc looked to me for help. I tried to interject something light into the conversation by announcing my pregnancy. Czar was–"

"Ali, how can you be so offhanded about having another baby? Oh, my God! I'm so happy. Czar will have that brother or sister that you never did. When are you due?"

"In about six months. Sometimes toward the end of December."

"Then why are you so glum?"

"Mommy, don't you see? This is just the tip of the iceberg. If Czar is subjected to this now, what will it be like bringing another *black* child into the world?"

"I can't make this problem disappear for you any more than you can do that for Czar. There are problems in every relationship. However, your problem is visible. Unfortunately, you've no control over it. Your father and I were wondering how and when the color issue would surface. I'm sorry Czar had to be hit with this so soon."

"Mom, I feel for Czar but he's faced nothing like Marc's endured. Do you remember how the police tried to insinuate that Marc raped me and tried to blame someone else? Also, when I cut my shoulder, do you remember how the police tried to escalate it into a great big domestic episode? I'm more concerned about Marc than I am for Czar. Marc didn't have a strong family while he was growing up. He still managed to make a success of himself, but now his son has a rugged road due to society's taboos. If I were Marc, I might just throw up my hands and run away."

"I can appreciate how you feel, Ali, but you've got to be both supportive and positive for both of them. You can't fight either one's battles for them, racial or otherwise. You just have to ignore ignorance. Don't let this develop into something monumental."

"But Mom. It *is* monumental. Czar is going to face racial discrimination to an even greater degree than Marc did. Marc lived in a black section but was accepted into white circles. I'm afraid that since we're living white, Czar will be resented as trying to pass. I know I can't shield him forever, but I'm at a loss about how to handle it."

"Take it one day at a time. Throughout the years, your dad and I faced many prejudices mostly by actions and innuendo. If you maintain a strong family unit, you'll be able to handle it … all of you."

Even though Tessa was reassuring in her speech, she, herself, was filled with doubt. People could be cruel. She knew that firsthand. Although Ali and Marc were superficially accepted, she wondered how many of their friends would someday permit their daughters to date Czar.

Ali busied herself, along with her ecstatic mother, buying things for the awaited baby. Purchasing things for the new arrival partially eased the anxiety about further rejection.

A few days later, Ali was picking Czar up at nursery school and decided to say something to the principal, Mrs. Camp. She hadn't discussed this with Marc beforehand; nor had they had any further exchange about the black situation.

"Mrs. Camp, do you have a minute?"

"Sure, Mrs. Green. Come into my office."

"Mrs. Camp, there's no easy was to say this so I'll just get right down to it. Czar came home the other day and said some woman said that he was *b-l-a-c-k*. We've never made an issue of this at home so we were completely floored by it. I haven't noticed or heard about anyone shunning Czar, so I just assume it was an idle remark with no malicious intent. I guess what I'm trying to ask is, if you notice Czar being ignored or picked on, would you please let me know?"

"Mrs. Green, Czar is usually the center of all that goes on. He leads the other children in play, reading, lunch and rest time. Kids are colorblind. If I feel his color does become an issue, I'll let you know. How does that sound?"

"I don't think it could be better. Thanks a lot. It just makes me wonder if I shouldn't send him elsewhere. Eventually he'll feel societal pressures, but I'd like to hold it off for as long as humanly possible."

It wasn't long before Ali noticed a few subtle changes in Czar. He never used the black crayon while coloring. He never ate black licorice, black salt-water taffy or black jellybeans. He had also colored smoke black before but was now using gray. Ali decided to wait for the most opportune time to talk to Czar about this. One, day, while they were coloring together, she had her chance.

"Czar, please hand me the black crayon. I want to color the smoke."

"Here, Mommy. Use gray."

"I'd rather use the black."

"How about brown? It would be different."

"No. I'd prefer the black."

"I threw it away, Mommy," said Czar. His chin was down to his chest and his eyes were staring at the floor.

"Why?"

"I was afraid the black would rub off on my hands and I would turn black."

"That would no more change your color than if you used red, orange, green, blue or purple. We'll get you some more crayons and this time, we'll keep all the colors. For now, I'll take your advice. Hand me the gray please."

"Here, Mommy. You always color so pretty. I have trouble sometimes staying in the lines."

"You do fine. And you'll get better, you'll see."

A few days later, Ali and Czar were in the kitchen. Ali said, "Here, Czar. I saved you a black jelly bean, I know how much you like them."

"No thanks. I'd rather have red."

"But you always loved the black ones."

"I don't anymore. They'll make me turn black if I eat them."

"Honey, black jelly beans are no more going to turn your skin black by eating them than a black crayon would turn your skin black if you colored with it. When you eat a red or yellow one, it doesn't turn your skin, right? Why would a black one do it?"

"Daddy says that dark colors demonstrate."

"No, honey, not demonstrate.... Dominate. The only things that can change colors are bleach, dye and things like that. Eating black things and touching black crayons won't change you in any way."

"Are you sure? I don't want to be dark black like some people."

"Honey, being black isn't like being sick. It doesn't hurt you." As Ali said this, she knew she didn't actually believe it. She thought if things continued in this vein, she'd have to resort to different tactics to allay his concerns.

Ali had no time to dwell further on this because she started spotting and was mandated to bedrest.

Tessa came over and stayed throughout the days. She brought Ali breakfast, a mid-morning snack, lunch and an afternoon snack upstairs. Ali came down for dinner and Tessa brought Ali an evening snack upstairs. She did this and took care of Czar as well. Surprisingly, she wasn't tired. She rather enjoyed the feeling of being needed.

Czar adapted to having Tessa as his caregiver. They always had a close relationship and this cemented it even more.

However, he was curious and asked, "Why is Mommy in bed?"

"She's tired, honey."

Ali overheard this. Ali didn't want to contradict her mother, but remembering the disservice done to her when Tessa had lost the baby, called down to her mother. "Can you come up here a minute, mom?"

Tessa did so.

"Marc and I discussed this. We've have decided we'd tell Czar an abbreviated version of the truth.… The baby in my tummy isn't doing well and I have to stay in bed so it can be stronger. I don't know if I ever told you about how I felt when you lost my brother. I didn't know what to think. Even though I knew he was in your belly, I thought somehow he wandered away. I never knew he died until I was older. Sometimes kids are given an unintentional disservice when they hear whispers about what's going on. Most of the time, the anxiety surrounding secrets is harder than the actual facts."

Tessa was old-fashioned in her beliefs, one of which being children should be spared the truth when or if it's ugly. She agreed to abide by her daughter's wishes.

After a couple of months, Ali was permitted to resume a semi-normal way of life. She was permitted to work in maternity and/or the nursery at Linfield General. Her doctor didn't want her subjected to being on call so he wouldn't allow her back in the OR. After a while, Tessa visited less and less frequently. Czar was happy to have his mommy back.

Thanksgiving came before they knew it. Tessa usually prepared the Thanksgiving feast and Ali did Christmas. There was always something so much more festive celebrating Christmas in a house with children.

The night before Thanksgiving, Ali and Marc were completely alone. This was the first time in a long time. Thanks to Tessa, who took Czar.

Ali lit the fireplace in their den, then settled down to wait for Marc.

Marc was late getting home from work. At first, he thought the house was empty; there were no lights on. Then he heard Frank Sinatra music emanating from the den.

"Ali, Are you in the den?"

As he walked into the den, he saw his beautiful wife lying on a quilt in front of the fireplace. She had opened a bottle of champagne. She had crackers and cheese on the table near the sofa.

She said, "Hi, honey. I have some chicken in the oven but thought we'd start snacking here."

"I'm not really hungry," said Marc, playfully. "And besides, I'm more interested in my turkey in your oven than any old chicken."

"Well, here, have some champagne first," Ali said as she patted the space available on the quilt next to her. "I can have a drop. One tiny sip won't hurt."

Marc looked at her with lust. Her breasts were so full and inviting, he thought he could get lost between them.

As Ali moved to get Marc his champagne, she moaned, not with pleasure, but with pain.

"What is it, Ali? Are you going into labor?"

"No. My back's bothering me again."

"Wait, I'll get something to rub it with. Let's move this quilt closer to the fireplace and while I'm getting the lotion, you can take off your nightgown."

When Marc came back, the only thing he had on was his jockey shorts. He went up behind Ali, kissed her on the neck, while rubbing her upper back. He proceeded down slowly toward her buttocks. He rubbed one cheek first; then the other. He also rubbed the back and inside of her thighs. Once again, Ali moaned, only this time it was with delight.

She turned over on her side and very gently Marc began massaging her belly. He then went up to her breasts, which were sensitive ordinarily but infinitely more so during her pregnancies. He looked at the brown nipples, which were darker and much larger than usual. He never dreamed he would find a voluminous body so very tantalizing. He turned Ali on her back and carefully moved to her right side. He kissed her eyelids, the tip of her nose and rested his lips on hers, then slipped his tongue into her mouth. Their kisses were sending them to greater heights. She reached for his shorts, pulled them off and threw them into the fireplace. The flame this initiated was not as forceful as the heat they were experiencing. Gently, he entered her and they came together.

"Here's to a night filled with wild abandon." She took a slight sip of the champagne.

"I figured as much once you threw my shorts into the fire." He was laughing as he said this.

"Yes. You definitely won't be needing them tonight."

She gave him some cocoa butter and took some herself, encouraging him to follow her lead by rubbing her belly as well as her breasts with it. The smooth, slippery butter on her skin felt soothing to her but acted as an aphrodisiac to him.

As he lay on his back, she got up and got a small pillow for his head. He put his head on it as she straddled him with minimal difficulty. She got on her knees, then lowered herself onto his erection. They began bucking, gently at first, then with more passion and fury. It wasn't long before they reached simultaneous orgasms.

Ali got off Marc and giggled, "Do you think that our baby will be a horseback rider?"

"I don't know about the baby, but I think I'll buy you a pair of western boots."

"Marc, let's get a little rest. Maybe we can experiment some more later."

"Come over here," he said, lifting the afghan. "My battery won't take too long to recharge."

True to his word, Marc rose on one elbow, looked at his beautiful wife and asked, "Well, how about it? Are you game?"

The next day, they were both tired. They didn't get to the football game until half time. When they got to Gary and Tessa's house, Rita was in the kitchen, as usual. Tessa was setting the table. Becky was readying hors d'oeuvres. Gary and Jake were watching TV as Czar napped.

Ali immediately went into the kitchen; Marc flopped in front of the TV set.

The table was set with one of the embroidered cloths that Rose had given to Rita, who had, in turn, divided them between Tessa and Treva. Tessa had Lenox china and crystal. She had selected a plain white pattern with a gold border. The glasses were plain except for a small pattern near the stem. The candleholders were simplistic in sterling. Tessa had gotten a floral arrangement with autumnal colors. The effect was elegant.

It was time to sit down to dinner, and breathlessly, Treva walked in with her gentleman friend. They had been seeing each other for almost five years but no one dared mention the subject of marriage to either. Treva had been engaged twice before but marriage always seemed to elude her. This gentleman was owner of a fabric wholesale/retail factory, which was where Treva had met him. She and Tessa had numerous dealings with him throughout the years. When his wife died six years ago, Tessa played Cupid. Both Treva and Cliff looked extremely happy. Treva said there was no longer a reason for her to get married because her biological clock was not going to be conducive to bearing children. She was content to 'keep company.'

As Rita looked at her younger daughter, she saw a twinkle in her eyes, knowing then that something was up. She, however, said nothing. She planned to wait to see what enfolded.

At every Thanksgiving, before the meal, everyone would recite what he or she was thankful for. This holiday was no different. The adults started first, and now it was Clifford's turn.

"I am thankful for Treva coming into my life, and I am especially thankful now that she's consented to marry me."

There were oohs and aahs as Cliff placed the two plus round diamond in a gold setting on Treva's finger. Now it was Treva's turn.

"I'm thankful for my family, but also for my wonderful future husband, Cliff. He's the epitome of a perfect male; no slight intended to the rest of the men in the room."

Rita was beside herself with glee. She didn't want Treva to spend her life alone. Now she wouldn't be. Even though there was a distinct possibility that she and Cliff would have no children, Treva would be gaining three stepchildren.... Two girls and a boy. The children remembered how devoted and caring their father had been to their mother before and during her illness. They were glad that he was having another chance at happiness. The thanks were put on hold while everyone congratulated the newly engaged couple. Since it was Treva's first time around, they planned to have a big bash.

Treva looked at Tessa and said, "Tessa, we're going to be married in April. I'd like you to be my matron of honor." Then looking at Czar, she added, "Czar, honey, I'd like you to be my ring bearer. Would you like that? You'll wear a tuxedo, just like the big men."

"Wow, yes, Aunt Treva. It's okay, isn't it, Mommy?"

"Sure. That'll be great."

"It doesn't matter to Aunt Treva that I'm black, either. She still wants me."

Treva looked with astonishment at this comment. She saw by the expressions on the faces of others that this wasn't a new topic.

She looked at Czar and said, "Honey, I wouldn't care if you were a green Martian. You're still the same little boy I love."

Although the food was beginning to be served and Czar was busy with his turkey, the rest of the family realized that there was, indeed, a problem.

When dinner was over and clean-up had begun, Tessa insisted that Ali relax. Treva helped, as did Rita and Becky. Treva had been dying to broach the subject of Czar's outburst but she didn't want to upset Ali.

When the opportunity presented itself, she said to Tessa, "What's this about Czar's preoccupation with his blackness? I never thought it had been an issue with anyone."

"A while back, he overheard some women say he was b-l-a-c-k and it piqued his curiosity. We thought he'd forgotten it but evidently he hasn't."

"What has Ali done about it? Anything? Has she gotten any advice on how to handle it?"

"Not yet. We all felt that loving support would be the best approach but it still seems to be gnawing at him."

"I really feel bad for him, but mostly, I feel for Marc. He's probably feeling pretty rotten about it all."

"Ali said it doesn't appear to bother him as much as it does her. As a black man, he says he's inured to it all. But I don't know; his eyes betrayed him when Czar spoke out tonight."

"Maybe they should *all* go to counseling."

When Ali walked in for a glass of water, they all stopped talking.

"Aunt Treva, I'm so very happy for you. Cliff's a super guy. By the way, he asked Marc to be in the wedding, too. Now, all I have to worry about is a babysitter." She patted her humongous belly.

Cliff's son was going to be best man. Gary and Rita were going to escort Treva down the aisle. Rita only wished, as she did on all festive occasions, that Al could have been here. She believed he was looking down on her and their family, though. Whenever she was troubled, she went to the cemetery to chat with him. She always came away with a renewed feeling when she left him. She felt protected from society's ills. She was going to go in the morning to tell him the good news about Treva. She also thought she should discuss this thing about Czar with him. She knew that whatever disposition was to be implemented was up to her granddaughter and grandson-in-law.

Thirty-two

As usual, the days between Thanksgiving and Christmas flew by.

Ali had done her Christmas shopping around Halloween because she didn't feel as if her anticipated big belly would be conducive to crowds. She was glad she had because although she was big with Czar, she was *huge* this time. She waddled. She had trouble with stairs. She had trouble sleeping. In general, she was miserable.

The night before Christmas, Ali was relieved that she didn't have to go to Midnight Mass. She had always considered it an intrusion on her time. She maintained that the only people who went to Midnight Mass were the twice-a-year Catholics who also graced the church on Easter. Midnight Mass had always been a part of her parents' lives but for the life of her, she couldn't figure it out. It was too hot. It was too crowded. In days gone by, the family always had hot chocolate and cookies in the church hall after mass and Ali had to admit this had been fun. However, she hadn't adjusted to the formality of Midnight Mass and much preferred the 9 o'clock one, which she now attended with Czar. Marc didn't seem to mind. If Ali wanted to go, he would go. If not, he accompanied her to another mass. Tessa and Gary wouldn't think of missing the midnight religious festivities. Tessa knew how Ali felt about it though so she never insisted she and Marc attend with them.

On Christmas morning, Czar woke up at an ungodly hour … five o'clock … much to the chagrin of his parents. However, he was so thrilled with what he saw under the tree his enthusiasm was contagious. His parents soon got caught up in his excitement. His favorite gift was a red wagon seconded by his very own miniature redwood table with attached benches. Now, whenever the grown-ups were eating outside, he could have his little friends sitting with him at their very own table.

Marc got Ali an amethyst necklace. That was the birthstone of both Czar and her. In turn, Ali got Marc a gold ring with his initials enhanced in diamonds. They had gotten each other incidentals and necessities as well. After a breakfast of French toast and bacon, they got ready for nine o'clock mass.

When they arrived in church, the family sat down front. The priest read

'The Night Before Christmas' at this children's mass. Czar was always enthralled by this reading so he didn't squirm as he usually did during mass.

As they were leaving church, Czar stopped short in his tracks. "There she is," he said.

"There who is, Czar?" asked Marc.

"The lady who said I was b-l-a-c-k."

Marc and Ali recognized Linda's daughter, who was a little younger than Ali. They immediately realized the incident hadn't been as harmless as they had lulled themselves into believing. This was steeped in past malice surrounding Linda, Gary and Tessa. They had mixed emotions about what they should say, if anything, to the troublemaker. However, they decided if anything was going to be or needed to be said, now was not the time.

Rather than chance a confrontation now, they turned toward the other door, feigning a desire to see one of their friends. Czar went along with his parents. And though both Ali and Marc realized the woman who made the statement would make more trouble if she desired, they also knew there was nothing to be done about it now. They went home, where Ali planned to take a nap before all of the company arrived.

When Tessa came over to the house, she sensed that Marc and Ali were preoccupied. Since neither of them was forthcoming with an explanation, she chalked it up to pre-delivery anxieties. Ali didn't plan to mar her mother and father's Christmas by a ghost from the past, so she and Marc remained silent about the morning's episode.

The entire family followed shortly after Tessa and Gary. Ali didn't have to do any of the preparations. Rita, Tessa and Becky took care of everything.

On Christmas day, they always had quite a feast. This one was no different. They had salad, meatballs, lasagna, roast beef, Bordelaise sauce, mashed potatoes, turkey, stuffing, cranberry sauce, peas, broccoli and garlic bread. For dessert, they had a cheesecake, pound cake and a fruit salad.

Ali was exhausted by the end of the meal even though she had done absolutely nothing other than eat. Marc had cleaned the house. Alone he had trimmed the tree. He had set the table and wrapped the family's gifts. Ali just had to get dressed and relax. This was quite a chore, relaxing. If she moved to her right, the baby kicked.... If she was sitting, it seemed to be doing flip-flops. Czar hadn't been anywhere near this active.

The perfect Christmas had come and gone. Mabel also came to dinner. She wasn't permitted to help much. They didn't want to relegate her to the house nigger. Though Marc and Ali always encouraged her to visit, she seemed reluctant to do so. She said there was no point in advertising to those who didn't know that the house was part *colored*. Marc corrected her, reminding her she should say black.

"When I was growing up, no one would dare call us coloreds black. That was an insult."

"But Grandmom, times have changed. Black is beautiful, haven't you heard?" Marc asked in a voice laced with sarcasm.

"Well, Martin Luther King did a lot for coloreds, I mean blacks, but we still have a way to go. I still think it's best if I don't come over so often. That way, you and your family can *pass* easier."

"Anyone who knows us knows that I'm black and my son is too. That's a fact and it won't change if you visit or not."

Mabel did agree to come on other holidays in addition to Christmas. This pleased everyone because she was always considered family to the Rosens and Marenos.

The Christmas festivities had passed and New Year's Eve was fast approaching. Though Ali and Marc had always had a New Year's Eve party, this year, due to Ali's pregnancy, they'd foregone their usual merriment.

Ali woke up on New Year's Eve with back pain. Throughout her pregnancy, she had trouble with back discomfort so she didn't think anything about it. She got out of bed, showered and went downstairs. Marc heard her. He was surprised she was up at 6. The only time Ali beat him out of bed was on a Sunday. He showered, dressed for work, then went downstairs.

"Ali, are you okay?"

"My stupid back is giving me fits. I must have hurt it yesterday when I was putting the finishing touches on the baby's room."

"Why don't you see if your mom can take care of Czar today? You can just pamper yourself."

"Sounds good to me. She's an early riser so she's probably up already. I'll call her."

Marc went to the phone and called Tessa.

"Hello." It was answered on the first ring.

"Hi Mom," said Marc.

"Oh, is she in labor?"

"Not yet, but she's having a lot of back pain. We were wondering if you could take care of Czar until I get home from work. That way Ali could take it easy."

"Sure. How do you want to work it? Shall I come there or do you want to drop him off?"

"I think I'll drop him off. That way, Ali can sleep peacefully without him constantly going into her room."

"Great. I don't have to go to 'Mist' today.... We're closed until after the New Year."

"Okay. I'll see you in a little bit."

Marc packed up a traveling toy bag for Czar and got some of the things he liked for snacks. Tessa and Gary always had his favorite foods when they knew he was coming but since they had no advanced warning, they wouldn't have the things that were right for him ... at least right in his little eyes.

When Marc went to say good-bye to Ali, he asked if she would be okay alone.

"Really, Marc, I'm not helpless, just pregnant," she said with indignation. "You and my parents are just a phone call away."

"Okay. But don't forget. I may be in court this morning so you may not be able to reach me. Here's the number where you can try, okay?"

"Thanks, but I don't think this baby will come any time soon. This pregnancy is nothing like the other one. Everything is so different that I'm sure it will come out when it's damn good and ready."

Marc left the house with an uneasy feeling. After dropping Czar off at his in-laws, he went into work, where he all but forgot about Ali and the pending labor. It was lunchtime by the time he called home. When he didn't get an answer, he thought that Ali had probably turned the phone off to get her needed rest. To play it safe, he decided to call Tessa at home.

"Hello." It was Gary who answered.

"Hi. It's Marc. Is anything going on with Ali? I just tried calling and I can't get an answer."

"Marc, Ali went into labor a little while ago. Didn't you get the message?"

"No, I finished a little earlier than I thought I would and went to lunch with a few of the other lawyers. She's at Linfield General?"

"Yes. Tessa's with her. I'm here with Czar so no need to worry."

"Okay. I'm on my way to the hospital."

Since Tessa was a nurse, in addition to being Ali's mother, she was permitted to go into the labor room.

"Just relax between contractions, Ali. You remember that from Czar, don't you?"

"Mom, the contractions are just so different this time. It seems like just when I get over one, another one– Aah."

Tessa could see the violent movement of Ali's abdomen. She called the attending nurse, asking her to call Dr. Martin. The nurse checked Ali's progression and when she was satisfied that the delivery was near, she put in a call to Dr. Martin.

Coming back into the room where Ali and Tessa were, she said, "Dr. Martin is delivering a baby at another hospital so the resident is on standby."

Tessa didn't like the idea that Bob Martin wasn't around, but she realized babies come without a great deal of warning.... First come, first served.

The labor intensified so Ali was moved into the delivery room. The resident entered and asked, "Mrs. Green, Ali, do you need any sedation? As you know, it will be better for the baby and faster for you if you can possibly do without."

"I'm not a novice to this process, but with my firstborn, it wasn't nearly as bad as this. Do you think I could have a little something just to take the edge off?" Ali was breathless and she was perspiring profusely.... No, she was actually sweating. Her voice was emotionally charged. One could feel her intense pain and fear.

"Okay, nurse. Give her 25 mg. of Demerol." To Ali, he said, "That should help take the edge off as you so aptly put it. Now it's up to you, Ali. Come on. Push ... push ... push. Okay. Relax. Okay, not too much longer. Relax until I tell you to push again. That's it. Okay, now push. Push. Good girl."

Tessa was standing by Ali's head, mopping her brow. She always felt that an obstetrician was like a cheerleader and half expected someone to come out doing cartwheels.

"Come on, Ali. Atta girl!"

Just then Bob Martin came into the delivery room. It almost seemed that Ali had been waiting for him, because as soon as he got there, she gave an enormous push and out came a little baby. Tessa was amazed at the small size of the baby, considering how huge Ali had been. She looked at Dr. Martin and was about to say something when he said something to the resident.

"What's the matter, Bob?" asked Tessa. "Is there something wrong?"

"Not unless you consider a multiple pregnancy wrong."

"Oh, my God," exclaimed Ali. "Not twins."

"It looks that way, Ali. We really should have been suspicious after all the weight you gained and how pendulous your abdomen was. However, I only heard one heartbeat."

"Well, what's number one?"

"A little girl," stated Dr. Martin.

Tessa could feel the tears stinging her eyes. She was incredibly happy that Ali had accomplished something she and Gary hadn't been able to. She didn't want to blubber right then and there because Ali's job still wasn't over. She was getting antsy and could hardly wait until the delivery was completed. Then she could shout the news to anyone within earshot. She was anxious to see what the stork was going to bring next.

The doctor spoke to Ali. "Come on. Your work's not done yet. Don't quit on me."

"I don't think I have enough energy to complete this."

"Come on, Ali. I can't do this for you," encouraged Tessa. "Come on. You can do it." Now who was the cheerleader?

Ali pushed with all of her might and out came another baby.

"What's this one?" asked a gasping Ali.

"A boy, now." Tessa said this through her falling tears.

"It looks as if you have yourself an instant family," said Dr. Martin, who was preparing to deliver the placenta.

Ali said, "I feel like there's another one coming."

"Yup. You do have another one there. And here he comes now." Bob Martin knew it was a boy because he shared a placenta with the prior baby.

"My God, turn it off!" laughed Tessa, unbelieving what she had seen right before her eyes. "Triplets." Her heart was filled with delight. What a perfect family her daughter had.

Ali regained some of her vocal power. "Boy, I guess I don't believe in doing things halfway. What are we going to do with three babies?"

"Love them and take care of them, what else?" stated the practical Tessa.

"Are they all okay?"

"They look fine. A little small, but that's to be expected. I'll call the pediatrician and have him check them."

"Can my mother call Marc now?"

"Tessa, go and tell your son-in-law, please. Ali's work is over but Marc's has just begun."

"I think not, Doctor. His part is what started the whole thing in the first place." Ali giggled, still a little giddy from the sedation.

When Tessa told Marc, she thought for one awful minute he was going to pass out. He had just arrived at the hospital. He was completely taken aback by the multiple births. He didn't even ask the *sex* of his triplets.

Tessa said, "Marc, the girl is the oldest and then the two boys came."

"A little girl!" exclaimed Marc. "Ali said if we had a little girl, she wanted to name her Vera. I didn't want to disagree with her. I was so positive it was going to be another boy, I saw no point in upsetting her. But I was never too keen on the idea."

"Well, you have to decide that between the two of you. Right now I want to call Gary, my mother, sister and in-laws. Do you want me to call your grandmother or will you?"

"I will. When can I see Ali? When can I see the triplets? My God, that sounds so scary."

Tessa smiled, hugged him, then left to phone Gary.

"Hello," answered Gary

"Hi," said Tessa. "How are you and Czar making out?"

"We're fine. How's Ali? Did she have the baby? What is it?"

"She's fine. And she had the babies."

"What? She had twins? Okay, boys or girls or one of each?"

"Both, Gary. There's a girl and two boys."

"Triplets?"

"Yes, Gary. Isn't it wonderful?" Tessa said, beginning, once again, to cry.

Gary, on the other end, couldn't believe his ears. "God, Tessa. Did you or Marc call and get two other cribs?"

"My God, no. Will you take care of it? I'll go to the house tomorrow and wait for them to come. The babies are a bit small so I don't know when they'll be coming home from the hospital. But we should be ready for them whenever in any case."

"Okay. I'll take care of it right now. Shall I tell Czar?"

"Why not wait and let Marc do it?"

"You're right. He should. See you later."

After she hung up, Tessa called Rita, who was so completely overwhelmed that she could hardly put a sentence together. She then called Treva as well as the senior Rosens, who were equally thrilled with the news. Then, she went back to the waiting room and told Marc that Gary was ordering two more cribs.

"God, I forgot all about that. I think we're going to be very crowded in our house. We'll have to build an addition or buy another house."

"Marc, wait for a little while. The babies are going to keep each other up anyway, so why worry about them not having their own rooms for now? It's a bit premature to talk about uprooting the whole family. We'll take care of cribs for now. We'll worry about high chairs and rooms later; when they're ready for them."

Marc nodded. He was still in a state of shock. He told Tessa he was going to call Mabel and would be right back.

Marc called his grandmother.

"Oh, praise the Lord. Praise God. Are they okay? Is Ali okay, too?" Mabel was running her words together. She was thrilled about the little girl. Although one life couldn't be exchanged for another, she was glad she'd have a replacement of sorts for Vera. She repeated, "Are you sure they're all right? Are you sure Ali's okay too?"

"Yes, Grandmom. Everything's fine. I am so very, very lucky."

"I wish your mother were still living and could be here to see this. For that matter, I wish that she could have been here for everything.... Your wedding.... Czar.... How you finished school early.... Everything."

"Grandmom, somehow, I feel she's been with us for everything. Listen, I'm going to go. I want to call the florist and send my wife some flowers."

"Okay. I'll wait until Ali comes home from the hospital before I see her."

Although she didn't elaborate further, Marc knew Mabel didn't want to *color* their happiness. She had decided not to call attention to the fact that the children were of black lineage. There would be no doubt of this if she went to Linfield General as their grandmother. He didn't know what else he could do to let her know she was very much a part of their lives and public opinion didn't matter to them. He felt as if he were swimming against the tide as far as this issue was concerned.

The pediatrician gave all of the babies a fairly clean bill of health. Number one weighed 4 pounds.... Number two 4 pounds, 8 ounces.... Number three weighed in at 4 pounds 10 ounces. They would have to stay in the hospital for a short time after Ali went home. It would give her a chance to get back on her feet.

Now the big problem was upon them. What in the world would they name these three babies? They had numerous names picked out but felt there should be something in the names of the triplets to tie them together. But what?

Ali and Marc laughed. They said they should have a contest to see what people thought the children should be named. All along, Ali knew Marc wasn't keen on the name of Vera. Now, since there were two boys, she felt in order to name one after Vera, she'd have to name one after her grandfather, Al. But she had never liked the name Al, so....

"But Marc, I don't know if I like the idea of 'T' names.... Toni, Tommy and Terry just don't grab me."

"Maybe not, but we can't continue calling them A, B and C forever."

"Why don't we have their names start with the letters A, B and C? Let's think of a few and then let Czar decide. I don't want him to feel left out."

"Okay, but it's not as easy as it seems. Throw me the names' book again. Agatha.... Allison.... Amanda.... Antonia.... Ardis.... Ariel...."

"Barry.... Barton.... Brian.... Brent.... Bruce...."

"Now the C's."

"Let's see what the book has for that letter.... Casper.... Charles.... Charlton...."

209

"This is mind boggling. Shall we do AA, BB and CC?"

"May just as well."

"Okay, let's narrow it down and tomorrow we'll let Czar make the final selection."

"Fine. Bring him in tomorrow to meet his brothers and sister. We'll tell him he can have the thrill of naming them. And Marc, I want to keep the nametags on the boys. I don't trust myself to know them apart."

"Great. I was afraid I'd get them mixed up, too."

"Okay, then. It's settled. Now all we have to do is settle on some names."

"Well, since these are our last children, maybe we should name them X, Y and Z."

Playfully, Ali threw her bedroom slippers at him, saying, "And get out of here before you drive me crazy."

Marc kissed her, scurried out of the room while saying, "That would be a very short trip."

She pretended to be perturbed but was laughing inwardly.

Czar came to the hospital with his father the next day. He was so excited he talked all the way in the car. Marc remembered he and Ali had thought Czar was retarded when, at three, he still wasn't speaking in sentences. They realized he was now making up for lost time. His speech was in overdrive.

"Hi, Mommy. Daddy said he would take me to see my sister and brothers. He said you'll be coming home tomorrow but my brothers and sister have to stay. Daddy said baby C would probably come home first and my sister will probably be last. We have lots of cribs in our house. We bought a lot of diapers, too. Daddy said we might have to move. Daddy said he'd teach me how to give the babies their bottles.... Daddy said–"

"Whoa. Wait a minute, Chad Zachary Rosen Green. Take a deep breath." Ali laughed.

"But Mommy, there's a lot I have to talk to you about. I haven't seen you for a couple of days. We haven't had one of our chats."

Ali never realized how much their little chats meant to Czar. Ever since he was a toddler, she had sat with him each night before bedtime and chatted with him before reading him his stories. She had always looked forward to it but never knew whether Czar did. She was happy to see he apparently liked them as much as she did.

Ali walked with Marc and Czar to see her sleeping alphabet beauties. There they were.... 'A' Green, 'B' Green and 'C' Green, and they were all light in color with peach fuzz-topped heads.

Czar exclaimed, "They're so tiny. If I hold them, they might break."

Ali laughed, "No, Czar. They won't break."

"Mommy, are they black, too?"

"Yes. Do you remember? We talked about this before."

Marc was quick to change the subject. "Czar, when we get back to Mommy's room, you can help us name the babies. Okay?"

"Can I really? Can I pick their names?"

"Sure you can. We'll give you some names which Daddy and I like. You can choose from them."

"Okay. Let's go back to the room, now, then," said an anxious Czar.

They went back to the room and sat down. With diligence, Czar decided what the names would be. He felt important, which was what his parents had intended.

After they had decided on the names, they also made the decision not to tell anyone else. Since the children weren't coming home all at once, Marc and Ali had planned to have the christening party after all of them got home, at which time everyone else would learn their names. Until that time, it was going to be kept a secret.

Baby C came home two weeks after he was born. He had difficulty attaining the five-pound weight, which was what was desired. Ali had pumped her breasts to share the milk among her three little ones. Baby A got the most because she was the smallest. The rest was divided between the boys … with the smaller one receiving more that the larger one. When C got home, he was mostly on formula so it wasn't as difficult to divide Ali's milk between the two remaining in the hospital.

The first night that C was home, Czar's earlier enthusiasm turned to frustration. C cried incessantly.

Czar screeched, "Make him shut up. Puleeze!"

Ali went into his room. "Czar, honey. This is your brother's first night home. He's not used to his crib. He's not used to us either. You had to get acclimated when you first came home."

"Did it take me long to get activated?"

"Not activated, Czar. Acclimated. It means getting used to something."

"Did it take me long to get used to my home?"

"Not too long, honey. Now go back to sleep. Baby C is asleep now, too."

Two weeks later, Baby B came home. He put the family through more sleeplessness than his brother had.

Czar woke up the day after B had come home and said, "Mommy, I know what's wrong with B and C. They miss each other. They were used to being together with my sister. Didn't they all stay together in your tummy?"

"Yes. You may be right."

"Well, why don't we put one of my teddy bears with each of my brothers? That way, they won't be as lonely."

Czar ran to get his teddy bears and put one in with each of his brothers. They had been crying but coincidentally they stopped their crying. Ali let Czar think it was because of the teddy bears.

Ali was worn to a frazzle. She had hired a helper, but during the night, she was kept busy between her two little sons. She had no idea how she would manage when A joined them. Marc was a big help, but she insisted he sleep during the period between midnight to at least 5. She said he needed his rest if justice was to prevail.

Oddly, enough, when A came home, the boys calmed down a little. It was as if they sensed they were once again a unit.

Ali had convinced Marc to put all three cribs in the same room. At first, one baby crying would wake the other two. Eventually, it seemed as if their crying was their means of communicating with each other. Ali didn't mind listening to them.

Marc and Ali continued to build Czar up but noticed him studying the babies intently.

"What are you doing, Czar?"

"Just looking at their skin. How come they're lighter than me?"

"It's in their genes."

"But Mommy, don't be so silly. You know they're too young to wear jeans yet."

"Czar, genes are what you get as you're being formed. Some people have dark hair and blue eyes; some people have blond hair and brown eyes, some are fat and some are thin."

"But why are they lighter than me?"

"The boys are lighter than you but Baby A isn't. The boys will be the same color but A won't be the same as them. See, she's darker."

"Do you really think so, Mommy?"

"Sure, I do. Look at them."

Another discussion seemed to be put to rest.

Ali began readying everything for the christening. Tessa had knitted a dress for Baby A as well as matching suits for Babies B and C. She was anxiously awaiting the naming of her newest grandchildren. She, too, had been kept in the dark.

The day of the christening was bright, crisp and cold. Ali bought a two-piece hot pink dress with which she planned to wear black suede shoes and carry a black handbag. She had a silver fox jacket with a matching hat. Marc had gotten a new navy blue suit, blue and white striped shirt and a blue and green print tie. He had a black cashmere coat he planned to wear. Ali had bought Czar a brown suit, peach shirt with a brown and peach print tie, which delighted him to no end.

Although many mothers didn't go to church, Ali said there was no way she was going to stay at home and wait while her babies were being baptized.

As she watched the priest committing them to the Catholic faith, she allowed herself time to reflect upon her childhood. She knew the prejudice which she had faced would pale in comparison with those which Czar and his brothers and sister would encounter. She was not paying attention so she was stunned when she heard the priest speak.

And now I baptize you Althea Anne.... Benjamin Brad.... Colin Charles...."

She looked at the three of them and then at Czar, who was beaming with pride. She was hoping she'd be as strong as her mother. Marc had endured a lot. She had hoped by the time they had children prejudice would be passé.

Now that her babies had an identity, she was bound and determined not to let them feel any of her misgivings. She was equally determined to make them proud of their diversified heritage. And the *world be damned!*

Thirty-three

Treva's April wedding was lovely. This was the only real wedding in the family for Rita. It was at times like these when Al's absence was poignant. Treva, as she was getting ready to walk down the aisle toward Cliff; toward her future; leaving the past behind, was thinking about when they were planning for the wedding.

Cliff said, "Honey, this is the second time for me but I'd like it to be special for you."

"Just marrying you would be special enough. But I think my mother would like to be present at a full regalia for at least one of her daughters."

Treva hadn't wanted to disrespect her mother, but she thought how unkind Rita had been to Gary and Tessa. That's why there'd been no formal wedding. She didn't verbalize it. Despite this, she felt her sister and brother-in-law were the epitome of love, acceptance and tolerance. They were like a lighthouse, ready to assist anyone in distress. She was awakened from her reverie when Cliff spoke.

"My kids will love being in a wedding, especially yours and mine."

"You have raised them beautifully. They're filled with respect. You must've had wonderful parents to have learned such good parenting skills," said Treva.

"Parenting skills aren't easy to learn. Sometimes we learn from our parents what *not* to do."

Treva thought how discerning he was. She hadn't downed her parents verbally, but he knew what she was thinking.

She watched Czar walk proudly down the aisle, carrying the rings. He took his job so seriously. He looked adorable while doing it. He carried the rings as if they were uncooked eggs. He was an old man, so serious and yet with a keen sense of humor for a little one.

It was time for her to make the journey down the aisle. She had dreamed it for a long time. When she reached the altar, she and Cliff took each other's hands.

The ceremony proceeded typically.

"And now the rings."

Little Czar almost marched up to the altar military style. He gave the rings, which Ali had taped to the pillow. Then he went back and sat down.

With no dry eyes in the church, the ceremony was completed.

The triplets were flourishing. They were like the Three Musketeers, sometimes called the 'Musks.' They had formed quite a union.

Throughout her childhood, Ali missed the camaraderie of siblings. She'd been close to only Vera and now, she was determined to have her four children be close to each other. However, the battle lines were drawn at a young age. Czar was always odd man out. As sensitive as he was, Ali knew this hurt him deeply.

One day, as they were readying to go to the zoo, the division surfaced again.

"I want to go to see the bears first."

Colin said, "How about the monkeys? They're so funny."

"Sure" quipped Ben. "They look just like you."

"Not as much as they look like you." Colin wasn't going to be outdone.

"I want to see the birds first. I love the peacocks. They have such pretty colors." This was Czar's contribution to the discussion.

"We'll go where my *brothers* want to go."

"But Althie, Czar's your brother, too."

Ali saw the hurt in Czar's eyes as he said, "Mom, you know, I don't feel much like going. I think I'll stay with Grandmom Tessa. She was going to help me paint."

Although she didn't approve, Ali acquiesced, "Okay, honey. If you're sure, you don't have to go."

After Ali dropped Czar off at Tessa's, she took the trio to the zoo.

"Mommy, we'll go to see the peacocks, too, won't we?"

"Yes, Althie, we will. It's too bad Czar didn't come. He really would have liked to have seen the peacocks, too. You do know that Czar is your brother, too, don't you?"

"Yes, Mommy, but he's not the same as my other two. We have the same birthday."

"He's only four years older than all of you. I want you to be nice to him. We're all a family and families stick together."

"Yeah, not macaroni, but people and families," Ben cited a commercial quip.

Ali relayed the story to Marc later that night. "Marc, he feels left out. What can we do?"

215

"Well, for one thing, you shouldn't let him segregate himself from them. It alienates him even further."

"That's not always easy. Althie's so verbal. I have trouble believing she's only four. Sometimes she's downright nasty."

"Who does she remind you of?"

"Come on, Marc. I'm not as tough at my age as she is at four."

"No, but you were pretty much of a spitfire in your childhood."

"Perhaps we should get some advice from a professional. I'll check with the hospital social worker to see who she'd recommend.

After ascertaining that Dr. Brenda Morris was the one who they should use, Ali made an appointment to take the three kids to the psychologist's office.

When they were told they were going to talk to someone, mouthy Althie spoke up. She wrinkled her nose in disdain and said, "But Mommy, I can talk here. I have my brothers, Ben and Cole to talk to. We can all talk to you."

"Althie, I know that. You also have another brother and daddy, too. But this is different. She's going to help all of us get along better and understand each other."

"But, Mommy, my two brothers and I get along great. Czar isn't like us. He's always brushing his teeth even when you don't tell him. I remember how Grandmom used to play a game with us. She'd put the lights out after we brushed our teeth and told us they were so shiny she didn't need the lights to see. And he's always washing his face and hands before you even tell him to get ready for dinner."

Ali knew part of this rivalry was due to the fact that the 'musks' thought Czar was Tessa's pet. She thought perhaps this wasn't an apt description of how Tessa viewed her oldest grandchild. She had taken on the responsibility of Czar when Ali was on bedrest so they did have a lot more quantity of time than the triplets did. It was rather hard to divide yourself among three.... A lot harder than when there was just one. Althie was still talking and her mother decided to listen more attentively.

"He's no fun at all. The only time he's funny is sometimes at lunch when he tells you what he wants to eat. Remember? He says, a barking kangaroo. But that's an icky sandwich. Who would want a hot dog on pita bread? Yuck! And daddy is too busy for us. He talks to Czar more than he does us. He treats Czar different. He likes Czar better than he does us."

"If that's how you feel, we'd better all go to understand each other better."

"Well, I'll go if I have to, but I won't *talk*."

Ali knew this wasn't likely but she thought she should pick her battles.

She said nothing.

And the next day they were in the office, which was decorated in primary colors. The window treatments were blue, the plastic slide was red and the miniature table and chairs were yellow. There were puzzles and books on the shelves.

The receptionist who was seated behind a glass-topped desk asked their names.

Althie, who was going to remain mute, spoke right up. "I'm Althie Green. These are *my two* brothers, Ben and Cole. This is our mother, Ali Green and her other son, Czar."

The receptionist showed no sign of confusion, as she knew Althie, Ben, Cole and Czar were all siblings. When Ali had called for the appointment, she had explained the problem briefly.

Shortly after Ali filled out forms, the receptionist said, "Dr. Morris will see you now."

Althie led the way into the inner office.

"Good morning, everyone," said the doctor.

Before Ali could respond, Althie said, "Hi, I'm Althea Green. This is my brother Benjamin and this is my brother Colin. This is our mother, Ali Green, and her son, Czar."

"You mean your brother, too, don't you, Althie?"

"Well, he sort of is but he sort of isn't. It's hard to explain. Mommy, tell Dr. Morris about some of us being related and the rest of it."

"Althie, I've told you over and over again that Czar is your brother, too. We won't get anywhere unless you're willing to admit that."

"Okay, Ali," said Dr. Morris. "I get the basic picture. Let Althea tell me how she sees the family."

"Well, my two brothers and I were in Mommy's tummy at the same time. Since I'm older than they are, I can tell you all about the three of us. But Czar isn't the same as us. He's black like Daddy. Daddy talks a lot to him but not much to us."

Ali threw up her hands and said, "She's isolated herself and her two brothers from the rest of the family."

"Ali, I think perhaps I should see the children … separately at first. I don't think they'll feel free to talk with Althea in the room."

Ali agreed and set up an appointment for Marc and her. Then all four of the children would be seen individually.

Ali and Marc were sitting with Dr. Morris, who asked, "What do you perceive the problem to be?"

"It seems that our firstborn, who is only eight now, is considered an outsider by the others. Don't get me wrong. Although he's sensitive he doesn't seem to mind this too much. He's always been able to amuse himself. He found activities to ward off any slight he may have felt from his siblings. He would go to my mother's and paint or do other things with her."

"Althie has formed a circle of three and won't let Czar in."

"Does this make him unhappy in any way?"

"I'm not sure. Sometimes it appears as if it does. Superficially, he seems to be able to insulate himself from her venom. My daughter can be rather cruel. Czar always can find humor in many things. He's quite funny. I think Althie knows this because of what she said about Czar and the barking kangaroo. She resents it when he can get a laugh from their brothers."

"I agree with Ali. Our daughter thinks she's being funny with her slurs and slights but sometimes, I honestly feel she's cruel. Czar did get a lot more undivided attention because he was the first as well as the only one. Ali had three all at once."

"Also, I think I became more relaxed when the triplets came. Marc was busy so I had the major responsibility of them. I did with Czar also but that was different in a lot of ways.... Not just the numbers. I thought my firstborn had to be perfect. I think I tried to make him into Little Lord Fauntleroy. But when the others came, I had so many other distractions I didn't mold them completely the same way. I was definitely more relaxed with them."

"Well, I'll begin with Czar."

A week later, Czar was alone with Dr. Morris. She had him draw a picture of his family. He depicted three kids together building a snowman in the freshly fallen snow while a little boy looked out of the window, watching them. She ascertained this was a self-inflicted situation. It had been fostered by the attitude of his sister who had formed a clan with her two other brothers.

Next came Althea. She drew a picture of Czar with his father, playing a game of cards.... Fish. She drew her brothers and herself just watching this game.

Ben was the next one to be seen. His picture showed his two brothers and him playing a game, which was interrupted by his sister.

Then came Cole. He drew a picture of Althea, Ben and himself playing a game with Czar looking from a distance, crying.

After the initial sessions, Dr. Morris met with Ali alone.

"Why not try organizing activities for Ben and Czar? Let them go out to play. Occupy Althie by baking cookies or doing something she'd like. Then

218

encourage Cole to go out and join them."

"As long as I can occupy Althie, it will pre-empt her from ostracizing him. Eventually, he'll be assimilated into her clan."

"That's the idea. She may feel threatened by him. By keeping him out she may relegate herself as the true leader of the group."

"Okay, I'll try anything to create a harmonious coexistence within our home."

"Also, try having Cole and Czar do something together. Maybe the boys will be won over. Althie will probably follow suit if she's outnumbered."

Because Dr. Morris was concerned that Czar viewed himself as the only black child, she wanted to see him again. She suggested a few more sessions, feeling he was permitting the situation to remain. He was segregating himself. This was the same thing Marc had often said to Ali.

Ali began implementing the psychologist's recommendations.... Separating the triplets as diplomatically as possible.

She had Marc take Althie to buy some clothes. She, in turn, took Czar, Ben and Cole to the movies together and then to McDonalds. By the same token, she took Althie and Czar out together to try to develop congeniality between the two, thus helping them relate to each other.

Tessa also got involved in the plan. She picked up Althie and took her to a playground. She did the same thing with both Ben and Cole separately. She knew in her heart that Czar did have a special place because he was hers, secondhand, but nonetheless, hers for a few months.

Through the concerted effort of the entire adult family, the children were intertwined seamlessly. Thus Czar's status of odd man out was eliminated.

But not long after, Ali received a call from Czar's teacher.

"This is Mrs. Gold calling. There's a problem with Czar. I'd like you to come in to discuss it."

"Can you give me an idea as to the nature of the problem?"

"He's disrupting other children while they're at work on a project. He's been accused of stealing the ideas of his classmates and passing them off as his own."

Ali was a bit surprised about the latter accusation because Czar was creative in his own right. She agreed to set up an appointment with Mrs. Gold.

When Czar came home from school that day, she spoke with him.

Czar got upset. "Mommy, I really didn't do that. Susie and I were talking and I told her about my idea. Then she copied it and said it was hers."

Ali felt a knot of dread in her stomach. Susie was being raised by her grandmother…. Linda.

That night she relayed the story to Marc. "I just don't know what to do. If I go to school, Linda will probably be there too. I don't know if I want to have an encounter with her."

"Ali, are you asking me to go?"

"I'm not sure. If I don't go it'll look like I'm intimidated by her."

"And? Are you?"

"That's not fair, Marc. You know our families' history. I always carry that little extra bit of baggage."

"I don't mind going but I've never known you to run away from a situation."

"I'm not running from the situation. It actually feels like I'm running hurdles."

"Come on. Life has lots of hurdles. If you let these little ones get you, how are you ever going to be strong enough to leap over the others, which may be even higher?"

"I thought you knew me well enough to know I take the bigger ones in stride a lot easier than the small ones. Okay, I'll take care of it."

The following morning, she phoned Czar's teacher and suggested having a meeting with either the teacher and her or else have one with the teacher, Linda and herself.

Mrs. Gold opted for the three people meeting, feeling that a face-to-face encounter would be better than solving the situation secondhand.

Hence, it was the following Monday that Mrs. Gold, Linda and Ali were in the conference room discussing the difficulty between Susie and Czar.

"Okay. From what I understand, each child is claiming the project is his or her own idea. What's of concern is that Czar struck Susie and she struck him back, or vice versa. These are two of my best students so I'm surprised to be having a problem with either of them, never mind *both*."

"Well," said Linda, "it's always been my experience that nig– Ah … roes always resort to violence. Perhaps by hitting Susie, Czar is yielding to the black aspect of his heritage. After all, he is multicultural."

Ali glared at Linda. She was just about ready to explode. Then Mrs. Gold raised her hand and said, "We really have no need to bring race into any of this. Children are just children. Being children, they learn best by example. I didn't want this discussion to take a turn like this. We've two young human beings who, for one reason or another, have resorted to harassing each other. Yes, each other. Czar isn't always the perpetrator. Susie, in a covert way, does, and yes, even says things to rile him up. He may not react immediately, but the reaction does come nonetheless."

Linda was ready to interject something but Mrs. Gold continued.

"I don't want the two of you to start trading barbs or stories. I want to handle this rationally. First, I'll bring Susie and Czar in by themselves and try to work out a truce. Second, I'll separate them in the classroom. Right now, they are sitting next to each other. After a few days, I'll get back to you both with a full accounting of what's ensued. Is that satisfactory to you both?"

"Yes, Mrs. Gold," said Ali. "That's an excellent plan."

"I guess so," said Linda, "but I still think it's genetic."

Ali, much to her surprise, ignored the slur, turned to Mrs. Gold and said, "Thank you for your time and consideration." Saying nothing further, she left.

Later, as she relayed the story to Marc, she said, "You know, Mrs. Gold as much as called Susie a sneak. She made reference to Susie's covert behavior. That very word said more than anything else did. I also wonder if Susie ever calls him any names. Czar probably wouldn't tell us because he wouldn't want it to be hurtful to us."

"If what Linda said in the office is any indication of the racial slurs within the house, that's quite possible. Let me take Czar out for a pair of new shoes tomorrow. I'll see what I can pry out of him."

At breakfast the next morning, Marc said to Czar, "I'm going to pick you up today after school. That way we can buy you the new shoes, okay?"

"Okay. I just might be a little late. Mrs. Gold said she wants to talk to me."

Thus, after school that day, Marc was waiting outside the building for his oldest child. As he waited, he saw Linda leaving school with a crying Susie.

Czar came out shortly thereafter.

"Hi, Daddy. I wasn't as long as I thought I would be. Mrs. Gold wanted to ask me a few questions."

"Such as?"

"She asked why Susie and I couldn't get along. I decided I would finally tell her that Susie called me a black nigger. She kept saying it and saying it until I got so mad I finally hit her. Mrs. Gold said that hitting someone doesn't solve anything. She hoped both Susie and I would learn how to cosist."

As Czar was talking, Marc realized how the actual word, *coexist*, was elusive when you were a black make in a white-male-oriented society. However, he felt Czar's struggle would be less than his.

"…so anyhow, Mrs. Gold changed our seats. She also reprimed Susie and told her it's not right to call people names. She said that America is for all of

God's children, not just for the ones who look like Him."

Marc decided he wouldn't ask anything else of Czar... nor did he correct his word for reprimand. He thought that was probably the reason Susie was crying. He realized much of the situation was buried deep within Linda's mind and was passed on to Susie. Just as his father-in-law had penetrated Linda's body, so had intolerance embedded itself within her soul.

Thirty-four

Another school year came. Mrs. Spellman was talking to her class about famous African Americans.

Czar raised his hand. "My dad is a successful African American."

There was snickering within the classroom.

Following this episode, Czar came home with a terrible report card.... D's and F's. Ali was completely unprepared for this and asked Czar what was wrong.

"I don't know why but I just can't concentrate in school. We were doing this project on famous Afro-Americans. I brought up daddy's name and the kids, who didn't know I was black, were mean. I guess they never knew someone who was black and white at the same time."

"Okay, but what does that have to do with your report card? Your father has never used color for an excuse. We're certainly not going to tolerate that from you."

"But Mom, they put pictures of apes on my desk with my name under them. And they called me nigger. Whenever I come into the room, they either shut up or say, 'Here comes nigger boy.'"

"Czar, have you told your teacher about this?"

"I don't want to be a tattletale. You and Dad have always said we should handle our own problems. That's what I'm trying to do."

"But this isn't a personal problem. This isn't a disagreement you had with another student. This is a problem built on prejudice and hatred. I know we've always insisted you handle things on your own. However, this is a problem which even adults can't handle alone. You've mentioned this started with the famous Afro-American program. Evidently these kids have hang-ups about blacks; probably from their parents. Maybe your father could come in as a guest speaker. And you could provide the class with some information about such Afro-Americans as Crispus Attucks, Adam Clayton Powell, Martin Luther King, Malcolm X and Fredrick Douglas."

"Mom, that's a lot of work."

"Granted. But when people are ignorant, they have to be educated. That's how intolerance gets beaten ... by understanding. I'll help you with it and

223

I'm sure Daddy will, too. Will you talk with Mrs. Spellman tomorrow?"

"Okay, Mommy. I'll try."

Unbeknownst to Czar, Ali called Mrs. Spellman in the morning.

"Mrs. Spellman, this is Ali Green. I'd rather that Czar didn't know I'm calling. Some students, who were apparently unaware of his black heritage, have been anything but kind to him ever since they found out. They are harassing him. I suggested he prepare a small report on some prominent Black Americans and present it to the class. Also, I thought his father, along with some other Afro-Americans, could come in to speak to the class. Will that be okay with you?"

"Mrs. Green, that's an excellent idea. As a matter of fact, I'm going to follow through. I'll have representatives from different groups who have been stereotyped. Just the other day, Johnny Camero was in tears because the students were tormenting him about *The Untouchables*, which they see on TV. I think your suggestion will help pave the way for more ethnic tolerance. This is actually pretty exciting. Why, I may even have a favorite-person day when they can wear the clothing of their ancestors."

"Thank you. I'm sure with your help, we can forestall any future problems."

Marc, of course, consented to do a guest stint in Czar's class. Ali and Czar went to the library and she helped him look up some of the black men. They decided to include Jackie Robinson.

After Czar submitted his paper, Marc made arrangements with Mrs. Spellman to speak to the class. This was planned to coincide with Czar's reading of his report. Ali wanted to be there but thought it best to absent herself.

The report seemed to make an impression on the young people. It was kept simple so it wouldn't appear as if something was being forced down their throats. It made quite an impression on the kids in the class.

And now it was time for Marc.

"So, young people, you're no different from adults," Marc began. "If you aren't used to being around people who are different from you, you don't feel comfortable. So you stay away from that person or group. There is a word called tolerance ... spelled t-o-l-e-r-a-n-c-e, which means allowing those who are different to express their views and live their own lives as they see fit. That is as long as they don't try to take away the rights of anyone else. In other words, we should all live and let live. If anyone has any questions, I'll be happy to answer any of them now."

"Why do some grown-ups call people nasty names? I hear some people say 'mick', 'heeb', 'wop' and other things like that."

"You left out one other very much used one.... Nigger. I really can't explain why people say such things. Each of us is born with a brain as clean as an erased chalkboard. Facts, thoughts, beliefs and words are like tattoos in the brain. By the time a person becomes a teenager, many of these things are hard to unlearn. Getting hit hurts.

"But words can be hurtful too. I don't know how we can get people to stop name-calling, but each one of us can promise not to start doing it. And if anyone of us has started, we can promise to stop."

"Were your family slaves?"

"My grandmother has told me they were, and I'm sure it was awful." Marc smiled. "How would you like to be told what to do all of the time?"

"But my mommy and daddy do that all the time."

"Yeah," chimed in most of the class.

Mrs. Spellman was about to answer when Marc interrupted.

"Parents do that for your own good. They're guiding you into being model citizens. They care about you and want your lives to be the best they can be."

"Well, class. Mr. Green has to leave us now. Thank you very much," Mrs. Spellman continued, as she faced Marc and extended her hand.

"You're quite welcome," replied Marc as he waved good-bye to the class. He then left to go back to his office.

After Marc left, Mrs. Spellman spoke with the class about tolerance. She knew the afternoon had been successful when she noticed some of the children had crossed their mental barrier. Once again, they began congregating around Czar's desk.

Marc gave Ali an overview of what happened in school that day. She was looking forward to a respite from problems.

Ali appreciated what Marc had done in school. She had always respected him and her respect had grown through the years. Even though their past wasn't easy, they managed to muddle through everything together. She felt that when they were young, they were not actually in love, but in lust. At that time, the chemical reaction was the driving force behind their relationship. Although they hadn't acted upon the great physical attraction until Czar's conception, it was a strong force between them. More and more each day she appreciated the person behind that electric charge. Today had definitely been one of those days.

When Tessa was apprised of this latest situation, she felt Ali was still not in tune with the events surrounding her kids' acceptance or lack thereof. However, she'd never been one to say, 'I told you so,' and she wasn't about to start now.

"And so, Mom, Marc felt that it was a worthwhile afternoon. Mom, are you paying attention?"

"Yes. What? Oh, I'm sorry, Ali. I'm afraid I wasn't."

"Am I boring you?"

"No, of course not. Please continue."

"Well, Marc has such a great way with words. He really impressed those young people."

"But Ali, you and Marc aren't going to be able to run interference for the kids all the time."

"It won't be necessary."

"How do you figure that?"

"Well, here in Linfield, Marc and I are accepted the same as any other couple."

Tessa thought, Where could the young people in Czar's class learn prejudice and discrimination if not from Marc and Ali's so-called friends? But discretion prevailed and Tessa held her tongue.

Later, when speaking with Gary, she gave vent to her thoughts.

Gary responded by saying, "Tessa, everyone has problems. With Ali's kids, the color divergence is right out there. With you and me, it was religion. We certainly had our share of problems surrounding that. We overcame them together. I'm sure Ali, coming from a mixed marriage, faced some things that she didn't share with us."

"Perhaps you're right. Maybe she's interfering too much in the lives of her children. Maybe she *is* being overprotective. I had hoped she and Marc went into this relationship with their eyes open. All children of different mixtures have pressures. For that matter, children with similar backgrounds aren't immune from unpleasantness. I think Ali should just back off and let the kids take their lumps."

"Gary, these are your grandchildren you're being so blasé about."

"I'm not being blasé. Ali can't be their offensive as well as defensive lineman. She has to cut the cord before she can't distance herself enough from them to allow them to grow. It's funny she can't see what she's doing by being overzealous."

"Well, if you're so sure about this, why don't you talk to her about it?"

"I just might do that," responded Gary.

A few months later, after giving the incident time to blow over, Gary called Ali.

"Hi, Ali. I'd like to take my favorite daughter to lunch. How about this Saturday at the Linfield Country Club?"

"Okay, Dad, I'll meet you there. What time?"
"How about 1 o'clock?"
"One it is."

Thirty-five

At 12:55 on Saturday, both Gary and Ali pulled into the valet area at the country club.

"Hi Dad," said Ali as she kissed Gary's cheek.

"Hi sweetheart," Gary said, looking at his daughter. She looked lovely. She had on a sky blue pants suit with a light blue sweater. Around her neck, she wore a single gold chain, which had a round diamond pendant in the center. She wore her diamond stud earrings along with a gold bangle bracelet. She looked simplistically elegant.

They walked into the dining room with Ali in the lead. The maître'd showed them to a table overlooking the swimming pool. The trees in the background were a perfect contrast to the periwinkle blue of the water.

The dining room was a study of peach, brown, and beige. The tables had a peach candle housed in a brown candleholder. Although the overall effect of the room was peaceful, it wasn't in keeping with Gary's mood.

Ali sat facing the pool with Gary to her right. He waited until they had ordered before they spoke.

"Ali, there's something that's been troubling me...."

"Dad, you sound so serious. What is it? Are you getting a divorce or something? Are you being arrested for tax evasion? Do you have a body buried in the yard? What is it?" Ali was giggling.

Gary cleared his throat. "I'm concerned about your involvement with the racial difficulties Czar and the Musks are experiencing." He put up his hand as she began to protest and continued. "It's natural to want to protect them from anything that hurts them, but sooner or later, they're going to have to learn to stand up for themselves. Either that or ignore the slurs. You know your mother and I try not to interfere. When you were younger, we let you go to the edge of the crevice, praying you wouldn't fall over. However, if you did happen to fall, we were right there picking you up.

"We taught you to fight your own battles but were always around to back you up. Likewise, your kids have to make their own way in the world. You've given them a solid foundation.... Now it's up to them to build on it. I know it's hard to watch them go on a collision course but that's how they grow. Kids have to leave the protection of the nest."

"I didn't know you were ordained a priest." Her voice was laced with sarcasm.

"Just a minute," Gary said.

"For what? For you to continue to berate me? Shall I just put them out in the streets and let them fend for themselves?" Ali's voice rose in octave and tone.

Gary put his hand on his daughter's and said, "Ali, I know you're upset. But when you calm down, you'll realize the messenger loves you and the message is true."

"Just leave me alone!" Ali said. As she bolted from the table, her right hand knocked over her water glass, which broke. Its contents spilled all over Gary and the table.

Gary rose to go after her, mindful of the fact that the entire dining room was looking at them.

Ali was crying silently as she ran to get her car from the valet. Her eyes were so blinded by tears she almost ran into the path of an oncoming car. Gary was close on her heels.

Although Gary's eyes weren't overflowing with tears, his brain and heart were. So intent was he on reaching his daughter, he was oblivious to all of his surroundings save the sight of the blue-clad lady running a good distance ahead. However, he was in good shape, wasn't the least bit winded, and continued pursuing his daughter, who had quite a head start.

He was completely unaware of the car coming in his direction. He heard the engine but didn't see it, as he was looking ahead toward Ali. The next sound he heard was the loud thump as his body collided with the steel. He was no match for the car. He unwillingly yielded to it, falling hard on the asphalt.

Ali didn't even realize the steel had made contact with her father's flesh. She was so forlorn she was unaware of anything but her own feelings. She heard someone shout. "Call an ambulance."

It was then she turned and saw her father, lying unconscious in the country club's driveway. She ran back to him but the crowd blocked her. A woman, who was also a nurse, took charge. This nurse got people to step back so Gary had air room. She recognized Ali, who was frantically struggling at the circle's perimeter, trying to get to her father. When she finally made it into the center of the circle and saw the blood streaming from Gary's face and head, she promptly fainted.

A good Samaritan broke her fall, but she was out cold.

The nurse, who was present at the scene, monitored Gary's pulse and respirations. He looked horrendous, but his breathing was strong and his pulse was steady. However, he remained unconscious.

During the ride to the hospital, Ali awakened approaching hysteria. She saw her father's bloodied face. She felt responsible for his condition.

When they arrived at the hospital, Ali got out immediately. She hastened to the phone.

"Marc, oh, Marc," cried Ali, breathlessly.

"Ali, what's wrong?"

"Oh, Marc, there's been a horrible accident." She could no longer speak. The phone dropped and hit against the wall, dangling from its short cord.

Marc shouted into the phone. "Ali, Ali, pick up the phone. Where are you? I'll come and get you. Ali? Ali?"

Marc regained his composure and hung up the phone, then picked it back up and dialed.

"Linfield Police Department," the voice said.

"I just received a call from my wife, Ali Green. Is there any way you can tell me if she was involved in an accident? She said something about a horrible accident then began sobbing so I couldn't understand what she was saying."

"Just a minute, please."

After what seemed like an eternity, a voice came back on the line.

"We had a patrol car and an ambulance dispatched to the Linfield Country Club within the last half hour, sir. But I have no names or follow-up at this juncture."

"That would seem whoever was involved would have been taken to Linfield General Hospital, right?"

"Yes, s–"

Before the officer could finish his statement, Marc replaced the receiver on the hook, grabbed his keys and drove to Linfield General.

After he parked the car, he went into the emergency room, where he saw a catatonic Ali.

"Ali, are you okay?"

She nodded mutely.

"Ali, is it your dad?"

Once again, Ali nodded.

Realizing it was going to take entirely too long to get the facts in this manner, he walked her over to a chair, sat her down and said, "Whatever you do, don't move!"

He went to the ER desk. "I'm Marc Green. I believe that my father-in-law is here. Can you check, please?"

"Name, please," said the clerk without even looking up.

"Gary Rosen."

"Yes, sir. He's here but he can't have any visitors. Can you please contact his wife for us?"

Of course, thought Marc. Ali hadn't been coherent to tell him so she certainly hadn't called Tessa.

"Sure."

"Thank you, we haven't gotten any answer at the home."

"Shit," said Marc, louder than he intended.

He went to the phone, dialed and heard Treva answer, "Italian Mist."

"Treva, it's Marc. Is Tessa there?"

"Yes, Marc. Shall I put her on?"

"No. Listen. I know nothing further than this. Gary's been in an accident. Ali, he and I are at Linfield General. Please drive Tessa here."

"Anything else?"

"No, hurry though. I don't know if he's dead or alive." Marc hung up.

"Tessa, listen to me." She continued, "Gary's been in an accident. I'll drive us to the hospital. Hurry. Come on."

Tessa's mouth dropped open in astonishment. She fiddled with her hair, brushing imaginary strands back from her forehead. She said nothing in response to her sister's statement, determined not to fall apart. Gary would need her to be calm now.

After Treva locked up 'Mist,' they got into her car. As they rode, Tessa closed her eyes, willing the car to go faster. Tessa played with her keys aimlessly. They finally pulled into the hospital parking lot. Tessa jumped from the car almost before it stopped. She fled into the ER, where she saw a mesmerized Ali along with Marc. She suspected the worst.

"Marc, is he.... Did he.... What happened?"

"Mom, I don't know anything other than when he was brought in, he was unconscious and bleeding from his head wound."

Tessa turned to Ali, trying to ascertain what had happened.

Marc faced Tessa and said, "I haven't been able to get anything that makes sense from Ali. All I know is that they were at the country club but hadn't eaten yet. She seems to be hazy about details."

"Are you Mrs. Rosen?"

Tessa looked up to see a clerk standing above her. She just nodded in assent.

The clerk spoke to her again. "Fill out these forms please."

Tessa numbly did as she was told.

"Mom, Tessa. The doctor's here and wants to talk to you." Her son-in-law was speaking to her.

Tessa looked up from her chore to see Dr. Dawson, a general surgeon, standing in front of her.

"Tessa, it appears as if Gary has a severe concussion. That in itself is a bit problematic, but one that's likely to resolve without any difficulty. He has no skull fracture. However, there's something worse at this point. One of his ribs has impaled itself in the spleen. It's acting as a tamponade. That's why there's been no excessive bleeding up to this point. Since the rib is embedded within the spleen, we must operate as soon as possible to remove the spleen and the remaining part of the rib so it won't damage any other organs. Of course, I'll need your permission to operate."

Tessa just nodded while saying, "I'll sign, of course. What are his chances?"

"Well, he's relatively healthy. But I really won't know anything until after surgery."

"I'd like him to be seen by a priest." Even though Gary hadn't converted, she knew it would be okay with him.

"He has already been seen by one. One was in the ER visiting another patient and I asked him to see Dad," Marc announced.

"May I go in to see him, now?"

"Yes, but only for a few minutes."

Tessa, assisted by Marc, walked into the area where Gary was being treated. Though she'd worked as a nurse for years, she was still unprepared for what she saw. Gary had tubes running in and out of him.… It seemed to Tessa they were everywhere. He was no longer unconscious but was dazed.… A bit disoriented.

He gave a half smile when he saw his wife, "You should see the other guy," he whispered.

Tessa managed a brief smile and said, "I can imagine." She was determined to keep conversation light. "Dr. Dawson's going to operate soon. I'm going to sign the consent form. There's a rib impaled in your spleen. Both the rib and the spleen must be removed as soon as possible."

Gary lapsed back into his semi-stuporous state. Tessa wasn't even sure if he had comprehended or even heard her words. She went back to the desk to sign the form, and then asked about her grandchildren.

Treva said, "I'm going over to the house now to tell them before they hear it on the news."

She had planned to pick up her two little ones along the way and tell the kids all at once. Marc said he would call Gary's parents to let them know. And, of course, he would call Mabel. Tessa also requested that he call Rita.

Marc went to where Ali was sitting, "Hi honey. Did you hear what Dr. Dawson said?"

Before he could finish, Ali cried out. "It was all *my* fault. If I hadn't run out of the country club that way, my dad wouldn't have followed me blindly. I acted like a spoiled brat. If he dies...." as she said this, the sobbing accompanied the tears that up until now were silent, "...I'll never forgive myself."

"What upset you so much that you couldn't sit and talk it over?" Marc was gentle with his question.

"He was telling me I should back off with Czar. That I should let him fight his own battles. The same thing you've told me time and time again."

"Ali, your dad's in good shape. He's got a lot more resilience than men half his age. He'll be fine.... We all will. We'll get through it together."

"Marc, can I see him now?"

"Let me check with the nurse."

Marc came back in and said, "They said just for the briefest time. Come on. Brace yourself, now. He looks rotten."

Ali said, "Marc, would you mind if I went in alone?"

Although Marc had misgivings about this, he agreed.

Ali walked into the cubicle where her dad was lying. She had a slight intake of breath when she saw him. She almost faltered a second but continued walking toward the gurney.

"Hi, Daddy. I know.... I should see the other guy. You'll be fine. I want you to know that I'm sorry for how poorly I behaved today."

"Princess, don't be sad. I'm going to be okay."

Ali bent down and kissed Gary on the cheek; her tears spilling on his face as she did so.

"See ya later, Dad," Ali managed to say. She remained composed until she got out of the room and fell into Marc's arms.

"It's okay, Ali. It's okay."

"Do the kids know yet?"

"Treva was going to the house to tell them. Do you want to go to them or would you rather stay here?"

"I want to stay here to be near Dad and help Mom if she needs me. Do you think the kids would be better off if Treva brought them here?"

"That's a judgment call, but I think it'd be better if they stayed at home. I'll bring them in to see your dad as soon as possible."

Ali nodded, and then asked, "Where's Mom?"

Marc said, "The chapel. Just where you'd expect her to be. Do you want me to go with you?"

"No thanks. I've got to do this on my own."

When Ali approached the chapel, she saw her mother deeply engrossed in either thought or prayer. She didn't want to interrupt so she merely sat down next to her mother in the non-sectarian chapel and gently put her hand on top of her mother's praying ones.

Tessa turned to her daughter and said, "Don't worry, Ali. Daddy's going to be fine."

The two women embraced each other in silence.

Marc was peering into the chapel. He had to suppress the tears which were welling up in her eyes. He knew somehow they'd all survive this, no matter the outcome. He had such tender feelings toward Gary he didn't dare allow himself to face the worst possibility. He walked back to the ER just in time to see them wheeling Gary to the operating room. Once again, Marc realized life is extremely fragile. He said a silent prayer then began the lengthy waiting process.

Meanwhile, Treva had the unenviable task of telling the children about their grandfather's accident. She didn't elaborate or divulge all of the details. She just told them Gary had an accident. That he was hit by a car. Everyone was at the hospital waiting for him to be operated on.

Czar queried, "When can we see him? Or at least talk to him?"

"Czar, I don't know the answer. We'll have to wait and see. Your mother and father will let us know."

Althie said, "Why wasn't Grandpop more careful? He always tells us to look carefully in the street and the parking lot before we walk."

"Well, Althie, that's why these things are called accidents. Sometimes things can't be explained. And sometimes the unexpected happens."

At the hospital, the family waited for Gary's surgery to be completed. His spleen was going to be removed, but barring any other damage to bodily organs, that was the only thing the doctors had anticipated doing.

Within a reasonable time, Dr. Dawson appeared in the waiting room door. He looked at Tessa and said, "Well, it looks as if the spleen was the only damaged organ. There was minimal bleeding and no other trauma to surrounding organs. Barring anything unforeseen, we're expecting a complete recovery."

Tessa just nodded as tears filled her eyes. "Thank you, Dr. Dawson. When may I see him?"

"Well, he's in recovery now, but you can see him for a minute or two."

Gratefully, Tessa once again nodded. She followed Dr. Dawson into the recovery room.

When she saw Gary, she was relieved to see that he was apparently experiencing no notable pain. He was in a totally relaxed state.

She bent over the bed, kissed his forehead and left the room.

"Well, let's go home and tell the kids their grandfather will be okay," said Marc when he saw Tessa emerge from the room.

"Marc, you go ahead with Ali. I'm going to wait until I can have a real visit with Gary."

Marc knew there'd be no dissuading her from this plan of action. He acquiesced. He took Ali home.

When they arrived at home, the kids were all waiting around. The TV wasn't on and they weren't playing any games. Surprisingly they were doing their homework.

Czar was the first to see his mother and father. He ran to the door to greet them.

"How's Grandpop? Can I see him? What happened?"

Marc responded, "He's doing fine. They had to operate on him. I think you can probably go to the hospital in a few days as long as he continues to do well."

"How did he get hurt?" asked Althie.

"He was running in the parking lot and didn't see the car coming. It hit him in the belly. Then he fell and hit his head."

"But Grandpop's always so careful when we're with him. That doesn't make any sense."

Marc looked at Ali, ready to follow her lead. She spoke up almost in a whisper.

"Althie, Grandpop and I had a small misunderstanding. He was running to catch up with me."

"But Mommy, you always tell us that we shouldn't argue in public; that what happens with us is no one else's business; that it's not polite to be loud when you're out; that children shouldn't talk back to their parents; that–"

"Sometimes things can't be controlled. For some inexplicable reason, things just happen. Okay, kids, who wants pizza for dinner?"

The boys accepted but Althie shrugged her shoulders, not really caring.

Treva had been standing in the background with her own children and took Ali aside. "Why don't you go up and lie down? Marc and I can handle dinner as well as field any questions which may come up."

"Aunt Treva, I'll go and take a shower, but I want to be here for dinner with the kids. They've always been so close to Dad. I want to be around in case they need me. And by the way, thanks for not asking what happened. I'll explain when I can. It was all my fault."

"I only know your father was talking to you about Czar. I know this is a tough subject for you. You live it 24 hours a day. We just get smatterings of what's happening daily. I also know both your mother and father are deeply troubled about the taunting as well as the nastiness Czar's had to put up with. What I don't know is what I would have done under the same circumstances. Whatever happened today was a result of love. When this ordeal is over, you can sit down and calmly work things out."

"Aunt Treva, I know what you're saying is true, but I still have to take complete responsibility for what happened to my father. I won't be able to live with myself if he's not okay. I was completely useless today at the E.R., knowing if I hadn't gotten so mad and run from Daddy, he wouldn't have gotten hurt."

"Maybe if I was in your situation, I'd look at it the same way. But taking the blame is not the important issue here. What's important is you understand what your father was saying. If he got that message across, that's one less obstacle your family will have to overcome." Treva gave her niece a hug and helped her make her way up the stairs.

Thirty-six

A few days after the surgery, Gary was spiking a temperature of 103^0. The doctors hadn't anticipated this post-op problem because the operation itself was so uneventful. They met with Tessa.

"This is something we didn't anticipate but it does happen. We have been giving him prophylactic antibiotics since he was admitted."

"What's next?"

"We're going to do a blood culture to determine what other antibiotics to give him. As soon as the blood is drawn, we're going to start him on some additional ones and change them if the blood culture shows something else may be more effective. He's a pretty sick guy."

Tessa remained mute throughout this exchange when she learned just how sick Gary was. He was septic. She began to feel she was spending more time in church than the priests were. She went to mass every day. She often went to the hospital chapel when she visited Gary. Never had she prayed so hard in all of her life. Ali had retreated into herself so much so that Marc insisted she accompany him to the hospital, where he had set up an appointment with a psychologist. The kids were getting by pretty well with Treva's help. The hours crawled by. The days did likewise.

Gary's temperature hovered around 103^0 to 104^0 for a few days. Once again, they met with the doctors.

"Tessa, he's not responding to the antibiotics. Hopefully, when the culture comes back, we can switch him to something which will do the trick."

"And if not?"

"Let's not cross that bridge until or unless we have to."

The antibiotics were changed and within a week, Gary's temperature was returning to normal. He was going to recover.

Tessa was afraid Ali and Gary would be estranged after the accident. Thankfully, she was wrong. The underlying factor of the accident was resolved. Ali began backing off from her children's problems.

Tthirty-seven

By now, Czar was in the eighth grade and he was a finalist for the American Legion Award.

Ali hoped that he would win, but she tried not to show him this. She didn't want to make winning awards or prizes overly important to her children. There was something to be said for a job well done for which there was nothing won. She always tried to teach the kids to do their best. She also taught them everyone was special within his own right. The fact that Marc earned a more than adequate income made them more able to appreciate the finer things of life, but it didn't make *them* finer.

The day had come for the much-anticipated graduation. Czar was getting dressed for the event when he heard a knock at his bedroom door.

He opened it and saw both of his parents standing there.

"Hi Mom. Hi Dad. What's up?"

"We wanted to give you your graduation present before school so you could wear it," said Ali as she handed him a box wrapped in blue paper with a lighter blue bow. As he'd been taught to do, Czar opened the card first and read it.

You've finished grade eight,
Now it's time to graduate.
You're going on to grade nine,
Where you'll be just fine.
Remember while in high school,
Education is the tool.
To ready you for the years ahead,
To provide fun, butter and bread.

There was a note in his mother's handwriting telling him how proud they both were of him.

Czar then permitted himself to finally open his present which was a gold signet ring – CG – with a tiny diamond-shaped amethyst, his birthstone, in the center. He was thrilled with his ring, which fit him perfectly.

"Geez, Mom. Geez, Dad. This is really cool." He didn't care much about jewelry but knew his parents wanted him to have a special something for his eighth-grade graduation.

"Great, Czar." Marc hugged his son.

"Let's go." Ali grabbed his hand.

Later, in the school auditorium, the announcement was made.

"The winner of the boys' American Legion Award is Chad Green." Czar, who was daydreaming, stood up and walked to the stage to accept his award. His parents and grandparents were bursting with pride. Tessa in particular was pleased. Czar was special to her not only because he lived with Gary and her when his father was doing undercover work, but also because she'd spent so much time with him when the triplets were expected.

Czar stepped to the podium, took his award and said, "Thank you very much." He didn't deviate from his modest shyness.

After the ceremony, the junior and senior Rosens, the Greens and Rita went with Czar and the Musks to the country club for lunch. Ali hadn't been to the club since the fateful day of Gary's accident. But to please the family, she went.

That night, there was a dance at the school. Czar wasn't going to go but changed his mind at the last minute.

The gym was decorated in burgundy and gray. There were two picnic tables; one with a burgundy tablecloth; the other with a gray one. In the center of each table were two trays of cookies along with two bowls of punch. There were paper cups and burgundy and gray napkins at each end of the table.

Czar spent most of his time around the refreshment tables, periodically drinking punch and eating cookies. He'd never had much interest in dancing. However, when lady's choice was announced, girls flocked his way. He danced, happily dividing his time among the throngs who were waiting their turn.

When the dance was over, Czar and his friends all walked home together. He could hardly sleep that night because of the day's happenings. He was also full of excitement about what the coming year would bring in high school. He knew he wanted to play football, almost as much to please his grandfather as to please himself. It had been Gary who taught him how to throw a football, how to tackle and perform other skills which were necessary to possess in the game.

Thirty-eight

The weekend before beginning his freshman year, Czar was going on a camping trip. The local 'Y' was sponsoring it. He was looking forward to it. He was packing his clothes for the overnight excursion when his mother called him to the phone.

"Hello."

"Czar, this is Susie."

Surprised at who was on the other end of the line, Czar just said, "Oh, hi, Susie."

"There's a dance at the Linfield Community Center this Saturday and I was wondering if you'd like to go."

"I'm sorry, Susie. I'm going camping with a group from the 'Y'."

Susie was still miffed and smarting from it the next day as she was swimming at the housing development's pool.

"Are you coming to the dance?" asked another would-be freshman.

"No. I don't think so. The black faggot can't come and I can't think of anyone else to ask."

Althie, who was within hearing distance of this exchange, became so livid that she almost went after Susie. She thought it would make it more uncomfortable for Czar if she did. She decided to talk to the Musks about it.

"Susie called Czar a black faggot. I'd love to bring her down a peg or two."

"So what's the difference?" asked Ben, who then added, "You're too sensitive."

"No. I'm not. I just think it was a rotten thing to say. There aren't many other black boys Czar's age so everyone right away knew who she meant."

"I repeat, so what? Don't you know why she was pissed?"

"Gad, you're so crude. Yes, I know why she was mad. He refused to go to the dance with her."

"Right. She couldn't understand why he preferred bugs and tents over cunts and boobs."

"Every time you open your mouth, you get cruder by the minute. What should I do about it? Shall I tell Czar?"

240

"Do what you want. When have I ever tried to tell my *much* older sister what to do?"

"Oh, shut up. Neither of you are any help at all."

Ali walked in on the latter part of this and after seeing that Althie was upset, asked, "What's wrong?"

"Oh, nothing, Mom. Just Susie stirring things up again."

Ali wasn't able to get anything further from her so she knew the subject was closed.

Meanwhile, Althie decided not to say anything to Czar. Happily, he went off on his trip.

And now the much-awaited first day of school had come. Linfield High School had kept abreast with the times; had been refurbished throughout the years. The ivy-clad building was truly an architectural masterpiece.

While walking up the steps, Czar was accosted by an older student saying to him, "Hey, freshmen are supposed to let upperclassmen into the building first."

Czar turned, bewildered, "Are you talking to me?"

"What are you? Robert DeNiro or just a wise guy? Do you happen to see anyone else standing around here?"

"I guess not. Go ahead. Be my guest."

"Here, you can take my book, too, while you're at it."

"Is that a policy, too?" Czar asked, not meaning to sound challenging. But he knew the words weren't going to endear him to this bully.

With that, a teacher came by, and said to the bully, "I hope you're not harassing this freshman, are you, Conrad?"

"No. Go ahead. Ask him yourself."

"Young man, is he bothering you?"

Figuring he was taking the path of least resistance, Czar said, "No."

"Okay, guys. Don't be late."

"Hey, man, that was okay. You're pretty cool. My name is Conrad Richards, but you can call me Rad, like all of my friends do," said Rad while extending his right hand.

"Chad Green. My friends call me Czar."

"Okay, Czar, catch you later."

Czar knew he had escaped a few months of hell, just by chance. He eventually learned Rad was one of the macho guys in school. He was too cool to play sports or study. Girls, of all ilks, were his forte … or so the story went.

It's funny when you think of it. So much of life is based on timing and/or chance. So far, Czar had lucked out on his.

Czar had already decided to join the freshmen football team, which he knew would please the men in his family. But since he was also an artist, he knew the females wouldn't be thrilled with his decision. Linfield was a big sports school and supported three football teams.... Freshman, JV and varsity.

"But what if you get hurt and can't paint?" asked his mother.

"I'll get my hands insured so it won't be too much of a loss."

Althie ran and got the phone book.

"What are you doing with that?" asked her brother.

"I'm looking up insurance companies to see who'll insured your hands."

"God, are you gullible!"

The football season was in full swing, but not for Czar. He actually had broken his right hand in one of their first scrimmages. Art class as well as football were both put on hold for a while.

"Oh, I was afraid this would happen," was the comment from his mother as they were waiting in the ER for an orthopedic surgeon.

"Come on. It's only going to be 4 weeks at the most. I'll just have to work twice as hard when it heals. I'll get no rating this quarter in art, but my hand will heal soon enough." (He eventually managed to get an 'A' the next quarter so he went into the third one with two 'A's under his belt)

Speaking of quarters, the football team was undefeated going into the final game of the season. Czar didn't know if he was going to be permitted to play. The doctor was going to see him but wasn't definite about allowing him to play; let alone his original position of quarterback. Since no one was sure if his throwing arm would hold up, the coach decided to switch him to a wide receiver. Since Czar was a fast runner, this was no problem. However, he wasn't sure he could catch well enough but figured he could use both of his arms and pull the ball into his body like his grandfather had taught him.

In the third quarter, Linfield was down 21-7. Czar was finally put into the game. The quarterback threw high into the end zone. The ball was so high he would have had to have been a kangaroo to jump up and reach it. Linfield lucked out, though, because there was a penalty against the opposing team. They repeated the exact play. The team members connected. They were now trailing 21-13. The coach preferred kicking instead of going for a two pointer. Everyone second-guessed him, but since the score became 21-14, who could fault his decision? Besides, he felt his team still had another quarter to go so they could combine their luck and skill once again.

Amazingly, the Linfield defense held their opponents to zip in the fourth quarter. Their opponents almost returned the favor. With less than a minute to go in the game, the quarterback threw again and connected with Czar, making the score 21-20. The ball was definitely in Linfield's court now ... oops ... wrong sport. Anyway, this next play meant one of three things.... A win ... a tie ... or a loss. The coach called the play and the onus was on the Linfield Lions to execute the play to its fullest extent. The final play was to be a pass for the two-point conversion. Two of the Lions (one of whom was Czar) headed for the end zone. Czar's cohort tripped and the burden became his alone. He almost held his breath but figured he'd get weak. Czar lunged, jumped and caught the ball! The Lions had done it. They won the game 22-21.

Czar received one of the coaches' awards at the freshmen banquet. He got most courageous player. Even though his season was short, the other players didn't mind his recognition. Many of them were also honored. The Lions had a special camaraderie. There was no jealousy amongst them.

When Czar saw how the team responded to his award, he felt it was too bad that life, in general, couldn't emulate the team spirit found in sports. But then, perhaps, life would be boring. However, sometimes boring wasn't so bad. Sometimes he wouldn't mind life being boring.

Thirty-nine

The fall sped by. At Christmas time, Tessa and Gary gave the four Green children a trip to France, which they planned to take during the spring break. Czar was so excited. He was anxiously waiting to visit all of the places he had studied, especially the art museums.

His football coach approached him shortly after the Christmas break. "Czar, are you going out for a spring sport?"

"I don't know yet. Why?"

"Well, I like to see my athletes stay in shape. What better way is there then to condition for another sport?"

"Well, coach, there's a little problem. Some of my family's going to France for ten days around Easter. I know there are games scheduled then."

"You're right. But the vacation schedule's light. You'd only miss three games, plus practice."

"I'll let you know."

Two days later, Czar went to the coach.

"I think I'll just stick to football this year," said Czar. He didn't have the nerve to tell him that his art took priority over baseball at this point.

"Okay, if that's your decision, we'll have to live with it. Can't say I'm happy about it, though."

Although the coach didn't express it, Czar felt the shift in the coach's focus from him. In the coach's eyes he had copped out.

Spring came and the family was all excited about the pending trip. Althie walked around the house saying 'bon jour' and 'à demain', not very sure about her pronunciation.

"Can you help me with my French?" she asked her older brother.

"Most of my French is limited to grammar. I don't think conjugation will help too much if we're hungry or need a bathroom."

"Well, how about some basic phrases, then?"

Together they managed to figure out how to say where is such and such a place and how much does this cost.

The family all boarded the plane for the flight. The plane left New York in the evening and since France is ahead of the US by roughly six hours, they were going to arrive about ten a.m. They went to their hotel, where they dropped off their luggage. By this time it was noon.

They walked across the street to a little café. It was kind of funny because Tessa, who wouldn't deliberately hurt anyone, offended the waiter.

"Can we get a sandwich for lunch?"

"Madame, this is a café, not a snack bar. We do not serve sandwiches here. We serve whole meals, not the fast food you're used to in America."

"Oh, oh, I see. Fine. We'll have a meal then. Is that okay with you kids?"

Everyone agreed, though the kids probably would've preferred a Big Mac. Tessa sat down and requested wine.

"Would you like Kir, madam?"

Tessa, already intimidated, said timidly, "I'm not quite sure what that is."

"A Kir is white wine and Crème de Cassis. A Kir Royale is champagne and Crème de Cassis…. One is sparkling wine, the other is not. It's a matter of individual preference."

"Well, in that case, I'll have a Kir," said Tessa, who then also ordered her meal.

The family decided not to sleep other than just take a catnap, so they could more easily adjust to Parisian time. They decided to walk around a little. Then they'd unpack and lie down for about an hour … just enough to recharge their batteries.

Gary teased Tessa about the two places she had been hounding him to take them to. The first was the famous Paris flea market. Tessa said she had read in order to get bargains, you had to get there early.

Lucky for her, they overslept. When they arrived at the flea market at nine thirty, the wares were just being put out. You can imagine how relieved she was that they hadn't gotten there earlier.

Tessa walked up and down the aisles for what seemed like forever. She didn't even buy anything.

Gary asked her, "Why didn't you buy anything? You certainly hounded me enough about it. Honestly, I was surprised you even wanted to come here. Whenever I suggest we stop at one at home, you always protest. You tell me that flea markets make you itch just by hearing the name."

"I just wanted to experience some of the local flavor."

"Well, next time, when I ask you to go to one at home, I hope you'll be willing to experience *that* flavor, too."

The four kids laughed at this along with their grandfather. Tessa was a good sport about all of the teasing. She was used to it by now.

Tessa had mapped out the whole trip. Because of her strict schedule, the whole family had to go to see the Eiffel Tower in the middle of a northeast storm. Needless to say, they were the only ones who ventured to the Northeast section, let alone the top at all. They all agreed they would like to return someday, especially Czar, who wanted to paint some Parisian sights.

The following day, the group went to Versailles. The weather was disastrous that day, too. But since they had access to a great selection in rainwear, the family had brought lightweight 'Mist' gear along. They were protected from the elements.

The next day was nicer. The grandparents and their four charges went to see the sewers. This was a must for Tessa, who was an avid fan of Victor Hugo's *Les Miserables*.

"What do you expect to see there in the sewers? Rats?" Gary was teasing his wife again.

"Gary, I've heard how clean they are. Besides, aren't you curious to visit a place that an area is noted for?"

"I'll tell you what. Let's go visit our waste plant as soon as we get home. Linfield has one of the best waste systems in New Jersey. If you are interested in the wastes of Paris, why not show an interest in ours as well?"

"It's not the same and you know it," Tessa said, pretending to be perturbed, but secretly delighting in the frivolity of the conversation.

Before leaving the United States, Gary and Tessa had decided to see the show at the Lido but felt it wasn't for the children. The show was topless, so it wasn't the right atmosphere for the kids.

The night Gary and Tessa went to the Lido, the kids went for a trip on the Bateau Mouche. They got a seat on the upper deck. They were overwhelmed by Paris à la twilight.

The kids had taken a cab to the boat. Naturally they were also going to take one home. They had a minor problem. On the way to the boat, the fare was four francs, but on the way home, the driver wanted more.

"Fourteen francs, please," said the greedy driver, anxious to take advantage of four kids.

Czar was trying to reason with him. Althie had a better idea. She stood in front of the cab while the three boys tried in vain to lessen the fare. She got out a note pad and paper. She knowingly looked from the cab's license tags to her paper, presumably writing down the registration number. The cab driver got her message loud and clear. He recanted and took the four francs as a fair fare. He'd never run into the likes of Althie Green before. Needless to say, he got no tip.

Everyone had his or her own favorite spot in Paris. Czar's was naturally the Louvre.

"No matter how much I've read about it or seen pictures of it, I was so impressed by the reality of actually seeing the Mona Lisa and Winged Victory. They actually left me speechless. Maybe one day, I'll have paintings hanging in the Louvre."

"Life is full of dreams. If not for them, so much would go untried and unchallenged. Hold fast to your dreams, Czar."

"I will, Grandmom. I will."

The trip was over all too soon. Enter the real world once again.

Forty

Before long, Czar's freshman year was over. He never remembered anything else in his life going so fast.

He wanted to get a job for the summer but knew, due to his age, he'd have a hard time. It was because of this he went to see Gary at 'Down Under'.

"Grandpop, can I work at one of the sub shops? I know I'm too young to work late at night, but can you use me other times?"

"Let me see who I have coming back from college. I'll let you know. I'm almost positive I can work something out for you."

A few weeks later, Gary called Czar and said, "I can use you. I don't think you'll be working straight day work. You'll probably fill in during the times when I need someone."

"Okay. If I work a split day, I can go to the beach or paint in the afternoon."

He drew the split shift.

Czar was taking his work very seriously. He spoke with his mother about how much he wanted to please Gary.

"Mom, I don't want anyone to think that I'm just working there because my grandfather owns the place. I cut the bread, tomatoes, and onions and tear the lettuce. The only thing I don't like about the job is I smell just like an overripe onion."

"When you come in from your shift, just shed your work clothes in the laundry room, shower and put on fresh clothes. And why don't you keep some old jeans out just for working at 'Down Under'? Grandpop provides the 'Down Under' tee shirts so that's no problem."

"The hard part about this job is when my friends come in. I try not to goof off when they do because I don't want Grandpop to be disappointed in me."

"You're a good kid and your grandfather knows it. He'd never be disappointed in you."

"I hope not because I respect him. I hope he respects me, too."

Ali was so pleased by this exchange it left her speechless. But Czar had bolted from the room so it didn't matter she couldn't find her voice to tell him how proud she was of him.

The summer was practically over. Czar's sophomore year was about to begin. With it came another year of summer football practice. Gary was very accommodating to Czar. He arranged Czar's schedule so he could work and not miss practice. Gary was so proud of his first-born grandchild when he went to see him practicing. He gave him tips about the game he loved. Naturally he was too old to play it, but he watched many games on a regular basis.... High school college, professional, etc

"Grandpop, I like it when you come out to practice. The other kids couldn't believe you're my *grand*father. You seem so much younger than the grandparents of my friends."

Gary eagerly relayed this to Tessa that night and she said, "But you must know that you look and act a lot younger than some of your contemporaries. I'd better watch it or I'll lose you to a cheerleader."

"I have the only cheerleader I've ever wanted or ever will want." Tessa blushed coyly and they both went about whatever they were doing.

When the football season and his sophomore year began, Czar was a starter for the team. His grandparents came to every single one of his games. His parents made almost every one. His triplet siblings came a lot, too. Althie was more interested in the band, cheerleaders, and cute guys instead of in the games.

"Althie, do you know anything at all about football?"

"Sure I do. A touchdown is six points and the kick after is one. Each team has four chances to go ten yards. The guys move the sticks when the ball moves. What else is there to know?"

"At that rate, you could coach the team," said Cole, jesting.

"I don't think I'd like that. I'd rather watch the band and cheerleaders," said a very serious Althie.

Cole looked at Ben, shrugged and said, "What do you expect? She's just a girl!"

This football season, as the one prior to it, sped by. Czar was the recipient of the MVP award this time. He was now ready to help with the props for the school play.

This year's play was going to be Romeo and Juliet. Czar truly enjoyed working on the balcony. He liked these team-like activities because he felt projects were fun for everyone. They were like a family grouping or a football team.... All going for one goal.

It was around this time Czar and Susie finally resolved their differences.

After the last night's performance, Susie approached Czar, "Would you like go to the cast party with me?"

"Sure, that'd be fun."

After the party, Susie and Czar walked along the beach, looking at the ocean. They sat down at the water's edge. Timidly he put his arm around her. Before long, they kissed. At this point they both knew there was no chemistry between them. They may have been kissing a sibling for all it meant to either one of them. They giggled and talked.... Something they'd never done before ... except when they taunted each other in the lower grades.

"Well, I guess we were meant to be either enemies or friends," said Susie. "And nothing else."

"Suze, I'd much rather be friends than go back to how we used to be. Remember all of those fights we had? We did and said some rotten things back then."

"I don't have the faintest idea why I felt so much hatred toward you. It's almost as if I was born with it. I felt like the little girl in the movie *The Bad Seed*. Of course, I didn't push you off a pier and drown you but I think maybe I would have liked to."

They both got a chuckle out of this.

"It was like there was a recording playing every night extolling the other's negative qualities."

"Have you.... Well, maybe I shouldn't ask."

"Go ahead."

"Have you ever wondered why our grandparents seem so antagonistic toward each other?"

"All the time. I was going to ask my mom about it but I always thought it was something that she wouldn't want to talk about. Anyhow, I don't see much of her."

"It's never been what's actually been said, just innuendo."

"One of these days, one of us will have to find out." Teasingly, he added, "Let's flip for it.... The loser gets the job."

"I'll see what I can uncover. You've no idea how glad I am we had this talk. Just think of the time we've wasted being enemies, undermining each other. We really could have been quite a team all of these years."

"Well, we can't erase what happened. What we can do is become friends."

"Shall we sign something in our blood?" Susie giggled as she playfully asked this.

Then they kissed platonically and went home. They became as commonplace as Ozzie and Harriet, Lucy and Desi, Burns and Allen, ham and eggs, bagels and lox, etc. They were finally at peace with each other.

And what a beautiful peace it was. They knew they could call upon each other. They could count on the other being there to offer any needed help.

Even Ali had to admit Susie did a great job as Juliet.

"I was really surprised about how good a Juliet Susie was."

"Her grandmother was a pretty good actress or perhaps she was just a good liar."

"Well, to be a good liar, you have to be good at acting or else you could never pull it off."

"That's true. By the way, she and Czar seem to be hitting it off now. There's been a truce. They even went to the cast party together."

"So there's no more tension between them. Isn't that great?"

"Yes, but did Althie ever tell you about the conversation she overheard?"

"No, Mom. But Althie is always overhearing conversations. It's almost as if she puts a glass to the door and listens in."

"She definitely has a keen sense of hearing."

"What about the conversation?"

"I'd prefer it if she told you herself but I guess it won' t hurt. She heard Susie calling Czar a black faggot."

"*NO*, not again."

"Actually this was quite a long time ago. The only reason I mentioned it was to show how far these two have come in their relationship. Now, they don't resort to under-cutting or name calling."

"It used to be so hateful. Going to the cast party is definitely considerable progress."

In the spring of his junior year, Czar got his coveted driver's license. Ali never saw him so willing to go to the grocery store or the cleaner's or even to the dentist. He didn't moan when he had to pick up his sister after her piano lessons, Ben from basketball and Cole from swimming.

Ali and Marc had discussed buying him a used car, but didn't want to give him too much independence.

Susie wanted to work at 'Down Under' during the summer break. Czar was going to put in a word with his grandfather, but Gary approached Czar about it.

"Did you tell Susie to apply for a job here?"

"No. Did she say I did?"

"No, but I wondered why, all of a sudden, she has a burning desire to work for me."

251

"Maybe because she and I are friends now. You know, she's a good, honest worker. If we had the same shift, we'd still be productive. Do you think that you'll be able to hire her?"

"I'm not sure. If you talk to her, tell her to keep all of her other applications open."

"Okay, but I sure hope it works out for her."

A few weeks later, Czar was walking by his parents' bedroom and heard them talking.

"Ali, did I hear you say that Susie applied for a job at 'Down Under' for the summer?"

"Yes. Mom hasn't said anything to Dad about it but I know she's not happy. She says it has to be his decision."

"That sounds like Tessa. She never was one to offer a negative opinion. I remember the first time I met her.... It was Vera's funeral. As a matter of fact, that was the very first time I saw you."

"I don't know if I could have held my tongue all of these years the way she has. It was enough when Dad and Linda had an affair but Susie's uncle looks so much like Czar, I swear he's Daddy's son."

"How did you come up with that?"

"Come on, Marc. I'm not as dumb or as air-brained as I might seem. God, I don't know how Linda had the gall to name him Garrett!"

"Garret is Linda's maiden name. A lot of people name kids that way."

"Oh sure. And just conveniently they shorten his name to Gary or Gar. Anyhow, remember what happened the night that I found out about Dad and Linda? That was the night Czar was conceived. Marc, are you blushing? Do you remember the sex that night? Come here. I'll refresh your memory."

Czar couldn't believe his ears. Not only had his grandfather had an affair with Susie's grandmother and gotten her pregnant, but if it hadn't been for that, he may not have been born. He thought the story about him being a preemie was far-fetched but.... He felt sorry for his grandfather. No wonder he didn't want to hire Susie. He felt soiled in some way. He wasn't sure why. He didn't know if it was because he was ashamed he was an accident or the fact he had eavesdropped. He wasn't going to tell Susie. At least not now.

He was completely taken aback when Susie exclaimed, "Guess what? I got a job at 'Down Under.' Your grandfather called me today."

"Great, Suze." He said this devoid of emotion.

"Yeah. You don't sound as if you think it's so very great. What's the matter? I thought you said it was a good idea."

"I'm sorry. It's just that I have something else on my mind."

"Anything you'd like to share?"

"No. I … I've got some sorting out to do first."

"Okay. Listen, we can have a summer of fun. This is our very last carefree one.… Next summer we'll be readying for college. Have you decided where you really want to go?"

"I haven't even decided if I *really* want to go, period."

Thankfully, Susie changed the subject because Czar wasn't ready to divulge what he had discovered.

That truly was a beautiful summer. They worked hard but they played just as hard. They went boating, to the beach, fishing, water-skiing.… All the outdoor things people do in the summer. They often referred to that summer as one of complete happiness, the transition from childhood to adulthood. They knew this would never come again. But for that matter, what does?

Before long, Czar was a senior at Linfield High. He had done exceptionally well on his SATs (1450) and was readying his college applications. He planned to apply to Duke, Harvard, Princeton and Penn for his first choices. William and Mary, Georgetown, Penn State and Villanova were his additional choices.

Ali didn't want to influence his choice so she remained mute. The only thing she wanted to suggest was for him to apply as a minority. Marc was vehemently opposed to this. He felt Czar could hold his own with the rest of America's seniors. He didn't want him to hide behind his color.

It never even dawned on Czar to do this. He applied in the usual way, convinced merit would prevail.

Despite any misgivings she may have entertained, Ali was proud her son wasn't going to use the practice of claiming minority status to achieve majority success.

As in the past, Ali decided she would have Thanksgiving dinner. She, Tessa and Treva always prepared for the family feasts, no matter whose house was hosting them. This year was going to be the last time all of the family was intact. No one was completely sure where Czar was going to go to school so it wasn't certain when he'd be home for Thanksgiving again.

Two days before Thanksgiving, Tessa and Treva came to Ali's house to start preparing the food.

Treva's job was to make the pies (pumpkin, sweet potato and mince), the pumpkin cheesecake, the decorated pound cake and the rolls.

Tessa was going to make the homemade pasta, marinara sauce, cranberry sauce, watercress sauce, broccoli casserole and the two stuffings (apple/raisin bread as well as the traditional celery/onion/bread one).

Ali's job was mostly last-minute stuff.... Mashed potatoes, turkey, ham, cranberry Jell-O mold and hors d'oeuvres.

Czar walked into the kitchen after school and football practice, saying, "Wow, it smells good in here. What can I have?"

"Get out of here, Chad Zachary Rosen Green, before you nibble on something you shouldn't." They were all laughing.

"You have enough food here for an army. What regiment is coming?"

"Czar, there are six of us," said Ali. "Grandmom Tessa, Grandpop Gary, Grandmom Becky, Grandpop Jake, GG Rita, GG Mabel, Aunt Treva, Uncle Cliff, his three children and your two cousins. With your math acumen, you know the total's 19."

"Well, it looks as if there's going to be enough for twice that. A little piece of Aunt Treva's pumpkin pie won't be missed. Right, Aunt Treva?"

"Czar, how do you suppose it will look on Thanksgiving if I serve a pie with a piece missing?"

"Well, I've a better idea. Bake two and you can give me that one now."

"If that's the only way to get rid of you, gladly. It's a wonder you can run around the football field with all you eat."

"I don't eat much, I just eat frequently. At least that's what my mom always says about me. Anyhow, when can I come back for my pie?"

"Okay, Czar, give me an hour and you'll have your pie."

Czar playfully pinched his Aunt Treva on the cheek and said. "I knew you'd see things my way."

The cooks remained busy throughout the day. They froze the cakes, pies and rolls, figuring they would keep better. If there were any leftovers, as there was bound to be, they would be fresh. Likewise the broccoli casserole was frozen, as was the marinara sauce and the stuffings. The other things were going to be made Wednesday and Thursday.

After preparing the batter of the baked goods, Treva brought them to 'Down Under' to bake them in the commercial ovens. That way they would all get done at approximately the same time. She did use Ali's oven for the one pumpkin pie that she had promised to Czar.

Tessa also prepared her freezeable portion at Ali's and likewise, brought them to 'Down Under' for the same reason that Treva did.

Ali merely oversaw their projects because her assignments had to be completed later.... Perhaps Wednesday night.

Althie was nowhere to be found. She always had after-school activities and besides, she really didn't like kitchen work ... as she called it.

Her job would be to set the table and help serve.

Preparations aside, the day of the game had arrived. Czar was the quarterback for Linfield High. Determined to go to her son's senior game, Ali got up at 5:30 and put her turkey in the oven. She had made the mashed potatoes the day before as she had learned that they did well being warmed in the microwave. She also prepared everything else the day before, save the vegetables and dip, the melon and prosciutto, pepperoni and cheese.... All the good-tasting things that played havoc with cholesterol.

Ali got the kids up at 8:30 so they could eat in ample time ... especially Czar. Althie still had to perform her chore.... Setting the Thanksgiving table. She didn't mind this because she loved the autumnal colors. She mixed the green, orange, brown and rust napkins atop a beige, burlap tablecloth.

The large table was for the senior members. The picnic style for the mid to older kids and the smallest for the triplets and Treva's kids.

After a hearty breakfast of chipped creamed beef and/or an omelet with mushrooms and cheese, Czar readied himself to go to the football locker room. Althie was going to go with her mom and dad. Since Rita was not a football fan, she was staying at her granddaughter's house with Mabel to turkeysit.

At last the football team was introduced and the national anthem was sung.

The brisk November air was invigorating. Linfield High was touted to lose. However, their defense really held Norwood High. It was the final seconds of the fourth quarter.... Norwood 13-Linfield 7. The ball was on the Norwood two-yard line. It was fourth and goal. The quarterback, Czar, passed the ball successfully to the wide receiver. The crowd went wild. Suddenly out of nowhere, there was an offensive call. The yellow penalty flag never appeared so stark as it had now; besmirching the integrity of the green playing field. The crowd waited as the five-yard penalty was imposed. Czar was outwardly cool but his stomach was doing flips. His teammates lined up, bound and determined to give it their all.

The ball was snapped to Czar from the center. Czar scanned the end zone and saw his men had double coverage. Then, the center began plunging through the maze of Norwood players with Czar carrying the ball, following on his heels. As Czar approached the one-yard line, the big defensive tackle from Norwood clutched him about his waist, trying to bring him down. It was only through a huge second effort and supreme determination that Czar victoriously crossed the goal line, thus tying the score. The crowd broke into a boisterous roar.

After the raucous uproar, silence reigned upon the crowd. It was time for the extra point. The center snapped the ball to Czar. He faked left and threw right. The wide receiver juggled the ball, then grabbed it tightly, pulling it into his chest. Final score.... Linfield 15- Norwood 13. Linfield and Czar had pulled it off.

The Linfield players were jubilant. Before they were let go to celebrate, the Linfield band played the Alma Mater and the crowd sang;

There is a place where we go to learn....
Preparing for a happy future which we yearn....
It is hidden by trees within the street....
Near a fountain where we all meet.
A building which towers above the rest....
Linfield High, you are the best.
We love your colors of green and blue....
But most of all, we love you.

When the crowd had come to the word green, the students let their green and blue balloons fly into the air. Ali hugged Marc tightly. She felt her eyes fill with tears when the offensive linemen hoisted Czar and the coach on their shoulders, carrying them both into the locker room.

After making his way through the crowd, Marc joined the other male parents in the locker room. He saw Czar was in the center of the group. Marc thought his heart would burst with pride. He worked his way through the crowd of fathers and gradually got to Czar. Czar's face lit up when he saw his dad. He hugged Marc tightly. Never was the bond between them stronger than at that moment. Never would it be the same again.

Almost everyone had arrived at the Green household by the time Czar came in. The family gave him a hero's welcome. The triplets wouldn't let him alone, until finally, Ali called them all to the table. The Thanksgiving festivities were about to begin.

Ali looked out over her table to the other tables and her heart was overflowing with pride and love. She wasn't paying attention until she heard Marc's voice saying, "...and so we've had much to be thankful for throughout the years. Today's victory, as well as Czar's athletic prowess, were both sweet, but the best reward is we're all here ... healthy, happy and eager for more of what life has to offer. Now let's bow our heads and repeat The Lord's Prayer."

After that, everyone dug in, ate and chatted.

That night, the triplets had a birthday party to attend and Czar had a victory party at Susie's house. Though both sets of grandparents were bitter enemies because of the history, they didn't express any displeasure. If the two ever became an item, they didn't want an aftermath of additional hard feelings.

The shy Czar went victoriously, yet timidly, to the party. He was always insecure at these social fetes. He was uncomfortable making small talk.

As he was walking toward the house, he almost bumped into another partygoer who was, likewise, heading to the house from the opposite path.

"Hi," said Julie.

"Hi," replied Czar. "Do I know you?"

"Not really. I didn't go to Linfield. I did see that game today. Nice going. My name's Julie Martin. I live near here and know most of your classmates."

"Czar Green, but I guess you already know that."

They shook hands, not knowing their lives had been changed forever. Both of them felt the electrical charge between them.

As soon as Czar entered Susie's house, the teenagers already gathered burst into a rendition of *For Czar's a Jolly Good Fellow*.

With that introduction, Czar became more comfortable and secure.

A few weeks after Thanksgiving, Mabel had a massive heart attack. She was pronounced dead at Linfield General. Czar asked his father if he could give his great-grandmother's eulogy. Marc was pleased his oldest child wanted to do this.

"Let me introduce myself to those who may not know me," Czar began, with his quivering voice showing he was on the verge of tears. "I'm the first great-grandchild of Mabel Green. Yes, there are some among you who may not have known the relationship she and I shared. Believe me, it's not because my father and mother, or the rest of our family, tried to keep it a secret. We always encouraged GG Mabel to come to our house, but she only consented to make her rare appearances at Thanksgiving and Christmas. She felt we could pass ourselves off as being white if she stayed out of our lives. That's not something we wanted to do. Some among you may not have known of our black heritage. Does it matter to you, now that you do know? I'm not naïve enough to think it doesn't matter to some of you. However, I would hope those of you are in the minority.

"My great-grandmother truly was a wise, kind and gentle woman. She turned to God when many would have felt abandoned by Him. She had many losses in her life; not the least of which was my Aunt Vera, who died out of an act of violence. Some here may remember, all too well, what happened in that instance. I'm not going to expound on that issue. Today we're celebrating the life of a woman who was wise beyond her educational level, who was tolerant when others may not have been, who was selfless in all of her actions. She worked for many of you in the past. Because of her work ethic, it's just been recently she consented to stop working. You see, work ethics are either a part of your being or altogether absent.

"It doesn't matter if you are white, black, oriental or any other minority, you either have self-respect or you don't. You either join the human race or you don't. I know a typical black person is depicted as lazy and shiftless with their hands held out to Whitey, waiting for reparation for the injustices of slavery to be equalized. Well, if some are, they're going to have a long wait. The ancestors of many people here in church came to America after slavery was abolished. Some have not been in America as long as my great-grandmother's forefathers. I know my other set of great-grandparents came over in the early nineteen hundreds. Can we in Black America expect them to know what slaves had endured? For that matter, could any of us in America fathom what the Jews endured in World War II when Hitler was on the rampage?

" I guess what I'm trying to say is, instead of wasting time bemoaning the life of her ancestors, my GG Mabel thanked God for every day she was able to provide for herself and my father. She lived her life the way she would have expected any decent human to do, never discriminating against anyone less fortunate than she and always willing to lend a helping hand wherever and whenever it was needed. I'd like to say thank you, GG, for a job well done."

At the end of this eulogy, Marc hugged his son. He then buried his face in the young boy's shoulder and cried.

Mabel was put to rest in the same cemetery where her granddaughter had been interred many years before. Those attending the funeral were many of Mabel's employers. While some of them did know the link between Mabel and Marc, the ones who didn't admired Czar's courage in apprising people of his lineage.

Before long, it was April. Czar's college acceptances were rolling in. He had a decision to make. Although he knew what he wanted to do, he hesitated telling his family. He knew it would upset them. He decided to try it out on Grandmom Tessa first.

"Grandmom, I really don't want to go to college right now. I'd like to take a year off, go to California and learn art on the streets."

"Czar, I can't tell you what to do. I do know all these years, your parents have counted on you going to college. They'll be pretty disappointed."

"I don't mean I won't go to school. I'm just postponing it. I've been in my parents' home all these years and I'd like a taste of life on my own before I settle down to get ready for my working life."

"You're the one who has to live your life. I can't tell you what to do. One thing to remember is that sometimes, when you take time off to do something, you never go back to your original path."

"But I have to learn by my own mistakes. Mom's told me a million times about what happened when you and Grandpop got married. Look at all the time wasted by not letting kids do what they wanted to do."

"That was different. Our parents were afraid of the obstacles we'd have to overcome. Interreligious marriages weren't an everyday occurrence back then."

"But when Mom and Dad got married, neither were interracial ones."

"True. Look, I can't give you my blessing on this. But I won't do anything to stand in your way, either."

"Well, at first, what I really wanted was for you to tell my parents. But maybe if you're just there when I tell them, it won't be as hard."

"I'll be there with you. Just let me know where and when."

"Thanks. You're great!" And he kissed Tessa on the cheek.

And so, Tessa, Ali and Czar were sitting at the Linfield Country Club. After they ordered, Tessa nodded to Czar to begin.

"Mom, Grandmom knows what I'm going to say. I want to postpone going to college. I want to go to California for a while to learn more about painting by doing rather than sitting in a methods class. When I come back, I'll go to college."

Ali's mouth dropped open. "I'm speechless. This has taken me completely by surprise. What makes you want to do this? How did you ever decide this?"

"I just feel I'm too limited in my approach to art because I haven't done enough living. I've never tasted the real world. I want to feel life so I can paint it better."

"Czar, painting is a difficult field to enter and be successful. Why can't you start college this fall? Dad and I will be happy to send you to California during the summer after your freshman year."

"But Mom, you don't understand. I *really* want to do this. I'm sure I can get a deferment from my college acceptances."

"I know I'm speaking for your father as well as myself in telling you if you choose to follow this path, we won't finance it. Sorry, but that's just the way it is."

Tessa then entered into this exchange as she looked at her daughter and said, "Wouldn't you rather he be up front with you, instead of going to college and taking up time, space and money?"

"I just hate to see him waste his time doing this scheme."

"I wish you'd stop talking about me as if I'm not here."

"We're not deliberately ignoring you. I'm trying to present your side to your mother, even though, in essence, I agree with her."

"Mom, you don't have to explain yourself to him," Ali admonished. She turned to Czar and said, "I think it was unconscionable for you to go to your grandmother to have her run interference for you! Why didn't you talk to Dad and me? Your grandmother has always acted as buffer for you. I think it's high time you stood on your own two feet."

"Did you ever stop to think maybe you don't listen to me unless someone else helps me present my wishes?"

"That's both untrue and unkind," interjected Tessa.

"That's all right, Mom. Let him talk. Maybe we can clear up a few things."

"Mom, you always let me shift for myself. You're always fussing with Althie and the boys. You never really have time for me and my problems."

"Listen, young man, if you'll remember, Grandpop Gary had quite a severe accident a few years ago because of just the opposite. I thought we reached a happy medium."

"Ali, Czar, rehashing all of this isn't going to do any good. Let's deal with the situation at hand."

"Which is that my firstborn has decided to forego college and flit around San Francisco with a brush, easel and paint!"

Czar just rolled his eyes and said, "Never mind, Grandmom. She won't even try to listen. I hope I have better luck with Dad, but I doubt it."

True to his words, Marc was not an easy sell. He secretly admired Czar's gumption but wouldn't verbalize it. He felt the chances of Czar pursuing college after being on his own were slim to none, but he didn't pull the carpet out from under him.

The family gave him a half-hearted blessing, knowing he, too, had to do what he felt was right.

Graduation day came. Czar and Susie were speakers for the commencement exercise. Czar made his announcement from the podium.

"…and so, fellow classmates, we're at yet another beginning…. The preparation for our future lives. Many are going to college. Some are going directly to work. Some are going for technical training. I'm going west to paint the realities of life. Hopefully, one day, you'll come to a showing of my works. Good-bye, good luck and God bless you."

Susie was the first to start the standing ovation. Other classmates stood and the guests in the audience followed suit. Whether the reason they were applauding so vehemently was his courage, commencement itself or the end of the ceremony was unclear.

The day came for Czar's departure. He had worked mostly all summer and saved enough to get started in San Francisco.

The day was clear and bright as they drove to the Philadelphia airport. Gary and Tessa had the triplets with them while Ali, Marc and Czar went in the other car.

Althie, to the surprise of everyone, including herself, cried, "I'm going to miss you so much. I'm afraid you'll never come back here to live." She gave Czar an afghan as a going-away present. She had crocheted it herself. She was proud of the alternating blue and green colors of Linfield High she had placed within the work.

The older adults remained stoic while Ben and Cole showed more interest in the plane than their brother's departure.

"We'll come visit," said Ali. "I don't know when, but we will."

"I'm counting on it. How about you, Grandmom? Will you and Grandpop visit me?"

"We'll try. But surely you'll come back east to settle down eventually."

Since Czar didn't want this good-bye to be confrontational, he said nothing. He knew his grandmother was sincere in what she said and wasn't trying to open up an unfriendly discussion. He just hugged her tightly. One could feel the mutual love between these two kindred spirits.

Czar spent the first week sightseeing, riding the cable cars and doing all the things first-time visitors do.

He had gotten a room where a lot of the other would-be painters lived. Gradually, he made friends.

One day, he was walking along the wharf when he heard someone calling his name.

"Czar. Czar Green, Yo, wait up!"

Czar, deep in his thoughts, racked with homesickness, looked for the person who was calling his name.

"Czar, over here. It's me Julie Martin from Linfield."

"My God! You're the very first person I've seen from home. It's good to see you."

"Same here. Listen, I have to hurry to an appointment, why don't we hook up later?"

"Sure, how about dinner?"

Julie agreed so they met later that night.

"I'm here to learn all I can about painting. How about you?"

"I came to establish residency and eventually go to college. In the meantime, I'll take photographs. I enjoy doing that. Besides, I can earn money by selling pictures. When I was little I got a disc camera and then took a photography course. Have you ever seen some of the pitiful pictures people take on vacations? They'd be better off buying picture postcards and either check or chuck their cameras."

Czar listened to Julie's every word. He realized perhaps, he, too, should follow the same path and establish residency. He could always attend college out here. He and Julie walked and talked. Eventually they ran into a girl named Kate, who Julie had met upon arriving in California. The three of them went to Czar's room, where they talked, played music and drank beer.

Before long, Kate began massaging Czar's back, while Julie began massaging Kate's. Kate kissed Czar, after which Julie started massaging Czar's back, chest and waist. Czar was becoming tumescent. Before he knew what was happening, Czar was performing oral sex on Julie while Kate was doing the same thing to him. Czar was the first one to achieve orgasm. He was slightly embarrassed about losing control. The others didn't seem to notice or care. They were raring to go so they continued.

Next time, Julie took Czar orally as Czar fondled Kate's genitals. Before long, Czar was ready again. He entered Julie as Kate tickled his tongue with hers.

He exploded within Julie. This was the most wonderful feeling he ever encountered. Although he was spent, he welcomed Julie's tongue in his mouth as he gently lowered Kate onto his upright member. Czar never dreamed real sex could be this good. He'd always thought the locker room talk was just a bunch of bull.

The trio continued throughout the night. The closeness of someone helped to ease Czar's homesickness..

The next night, he called home.

"Hi, Mom. How are ya doing?" asked Czar with a definite lilt to his voice.

"Hi, Czar. My God, do you feel as great as you sound?"

"Oh, yes. I'm making friends every day and getting acclimated. I'm going to check about getting a job in a restaurant either bussing tables or waiting them.... Whichever I can get."

"You know your grandfather waited tables when he and my mother were expecting me. They didn't have it easy at first because my father had no formal education." As soon as the words were out of her mouth, she regretted them.

"Mom. Please. I'm about 3000 miles away from you so don't berate me."

"I'm sorry. That's not what I meant to do. Althie is crocheting you another afghan. The boys are giving her grief about it because she's yet to make one for either of them. How's your painting coming? Are you making any headway?"

Czar had a private chuckle. He had much headway within the past twenty-four hours, but somehow he didn't think that was what his mother was talking about.

"Not really. I'm still getting the feel of it."

"Dad and I may come out in September. We'll let you know when, as well as where we'll be staying once we've made our plans."

"Great. Listen, I've got to go. I'll call next week, okay?"

"Fine. We all love you."

"I love all of you, too, Mom. So long."

When Czar got off the phone, he felt a little blue so he called Julie and Kate. Kate was busy, but Julie agreed to meet him.

Julie and Czar went to a local hangout. Julie saw a girl named Dana. Both of these young people suggested Dana accompany them for a night of fun. The three of them spent hours traipsing from one bar to another.

Instead of winding up at Czar's, they ended up at Julie's place. Dana was really turned on. She had a zest for sex. She was actually quite proficient at it. She went back and forth from Czar to Julie, performing expert oral sex on both of them. She stopped short of having them climax, making them beg for more. Czar and Julie could no longer contain themselves. Czar entered Dana, who was bringing Julie to a climax orally. It was because of this expertise Julie and Czar dubbed her as the girl with the dancing tongue. This scene was repeated nightly for a while until Dana got bored.

Czar thought he and Julie should cool this activity for a while and get down to work. Julie had planned to paint but decided on photography instead. They both ventured out to try their hands at their chosen fields. Julie went to take pictures and Czar began painting in earnest.

Julie introduced Czar to drugs, or as they called it, recreational relief. Since Czar was health-conscious, he didn't continue using them. And Julie was afraid of the legal consequences so their drug usage was short-lived. So they relied upon alcohol as their drug of choice.

Together they spent many evenings choosing different girls to join them in their sexual experimentation. Sometimes, it was both a guy and a girl, making their duet, first into a trio, then a quartet.

Whether his sexual release was the reason or not, Czar's painting went on to a greater depth. Initially he felt his painting had looked more like paint by numbers. As he threw himself more into his work, it began to take on a greater height. The days flew by. Before long, his mom and dad came to visit. He virtually abandoned his friends to spend all of his time with his parents.

He and Marc had a private conversation away from his mother's ears.

"I know your plans are indefinite, but secretly I always wanted you to go to law school. I'd eventually go into private practice.... Green and Green.... A criminal defense team."

"I've never even entertained the idea of law school. Don't take this wrong, but I'm not a good liar."

"Where'd you get the idea a *good* lawyer has to lie?"

"Well, if you know your client's guilty, you'd be lying by defending him."

"First of all, you don't necessarily *know* that your client is guilty. Second, you can't knowingly lie. Everyone's innocent until proven guilty beyond a reasonable doubt."

"Well, I'm not a good poker player because I don't bluff well. What's on my mind is written all over my face."

"It takes practice to develop a stone face. That comes with time. But let me point something else out to you, two people, as innocent bystanders, could view something in two entirely different ways."

"Well, anyway, don't wait for me, Dad. Law is definitely not an option."

Marc was silently relieved he had chosen to have this encounter when Ali wasn't around or it would have escalated into World War III.

Soon it was time for Marc and Ali to bid Czar a fond farewell. Ali, who had held her tongue so far, said, "You've been here about three months now. If I understand correctly, you're considered a resident after six. Do you think you'll enroll in classes soon?"

"Mom, don't pressure me. You, yourself, said that my painting had potential. I'd hate to stop painting now. This is *my* life and I have to do what's right for *me*! I can't be molded or pressed out like one of your Christmas cookies."

"Czar, hold on a minute. There's no need to talk to your mother that way. Especially since we're leaving today. That's no way to part from loved ones."

"Then maybe you'd better lecture your wife."

"Being a smart ass will get you nowhere. My wife, if you'll remember, is still your mother. I'm sure you've heard you should honor thy father and thy mother."

"Maybe an adjunct to that should be; honor thy father and mother when and if they honor you."

"Okay, that's enough. Do you think you'll be coming home for Christmas? We'll gladly send you airfare."

"I really can't say. It depends on what I'm working on at the time."

"Well, the welcome mat is always out; either for a visit or a return to your home." And she embraced her firstborn tightly.

"Dad, Mom, I can't begin to tell you how much I've enjoyed your visit. I wish the rest of the family could come out here, too. I know that GM and GP were here for their twenty-fifth anniversary in 1978. The triplets haven't been here, though. Talk to GM and GP. Try to convince them to take a break and come out."

"I will. They might just do it."

Czar said good-bye and his parents left on their scheduled flight. He was eager to get back to Julie. During his parents' visit, he had spent all of his time with them in exclusion of all of his newfound friends.

When Czar returned home, he was stunned to see a note in his mailbox from Julie. Julie and four or five others were hitchhiking to the northwestern part of the United States, determined somehow to get to Alaska. Julie had always been a lover of animals and wanted photos of them in their natural habitat, Denali National Park. In the letter, it said the group was going to sign on a cruise ship in Anchorage going on to Juneau, Sitka and other ports, planning to disembark in Vancouver. No one likes to think of their lover as testing other waters but he was sure that Julie was doing just that. It didn't appear as if their relationship was exclusive up to this point. Something he hoped to rectify soon.

Czar was heartbroken he hadn't been included in the group. He realized the pain he was feeling would enhance his painting even further. He delved into his work with an exuberance he didn't know he had. He had deferred his sexual encounters, not wanting to have any deterrent to his blossoming easel.

He had painted a portrait of his sister and two brothers, which he took from a family photo. One of his best works was done during this dark period of his life. It was a portrait of his mother and grandmother. He entitled it 'Beauty in Memory.' He eventually sent them a photo of it. He heard when they saw it they both cried. He felt it was easy to make them beautiful because they both had supreme depth. Even if he was hard pressed for money, this was one painting on which there would never be a price. He didn't know which one to give it to so they'd eventually have dual ownership.... Six months in one house and six months in the other. Another of his favorites was entitled 'Fleeting Life.' It was a picture of a rose, first as a bud, which slowly bloomed in the next frames and progressed to a bare stem in the final segment.

He did stills of the wharf area, expertly catching the area's unique beauty. He thought perhaps he was ready to go to some art dealers to show his work. He was devastated when most of the dealers didn't share his enthusiasm; but he was heartened when one of them finally agreed to take a couple of paintings to see what the market would allow.

Excited, Czar called his grandmother, who had always encouraged his artistic endeavors.

"Hi, it's me. Czar."

"Czar, for goodness' sakes. I know who it is. It hasn't been that long. Is anything wrong?" Tessa was wary because it seemed that he only phoned when he was in need of something.... Money or medical advice.

"No, actually something is very right. I dropped a few of my paintings to a dealer who thinks he'll be able to sell them. I called you before I called home because I remember how you always told me talent would eventually win out ... that cream always rises to the top. I can't tell you how glad I am I came out here. It's like a whole new world has opened up for me. Living on my own, I'm learning more about art than I ever could have at a university. I guess what's really changed is the depth of my feeling."

Tessa shuddered. She was worried that Czar had endured some sadness in his recent life, which had increased his insight. Not wanting to dampen his spirits, she didn't vocalize her fears.

So she merely asked, "How are you signing your works?"

"Chad Green. I thought I'd be taken more seriously that way. Besides, I'm sure Mom and Dad would like it that way."

"Czar, as long as you're happy and content, I'm sure your parents will be likewise. I prefer the idea of just 'Czar' on your paintings. It has a dramatic flare. But sign them however you're most comfortable. Do you plan to come home for Christmas? It doesn't appear as if we can make it out there before spring."

"I'm disappointed. I thought maybe someone in my family could come out for Thanksgiving."

"I don't like to leave my mother on holidays. She and Dad always especially loved Thanksgiving. I'd feel as if I was forsaking her if I came out there."

"I understand," said Czar, who wondered if he really did. "I'll let you know about Christmas."

After bidding each other good-bye, they hung up.

Czar knew that he hadn't really fooled his perceptive grandmother. He hadn't told her how alone and lonely he was without Julie and company. He knew she detected something was amiss. He tried to rise up from the doldrums but the more he tried, the deeper he descended. He remained in a blue frame of mind until a few days later when he received a letter from Julie.

Dear Czar,

This is great! I got a few snaps of a bear in Denali and some of the whales playing hide and go seek in the water with each other. I'm sorry you couldn't come. The glaciers are stupendous, especially the great one.... Mendenhall in Juneau. I felt as if I had skipped to the moon; that's how foreign the walk was. I haven't done any painting but if I'm inclined to do so, will use my pictures as well as my imagination. If not, maybe you can create some masterpieces from my shots. We'll be home in a couple of weeks.

See ya,
Julie

Although aware of the casualness of the letter, the mere fact Julie had even written lifted his spirits so high he realized what had been gnawing at him since the gang departed. He was in love with Julie. He was eager to see, after he professed his love, if the feeling was reciprocated.

The day after the letter arrived, he went to the dealership to discover that one of his paintings had been sold that morning. If that wasn't enough, the person had requested a different view of the wharf and had left some snapshots of what he wanted.

Czar was ecstatic! He wanted to share the news with his grandmother but called his mother and father first.

"Hi Mom, guess what?"

Biting her tongue so she wouldn't reply, 'You're coming home,' she asked, "Are you okay?"

"Mom, I sold a painting! I actually sold a painting. The person wants me to paint a few more, too. It looks like I'm on my way."

"That's terrific. Now you can come home, go to school and continue painting on the side."

"Mom, I think that San Francisco is my destiny. I've become more aware of what goes into a good portrait. I watch how people hold their hands, how their eyes twinkle, how they cock their heads.... All things that go into making me a better painter. I am not as stilted as I would be in a methods

267

class. I've become a people watcher. If you don't do that, you may just as well as buy a good camera and take some pictures. When you paint a portrait, you capture the soul of the person. I may enroll in a few classes here, but as far as coming home, I just don't know. It would be different. I don't think it's a good idea. I'm not your little boy anymore."

Ali thought hard and long before she responded, "It appears as if 'Go West Young Man' is something I guess you've taken quite seriously. Well, God bless you. Please visit us at Christmas." Ali forgot to give him the latest news. She had taken a job as a school nurse. She'd have to remember to tell him next time.

Czar felt freer after this conversation than at any other time in his life.

Forty-one

Czar had already spent a year in California. It was then that it became apparent that college was way off in the future, if at all.

Susie came out for a visit. It was during a break from her nursing school. However, she fell in love with the area and decided to transfer her credits and finish up on the West Coast. Her grandparents were okay with this and God knows where her mother was. They said as long as she continued her education, she could stay.

Anyhow, Susie made sure Czar took better care of himself. He used to eat on the run and sleep only after completing a piece that he wanted to get just right. The canvas had to speak to him, or so he said. Susie encouraged his work, acting as a critic. She wouldn't let him consider something done until he had captured what he told her he was trying to achieve. Sometimes, she was brutal. But when she liked it, she was effusive with her praise. Something which drove Julie absolutely crazy. They got along like prickly porcupines.... Neither wanted to get too close to the other. They were pretty sarcastic in all of their conversations. In their own way, they were possessive of Czar. He hated to be in their company when, on rare occasions, they happened to be together. It was hard juggling these friends.

The letters from Linfield were always a welcome sight. He remembered one in particular, that he got from his grandmother. She and his grandfather always went into New York to see shows. One show upset her so much that they walked out. It was *Torch Song Trilogy*. It was about gay people. She felt people are too harsh on them. She said love was so fleeting one should accept it whenever they can. As long as no one deliberately hurts another, people should cling together and face the world together. That's how Czar's parents and grandparents had done it. Strength comes in unity. She went on to say she had been upset because Althie was seeing a young Pakistani who not only was dark, but also had different customs. However, she knew she was being foolish because who knew how many other young men of different cultures, beliefs and family values Althie would see before finding Mr. Right.

That was the one letter he kept in a safe spot because it made him see that no matter what path he took, she'd always be in his corner. For that matter,

269

his entire family's love was given unconditionally. He never had any doubts
about that.

And once again, Julie was off to God knows where. Although Czar didn't
like this, he was the beneficiary of many pictures he could use for paintings.
By this time Julie had sold many pictures and was in demand for various
photo shoots.

So Susie and Czar hung out. They went to Disney Land and had loads of
fun. They were as close as brother and sister, without the sibling rivalry.
They both loved the Matterhorn and Fantasyland.

They had fun composing some poetry when they got back.

The life of a child is fun to recall. ...
It's really a small world after all.
The laughter of the young is delightful to hear. ...
The sound of their voices extremely dear.
If you want to see inhibitions fly away. ...
Take the kids to Disney Land today.
If in a depressed or grumpy mood. ...
A fantasy life will cease you to brood.
We all grow up, at least, we hope.
But why not explore things within your scope. ...
Of the happy go lucky world of the young?
Because adult life can be full of dung.

They had a great time writing and laughing but before long Czar got
despondent and composed this eerie poem.

The sound of death is ringing in my head,
It's a sound that I really don't dread.
The poignant silence of a corpse grown cold,
Makes some of the bravest of us no longer bold.
The crying around the coffin and hearse. ...
Just seems to make many feel worse.
The gladiolas are arranged around the funeral bier. ...
With the smell of the flowers dispelling some fear.
There is nothing that can take the place of a life. ...
Even though it is no longer burdened with strife.
When the time comes for one to depart. ...
They may readily take a piece of your heart.

Do not cry for me, now I am free. ...
To go to heaven and live happily.
None of us knows when the end is near. ...
So please, live for now and not for next year.

Susie said, "That' so morbid." And she began to cry.

"Have you ever thought about your death and how people will be affected by it?"

"When I was a little girl and my mom made me mad, I would pretend I was dying of something horrible. Then I'd visualize her as being very sad at my funeral and sorry how she treated me."

"Well, I'm not afraid of dying. At least I don't think I am. I wonder how it'll happen, though, and hope I'm ready when it comes." Czar became pensive, thinking about how poorly he had been feeling, but at the same time refusing to let his fear of a pending illness enter into their conversation.

Times with Susie usually weren't serious. They had fun together but Czar's chemistry didn't react to her, nor for that matter neither did hers to him. He lusted after Julie like a puppy after a little ball. But since Julie was away, he and Susie took another one of their explorative trips. They went to Mt. Rainier National Park.

"Oh, look at the view from here," exclaimed, Susie who was always thrilled with nature's wonders.

Czar looked out over it and agreed that it was a sight to behold. He did much of his dreaming on these trips with Susie. They both remembered how they would climb to a tiny mountaintop in Linfield and pretend they were kings of the hill.

They toured the rest of Seattle by bus. It was rainy and the bus driver encouraged them to think of that as liquid sunshine.

Czar, who was always quick with the quips, said, "I prefer my sun in rays, not sprays."

When they stopped to visit the University of Washington, they were impressed that boats could be docked near the sports complex, enabling boaters to 'park' near the event.

Czar and Susie thought the northwest was beautiful; whereas Julie just viewed it as a place to take some cool saleable shots. In that young person's eyes, everything was superficial.

Unavoidably, there was a trip coming up which included both Julie and Susie. It was to Yellowstone National. Czar was being tugged in two different directions. But Julie made it easy for him. Julie was going to tent with some others in the gang. Naturally this left Czar out in the cold.

Julie said Czar wanted to get up at dawn but Julie and the rest preferred to view the park at dusk as well as under the stars. Anyhow, that was the explanation offered.

"For God's sake, Czar. Stop pouting. You don't own me. Don't fence me in. I don't want to be permanently in your corral."

Czar could have bitten his tongue if he could only have taken his words back that had provoked this exchange; but like yesterday, the spoken word can't be retracted.

The whole group was viewing Old Faithful when it erupted.

Susie was biblical in her opinion of the sight. "Look, it's like a cup overflowing with happiness."

Julie looked at her like she was from another planet, thinking how corny, and added, "More like a guy masturbating."

Things such as this turned Susie off. She chose to absent herself from Czar for a while so she wouldn't have to be exposed to Julie … or the DO…. Despicable One.

Before long San Francisco was starting to look like a miniature Linfield. Rad Richards had moved here. Czar hadn't come across him until recently. Rad was a very successful stockbroker. He was going to marry a girl who had graduated from Linfield High a few years after him. Ironically enough, they'd never met in their hometown. They met at UCLA where they both received their degrees in business. Czar and he always had a special connection. They hadn't seen each other for a while, but like all true friends, they picked up where they left off.

Julie was away again but Czar had no time to miss his friend. Between his painting and not feeling well, he was preoccupied. He had swollen glands in his neck and ran a fever periodically. He had a sore throat and had depletion of energy. He didn't have time to go to a doctor so he just ignored his symptoms.

Susie's grandmother came to visit. She knew how close the two had become so she told Susie to invite Czar.

This was the first time they'd been together since the Yellowstone trip, which was quite a disaster.

After they dropped Czar off, Linda asked, "Susie, what's wrong with Czar? His eyes are sad and expressionless. Is there anything wrong with him?"

"I think you're reading something into it. He's been busy with his painting. He probably doesn't eat right or get enough sleep."

"Well, I hope that's the case. I know that you two are close." And with that, the conversation ended.

But Susie's grandmother had piqued her brain. So she called Czar.

"Are you okay? My grandmother was worried about you. She thought you looked sick."

"I'm fine."

"Are you sure?"

"How many ways can I say it? I am *fine!*" With that he hung up.

Rather than confront her fears, she remained in denial, taking him at his word.

Forty-two

Some months later, she saw Czar again. It was at Rad and Liz's wedding. Czar was an usher.

The ushers all took turns toasting the newlyweds and before long it was Czar's turn.

He stood, raised his glass and said, "May Rad and Liz live to a ripe old age together and meet their Maker surrounded by their children, grandchildren and some friends, not the least of whom I hope will be me."

The toast was so ominous that Susie felt a chill go over her but the room temperature was about 70^0. She tried to make eye contact with Czar but by then, he was on the dance floor doing the electric slide. Julie wasn't there so he was less inhibited and became one of the gang.

Susie didn't know where to turn. She knew even if he were sick he wouldn't consciously do anything to put his painting on hold. Even if it meant sacrificing his health. She played mental gymnastics with herself but decided not to act. Later she would view this as neglect. She especially regretted her silence when a friend told her she had seen Czar and Julie at the movies. The girl was appalled at how horrendous Czar looked. He could have been on a Holocaust poster, he was so emaciated. Also, one side of his neck had a lump somewhere between a golf ball and an orange. And it was then that it hit her!

Julie came back again after doing a camera shoot at Alcatraz. Susie knew when she and Julie were together it made Czar nervous. But she didn't care to be in Julie's company anyhow so she chose to absent herself.

"You missed Althie and the boys," said Czar in his pouting mode.

"So, maybe I'll see them next time," said Julie, having no real desire to see any of Czar's family. Czar was too emotionally entwined with his siblings as far as Julie was concerned. Julie had no time for this. Family was something you only had to see on special occasions but other than that, who cared?

Czar picked up on the indifference immediately and although hurt, he didn't express his views. Instead they got off on a tangent. He did admit to himself he enjoyed some philosophical conversations he and Julie had. Susie was more fun, but Julie made him think.

"So Czar, what would you like to be reincarnated as?"

"I don't know. Probably the same starving artist."

"Oh, yeah. Like you don't make enough money at the restaurant."

"But at this point, if I had to depend on my paint sales for money, I'd be a starving artist."

"Well, if not an artist, then what?'

"Give me time to think. I assume you have an answer."

"You got that right."

"Well, what did you come up with?

"I'd like to come back as a diamond."

"A what?"

"Diamond. Just think about it. Even if it isn't a perfect stone, it never gets mistreated. It escalates in value. I don't know if it feels pain when it's getting cut but that's a one-time deal. Then it's revered and admired. It's usually kept in a safe or if not a safe, a secure place. When it's worn, all feedback is positive."

This pointed out how shallow Julie was but Czar was blinded by love. "You may have a point there but I'd personally rather have more interaction with people. I like to feel … even though sometimes those feelings hurt. I like to think, even though thoughts can be painful. I crave feedback, preferably positive, but I've learned to take the negative too."

"Enough already. What did you decide?"

"I'd still want to be a painter but instead of a waiter, I'd like to be a meteorologist."

"Why?"

"Because it's the only job I know that you can be wrong consistently and yet people still turn to you when making plans."

"Yes, yes. I know. What you really want is public acclaim."

"Not necessarily. It's just I know I'd never get fired. Listen, how many times has the local meteorologist been wrong? What does he do about it? Nothing. He blames Mother Nature, but most mothers don't treat their children that way."

Conversations with Julie were never of a personal nature … just thought provoking.

When Czar heard Julie had skipped high school graduation he was appalled. The Martins were upset, especially due to the fact Mrs. Martin was a teacher at the very same private school. Talk about emotional detachment and hedonism. Despite that, Czar hung in. He liked the chase but knew he'd

275

never get the brass ring.… Julie.

One time their conversation turned to various languages.

"I think the hardest thing about a foreign language is all of the different inflections. They change an entire meaning."

"What do you mean, foreign ones? How about English?" Julie questioned.

"What about it?"

"Just take a simple sentence like 'I never said he took the money.' The meaning changes whenever you accent a different word. Look, if you accent *I*, it eliminates the speaker as the one who's spreading the story. If *said* is the focal point, the person may have thought it but never uttered it. Just think about the different connotations one sentence can elicit."

"I never gave it a thought. I just take English for granted because that's what I grew up with. I never stopped to think about semantics. It's like it's good if someone is loaded with money but bad if loaded with alcohol. And red and read.… To, two and too. It never entered my mind before."

Julie was thinking by hanging around with Susie, Czar was getting as addlebrained as she was. Although Susie wasn't stupid, she only engaged her brain when absolutely necessary. To her, life was fun. She saw enough heartache at the hospital where she was still receiving her training.

Susie didn't like their morbid conversations. She was present when they had one about suicide. They asked each other how they would accomplish it and tried to draw her into the conversation but she wasn't buying it.

"As far as I'm concerned, suicide is a permanent solution to a temporary problem. You two are no better than the guys who produce and direct soap operas. They're the ones who make death look like a temporary thing. Where else but on one of them do you have someone jump off a cliff and then return later, hale and hearty? Also, how about having the season end with someone dying only to appear the next season as if it were just a dream!" With that, she turned on her heels and walked out of the apartment.

"Well," said Julie. "I guess she doesn't want her air-head to be picked."

Czar didn't defend Susie because he didn't want to alienate Julie. He knew he was just treading water with their relationship.

And then the glib Julie continued, "How would you go about it?"

"I haven't given it a thought." And biding time, he asked, "How would you?"

"Well, I sure as hell wouldn't stab or shoot myself. I wouldn't drown myself or set myself on fire. I'd be hesitant to take sleeping pills because what if I didn't succeed? I'd hate to be a vegetable but then again, if I were, I wouldn't know. As far as driving my car into a brick wall.… No way. I'd hate the anxiety of waiting for the crash. And as far as jumping out of a building, yuck! What if I changed my mind on the way down?"

"Did you ever think of putting a plastic bag over your head and suffocating yourself?"

"No. That would be unthinkable. Can you imagine the panic of not being able to breathe? Have you ever seen an asthmatic during an attack?

Rather than answer the proffered question, Czar countered with, "How about electrocution?"

"You mean like walking on the third rail on a subway track?"

"No, that wouldn't be such a good way to go. I'll have to give it more thought."

Seeds were planted and the conversation was ended.

Forty-three

It was a cool January night. Czar was aimlessly wandering around the docks. He had never witnessed anything in his almost nineteen years to equal the likes of what he saw on that particular night.

He was alone. Julie was God knows where. Susie was working, doing her ER stint, which was part of her schooling. He was walking along minding his own business. He heard anguished cries coming from an alleyway. In addition to that, he heard voices raised in angry taunts. He could feel the raw hatred in the voices.... Something to which he had never been privy. Concerned, he followed the sounds. He was in no way prepared for what was going on in the alley.

"Okay, you faggot. Have you had enough now? Don't you know enough to keep your germs and your girly ways away from here where decent human beings are leading a straight life? They don't need the likes of you prancing around here."

"Please. Please. I don't know how much more I can take," begged the victim, who was dressed in drag.

"Take? Talking about take, how about you enticing the two of us and hustling us for sex?" snarled the main contender of the encounter. In his hand he had a pipe, which apparently had connected with the victim's body many times … judging by the crumpled, almost inert body lying prostrate on the ground.

"But I wasn't doing that." There was no mistaking the fear in the breathless, pained voice. "I was just waiting for a friend and then the two of you *approached me*."

"That's not how I saw it," added the other perpetrator, who had once again entered into the fray. He resumed kicking the drag queen in the ribs.

The blood was now flowing even more freely than it had been when Czar first appeared on the scene. Although he had no idea who the macho men were or even if he could possibly stave them off, he was determined to try. "Hey, guys. Let up on him before you kill him!"

"So what would be so bad about that? It would be one less fairy in fantasyland. We don't care."

Czar said nothing.

"San Francisco is full of girl wannabes." Then he asked Czar, "Hey, fellow, are you one of them?"

At this point, Czar was honestly too scared to reply. He didn't know if he could muster enough volume to render an answer. His knees were shaking. He began perspiring with fear.

The victim, still on the ground and still conscious, said, "You'd better just leave while you still can. I'll be okay."

Czar managed to find his voice and confronted the bullies. "Do you want him to cry uncle? Exactly what do you expect him to do or say? Why don't you let up on him?"

"Is that an offer for us to take you on now? Or is the reverse true? Do you plan to take on the two of us?"

"I haven't planned anything other than help someone who is being beaten unmercifully simply because he marches to a different drummer."

"What are you? Some kinda lawyer or somethin'?" The thick speech was slurred. He definitely had one drink too many.

Although these words were laced with venom, it was evident the guys had lost their steam. They were losing interest in their mission.

"I'm not a lawyer. I just hate to see someone being beaten almost to death. Just stop and think how you'll feel if you actually do kill him? Is it worth it?"

Czar could feel them slowing down. Their momentum had abated. He tried one last shot. "Listen, guys, I can take over now. I'll see that he gets help. You can go away scot-free. How does that sound?"

The two of them had all the fun they could handle for the night. Though they were not strangers to gay bashing, it had never been this hateful before.

Czar thought maybe they had been embarrassed. Maybe they had mistaken him for a girl, thus making them more upset with themselves than with the object of their beating.

"Come on. Let's get out of here." The larger and more intense of the two bullies spoke to his friend.

Czar looked down at their handiwork. He wondered if they had indeed started the process of actually killing him. At this point he had lost consciousness.

There was blood coming from his nose, mouth and ears. After making sure he was still breathing, Czar ran to the end of the alley, managed to find a public phone and dialed 911. As he was waiting for the ambulance, he tried to control the bleeding. He wasn't as careful as he may have been but it was hard to stand there and not do anything. He was aware of the little cuts he had on his hand but didn't even stop to think of this guy's HIV status. For all

Czar knew, he may very well have been positive.

But this was a fellow human being who needed assistance so, stupidly, caution went out of the window. Although it seemed as if an eternity had passed before the emergency vehicle arrived, it was, in essence, under 10 minutes. Czar was never so glad to see them in his entire life.

"What was your part in this?" asked the first policeman on the scene.

"I was just walking by and heard the commotion. I went into the alley and lucked out. At least, I guess I did."

"You mean you actually got involved in this ugliness that transpired here? By the looks of the kid on the ground, I'm sure ugly is the right word."

"I had no choice. He needed some help and apparently I was the only one around."

The officers just looked at each other amazed that someone had enough courage to intercede in a brutal beating.

"Would you like to ride with him to the hospital?"

"Sure, if that's okay."

Upon arriving at the hospital, the first person that he saw was Susie.

"Czar, what's going on?" Susie saw all of the blood that he was covered with.

"I'm not hurt, Susie. He is." He told her this just as they were wheeling the victim into the ER.

"Was he hit by a car?" asked the voice behind the admitting desk.

The policeman went over to the desk and said the boy was beaten up at the docks. Obviously gay bashing. He pointed to Czar and continued, "This guy came to his rescue. He saved his life."

Susie turned to Czar and said, "Look at you. Your clothing is soaked with blood. So are your hands. So much for universal precautions."

"Who was thinking? I didn't have time to." He tried to explain that he was on an adrenaline rush and just did what he had to do.

Susie was inwardly proud of him but by the same token, wary for him. Czar knew any member of his family would have done the same thing and would have expected him to act accordingly. But he knew they also would have urged caution, which he did not exercise.

Not long after, Czar tested positive for HIV. It was a situation he chose to ignore. The victim tested negative, so who knows how long Czar had been positive. He now had an explanation for his mono-like symptoms.

A few weeks after his status was unfolded to him, he was having a conversation with his grandmother.

She must have expressed concern that something was wrong. She felt he was sick. She called to ease her mind.

"What do you think? Do you have psychic powers? No, I'm not sick. Just working hard. I can't allow myself to be sick." And that was how he handled his condition.... By denying it both to himself and others.

Forty-four

Susie went to visit Czar. If at all humanly possible, he looked worse than he did before. She tried not to show any emotion but it was hard not to.

"What's wrong?"

"I've had some pretty bad diarrhea."

She realized he would look horrible because he wasn't utilizing his food intake.

"Try small, frequent feedings. Don't eat or drink anything too hot or too cold. Be sure to drink a lot of fluids such as Gatorade. Eat food rich in potassium like bananas, apricots and potatoes."

"I know to cool it on lactose and caffeine, too."

"Okay. You've told me you know what to do, but have you done it?"

He smiled half-heartedly and in a sheepish voice, "No, I haven't been to the store so I've just been eating and drinking whatever's on hand."

"Is Julie around?"

"No."

"Where is the happy wanderer?"

Czar ignored the sarcasm and just said, "Mount Rushmore, taking pictures for some magazine."

"How long has Julie been away?"

"What is this? The Spanish Inquisition? Two or three weeks. What does it matter?"

Susie, much to her surprise, said not a thing. Instead she told him that she'd go to the store and get some stuff. She came back about an hour later and sliced some bananas and poured some Gatorade. When she left there, she called Rad to see if she could stop by.

It was the first time she had been to this very elegant house. A beautiful Persian rug accentuated the entrance. Rad told her he had designed the house with the study in the back so when he brought work home, it would be easier to have calm. They went into the study, which had dark ceiling to floor cabinets. The computer was on a large wooden desk. The swivel chair was covered with a rust velvet cushion. The skylight enhanced the lighting so he could work without artificial light if the day was bright enough. She was curious to see the rest of the house but didn't ask and they didn't offer.

Liz came into the room with tea. She started to leave when Susie spoke up, saying, "Liz, why don't you stay? I'd like you to hear this, too."

After they listened, Rad was the first one to speak. "I haven't liked the way he has looked for a while. We went to Adam and Steve's last week or so. He looked thin and tired but he said he was just busy painting. He didn't get enough sleep. He wasn't eating right either."

Adam and Steve's was a gay bar but a lot of straights went to see the show. They had great female impersonators. So convincing were the performances, it was doubtful if some mothers would even recognize their sons on the stage. Susie and Liz had gone with them on occasion. Since the Richards never liked Julie, they never extended an invitation in that direction. No one seemed to like Julie except Czar.

Rad told Susie he'd call Czar and make plans to see him. He wanted a face-to-face encounter to see for himself.

So it was the following week that Czar and Rad met in Adam and Steve's.

"Czar, how are things going? Just the other day, Liz was saying she hadn't seen you in so long. She wanted to have you and Susie for dinner."

This made Czar smile because the only way they'd ever invite Julie for dinner was as the entrée.

"Sounds good. First, let me check with Susie to see when she's available, okay?"

The conversation turned to sex.

"I've always had to feel a connection with someone first before I have sex with them."

"But that's not always possible. Especially if the one that you are connected with is out of the state let alone town. Sometimes I've had sex as a release. It seems when I'm not stressed out, I paint better."

"I think everybody does things better when they aren't stressed out."

Rad didn't bring up anything negative. He was afraid his friend would run the other way if the conversation became too heavy. He wanted to be there when he was needed. Only Czar could actually determine when that would be.

They had set up dinner and Susie was glad she'd be able to see more of the house than she had before. She and Liz were in the kitchen getting dessert. She heard the exchange between Rad and Czar just as she was about to enter the dining room. She hesitated and decided to listen.

"So Czar, what's going on? I understand that you're going to have a one-man show. Do you have everything just about done?"

"Not exactly. I've been held up with the final ones. I haven't told anyone yet but I have AIDS. Sometimes I'm so tired and racked with pain. So the painting is going slowly. My 'T' cells are better now because I've been taking my medication more regularly."

"You mean you haven't said anything to your family yet?"

"No, and I don't plan to either. Why have them worry every time the phone rings? They'll think it's one of you guys calling to say I'm in the hospital or worse yet, I've bitten the dust."

"Do you think it's fair to them to keep them in the dark?"

"I haven't even told Susie yet. I think she knows though. She's never backed me into the corner and questioned me about it. And she's really not at risk for contracting the virus. She knows all about universal precautions and is careful whenever there's blood around, no matter who it belongs to."

"How about Julie?"

"Well, we aren't as close as we used to be so who knows what Julie does or doesn't know. Some people enjoy playing ostrich, so who I am to yank their heads out of the sand? If this is your way of asking if I'd endangered Julie or anyone else, the answer is if I did, it was before I knew I was HIV positive."

"You amaze me. You really have your head on straight."

"Not really. I wake up in the middle of the night when I have my sweats or pain and wonder why this happened to me. I haven't cried though because when I'm upset, I can't give vent to tears. I try to reason things out, but I wonder.... Why me? In that respect, I don't think I'm any different from anyone else."

"I just think you're brave and tough to continue with your quest for a show, knowing it might not only be your first, but it may very well be your last."

"That's something only I can deal with. Don't ask me why I didn't take better care of myself when I was actually diagnosed as being HIV positive. I think I felt that since I'd apparently developed a positive status so quickly that I'd be sick with full-blown AIDS at a faster rate so why waste the money on all that medication? When I look back, and after researching it, I possibly could have controlled my destiny a bit better. I have read so much on it; I could have a doctorate on the subject.

"If I had started taking AZT when I was first positive, I could possibly have allayed the condition from developing. They recommend I take 200 milligrams around the clock and then go on a maintenance does of 100 milligrams every four hours. The dosage varies and the medication does present side effects ... not the least of which is bone marrow suppression.

That's why I guess I didn't go on the medication. You have to be checked every two weeks to see what your red blood cell count is. And I didn't have the time to spare. Stupid, huh? Am I boring you?"

In actuality this was a bit too much information for Rad at this juncture but he knew Czar couldn't talk with just anyone about this. So as a true friend would do, he kept that opinion to himself and said, "No. It's interesting." He thought he should have crossed his fingers when he said that.... Something he'd always done when as a child, he told a fib.

"I found out since I have black blood, I'm at a lesser risk of developing Pneumocystis Carini. I know my immune system is greatly compromised. I have read there is possibly a genetic predisposition as to who may develop AIDS. Some are born with bilateral protection from both parents so they may not develop AIDS no matter what their sexual proclivities are."

Susie had heard enough. She loudly walked from the hall so as to issue warning that someone was entering.

Rad thought she had heard much of this but he played dumb and changed the subject entirely.

"Are your folks coming out for the show?"

"I'm not sure. I think some of them may come but I don't know who."

Julie went to visit Czar a bit later. By this time his face was blotchy. Julie didn't know much about AIDS but thought, "I'd better get tested'. Since that test proved to be negative, Czar definitely hadn't gotten the virus from Julie. Julie also tested negative when re-tested six months later. But they hadn't been together biblically for quite a while now so when the first HIV test was negative, the second was bound to be.

Czar had developed Kaposi's Sarcoma and was fighting a losing battle with trying to keep the lesions hidden. However, topical Kaposi's Sarcoma wasn't fatal. It was only so if it was of the pulmonary type. He tried to convince himself and others his lesions were due to a shellfish allergy. This was how he explained the blotches. Deep down he knew they didn't believe him.

One day, when she visited, Susie saw various pamphlets strewn about the apartment ... all AIDS-related. They weren't in plain sight and she wasn't snooping but she did see them. She didn't pursue them.

She called to the cat.

"Tiger. Tiger. Where are you?"

Czar, who was finishing one of his paintings, called out, "Susie, I gave her away. I couldn't take care of her anymore."

Susie almost hit herself in the head, because of her stupidity. She was trying to knock some sense into herself. Of course he gave the cat away. People with AIDS were more susceptible to Toxoplasmosis. Cats can be a source for this.

She saw it was too much for him to paint that day. His neuropathy was acting up and the pain was excruciating. He had tried relaxation techniques and had done Yoga but there were some days that nothing seemed to work.

The next day, she visited once again. He was doing pretty well and was able to paint, which was one of the major things keeping him going. In the recent past, he had pancreatitis, which subsided. He just wasn't taking care of himself.

She then made a well-thought decision. She was going to take some time off. She had some time coming to her and she could extend it with a leave of absence. She knew Czar needed someone and since he refused to say anything to his family, she was an adjunct.

Susie went to see the DON and asked if she could take her vacation time due to a family emergency. She said she might also need additional time. When her request was granted she approached Czar.

"I'm taking some time off nurses' training. I have vacation time coming. Sometimes I'm not sure if I want to stay in nursing."

"That would be a waste if you dropped out of training."

"Well, it's not definite that I plan to leave…. Just temporarily. Why don't I move in here for a while? That way I won't have to pay rent any place else. I can also run errands for you, if you'd like."

Czar was glad she had offered. Some days, it was just too much to get his meals ready let alone do the exercise program that he was supposed to maintain. As healthy individuals, people are told to push themselves somewhat to complete their exercises. That's not the case with some who have a chronic problem.

So, Susie had moved in … allegedly to save money but deep down Czar knew it was because he was sick. She wanted to help. She was determined to let him keep his dignity. She never broached his AIDS even though she knew it was in full bloom.

Whether it was because he had company in the apartment or his determination to finish what he needed for his show, Czar was improving. Since he was on Tegrotol, he was seizure free. That was definitely a plus.

Forty-five

Czar was doing better since Susie was monitoring his medications, diet and rest. His 'T' cells were higher than they had ever been since being diagnosed. He still had pain and fatigue but overall, his condition was fairly good.

One day Susie had to go to the store to buy supplies. One of the things on her list was batteries for the electric/battery-operated CD player. It just so happened Czar was in excruciating pain. He was going to take a soothing bath while she was gone. Since he was sensory deprived, Susie always regulated the water for him so he wouldn't get burned. She also arranged his CD player near the tub so he could listen to classical music.

When she got home from the store, she put the supplies away. She then called through the door to him. She got no answer. At first, she knocked gently. Then she knocked louder while calling through the closed door. Still no answer. She tried the door and to her dismay found it was locked. This was a bit surprising because they had an agreement…. Whenever he was in the bathroom he wouldn't lock the door in case he had a problem. She certainly couldn't break the door down.

She breathlessly went to the phone and called the building supervisor but got no answer. So she called Rad.

"Hello."

"RadthisSusie. Czarhaslockedhimselfinthebathroom." She was so agitated that her words ran together

"Hold on a minute. You said he's locked himself in the bathroom. Have you been able to speak to him?"

"No. He doesn't answer. And I've been banging and banging on the door. I tried to get the building supervisor but he doesn't answer."

"Call the police. I'm on my way."

"I already did. Hurry. I'm afraid there's really something wrong."

The police and Rad got there at the same time.

Since Rad had called Liz, she arrived there shortly after him.

When they got the door open, they saw that the CD player had fallen into the tub, apparently electrocuting him.

No one knew how it happened. Susie was sure he had taken his Tegrotol

287

so she felt he didn't have a seizure. But it remained a mystery. She was puzzled as to why he had locked the door. But it wouldn't have mattered anyhow. He was probably electrocuted within seconds. So even if she had been there, he would have died.

It was then that Susie fell to pieces. For all intents and purposes, he was her best friend. Thank God for Rad and Liz. They came to her rescue.

At best it wasn't going to be easy to tell anyone in the family so they had all decided to call Treva at 'Mist.'

"Italian Mist."

"May I speak with Treva? This is Conrad Richards, calling from California. I'm a friend of her nephew's, Czar."

"One minute please."

"Hello, this is Treva. What's wrong?" His friends never called so she knew there was definitely some kind of problem with her nephew.

"This isn't an easy thing to tell you. Czar had a fatal accident. He's dead."

"Czar? What? Oh my God. Oh no! What happened?'

Rad could hear the intake of her breath as she began sobbing. He pressed on. "Susie, his roommate, had gone to the store. He was feeling weak and decided to take a bath to relax. When she came back, she called through the bathroom door to Czar. When she got no answer, she tried to get in but the door was locked. She called me as well as the police. Apparently Czar was listening to music on his CD player. Evidently it fell into the tub. He was electrocuted instantly."

"Oh my God!"

"We decided to call you because we thought you'd be the best one to break the news to his parents and grandparents."

After exchanging phone numbers, Rad hung up.

In a little while, Gary called. "Is there anything else you can tell us that you didn't tell my sister-in-law? She mentioned that Czar was weak. Why?"

Rad felt the awkwardness of this conversation. He didn't know what to say. As he hesitated to get the right words, Gary continued.

"We were planning to come out to visit a few months ago but he discouraged us. He said he was too busy getting ready for his show to actually spend any time with us. But tell me, why was he weak?"

"This is difficult to tell you. Czar's had AIDS for a while now."

"Is this some kind of sick joke?"

"NO, NO. Of course not. Wait a minute, I'll put Susie on."

"Mr. Rosen, this is Susie. Czar's been sick for a while. He didn't want you and your wife or his parents to know. He was afraid you'd all want to bring him home. He jokingly said the fleet would swarm in and take him back to Linfield. He had been doing better even though he had a recent bout with pancreatitis. Today he was weak and his body ached. He decided he would soak in the tub. He was so very excited about his show. His painting was going well despite the fatigue and pain. The CD player's batteries were dead so he used the electrical current. The building is old so the outlet and the CD player didn't automatically turn off." Susie didn't know how she managed to get all of this out without breaking down.

Gary was still zeroed in on the AIDS thing. "How did he ever get anything like that? He never even hinted anything was wrong."

"I know. Forgive me for not telling any of you but I promised Czar that I wouldn't. Those were his wishes. Honestly, he was doing very well. This comes as a complete shock to all of us, too." She could no longer speak intelligibly as she was racked with sobs.

Liz grabbed the phone. "Mr. Rosen, this is Liz Richards, Rad's wife. Susie and Rad aren't in any condition to speak any longer. First let me tell you how very sorry I am. What can we do?"

"I have to talk to my daughter and son-in-law to see what their wishes are."

"Well, the coroner has Czar now. They said that by law, they have to do an autopsy."

"Let me talk to his mother and father first. Treva, Tessa and I will give the news to my daughter and son-in-law. We're just getting our heads on straight, though I'm sure that none of us are thinking too clearly. We'll get back to you. Don't make any plans out there."

"Of course we won't do anything. When you call back, we'll do whatever you'd like us to do."

Liz, too, was on the verge of falling apart. On the other end, she heard Gary's voice was quivering. She knew he, too, was on the same verge.

Ali was sitting in her nurse's office going over immunization records. The phone rang.

"Nurse's Office. Mrs. Green."

"Ali, sit tight. I'm dropping by."

She didn't have time to respond to her father. Before she knew it, Gary and Marc were walking through the door. Gray's skin was as gray as his hair. And Marc's eyes were swollen. She braced herself, knowing her world was going to be radically changed.

Neither of her two favorite men spoke.

Immediately thinking of her mother, Ali asked, "How? How did it happen?"

Gary looked to Marc for succor. Marc went over, wrapped his arms around his wife and in a faltering voice whispered, "He was electrocuted."

Ali looked from Marc to her father. "He? Who? I thought it was Mom." She grabbed Marc's shirt and shook him. "Who? Answer me, damn it! Who?"

Gary walked over to his daughter, who was leaning back on her desk, still tugging at Marc's shirt.

"Czar."

"My baby. Oh, Noooo." Ali let go of Marc, screamed then slipped to the floor.

Norman Williams, the school principal, rushed into the room. He'd been apprised by his secretary that Marc and Gary were coming to take Ali home. He already knew about Czar's death.

"Can I help? Do you want a wheelchair?"

"No, thanks. My son-in-law and I can manage." Just as they had many years ago after the rape. "Is it time for the bell?"

"No, this period has just started so the halls should be relatively clear."

As they were waiting for Gary to call back, Liz and Susie had cleaned the apartment. They used Susie's handy bleach bottle for disinfecting surfaces. They got Czar's paintings in order. He'd already done much of that himself.

They discussed Czar's AIDS. Even though Julie had tested negative, they still felt that's where the responsibility lay. If not physically, at least emotionally.

Then they reminisced about Czar and his keen sense of humor.

"...and how about the time he told me I was too thin? I was actually gaining weight and he just laughed at me."

"Oh yes, wasn't that the time he wrote the Susie psalm? That was really cool," added Liz, as she laughingly recited it.

The scale is my enemy....
I shall not weigh.
It makes me hide it in the closet....
It has me walk by it in a futile attempt to forget it.
It tempts me not.
My Twinkies and M&M's are with me.
I shall eat my peanut butter and chocolate with abandon.
My friends shall tempt me as well.
We will feast at the table set before us....
Yeah, though I walk through the 'Valley of the Fatties'....

It shall not bother me.
I will ignore the scale all the days of my life. ...
And I shall dwell in the 'Valley of the Fatties' forever.

They all laughed so hard they began crying. Through their tears, they joined hands and prayed together for their dear friend.

They all remained quiet for a while until Liz asked, "Has anyone thought to call Julie? That's what Czar would have wanted us to do."

"Julie's out of the country."

And that's the way it was left. No one ever brought the name up again.

Forty-six

The next day, Gary called from the airport, asking for directions to the apartment. Gary, Tessa, Marc, Ali and the Musks had all come out to California. Czar's friends offered to pick them up. Gary had rented a car. Both Liz and Rad drove to the airport. Susie was a passenger in Liz's car. It was predetermined that Susie was going to come back with Gary and Tessa so they wouldn't get lost. Marc and Ali went with Rad and the Musks went with Liz.

Not surprising, Liz had the toughest carload. The kids kept crying. They had been to California once before during a much happier time.

When they got to the apartment, Susie offered them food. But they declined, stating they'd eaten on the plane. No one really expected them to eat as their stomachs surely were tied up in knots.

Gary was the spokesperson for the family as he was superficially calm. But if one looked beyond the calm, his deep sorrow was etched in his sad eyes. He was in a bad state but managed to hold it all together. He and Rad had a conversation aside from the group.

"As soon as it's permissible, I've made arrangements to transport him to Linfield. I have made contact with my friend, Jeff, who's an undertaker in Haddon Heights. We have tentative plans for a mass in Linfield. Of course, the date hasn't been determined. What I'd like to do is see his art dealer." Gary was committed to follow up on the art show because Czar had worked so hard to achieve it.

The group came back into the room, where Gary had begun viewing the artwork of his grandson.

Susie didn't know what to say to ease their sorrow. She thought they might want to hear some stories of his last few months.

"You would have been so proud of him. When he wasn't painting, he did volunteer work for the AIDS Hospice. He also answered a hot line for AIDS Anonymous. Those calls were mostly from people who were afraid to get tested. Czar encouraged them to get tested. He even went with some of them. The ones who proved to be positive would call often.

"Czar was one of the best crisis intervention people they had. He didn't

292

hide the fact that he, too, was positive. He stressed the fact that due to his denial, he failed to get treatment and developed full-blown AIDS. However, he did tell them he was doing fairly well. He never skirted any question but tried to answer them succinctly and honestly."

Tessa just beamed with pride about how her grandson had turned his tragedy into something beneficial to others. Although she regretted she didn't know of his condition, she thought maybe he had been right to keep it from them. What he had said in jest was probably true. They would have wanted to transplant him from California and bring him back with them to Linfield. This would have given them more time with him but he would have been miserable.... Too much hovering.

"I should have made it my business to come out more instead of just that one time. I would have seen him failing." Ali was bemoaning the fact that she had neglected her son.

"Honey, what good would that have done? He was proud. He wouldn't have wanted your concern or pity. Besides, it wasn't AIDS that killed him.... Just a horrid accident." Even though Tessa said this, Ali's crying became more intense. She realized there are not many things worse than losing a child. She shuddered as she thought she'd never see her green-eyed, curly-haired grandson. She'd never hear his voice emanating from the other end of the phone. Gary came to her side and quietly held her hand. Sometimes there were just no words left.

The practical Gary went to see the art dealer. Together they decided to postpone the show. They were aware the value of the paintings would escalate. After all, there would be no more forthcoming.

Forty-seven

The funeral was held on a pleasant October day. It was the kind of day that was too warm for heat and yet not hot enough for air-conditioning. It was just a day that Czar would have loved; a day in which he could have done his painting outside.

Susie thought about what Czar had said about funerals. He said he couldn't understand why the word that denoted sadness began with the word fun. Well, this was going to be anything but.

The Mass was held at the same church where the triplets were baptized. The church was filled to capacity. Althie gave the eulogy....

"Most of you need no introduction to my beloved brother. He and many of your kids played together as he was growing up in Linfield. He was a star on the Linfield High football team. That was the public side of Chad Zachary Rosen Green. I'm hoping to give you a more private slant on him

"Our brother," and she nodded to Ben and Cole while saying this, "was filled with love and understanding. He was old when he was young. He always interceded for us whenever it was necessary. He had a practical approach to everything. Even while racked with pain, he completed some of his most brilliant works of art. Anyone who saw him at work can tell you his art was the most important thing in his short life. Because of his attitude and determination, he remains an inspiration to my brothers and me.... To all of us.

"For those of you who don't know, let me tell you so there won't be any mistaken whispers. Czar had full-blown AIDS. I can hear the gasps of disbelief in the audience. I don't know if it's because he had AIDS, or if it's because I am mentioning it at this very private time of death. I know many of you think of AIDS as a gay disease so I won't even try to dispel the thoughts you're harboring. To those of you who are more discerning, I say this; does it really matter what takes the life of someone we love? Czar was ill, yes, but his actual death was an accident.

"Czar never hurt anyone deliberately. I don't know why God chose to take him from us. I've been taught never to question His will. But I'm angry that He took my brother. It' s not fair he had to die at such a young age.

"His unique personality was shown by the volunteer work that he did for the AIDS hot line. Even though racked with pain, he never neglected his duty of answering the phone. He devoted much time to many who were enduring the same type of emotional turmoil he was.

"My brother would want to be remembered as just a normal guy who lived a good life; never looking for accolades. Czar was a private, shy guy who didn't enjoy center stage. He always considered himself a background person.... A wallflower.

"Czar would be the first to volunteer for a project such as gathering food or toys for the needy. He would shovel the sidewalks of the senior citizens in the neighborhood, many of whom did not know who had been the Good Samaritan. He loved little kids. He used to help them with their athletic endeavors.

"My mother told us he would go to the pharmacy for some of the neighborhood people when they were too ill to go themselves. He once found a disabled bird and kept it safe until he could take it to a wildlife federation. These are sides of Czar few people knew. He never beat his chest proclaiming to be great. That was never Czar's style.

"When you leave here today, I only have one request. Please be more tolerant of those around you. I'm not suggesting you take the troubles of the world on your shoulders. I'm only asking you to try to find within yourselves the tolerance to accept and help those who are less fortunate than you are. If even one of you could do so, then my brother's short life would not have been in vain."

Althie had amazingly held it together until the last word. Her grandfather had to go up and help her from the altar. Her eyes became blinded with the tears that she couldn't afford to shed until after she read her tribute to her late brother. She gave full vent to all of the pent-up emotion and the silence of her sorrow now found a voice in her loud sobs.

Althie wasn't the only one displaying sadness. Many of those congregated there were crying loudly … even the men. Those who did not show this overt reaction just cleared their throats, sniffled and reached for tissues.

Forty-eight

A few months after the funeral, there was a knock at Ali and Marc's door. Tessa and Gary were also there. They were formulating plans for the hospice they were going to establish in Czar's memory.

Tessa went to the door, where she saw a classically handsome young man with long, flowing blond hair.

"Can I help you?" Tessa asked.

"I'd like to see Mr. or Mrs. Green, if that's possible."

"Come in."

The young man hesitated before he moved. Ali came to the door where he remained standing, hesitant to enter. Finally, after a long, awkward pause, he said, "Mrs. Green, I know Czar would have wanted you to have this."

Ali looked at what the young man was showing her. It was Czar's ring.... The one she and Marc had given him when he'd graduated eighth grade.

Tears came to Ali's eyes immediately. She had all but forgotten the ring, which Czar had happily accepted and worn with pride.

Marc came to the door. "What's this about the ring? We had forgotten about it."

"Czar gave this to me a while back. My name is Jules Martin. But you've probably heard me referred to as Julie."

Forty-nine

Tessa met with her lawyer to discuss the lawsuit.

"Do you think we have a case?"

"It's not clear cut. Remember, not only did you initial each page, but you also wrote a short note authorizing the areas of the book you gave to Bette. We probably have a shot with the information she got from Czar's journals, though, because his parents have control of them. Also, have Susie, Julie and Rad signed off on their input?"

"Other than give their interviews, I'm not sure what they've done."

"Do you want my advice in addition to my opinion regarding the lawsuit?"

"Yes."

"Well, if you sue and delay the publication, your anonymity will no longer be protected. In other words, even if you win, you lose. What could be more appealing than airing someone's troubles via the tabloids? If you abandon the suit, even though some people may know it's your family encapsulated in this book; many will not."

It was because of this statement that Tessa gave up the fight.

Bette was at home, reviewing her text, when her phone rang.

"Hello."

"This is Mr. Gross' office calling Bette Gilmar."

"Speaking." As she heard her lawyer's name, she felt her mouth get dry and her palms began to sweat.

"One minute please."

And then Mr. Gross was on the line. "I have the news you've been waiting for." She thought she'd have to draw it out of him but he finally continued. "Tessa Rosen has withdrawn her lawsuit."

"Phew! Thanks. That's great news! You have no idea how great." Without adding anything further than a hasty good-bye. Bette hung up the phone. Not wanting to plant any seeds that may take fruit, she wanted to delete the part about the suicide discussion and then write the epilogue.

Epilogue

Dear Grandmom,

If you are reading this letter, it means I've gone to the artist colony in the sky. I don't feel as glib as I sound but knew you may have to read this before too long anyway.

Susie has assured me if I die before my time, whatever that may be, she'd see that you got this letter.

Of all of the people in the world, you've known me best. ... At least it always seemed that way to me. So what I'm going to say to you now won't be as shocking to you as it may be to others.

One of the reasons I moved to California was the fact I felt different than all of you would have liked me to be. I don't mean to say I felt any lack of love emanating from any of you, it's just I felt it would be easier for me to explore myself and my beliefs and desires away from where I may have embarrassed you.

Yes, you've read between the lines correctly. I am gay.

It's funny how some people view a gay lifestyle. Some feel it's a phase that some may go through. Others feel it's something like chicken pox and one will get over it. I'm afraid that's not the case at all with me.

If I could be different than what I am, it would be much easier. Society frowns upon me. I don't think my father and grandpop would understand how someone who was such a gifted athlete could have more pink in him than blue.

You've always taught me to be tolerant of others with their differences. I don't feel I've been the recipient of that same degree of tolerance which I've given to just about everyone I've encountered.

A while back, I witnessed a gay bashing which I found to be horrifying. It was then, because I went to the aid of the victim, that I got tested for HIV. You can imagine my surprise when I tested positive immediately. I had no idea I was sick. I attributed my lack of energy to my irregular hours and erratic eating pattern. Not the case at all.

This isn't meant to be a woe-is-me letter but I just wanted you,

298

above all, to know the turn my life had taken.

You have often heard me speak of Julie ... having never met him. Yes, it's him. But don't think Julie was the one who infected me. Julie has tested negative for HIV and as far as I know practices safe sex.

This isn't meant to be a rendition of my sexual encounters but just an honest telling you of my so-called deviant behavior.

It may not be a good idea to tell any of the male family members because they'd be upset about this and wonder what they could have done differently.

I can't think of anything different that anyone could have done to make me turn into a more acceptable person in mainstream America.

My childhood, although not perfect, was great. The love I received has helped sustain me now, during my pain racked days.

Susie, of course, knows my sexual orientation. She's been so wonderful to me as have Rad and Liz. They've given me unconditional friendship and love, as have you.

Some day, not evidently in my lifetime, perhaps people in general will be more accepting and charitable toward those who are different.

Don't be disappointed in me or for me. I followed the path my life has taken, although not always happily, at least with some degree of contentment.

I'll be looking down on all of you and will always love all of you.
Love,
Czar

The family once again encountered a societal taboo. Czar had been living an alternate lifestyle of which they had no idea. They faced this new strife together, maintaining a public aura of calm.

Tessa was the first to regain her composure. Suspecting Czar's sexuality all along, she wasn't completely surprised by the revelation.

The Czar Hospice, which the family had established, was a tremendous success. Susie, as director, did a magnificent job of caring for those downtrodden and hopeless. The center, which offered many services, concentrated on a more positive approach to HIV and AIDS, to those who had all but given up on life. The new strides in AIDS research revived the zest for life, which many patients had lost.

Czar paintings kept increasing in value and were coveted pieces to own.

Tessa and Gary opened another sub shop near the hospice. They donated a percentage of their profits to the institution and also sponsored an annual art exhibit/sale to help both the artists and the hospice.

Before too long, Ali and Marc were occupying the governor's mansion. He became one of the increasing numbers of black governors in the country. Ali works in Linfield Junior High as a school nurse.

Tessa and Treva are still running 'Italian Mist,' which is now on the public stock exchange. They have branches in Europe, South America and Mexico.

Becky and Jake moved to Israel to spend their waning years. Their son Harry was teaching at a kibbutz. Their daughter, Jennifer, was a top model in New York. They all return to Linfield periodically to see Gary, Tessa and the rest of the Rosen/Mareno/ Green group.

Rita did volunteer work at the hospice.

With her husband, Garrett, Althie had a bouncing baby boy who she named Czar.

Upon graduating from medical school, Ben and Cole both plan to specialize in infectious diseases.

Julie was a prominent photographer. He became active in the Czar hospice after moving back to Linfield. The family welcomed him into their fold.

Liz and Rad remained in California. Rad opened his own brokerage firm and assists the family in overseeing the investments for the Czar hospice.

The family and its extensions are all alive and well.

THE END

Printed in the United States
1295600003B/261